GHETTO DOGS

by Steve Romagnoli

Advance Praise for *Ghetto Dogs*:

Kirkus Reviews:

"Ambitious and sprawling, this compelling book delivers critiques of American institutions, from family and education to law enforcement and criminal organizations. Romagnoli is adept at dislocating the reader within a real but unfamiliar world, as in the tale's opening scene: a tree full of hanging dogs, some living and some dead. He has an ear for dialogue and a gift for establishing character with a few short clauses (one character, Ivory White, is introduced as a former "member of Rosco's high school basketball team until he got expelled for pimpslapping a referee")."

Kate Christensen, winner of the *2008 PEN/Faulkner Award*:

The opening scene of Ghetto Dogs is so riveting and surreal it launches the story right off the runway. The story sails airborne straight to the weird, poetic end, and the characters crackle with appetites and opinions, the dialogue is masterly. The book's density is vertical rather than horizontal, so that each page is spare and understated, but it all stacks up into something rich and full of soul, sad, funny, intelligent, and streetwise. Romagnoli is the Lester Young of writers; his virtuosity feels effortless.

Mark Caldwell, author of *New York Night: The Mystique and Its History*:

Steve Romagnoli's Ghetto Dogs is both a terrific read and a literary achievement, moving with ease and authenticity through the chronic clash and sudden concords of white and African-American culture in New York from the 1970s to the 1990s. Ghetto Dogs has the suspense (and violence) of a thriller—but with a precision of detail, a surreal moral seriousness, and large cast of fully imagined characters almost unknown to the genre. In its mastery of dog-fighting culture and intensity Ghetto Dogs recalls Jesmyn Ward's Salvage the Bones, but Romagnoli's canvas is larger, with a Brueghelesque mastery and a wider social sweep.

Francis Levy, author of *Erotomania: A Romance and Seven Days in Rio*:

Steve Romagnoli's Ghetto Dogs has the ambition and scope of a nineteenth century Russian novel, only it's situated in twentieth century Harlem. Instead of Pierre and Andrey, Natasha, Sofia, Vronsky, Levin and Anna, Romagnoli's characters are named Antoine, Tyrone, Rosco, Ivory, Desiree and Marisol. In place of duels there are dog fights and basketball and the most spiritual characters are now a recovering addict who teaches in a tough public school and the ghost of a three legged fighting pit bull, Redrum, whose name recalls The Shining. Scarface and Nietzsche's "will to power" fight for the souls of Romagnoli's characters. His gritty realistic style and gift for rendering the poetry of Ebonics does for millennial novel writing about the "hood" what the Ashcan school of painting contributed in its portrayal of an earlier era of New York street life.

Alternative Book Press
2 Timber Lane
Suite 301
Marlboro, NJ 07746
www.alternativebookpress.com

Originally published in electronic form in the United States
by Alternative Book Press.

Publication Data
Steve, Romagnoli, [2016]
Ghetto Dogs/ by Steve Romagnoli.—1st ed.
p. cm.
1. General (Fiction). I Title.
PS1-3576.S74R663   2016
813'.6—dc23

ISBN 978-1-940122-28-1
Printed in the United States of America
10 9 8 7 6 5 4 3 2 1

In Loving Memory Of Coffee
"The only one that ever listened to me."
RIP

"Me, I always tell the truth—even when I lie."

Scarface

CHAPTER ONE

In Harlem three legs kick hopelessly, the body jerking against gravity and death. Rum was great once, a champion who went on winning despite his handicap. But tonight it's a different story. Tonight, Rum has been strung up by the neck and hung from the Losing Tree. Rum is not the only strange fruit hanging here. Three other dogs dead and two near dead slowly twirl on leafy branches, their forms spinning shadows by the full August moon. Before the night is over the tree will be blooming, its thick limbs straining from the weight.

While the tenement has long been trashed and abandoned, its backyard is filled with noise and excitement, the air thick with humidity and the scents of reefer, fried chicken and raw blood. Most all fights are between pit bulls who, like boxers, must be weighed-in before each contest. A winner is declared only when the other dog is killed or is no longer able to fight on. When Rum lost to Bandit, it was not that he lost the will to win. Rum had an adverse reaction from the anti-inflammatory shot injected during the "scratch." A scratch is when the dogs are pulled apart and allowed to rest—similar to a break between rounds.

When Rosco passes by, Rum kicks harder. But Rum doesn't cry out, he doesn't whimper. It is not pain or fear that makes him struggle so, that makes him buck and briefly animate the other dead dogs in the tree beside him. It is a confusion of the mind stemming from a worldview he has never seen before: An entirely new and all pervading sense of doom born from the incomprehensible indifference of his master.

Without a final touch or word or even a glance, Rosco just walks on by. Right now, for Rosco, there is no time for thought on what has passed. Right now, Rosco must focus all his attention on his other dog, Felony, who's scheduled to roll against the Mighty Rye Rye in the next bout.

Rosco named him Redrum after he saw "The Shining." Redrum is murder spelled backwards. Rum is a red nose pit bull. He has a colossal head and a dense body of muscle. Unlike many of his peers, Rum has both ears intact (a jagged split in one repaired with super glue yet hardly noticeable). Rum lost his leg to a dog named Coffee in a fight people still remember to this day. Coffee was the best dog in Harlem with a perfect 14 - 0 record. Rum was new and untested against a dog of Coffee's caliber. Up until the first scratch, Rum's inexperience was obvious. Coffee tore Rum up every which way. Nobody, not even Rosco, thought Rum had a chance. Coffee was just too fast and too strong. What's more, Rum's hind leg was torn beyond recognition, the bone stabbing through the skin. But Rosco let him roll anyway, figuring it was either do or die. Coming out of the scratch, Coffee went straight for Rum's bloody leg. Rum made no move to defend the wound. In fact, Rum purposely turned to make it easier for Coffee to lock on. An offering of sorts. As Coffee occupied himself with Rum's leg, Rum contorted his body around and under Coffee's exposed neck. With two mighty shakes of his own massive head, Rum tore out Coffee's throat. It was an unprecedented performance. Nobody had ever seen a dog use his own wound as bait. As they dragged Coffee from the pit, Rum allowed himself to whimper. Without delay, Rosco shot him up with lidocaine, azium and baytril before having the mangled limb amputated the next morning.

A young dog not much more than a puppy, Rum healed fast, and despite the handicap, Rosco continued to let Rum fight. With the odds of a three-legged dog high in his favor, Rosco won thousands of dollars, many more thousands than the twelve thousand lost tonight.

Hungry and parched, Rosco fortifies himself with a chicken leg and a beer. He declines a hit off a blunt offered by Kelsey, a big fan of Redrum.

"Shame what happened wif Rum," says Kelsey.

Rosco nods, biting hard into the fried bird.

"I must have won near five thousand bettin' on your Rum in the past year alone. Shame to see him end up like dat."

Rosco shrugs and bites.

"Hey, Rosco... You think I might buy him offa ya?"

"Huh?"

"I wanna buy Rum."

Rosco looks at Rum still bucking in the tree across the yard. "Nigga, you must be crazy."

"He ain't dead yet. I could heal him up myself. Not to roll. Just for a pet. A watch dog maybe..."

"Rum's not for sale."

"Damn, Rosco... It ain't right Rum left to go out like dat. Not Rum. It's a shame is what it is. What you want for him? I got paper. I got plenty of paper. Most of it thanks to Rum."

Smiling at this, Rosco puts his beer on the ground. He reaches into his gym bag. Beside the syringes, gauze, sutures and shoestring is a loaded Tec-9, a gun capable of firing fifty rounds in a matter of seconds. Pulling the weapon from the bag, Rosco aims for Kelsey's throat. "Rum's not for sale. Rum is dead and, nigga, you gonna be dead too you don't get off this topic."

"Understood."

Still smiling, Rosco puts the gun away. He finishes the beer and sucks on the chicken bone. He yells at a man and his young son standing too close to Felony. Must be a newcomer. Kid could get his self killed like that. Starting when they're puppies, a pit is trained to attack small mammals. First they practice with rabbits and kittens—later with stray or wounded dogs.

Rosco leads Felony over to the fighting pit. The pit isn't really a pit but a fenced off space made of plywood. Around the pit stand those betting and watching, people screaming and rooting for the dog of their choice. Not unlike a block party, there's plenty of food, booze and weed. Harder drugs are also available as many of the local drug dealers sport pits of their own.

Rye Rye is owned by a kid called Nickel. Although Nickel has only a few hundred to bet, there are plenty others willing to put their money down on Rye Rye. A bottom dog, a dog known for breaking legs, Rye Rye weighed in at an even fifty-five pounds to Felony's fifty-three. In addition to Rye's weight advantage, many of the bets against Felony are just to see Rosco lose twice in the same night. Rosco hates to lose. He has always been like that and people know it. Back in the day, Rosco was the star of Wadleigh High School, leading them to a city championship at Madison Square Garden. His coach used to say he never saw a kid who hated losing more than he loved winning. Hate made Rosco a champion.

The two dogs charge, crash and tumble as Rye Rye manages to trap Felony against the wall before locking on a front leg. For a good ten minutes, Rye Rye controls the fight until Felony is able to get a hold on Rye's ear, breaking the lock on his leg. A scratch is called.

Nickel applies caustic powder to staunch Rye's bleeding ear. Rosco checks on Felony's leg. Wiping away the blood, he sees that it's nothing too deep, nothing to worry about.

Out from the scratch, Felony catches a lock on Rye's neck. Felony works that neck for a good five minutes. There is nothing Rye Rye can do. But in an effort to get a deeper lock, Felony slips his grip. Rye rolls under Felony, locking on to Felony's lower jaw and face. On his back now, Rye Rye keeps shaking Felony back and forth, the blood spraying against the plywood walls and faces of those leaning into the pit. After a few long minutes, Felony goes slack and the crowd goes wild but not too wild on account of Rosco's temper and loaded Tec-9.

Rosco smiles and people look away. When Rosco smiles he is not happy. When Rosco smiles he is ready to explode. Counting out hundred dollar bills, Rosco grins from ear to ear, his white teeth shining in the glare of the spotlights above the pit. After laying the money down, Rosco nods to Tyrone and Antoine who pull Felony from the pit.

Tyrone and Antoine will be in tenth grade this coming September. It is their job to hang losing dogs on the Losing Tree. They are also the ones who prepare the pit and clean up the yard when the night is over. Rosco watches as Felony is lynched beside Rum. Still smiling, he hands each boy a hundred dollar tip. They take the money and nod in thankfulness. Rosco crosses the yard for the hole in the wall that leads through the tenement back to the street, the frozen white of his grin disembodied by the blackness of his face.

Almost dawn and everybody is gone except Antoine and Tyrone. With heavy-duty trash bags in tow, they hand pick all the empty beer bottles, chicken bones and trash from the yard. Next, they disconnect the spotlights and walls of the pit to store back inside the tenement. Finally, they cut down the dead dogs, putting them each in doubled up garbage bags. Sometimes, if a dog is still breathing, they have to club the life out of him before throwing him away. But this is not necessary tonight. All these dogs are dead.

CHAPTER TWO

In the shadow of the Cathedral of Saint John the Divine, Morningside Park starts at 110th Street and runs along Manhattan Avenue in the valley below Broadway and Columbia University. The park serves as a moat separating two worlds of rich and poor. From the streets and tenements of Harlem, the grandeur of the great cathedral is omnipresent but rarely taken into consideration. It is from the other world.

If you enter the park at 112th Street, you can look up past the basketball court and see the angel Gabriel perched high on top of the cathedral. But he, like his horn, is earthbound and inert. A green speck against the endless sky.

Desiree imagines the creature spreading its wings and soaring into flight. She closes her eyes and the beating of his wings becomes a rhythmic roar suddenly pierced by the call of his trumpet. Like the swan and Leda, he is soon upon her, thrusting himself deep inside, his massive wings blotting out sun and sky...

Coming back to her senses, Desiree considers the angel once again, wondering why there are never any miracles anymore. Vague memories from her childhood still haunt her at times. Memories of angels and saints and miracles of fire and parting seas. Back then, such tales of walking on water and rising from the dead were as real as Aretha Franklin. Fantastic but true.

Sitting at a picnic table beside the small playground, Desiree checks on Clyde, her only child. He's a strange little boy, prone to walking on the balls of his feet.

Taking the joint from inside her pack of Newports, Desiree lights up, holding the smoke while discretely casting her gaze about the park. It's an early morning Monday. Those who work are working and those who don't are inside sleeping or watching the talk shows. Desiree hates those shows because she could have easily been a guest on one herself. Besides which, TV bores her. So Desiree gets herself out whenever possible. It's soothing to be in the park, especially when it's empty. Well, almost empty. There's always somebody or another walking the earth or passing time on a bench or fitfully sleeping in dark places beneath the trees. For Desiree, Morningside Park is rightfully named for the morning. It's peaceful and quiet and nobody will bother her until the sun goes back behind the cathedral, bringing on shadows and the usual riffraff with their rude looks and propositions.

After a final, deep hit, Desiree crushes the roach between her fingers. Savoring the burn, she lets the specks of ash and paper fall between her legs. She blows smoke and waves to Clyde. Hanging from the monkey bar, he waves back with one hand before falling to earth. Instantly up again, he heads for the arms of Mommy, running on the balls of his feet.

"You alright, Baby?"

Clyde nods his head.

"Give Mommy a kiss."

Clyde dutifully kisses her before running back to the playground. Desiree shakes out a cigarette. She lights up, watching a flock of pigeons descend about the old lady casting crumbs like confetti. But where are all the baby pigeons? How come you never see one of them? In all her days, Desiree has never saw a single baby pigeon. She's seen baby rats. Why not baby pigeons?

There goes a white man at the top of the hill. But not a cop because you can tell he's not pretending. Maybe one of them college kids looking to score. But it's way too early for that. Good luck, white boy.

There goes Carlos pushing his baby carriage filled with empty cans. Desiree once went to school with Carlos. She sat behind him in third grade. Sometimes she would hook her feet around the bottom of his chair and pull him back into her desk. He was a short boy who grew into a short crackhead. He doesn't look at her as he passes, but Desiree smiles anyway. Although he never looks at Desiree directly, she is sure he remembers her. He just doesn't want her to know it's him who he's become.

"Mommy!" In Clyde's hand is a black Frisbee. He holds the discus up. Desire smiles. Clyde runs to her with his newfound trophy.

"What's this?"

"It's a Frisbee."

"A frisbeen?"

"A Frisbee."

"It was over there. I founded it."

"Watch," she says. Getting up from the bench, Desiree takes one last drag from her cigarette, crushing it out on the side of the picnic table. She throws the Frisbee. It's a superb toss. They watch it float towards the lake and the willows, a soaring black hole curling back and softly descending in the grass about ten yards away. Clyde fetches it back to his Mom. Desiree takes him by the hand. They walk across the basketball court to the empty baseball field. Desiree throws the Frisbee high and far and Clyde runs to catch it. Then he tries to throw it himself. The Frisbee hooks forward and down, crashing on its side a few feet away. Clyde gives the Frisbee back to his mother. Better to catch than to throw. Clyde does not tire of this game and it's amazing to see the little man racing across the grass on the balls of his feet. Watching her son, Desiree is filled with an energy and happiness that, combined with the weed, makes her glow in harmony with the beautiful, sunlit morning.

As the game of fetch continues, Desiree notices that the white boy has been watching them. But he does not seem crazy or dangerous. Unlike her cousin, Marisol, Desiree does not hate white people. Desiree once had a secret crush on John Travolta. Not the fat John Travolta. The young one, the Brooklyn one, who knows how to dance. This white boy over there reminds her of him. Well, not really. Not at all. But Desiree pretends that he does and the park begins pulsing with disco, that old time disco her mother used to listen to back in the day... John Travolta reaches out. Desiree takes his hand. Twirling to the beat, they spin beneath the colored lights. He pulls her close and Desiree can feel his cheek on her cheek, his breath on her neck...

The music stops, the world jarred into violent discord. Desiree freezes as the white man races towards Clyde. Time and distance become slow and stretched like a bad dream. Charging in the opposite direction of the white man is the dog. A great white pit bull, his rope lashing the grass behind him.

Putting himself between Clyde and the pit bull, the white man swings Clyde up from the ground. He tries to run, but the pit is on him, tearing into his left leg. The white man stumbles and falls with the pit shaking his head like a shark. Focused only on the calf meat, the pit bull takes no notice of the little boy dashing to the arms of his mother. As the pit bull shakes his great head, the white man screams for help. But no help comes. With the dog locked on his leg, the white man struggles to his feet, shuffling forward, instinctively trying to get away but there is no getting away. It is a peculiar sight. The white man and the three-legged dog moving slow and steady across center field in the direction of home plate. Without the benefit of a second hind leg, the pit cannot set himself for a proper shakedown and so must follow the lead of his victim.

Exhausted and confused, the white man grabs the chain link backstop. He's dizzy from shock and loss of blood. Lucky for him, a squad car from the 28th Precinct is just now passing on Manhattan Avenue. Hearing the screams and shouts for help, the two cops hurry to the scene.

A small crowd forms around the white man caught by the pit bull.

"Damn," says one. "But that dog's got only three legs!"

"Must make up for it with them jaws," says another. "That shit's gotta hurt."

The circle of people makes way for the cops. One of the cops is black and the other is Puerto Rican. The Puerto Rican takes out his baton. He strikes the dog on the head. But this does nothing. The black cop follows suit. Again, nothing.

"How you doing?" says the black cop to the white man.

"Not good."

"Okay, just hang in there."

As the cops continue to beat the dog, the dog shakes harder, eyes rolled back into his head. The white man shrieking.

"Shoot the damn thing," shouts Desiree.

The two cops look at each other. They draw their guns.

"Everybody back," says the Puerto Rican.

"Yeah, get the fuck back," says the black cop.

Nobody needs the cops to tell them this.

"You wanna go," says the Puerto Rican.

"No, you can go," says the black cop.

"Just don't shoot me," screams the white man.

This sends a chuckle through the growing crowd of onlookers.

"White people sure is funny..."

"I can't shoot it in the head," says the Puerto Rican cop. "Might pass through and get the guy."

"Just pop him from the side, behind the shoulders," says the black cop. "His heart's gotta be round in there. Just make sure you angle it down."

Squatting, the Puerto Rican cop takes aim. He fires into the side of the dog. But the dog doesn't let go. The Puerto Rican fires again and again and again. Finally, the dog unlocks his jaw.

CHAPTER THREE

The name of the white man is Vincent DeRosa. Vincent is lying in a bed at St. Luke's hospital. Although he lost a lot of blood, he's not so bad off. Just a series of nasty rips and the stitching used to keep them closed. The window in Vincent's room has a nice view of Morningside Park. The park is filled with people. People playing softball and basketball. People smoking and drinking and barbequing various forms of meat.

Looking out the window is Vincent's father, Victor. Beside the father is the mother, Gloria. Father and mother think their son is asleep. Keeping his eyes shut, Vincent continues to let them think so.

"Look at those fucking animals," says the father.

The mother shakes her head.

"What the hell was he doing there? What was he thinking?"

"I don't know, Victor."

"Why the hell else would he be down there?"

"I really couldn't tell you."

"Fucking Zulu land."

"I wish you wouldn't curse."

"Don't start. Don't start with me now. We gotta do something, Gloria."

"Like what?"

Vincent coughs.

"Shush," says the mother, going to her son. "He's waking up."

Vincent opens his eyes. "Hi, Ma."

She takes his hand. "You okay?"

"I'm fine. Except for a headache and my leg."

"Does it hurt?"

"Of course it hurts," says the father.

The mother ignores her husband.

"What time is it?" asks Vincent.

"Going on eight," says his father.

"When can I go home?"

"The doctor said tonight. As soon as you feel well enough to move."

"I'll get the doctor," says his father.

"Check at the nurses station," says his mom.

"I know," says his father, leaving.

"You were very lucky," says his mom.

"Yeah."

"The doctor said it could have opened an artery. You could have died."

"I felt like I was going to die."

The mother looks to the door and then back to her son. "Your father's very worried."

"I'm fine, Ma."

"He's worried about you. About what you were doing down there."

"Down where?"

"Down in that park. In Harlem. What where you doing there? I don't understand it either."

"It's not what you think, Ma."

She does not answer.

"Ma, I wasn't buying anything. I'm clean. I swear to God, Ma. I was going for a job."

"A job?"

"Yeah."

"What, a park ranger?" says his father, just now entering the room.

"No," says Vincent. "A teaching job. I'm going to become a teacher."

"In the park?"

"No. At a High School on 114th Street."

"Jesus, Joseph and Mary..."

"Relax, Ma."

"On 114th Street?" says his father. "What the hell are you talking about?"

"I got off at 116th Street and Broadway. I didn't realize that the school was down on the other side of the park. So I asked somebody and they told me how to get there. I guess I should have taken the 2 or the 3 rather than the 1 train."

"I don't believe you," says his father."

"It's true," says Vincent. "It's true and I'll prove it to you. You'll see."

"What a waste," says his father. "All that money down the toilet. I don't know what to fucking do..."

"Victor, please!" says his Mom.

"He's lying. All over again. Right back in it, aren't you? Am I right?"

"No. I'm not. I'm not."

Veritas Village is a drug and alcohol rehabilitation center located in upstate New York. Vincent spent a number of months there to break a valium addiction. Vincent's father took out a second mortgage to pay for his son's treatment.

"She don't show it, but it's harder on your mother than it is on me."

"Dad, it's not what you think."

"You know what's like getting a call at work saying your son's in some hospital up in Harlem? No, you don't."

"But Dad."

"But nothing."

"I'm clean."

"Yeah, maybe you are. Maybe you're clean because that dog stopped you. Maybe it's a sign from God."

"What, the dog?"

"Yes. Maybe God's trying to tell you something. Like Saint Paul when he got knocked off his horse."

"Yeah, right."

"Yeah, it is right. Maybe if you still went to church, none of this would ever have happened."

"There's plenty of addicts who go to church, Dad."

"That's not my point."

"What is your point, then?"

"Without faith, you're lost."

"Who says I'm without faith?   How would you know?"

"It don't matter what I know.   That's between you and God. Only God knows for sure. He knows. He knows even if you don't."

"Maybe I'll ask him, then.   Ask him if I believe in him."

"Vincent," says his Mother. "Don't talk like that. It's a sin."

"Sorry, Ma."

"He don't care," says his father. "All he cares about is his next fix."

"I never did heroin, Dad."

"Drugs are drugs.   And a drug addict is a drug addict."

"Alcohol is a drug. So is coffee and cigarettes. That makes you a three time loser."

"Don't you talk to me like that! You're not so big I still can't slap the shit out of you."

"Your answer for everything."

"Please! The both of you, please stop. Please!"

CHAPTER FOUR

The overturned Frisbee sits like a black plate on the Formica tabletop. Desiree cleans her weed, carefully separating stems and seeds from the green sticky buds. Shaking the Frisbee like a minor panning for gold, the skunk smell fills the room. Across from Desiree is her cousin, Marisol. Although Desiree and Marisol look somewhat alike, Marisol is far lighter, the color of caramel to Desiree's licorice. Desiree rolls a joint with the Big Bambu. Marisol refills the juice glasses from an opened two-liter bottle of red wine. D'Angelo sings from a boom box on a milkcrate by the window.

Desiree has just put Clyde to sleep. Clyde sleeps in the same bedroom Desiree once shared with Marisol when they were young. In many ways, Desiree and Marisol are more like sisters than cousins. After Marisol's mom died, Desiree's mom took her in despite the fact that she hated Marisol's mom, her sister, more than anybody else in the world.

"So then what happened?" says Marisol.

"It died."

"What about the white man?"

"The ambulance took him. Pass me the lighter?"

Marisol sparks the fire. Desiree takes a big hit, holds the smoke, passes the joint.

"I didn't even thank him," says Desiree.

"Sounds like you didn't have a chance to."

"Maybe he's still in the hospital. I don't know his name..."

"Maybe he's dead," says Marisol, passing the joint over.

"You'd like that."

"What?"

"One less white man."

"Oh, please."

A knock comes to the front door. Marisol looks at Desiree. And another knock. Desiree gets up from the table. She goes towards the door. "Who?"

"Open up, it's me."

Desiree looks back at Marisol. Desiree peeps through the peephole. She puts the chain across the door. She locks the second lock. "You're not supposed to be here," she says to the door.

"I need to talk to you."

"You can call me. You're not allowed here. You know that."

"It's important, Dee Dee. Just open the door."

"I'm gonna call the police."

"I need to talk to you about Clyde."

"Clyde is sleeping. You gonna wake him up."

"I'll be real quiet. Just let me say what I gotta say and I'll be gone."

Desiree looks over at Marisol. Marisol shakes her head. "Don't let that nigga in," whispers Marisol.

"I ain't gonna let you in, Rosco," says Desiree.

"I'm not goin' nowheres until I speak to you."

Desiree closes her eyes. She puts her hands to her temples. Marisol creeps over from the table. She pulls Desiree away from the door. She speaks low but firm, "Do not let that nigga in. Girl, don't."

"What do you think he wants?" says Desiree.

"Who the hell knows. That nigga's crazy. You know that. I know that."

Rosco knocks on the door. "Will you open up? Please, Dee Dee, it's important!"

"Call the cops," says Marisol.

"Dee Dee!" shouts Rosco from the hall. "Just three minutes. And then I'll go. I promise."

"I can't," says Desiree, going back towards the door.

"Why not?" says Rosco.

"Because you's crazy."

"Girl, if I was crazy, I'd just kick the door in. But I'm not. So, please, just open up."

Desiree pulls back the chain. Marisol stomps her foot, crosses her arms. Desiree opens the door. Rosco stands at the threshold. "Can I come in?" he says.

Desiree steps aside. Rosco enters the apartment. Desiree closes the door. Rosco sees Marisol fuming by the bathroom. "What up, Marisol?"

Marisol turns her head away.

"I heard what happened in the park," says Rosco.

"Yeah, so?"

"I heard Clyde almost got torn up."

"Clyde's fine. No thanks to you."

"This is true," says Rosco. "And that's why I'm here."

"Nigga's talkin' shit," mutters Marisol.

"You! You, stay outta this," says Rosco, breaking into a grin.

"What's so goddamn funny?" says Marisol.

"Nuthin'. Absolutely nothin'," says Rosco, still grinning.

"Nigga be buggin'," says Marisol.

Rosco turns to Desiree. "Anyway... What happened in the park? I do believe it's an omen."

"Nigga's crazy," mutters Marisol. "Completely bugged..."

"Rosco, what are you talking about?" says Desiree.

"I'm talking about an omen. A sign. About the meaning behind what happened. It's an omen, Dee Dee. That dog? That dog was my dog and—"

"Your dog!"

"Yeah, just hear me out. Please! Yeah, the three-leg pit. His name was Rum, Redrum. I had him since he was a puppy."

"Well, your puppy almost killed my baby."

"I know it. I know it. And when I found out about it, I went crazy over it."

"Humph..." says Marisol.

"That dog? Rum? That dog was dead, Dee Dee."

"I know it's dead. I saw the cops shoot him."

"No. He was already dead. Not from the cops. Before the cops. He was dead on Friday."

"What the hell are you talking about?"

"Rum was dead and came back again. He rose up from the dead. You can ask anybody that was there. Hundreds of people saw him dead and hanging from a tree last Friday night. You can even ask Antoine. He was there."

"Don't you be bringin' Antoine into your mess," says Marisol.

"Will you just chill a minute! Damn..." says Rosco. "Antoine was there like everybody else. The dog was dead. Then, three days later, he's alive and tryin' to eat my only child. You understand? It's an omen. A sign from God. And I intend to do something about it."

"I don't know what to say to you, Rosco," says Desiree.

"You don't have to say nothin'. All I'm askin' is that you give me another chance."

"You must be out your mind. Another chance! Nigga, please..."

"I'm talkin' about with Clyde. I'm Clyde's father and I wanna do what's right by my son."

"He don't even know you."

"I wanna know him. I wanna do the right thing, Dee Dee. This thing with the dog has me all shook up."

"Crazy ass, nigga..." mutters Marisol.

Rosco smiles at Marisol. He turns to Desiree. "All I'm askin' you is to give me a chance. A chance to be his Pops. I barely knew my father. I don't want it to be that way for my son."

"I don't know..."

"Just think about it. Maybe I could see him once a week to start."

"I'll think on it."

"Thanks, Dee Dee. I guess I'll be goin' then."

"Alright, then," says Desiree.

Rosco goes to kiss her on the cheek, but Desiree feints back and away. Smiling, Rosco leaves the apartment. Desiree shuts the door. She looks at Marisol.

"You shoulda called the police," says Marisol. "That nigga's mad ass crazy."

CHAPTER FIVE

With school to start soon, Antoine and Tyrone spend as much time as possible at Sin City. Although they are underage, they never have a problem gaining entrance. Antoine drains his bottle of beer, washing down a handful of adrenaline pills. He sticks a hundred dollar bill into the thrusting crotch before his face. He grabs a tit and grabs an ass. He gets up for the door. On the way out, he and Tyrone shake hands with Shaka X, the porn director, sitting at a table with a small bevy of naked woman. Antoine gives a pound and a hug to the bald gorilla guarding the door. Tyrone does the same. They head outside.

The light in the parking lot sputters on and off. Antoine sparks a blunt, passing it to Tyrone. After puffing back and forth, Tyrone retrieves two baseball bats from behind the dumpster, handing one to Antoine. They walk over to where Shaka X's Jaguar is parked beneath the sputtering spot light. Antoine and Tyrone begin bashing in the windows and then headlights of the Jaguar. They are soon winded by their efforts. They throw the bats into the Jaguar via the shattered windshield. A shot rings out. Tyrone's head explodes. As Antoine runs for cover, a second shot rips through his kneecap. He falls hard beside the vandalized Jaguar. More shots are fired. The door bursts open.

"Shut that fucking thing off," says Marisol. "I wanna talk to you."

Antoine ignores Marisol, feverishly working the joystick, ducking and rolling away from the sniper fire blazing from the strip club's rooftop. Tyrone puts down his controller. He knows better than to mess with Marisol when she's heated like this.

Marisol stands between Antoine and the TV. Antoine cranes his neck to see. Marisol shuts the TV. Antoine tosses his controller onto the couch beside him. "What's wrong with you?" he says, picking up the blunt from the ashtray, relighting and blowing smoke between them.

Marisol goes to snatch the blunt. Antoine is quicker. He puts it behind his back. Marisol steps back. Antoine offers the blunt to Marisol.

"You're not funny," she says.

"I'm not tryin' to be," says Antoine, shrugging and handing the blunt to Tyrone who looks at it longingly, but not daring to partake until he sees how the whole scene is gonna shake out...

"I told you about Rosco," she says. "The nigga is dangerous. Dangerous and crazy."

"Yeah, so?"

"So, you hustlin' for him?"

"Hell no," says Antoine, turning to Tyrone. "We hustlin' for Rosco? For anybody?"

"Hell no," says Tyrone.

"Yeah, right. You swear and this nigga lies to it."

"I ain't lyin," says Tyrone.

"Who says we hustlin'?" says Antoine.

"Tell me you weren't with him last Friday night."

"What was we's doin' Friday?"

"I dunno," says Tyrone.

"Oh, Friday..." says Antoine. "Yeah, okay... But we wasn't hustlin'. You gotta get yourself some better info. We was there and Rosco was there. But we weren't working for him. Not exactly."

"Not exactly?"

"We was workin' the pit," says Antoine.

"Oh, yeah. Dat's right," says Tyrone, still staring at the blunt.

"With Rosco?" says Marisol. "I told you to have nuthin' to do with him."

"Yo, Sis, you gotta chill. All we was doin' was cleaning up after the fights. The only contact I had with Rosco was when he tipped me and Ty for pulling his dog from the pit. That's it. And that's all."

"No hustlin'?"

"No. Definitely, absolutely not. I'm not crazy. And anyway, Rosco don't sell drugs. Not no more."

"Yeah, right."

"He don't. Right, Ty?"

"That's right. Rosco strictly a money man."

"What are you talking about?"

"He a Shylock," says Antoine. "He lends out cash."

"You mean a loan shark?"

"Yeah. He makes mad money too. No need for him to hustle drugs."

"Well, the nigga still bugged," says Marisol.

"I know the nigga bugged," says Antoine. "But even if he wasn't, I got no interest in hustlin' for him or anybody else. I gonna blow up this year. Right, Ty?"

"Dat's right. Son's gonna make All City."

"So why I gonna take a chance with a nigga like Rosco? I got plans," says Antoine. "You know that. I gonna go D-1 on a full ride. Maybe play a year or two and then the NBA." Antoine takes a hit and passes the blunt back to Tyrone who now decides to partake. "Then, me, you, Ty, we all gonna live in style..."

"Dat's right," says Tyrone, blowing smoke.

"But who says I be hustlin' for Rosco?"

"I saw Rosco today," says Marisol. "He mentioned you."

"What he say?"

"Just some bugged out shit about his dead dog..."

"Rum?"

"I don't fucking know. Yeah, I think he said that."

Antoine looks at Tyrone. "So maybe it's true."

"What are you talking about?" says Marisol.

"Rum was Rosco's dog," says Antoine. "It got killed Friday night. Me and Ty put him in the garbage ourselves. But we be hearing rumors that he got killed again while chewin' up this white man in Morningside Park."

"That's stupid," says Marisol.

"Rum only had three legs," says Antoine. "Just like the pit that bit the white man."

"It's a miracle," says Tyrone.

"Stop talkin' junk," says Marisol. "You all fucked up anyway."

"True dat," says Tyrone.

"You both all fucked up."

"So is you," says Antoine, grinning.

"Don't you be worryin' about me," says Marisol. "Just make sure you two stay the fuck away from Rosco."

"I ain't got nuthin' to do with the nigga," says Antoine. "C'mon, sit down. Chill..."

Marisol takes the blunt from Antoine. She takes a hit followed by a sip from the warm quart bottle of beer sitting on the floor. Antoine picks up his controller. He turns the TV back on. A hand grenade is thrown into the Jaguar. As the car explodes, Antoine scales the chain link fence. In the alley below, a snarling pit bull gnashes his teeth. More shots are fired, pinging off the steel fence posts. Antoine pulls a knife from his boot. He drops into the alley.

"This shit is ridiculous," says Marisol.

CHAPTER SIX

Vincent is nervous. They will be coming shortly. He tells himself to calm down, that this is no different from the opening night of a play. Vincent sits behind his desk. The empty classroom is not unlike an empty theatre. Vincent stands and then sits again, his eyes trained on the rows of seats before him. Pretty soon, that door will open and the show will begin.

He looks at the clock. The bell's gonna ring in sixty seconds. The red hand sweeping. Vincent wipes his palms against his pants. Vincent tells himself to relax. You are completely prepared. You know what you have to do. But still, the nervousness will not go away. It will not go away and it seems to be getting worse. Vincent considers leaving. Walking out the door, down the hall and out the building. The urge is almost irresistible. The nervousness is overwhelming. It is so overwhelming because, deep down, Vincent understands why he is nervous and this understanding instead of calming him, only feeds his anxiety.

The bell rings. There is an instant of utter calm like the instant after a bomb goes off, before the destruction registers and the screaming begins. The door flies open. Vincent remains frozen behind his desk. They are here. They are coming inside. Tall ones, short ones, brown ones, black ones... Some glance his way. Most do not. A few have taken seats. Most others are clumped in small groups, chattering and loud talking. One kid holds a video game while two others look on as he plays.

Vincent stands up. Except for the nerds in the front row, nobody takes notice. Vincent looks to the door. Fight or flight? Vincent walks to the door. Fight or flight? He closes the door. The loud talking has gotten louder.

Vincent says, "Excuse me..." He raises his voice, "Can everybody please take a seat?"

The loud talking continues. The video game continues. One boy touches one girl's ass. The girl punches the boy in the shoulder. The boy puts up his hands and backs away.

Vincent opens the door. He looks down the hallway. Empty except for the security guard showing the custodian something in the newspaper. They take no notice of Vincent. Vincent grasps the edge of the classroom door. He slams the door with a tremendous bang. Heads turn. Movement stops. He has their complete attention. He must continue or lose it. Vincent says, "Please shut the fuck up and take a seat."

There is a long beat of dense silence.

Vincent says, "Yes, that's right. Please sit the fuck down."

The class is confused. But it is a proper confusion. Vincent feels this, he knows this. He says, "Please find yourself a seat. Thank you."

The students look at each other. Some smile, some mutter but they all find seats to sit in. They look at Vincent. Only seconds have passed but they are long seconds and Vincent must keep the flow streaming in his favor. Vincent goes to the blackboard. It is smooth and black and clean. He takes the chalk, breaks it in half and writes in large capital letters: "NO BULLSHIT." Vincent underlines the words. He turns back to the class. He says, "Can anybody read this for me?"

They stare at Vincent. A few smirk and a few suck their teeth. Vincent stares back at them. The nervousness is still there but now it's fueling his edge and advantage. Vincent does not blink. He says, "Somebody, anybody?"

From the far corner of the back row, a tall lightskinned boy stares directly into Vincent's eyes. Vincent can tell right away that he is an athlete by the confidence of his stare and the strength of his body language. Vincent nods, "Yes?"

"It says, 'no bullshit.'"

"Thank you," says Vincent. "And your name?"

"Antoine."

"Thank you, Antoine. My name is Vincent. Vincent DeRosa. I'm your teacher and this class will focus on what it says right there on the board. No bullshit."

"Cracker's crazy," mutters Antoine to Tyrone.

"Excuse me? Antoine? Did you say something?"

"Me? No. Nuthin'," says Antoine.

A hand is raised. The hand is connected to one of the nerds in the front row. Unlike the other boys, his pants are not baggy and his shirt is not triple-X. He is thin with a long neck and tiny, bat-like ears.

"Yes?" says Vincent.

"My program card says this is supposed to be a history class. It says, 'Humanities Elective HE4.'"

"And your name?"

"Drevone."

"Well, Drevone... That card is bullshit," says Vincent.

Laughter and various unkind barbs about Drevone's attire and general corniness.

"Alright," says Vincent. "Settle down."

But they are not settling down. Vincent may lose them yet. Vincent shouts, "Hey! Settle down! Damn... Fuck it..."

They are quiet again. But there is a general unease in the air like the tension generated when two predators face off over a recent kill. Antoine raises his hand. He says, "Why you gotta curse?"

"Curse? I don't have to curse. I don't have to do anything except breathe or die. But as long as I'm here, I'll say whatever comes to my mind so long as it serves the purpose of this class. This class of no bullshit. No lies. I'm gonna be completely honest with you. Nothing but the truth no matter how brutal that truth has to be. And I expect you to be the same way with me and with each other. No bullshit all around. That's the way it's gotta be and that's the way it's gonna be. Because, you wanna know something else: I don't give a flying fuck if they fire me today or tomorrow or the next day. I don't. So with that in mind, it makes it very easy for me to operate. You respect me, I respect you. You fuck with me, you're gonna get it right the fuck back. As far as you wanna go. You think I'm bullshitting, go ahead and try me. Okay? Good... So what the hell is this white man talking about anyway? You know the answer... But maybe you don't think about it so much. What I'm talking about is how your life, my life, mostly everybody's life is ruled by some kind of bullshit or another. And this is nothing new. Bullshit has been around as long as people have been around. As long as there has been a 'history' of man. I'm talking about way back, way way back to the Garden of Eden when that snake bullshitted Eve into eating the apple."

A girl raises her hand. She sits beside Drevone. But she is no nerd. She has long braids and a pretty face and her clothes match from her sneakers to her turned around baseball cap. She says, "You got some pretty eyes."

"Thanks," says Vincent, purposely not losing a beat.

"So you saying the Bible is bullshit?"

"And your name?"

"Aisha."

"Good question, Aisha. No, I'm not saying the Bible is bullshit. I'm talking about a story in the Bible. The story about Adam and Eve and how the Devil tricked them into eating from the Tree of Knowledge."

"How he do that?" asks Aisha.

"If I remember correctly, Adam and Eve were warned by God not to eat the fruit from the tree in the middle of the garden, the Tree of Knowledge. If they ate from this tree, God told them they would die. But the Devil, he told Eve that if she ate from this tree, she would be like God. That she would know everything and live forever. So she ate some and she gave Adam some to eat too."

"And then they got thrown out of Eden," says Aisha. "Right?"

"That's right," says Vincent.

"But they didn't die," says Antoine. "They just got thrown out. The Devil was telling the truth."

Drevone raises his hand, "Adam lived nine hundred and thirty years."

"Oh, yeah?" says Vincent. "How do you know that?"

"It says so in the Bible."

"You all be talkin' junk," says Antoine. "I don't believe any of it."

"You don't have to," says Vincent. "All I'm asking for you to think about it... To listen and decide for yourself: is this bullshit or is this the truth."

"Whatever," mutters Antoine.

CHAPTER SEVEN

They wait on a bench outside the park. After nearly an hour, Desiree takes Clyde into the park to play. While Clyde climbs the monkey bars, Desiree keeps an eye out for Rosco. She smokes a number of cigarettes. Inside the Newports box, a joint lies ready. But Desiree does not light it up. There is still an outside chance that Rosco will show and she doesn't want to be high in case he does.

As Desiree sits and smokes, she thinks about the white man. She pictures his black curly hair and pretty eyes. Bright blue bewitching eyes. She thinks how she never got around to looking him up at the hospital. She smiles to herself, remembering the dance... Touched on the shoulder, Desiree jumps.

"You scared the shit out of me," says Desiree. "You're late. What's wrong with you?"

"Sorry," says Rosco. "Hey! Hey, little man, c'mere. C'mere!"

In Rosco's hand is a gift-wrapped box tied with a big red bow. Clyde runs over.

"He shouldn't be runnin' like that," says Rosco. "It's bad for his back."

"What, you a doctor now?"

"No, I'm not a doctor. But it just makes sense. It's like he be wearin' heels. And everybody knows that high heels are not no good for your back. You know that, right?"

"I don't wear high heels."

"You used to."

"Not any more."

"Why, 'cause they hurt your back?"

"Stop talkin' junk, Rosco."

"Hey, little man," says Rosco, handing Clyde the present. "I'm your Daddy. And here's a little present I got for you."

"What do you say?" says Desiree.

"Thank you," says Clyde.

"Go on, open it up," says Rosco.

Clyde rips off the gift wrapping. It is a metallic cube. On the top of the cube is printed, "THE WORLD IS YOURS!" in bold, black lettering. On the side of the cube is a handle.

Rosco says, "Now turn that handle there. Go on, turn it around."

Clyde obeys. As he turns the handle, music plays. Desiree has heard that tune before, but she can't quite place it. Suddenly the lid flies open, a mini Al Pacino as "Scarface" popping out of the box. In his hands is a mini shotgun. "Say 'ello to my little friend," shouts Scarface. "Blam, blam, blam," goes the shotgun.

"That's just great," says Desiree.

"Isn't it?" says Rosco. "It's Scarface."

"I know who it is."

"Now push his head back inside," says Rosco. "That's it. Yeah. Now turn the handle and he'll pop out again. Go on."

Clyde does this again and again. He loves the Scarface-in-the-Box.

"You see what it says on the top? 'The World Is Yours!' That's what your Daddy lives by, little man."

"So did Scarface," says Desiree. "And look what happened to him."

"Scarface was a movie. I'm real."

"You sure are."

"Hey, little man, you wanna go to the zoo? See some lions and tigers and bears?"

Clyde looks up at Rosco and then at Desiree.

"I don't know, Rosco."

"What's there to know?"

"I'd rather not discuss it in front of Clyde."

"What's there to discuss? All I wanna do is take my son to the zoo. I'll bring him right back."

"You can spend time with him here."

"They got snakes at the zoo?" says Clyde.

"Sure they do," says Rosco. "Big giant snakes. Pythons and anacondas. Snakes as long as a bus. You'd like to see them, wouldn't you? Sure you would. It's educational, the zoo is... C'mon, Dee Dee. Nuthin's gonna happen. Not when he's with me. I swear. C'mon..."

"Five o'clock," says Desiree. "Not a minute later or I call the cops."

Clyde looks at Rosco.

"The world is yours," says Rosco. "C'mon, little man, we gonna have us some fun."

Clyde takes his father's hand. Desiree walks out of the park with them to Rosco's double-parked BMW across the street. Desiree helps Clyde into the back seat. For an instant and for the first time, she sees Rosco's face inside her son's face. It is a certain expression of the eyes and the mouth. An expression of curious attention. Despite herself, she glances into the rearview, taking notice of Rosco's fine looks. His full lips and smooth dark skin. She buckles Clyde up with the seatbelt. In his lap is the Scarface-in-the-Box.

Desiree says, "I swear, Rosco, you step an inch outta line with this, it's over. You understand me?"

"He's my son, Dee Dee. Nuthin's gonna happen to him when he's with me. No way."

"Clyde, you be good. Give Mommy a kiss."

Clyde kisses Desiree. He turns the handle. Out pops Scarface, "Say 'ello to my little friend!"

As the BMW drives down Manhattan Avenue, Desiree picks into her box of Newports for that joint.

CHAPTER EIGHT

Rosco brings Clyde back at exactly five minutes to five. He has outfitted the boy with a new FILA sweat suit and matching JORDAN sneakers. Clyde has a great time at the zoo. The only problem of the day was Rosco's displeasure with Clyde walking on his tiptoes. Rosco tells Desiree that if Clyde doesn't quit the habit, other kids will make fun of him. Desiree tells Rosco that the doctor said he'd grow out of it, that it wasn't something to worry about.

"What do doctors know?"

"Nigga, please. Didn't you do the same thing when you were little? Or did you forget you told me that?"

"I don't forget nuthin.'"

"So Clyde will grow out of it just like you did."

"My Moms beat it outta me with a ruler. That's how I stopped."

"Well, there's gonna be none of that here."

"Of course not."

Before Rosco leaves, he hands Clyde a hundred dollar bill. He says, "If you stop walking on your toes by next Saturday, I'll give you another one of those."

Desiree takes the bill from Clyde. "Go inside a minute, Clyde."

"Why? What did I do?"

"You didn't do nothing. I just need to talk to your Daddy a minute. Now do what you're told. Go."

"Go on, little man," says Rosco.

As soon as Clyde is out of sight, Desiree hands Rosco back his money. "Don't do that again," she says.

"What?"

"Be handin' him money."

"I was just tryin' to help him wif—"

"I don't care what you were trying to do. I don't want him thinking that money is the answer to his problems."

"You take it. I don't need it."

"I don't need it either."

"But that don't mean you can't use it. Use if for something he needs. New clothes or toys or somethin'."

"He don't need no clothes or toys, thank you. Clyde gets all he needs. I've been taking care of that his whole life and I plan to keep takin' care of it, all by myself, like I've been doin' without you or anybody else."

"You hardheaded."

"Maybe I am."

"Here, just take it," says Rosco. "Maybe buy some books with it. You still be readin' all them books like you used to?"

"When I can."

"So take it. Buy yourself a book."

"Thanks but no."

"I don't understand you."

"Nobody says you have to."

"True that," says Rosco, stuffing the bill in his top pocket, heading for the door. "Hey, I gotta idea," he says, taking out the bill again. "Why not buy some books for the boy? You know, start him a little liberry. What could be wrong about that? Huh? Boy's Pops buying him books for a liberry." Rosco lets the bill rest on the table top.

Desiree looks at the bill but says no more about it.

Rosco says, "I best be goin' now. Is next Saturday okay?"

"I suppose."

CHAPTER NINE

Rosco didn't show next Saturday or the Saturday after that. To make matters worse, he didn't call or send word, which only piqued Clyde's curiosity and hope.

"You think he's coming today?"

"I don't think so," says Desiree.

"When then? He said he was going to come on Saturday."

"Clyde, I got a headache. Alright? We'll talk later about this."

"You want me to rub your head?"

"Yeah, Baby. Okay."

Desiree rests her head on the pillow jammed against the arm of the couch. Clyde knows the routine. He stands behind her, massaging her temples. Desiree closes her eyes. Gradually, the pain subsides. She falls asleep... The phone rings and the phone is ringing and Clyde knows not to answer the phone. Desiree never answers the phone until she knows who's calling on the answering machine. Desiree does not like the idea of somebody suddenly talking inside her head without warning. Space is important to Desiree. In the olden days, people wrote letters and you could open them and reply to them when you were ready. Today, a person can just pop into your head and you gotta deal with it no matter what you're doing or thinking at the time. The answering machine clicks on. The answering machine says, "Clyde and Desiree. You know what to do and when to do it..."

"Dee Dee! It's me, Marisol. Pick up the damn phone!"

"Marisol?"

"Yeah, what up? I didn't wake you, did I?"

"Yeah, but it's okay. I guess I must have fell out."

"You got any smoke?"

"Yeah."

"I'm comin' over. Alright?"

"Yeah, okay." Desiree hangs up the phone. She can hear Bugs Bunny in the other room.

"Clyde! Clyde, turn down that TV!"

"WHAT?"

"TURN DOWN THE DAMN TV!"

"OKAY!"

Bugs Bunny fades... Desiree looks out the window. She sees a family walking up the block. They are dressed up for church. There are two little girls in bright pink dresses, their hair greased down and shining like their shoes. The mother wears a blue dress with yellow flowers. Her head is a sculpture of swirling braids that swoop up at least a foot above her brow. The father is tall and thin in a dark black suit. He is dark skinned like the girls and unlike the mother who is high yellow. The girls hold their Daddy's hand. The three walk a step behind the mother. Desiree watches them as they head up the block. Desiree used to go to church when she was little. She used to go all dressed up with her mom and Marisol after Marisol's mom was buried. The phone starts ringing again. The answering machine answers...

"Dee Dee! Dee Dee, it's Rosco. If you there, please pick it up. Dee Dee! Okay, alright then. Anyway, I'm in Jersey now but I'm on my way. I can explain everything. I had some trouble down in Atlanta but—"

Desiree picks up the phone. "Nigga, you must be crazy callin' here."

"Dee Dee, I'm sorry, but—"

"But nuthin'! Don't you be callin' here no more. Never. I musta been trippin' listening to your bullshit!"

"DEE DEE!"

She hangs up the phone.

Seconds later, it starts ringing again. The answering machine answers...

Rosco says, "Dee Dee, please, you don't have to pick up—just listen... I had some trouble. But now everything's fixed and I wanna make it up to Clyde for—"

Desiree picks up. "If you come by here, I'm gonna have you locked up. I still got that order of protection, Rosco."

"But Dee Dee, I—"

She looks towards Clyde's room. She lowers her voice, "Clyde don't need no Daddy who comes and goes whenever he feels like it. You gotta be committed, Rosco. And we both know that that's something you are incapable of."

"How am I supposed to be there when they got me locked up?"

"Your problems are not my problem. Or Clyde's. So listen... You show up here, you gonna be locked up again. I swear to God. I swear on Clyde, I will call the police. You got it. Good-bye."

Desiree hangs up. She goes down to Clyde's room. She peeks in on Clyde watching his cartoons. She goes into her room to get her address book. She looks under "R" for Adrian Raysor, a detective from the 28th Precinct. Desiree once went out with him. Adrian was a nice guy but it didn't work out because he was a cop who pretended he didn't care but who couldn't get over her smoking weed. Also, he had a girl's first name that Desiree secretly couldn't get used to or comfortable with (even though she knew it was a stupid reason). Not long after they stopped seeing each other, Detective Adrian Raysor got married to a Puerto Rican from Jersey City. Raysor showed Desiree a photo of his wife and the baby when they ran into each other on the street. Desiree had to smile to herself thinking how he could have named the girl Adrian and got away with calling her Junior...

Raysor knows all about Rosco. Everybody in the Precinct knows about Rosco. Raysor told Desiree to call him if she ever had any problems with him.

Desiree calls the Precinct first, hoping he's there because she doesn't want to call his house and risk speaking to his wife. Luckily, he's on the job. After a quick, "hello," Desiree gets right to the point. Raysor tells her not to worry, that he will send a car around.

Five minutes later, Desiree sees the patrol car parked across the street. Although she can't see them, they are the same cops who shot the three-legged dog. The black cop's name is Robert York. The Puerto Rican is Kenny Colon.

"The fucker makes one wrong move, I'm gonna waste his ass just like I did his dog," says Colon.

"You think he knows it's you who iced Redrum?"

"Huh? What?"

"That was the name of Rosco's dog. Redrum."

"Whatever..."

"I bet he knows it was you. Knows it was patrolman, Kenny Colon of the 2-8 who iced his beloved, Redrum. Probably has a picture of you with a target on it taped to his wall. We best keep a very close look out for the nigga. They say he's crazy. At least that's what I heard."

"Fuck you, York."

"Hey, check it! Damn! Check it out. Hola, Mammi."

The two cops hawk Marisol crossing the street.

CHAPTER TEN

Desiree blows the smoke out the window, passing the joint back to Marisol.

"Shit, look," says Desiree.

Rosco's BMW drives up the block but it doesn't stop on account of the police cruiser.

"Nigga crazy," says Marisol. "But he ain't stupid. At least he knows you mean business."

Desiree nods, blows smoke.

Marisol says, "So what ever happened between you and the detective?"

"Adrian?"

"Yeah."

"Oh… It didn't work out."

"He was fine…. Even if he was a cop…"

"He was alright."

The phone rings. Desiree freezes. Rosco comes on over the answering machine. "Dee Dee. I know you're there. I just wanna talk. That's all. I ain't gonna come by. I just wanna talk to you."

"Let me talk to the nigga," says Marisol, heading for the phone.

"Marisol wait."

Too late. Marisol has the receiver in her hand. "Come by? You ain't never coming by here. You done played yourself, nigga. You come anywhere near this building, those cops gonna bag you up. We saw your dirty ass rollin' through. So you best better keep on rollin'."

"Let me talk to Desiree."

"Desiree is unavailable. So—"

"Bitch, stop playin' and put her on the phone."

"Bitch? Who you callin' a bitch? You punk ass, nigga! I ain't no bitch. You must be talkin' about one of those little skank ass shorties you be blazin'. Not me, nigga!"

Marisol hangs up the phone. It rings again. She picks it up before the answering machine. "And you call here again they gonna pick you up for harassment. You got that—you punk ass, nigga!"

"Excuse me?"

"Oh, I'm sorry. Who this?"

"Is Desiree there? This is Detective Raysor."

"Oh, sure," she says, handing the phone to Desiree with a wince.

"Hello?"

"Hey, it's me, Adrian. Rosco's just went by your block but when he saw the patrol car, he kept on his way."

"I saw him from the window."

"I don't think he'll be back but I'm gonna have my men stick around anyway."

"Thank you, Adrian."

"Not a problem. You just give me a call—anytime—you have my numbers, right?"

"Yeah, I got 'em."

"Alright then."

"There go Antoine and Tyrone," says Marisol from the window.

Down on the street, York pushes the window switch. The glass slides down. York motions to Antoine. Antoine crosses to the cop car. Tyrone remains on the opposite side of the street.

York says, "What's goin' on?"

"Chillin'."

"How you look this year?"

"We gonna take it. Straight to the Garden."

"I think you may be right, Young Blood."

"You can bet your badge on it. All the way."

"That Tyrone over there?"

Antoine looks back to Tyrone and then to the cop, "Yeah."

"You gotta be careful. You gotta be careful who you associate with. 'Specially if you wanna go places."

"He alright."

"I hear he be hangin around Rosco and that Ivory White from uptown."

"I gotta go."

"Go on, then," says York. "And I'll see you next week. You got Manhattan Center, right?"

"Yeah."

The two boys cross the street to Desire's tenement. Once inside, Tyrone pulls a fat envelope from his pocket. "I'm supposed to give this to you."

"What's this?" says Desiree.

"It's an envelope."

"I can see it's an envelope, fool. From who?"

"Rosco gave it to me. He said to give it to you. He said to say that it's for Clyde's liberry."

"What liberry?" says Clyde.

"Antoine, could you take him inside and set him up with a movie?"

"Yeah, alright," says Antoine. "C'mon, Clyde."

Antoine takes Clyde by the hand. Clyde reluctantly tiptoes back to his room with Antoine.

Desiree says, "I don't want it. You take it back."

"I can't, Dee Dee," says Tyrone.

"Why the hell you take it from him in the first place?"

"Because he told me to."

"And you gonna do whatever the nigga says? You should stay away from him. He's all fucked up."

"Was Antoine with you?" asks Marisol.

"No," says Antoine coming back into the room.

"You stay away from him, Antoine," says Marisol.

Desiree goes to the phone. They all watch as she pushes the numbers... "Rosco?" she says.

"Yeah. You got it?"

"Tyrone just gave it to me. It's thick."

"That ain't nuthin'. I just wanted to let you know I'm serious."

"About Clyde?"

"Yeah, who else?"

"Why don't you come on back around?"

A pause. Rosco says, "What, you think I'm stupid?"

"I know you're not stupid, Rosco."

"Yeah, right. Come over there with 5-0 parked across the street?"

"I'm not saying for you to come up. I'll come down. I'll come down and tell the cops it's okay and then me and Clyde will get in your car to show them it's okay."

"What you sayin'?"

"I'm saying we should be able to discuss our issues like adults. We're not kids anymore, Rosco. We gotta be able to talk if we gonna be able to do anything."

"I'll be there in a minute. But you come down quick. I don't want any problems, Dee Dee."

Desiree hangs up the phone.

Marisol says, "Girl, you lost your mind?"

Desiree smiles. She opens the envelope. She thumbs through the hundred dollar bills. "No, I didn't lose my mind." Crossing to the window, Desiree sees the church family returning from church. They walk in the same formation as earlier in the day...

Rosco's BMW turns the corner, rolling to a stop about ten yards behind the police car.

"Shit, he back," says York, looking into his rear-view. He radios the Precinct for backup. "Let's go," he says. "And just take it real easy, okay?"

"I got you," says Colon.

The cops get out of the patrol car. They have their guns drawn. Rosco gets out of his BMW. He has his hands up high. He says, "I'm clean. Relax, officers."

"Just stay right where you are," says York.

"Yo, relax," says Rosco. "My kid and his moms are comin' down and we can straighten this whole thing out."

"Don't move."

"Yo! Yo, Rosco," shouts Desiree from her window.

Rosco looks up. The father from the church family also looks up.

"See, I tole you," says Rosco.

Desiree reaches into the envelope. She tosses the bills into the breeze. The wind catches the pieces of paper, swirling them all up and down 112th Street. It's a wonderful sight. A bright sunny day and the sky is raining money. Some bills flutter into open tenement windows. Others get caught up in a second wind that send them as far as Seventh Avenue. One bill gets caught in the tower of braids and the little girls grab the ones that get blown in their faces. Although the father keeps them moving, he can't help himself from stomping and then snatching the bills at his feet.

In less than a minute, the shower is over but the word is spreading. Within five minutes the street and surrounding blocks are full of people, stooping and scavenging like little kids on an Easter egg hunt.

CHAPTER ELEVEN

Detective Adrian Raysor sits by the table, across from Desiree. On the couch are Antoine and Tyrone. Marisol is inside with Clyde.

"Well, if that's what you say," says Raysor. "Then I guess I'll have to leave it at that."

"Thank you," says Desiree.

"Of course that means we have to let him go. There's no crime him driving up the street."

"I understand."

"But he bothers you in any way... Threats—whatever—you let me know and we'll pick him up."

"Thank you."

"Alright, then," he says, turning to Antoine and Tyrone. "And you two—you stay away from him. It's not worth it. No matter what he promises you."

Tyrone nods. Antoine nods.

Raysor says, "How's the jumper lookin'?"

"Smooth," says Antoine. "Like water."

"You think you can beat Lincoln this year?"

"Definitely."

"What about Grady?"

"Them too."

"Seems Brooklyn has all the powerhouses."

"Except for this year. This year, we the team to beat," says Tyrone. "Even niggas in Brooklyn know it."

"Well, keep workin' on that shot," says Raysor. "There's a million kids who can take it to the hole, but somebody who's got a shot and a handle? That'll put you in the big time."

"Hm-m."

"They say Larry Bird used to take 500 shots every day after practice."

"Larry Bird... White boy gotta be able to shoot 'cause he sure as hell can't do nothin' else," says Antoine.

"No doubt," says Tyrone. "He got all the hype 'cause he was white. If he was black, he'd be just another nigga in the NBA."

"Maybe," smiles Raysor. "But he could shoot. And he could shoot when the game was on the line."

As Raysor and the boys continue to talk basketball, Desiree remembers that Raysor has a large, crescent-shaped birthmark beside his belly button. Desiree sees him sitting naked in the chair. She sees the birthmark and his rounded belly and his hanging cock. Raysor looks back at her. Desiree looks away. Raysor stands. He says, "Alright, then. You all take care."

After Desiree closes the door behind Raysor, Marisol comes back into the living room.

"He sleeping?" says Desiree.

"Yeah, he out," says Marisol.

"Thanks."

"You know, you lucky," says Marisol.

"Why's that?" says Desiree.

"Dee Dee, you just don't get away with throwin' money out the window like that."

"Why not?"

"Because you ain't white and you ain't rich."

"So?"

"So where else somebody like you gonna get money like that? And," she turns to Tyrone and Antoine. "You two coulda been locked up if they caught you carrying it here."

"I didn't carry nothin'," says Antoine.

"Dat's right," says Tyrone. "Ant didn't even know I had it."

"You one dumb ass, nigga," she says.

"Why don't you just chill," says Antoine.

"Me? I'm not the one that need to be chillin'. You two are headin' for trouble you keep findin' yourselves in the same spots as that crazy ass, Rosco."

"Yeah, whatever," says Antoine. "C'mon, Ty, let's bounce..."

After Tyrone and Antoine leave, Marisol relights the joint. "You know, Dee Dee, you coulda kept that money. I don't see why you did that. I mean, I see why... But I don't think it was the best idea. You still coulda got your point across another way."

"Oh, yeah? How?"

"You coulda just kept it and had told those cops he threatened you and was on his way up here to bust you up."

"And what do you think Rosco would do knowing I did all that?"

"Nigga would be in jail."

"Niggas can still make phone calls from jail."

"Yeah... But he's probably just as mad for you throwin' it all away."

"He's mad. But he not gonna do nuthin' to me over it. I know the nigga. I know how his mind works."

"But you still coulda kept some," says Marisol. "A handful? You know what I'm sayin'? Just pocket a handful and toss the rest. You still coulda got your point across. No way he or anybody could tell if you hadda kept a handful for yourself."

"But I didn't want any. I don't need his money."

CHAPTER TWELVE

"WHAT DOES NOT KILL ME, MAKES ME STRONGER."

These words were written on the blackboard before they came into class. Each day, he'd put a quote on the board without further explanation. Then he'd have the class respond to the quote in their journals.

"You can write whatever you want in your journals," Vincent told them. "As long as you write something each day, you will pass this class."

"Whatever we want?" asked Antoine.

"It would be nice if you responded to what I put on the board. But if you'd rather write something else—a poem, a rap, a page about whatever's on your mind—go right ahead."

"And as long as we write something, we pass?" asked Marcus.

"That's right. What could be more simple?"

"How do you get an A?" asked Aisha.

"You get an A for putting down intelligent things in your journal, for saying intelligent things in class and for not getting on my nerves."

Vincent was well liked by his students. Although strict in one sense, he was still far easier than any of the other teachers in giving that passing grade. One kid only drew obscene pictures in his journal. But he passed. They all passed. For Vincent, passing was not the issue, a belief in conflict with that of Miss Betty McCool, the principal of Wadleigh High School.

McCool was hated by staff and students alike. She operated on a Stalinist model. Teachers were encouraged to spy on each other and report their findings. Those who came up with the best "dirt" were awarded the cushy positions. Those who fell into disfavor were banished to cafeteria duty and late afternoon study hall. At the end of the year, any unfavorable teachers without tenure were "excessed."

Vincent did not fear McCool because he was not afraid of what would happen if he lost his job. Everybody knew this. It was no secret. The kids, the other teachers, even the lunch ladies and the janitors all knew that Vincent didn't give a damn about what Miss McCool had to say.

It did not take long for McCool to be informed of Vincent's teaching tactics. But she held off her interrogation because it was early in the year and she had more pressing matters to attend to. Also, she didn't quite know what to make of him. Bold, but as far as she could tell, not insane, the man kept his classes well managed and in line. There were never any calls for help from Vincent's classroom. What's more, he had the best passing and attendance rate in the entire school. But, then again, she still had to let him know who was boss while, more importantly, letting the other teachers know that she was not about to be intimidated by this new upstart who walked the halls in sneakers and blue jeans and allowed himself to be called Vincent or Vinny by his students.

Vincent was summoned via a note in his mailbox. When he looked up from reading the note, he realized the secretaries had all been watching him because they all suddenly looked down. Smiling, Vincent tossed the missive into the trash, striding directly to the open door of Miss McCool's office. He knocked.

"Come in!"

Vincent took the chair across from her large desk, cluttered with piles of papers and textbooks, and a dirty ashtray in the shape of a swan. Vincent was repulsed yet irresistibly drawn to the sight of Miss McCool's spackle-white skin set off by short, yellow teeth colored from decades of smoking Bensen & Hedges 100s. Her head was large and turnip-shaped, the pointy side facing down. Although not technically obese, she safely qualified as slovenly. But what stood out most was her hair. Miss McCool was blessed with a luxurious mane of amber hair. If you judged Miss McCool solely by her hair, you'd swear she was Rita Hayworth.

Although smoking had been banned on school premises throughout the city, nobody ever said a word about this to Miss McCool. Miss McCool had been smoking for years. When it became illegal to smoke on school grounds, Miss McCool made no effort to stop. Yet, despite the telltale evidence of her teeth and the swan ashtray, nobody ever saw Miss McCool actually light up.

"Do you mind if I smoke?" said Vincent, removing a pack of Marlboros from his top pocket.

"Smoking is not allowed on school grounds," she said, her lipstick cracking in the cracks of her grin. "Didn't you know that?"

"Oh," said Vincent, glancing at the dirty swan. "I must have forgotten."

"A number of items concerning you and your class have been brought to my attention. Are you aware of what they are?"

"No."

"Let me get right to the point, then. This is a school. You are a teacher. It is your job to teach the subject you are contracted to teach. Profanity is not part of this equation. Tests, classroom assignments, homework and various other forms of student assessment must be administered and marked for a grade. Am I clear on this?"

"Absolutely."

"So, I can expect you to conform to the minimum standards as set forth by the Board of Education?"

"Excuse me?"

"So," she said, her smile withering like a flower in time-lapse photography. "You're going to start acting and start teaching like a teacher... Are we clear on this?"

"It's clear what you're saying, Ms, McCool. But, with all due respect, I'm not gonna change. I'm gonna keep on teaching them the way I've been teaching them because that's what I think is the right way to do it. And they're gonna listen to me because they know I'm not about bullshitting them."

"Maybe so," she said. "But ultimately, I'm in charge of this school. I'm the one who sets and makes policy here, Mr. DeRosa, not you or any other teacher who thinks they can do things according to their own whims. And if you or anybody else doesn't like it then—"

"You can fire them."

"Excess them."

"Excess?"

"It's like firing only we don't call it firing."

"Alright," said Vincent. "Fair enough. You can do that. But you're gonna have to find somebody quick, somebody to take over my classes... I wonder what the kids would have to say about that..." Vincent knew that all she had left to choose from at this time of year would be some lame burnt out shell of a substitute. "I'm sure my students will be most behaved for Mister Numbnuts who will begin by telling them to open their textbooks and take out their homework. Yeah, that oughta go over real big. But, if I were you, I'd want to get myself a backup just in case Mister Numbnuts doesn't survive the fall from the fourth floor window."

"You're sort of charming in your own way," said Miss McCool. "I see why they like you."

There was a long pause where Vincent stared into Miss McCool's eyes, neither of them looking away.

McCool did not blink until Vincent blinked first. "You can go back to your class for now... I'm not stupid. And I'm not one to back down either. If you decide to amend your policies, to perhaps compromise them to a degree, perhaps I can compromise too and you may well end up as one of the best teachers Wadleigh has to offer. But, and make no mistake about it, if you continue the way you are going, if you continue to defy me, this will be your first and last year here, Mr. DeRosa. Am I understood?"

"Absolutely, Miss McCool. And thank you for being straight with me."

"You're welcome," she said, reaching into the top drawer for her cigarettes and lighter. "You may go now. And please shut the door on the way out."

CHAPTER THIRTEEN

"Any volunteers?" asks Vincent. "Nobody? What about you, Rowland? We haven't heard from you in a while."

"I wrote nuthin' on that sentence," says Rowland.

"Well, what did you write then?"

"I wrote all about what I did wif my girl last night."

"Nigga be frontin'," says Shakia. "Nobody crazy enough to go for his ugly ass."

"What about yo momma?"

"Don't you be talkin' bout my momma," says Shakia, rising from her chair.

"Shakia, please sit down," says Vincent. "And Rowland, no mother talk."

"But she—"

"C'mon now, both of you. Your both acting stupid. Let's just move forward. Alright? Anybody else ready to read? Antoine? No? Okay, what about you? C'mon Tyrone, you write some very interesting things."

"Okay," says Tyrone. "I'll read." Tyrone opens up his journal. He reads: "'What does not kill me makes me stronger.' This sentence reminds me of a dog I used to know."

"Dat's his girl," says Marcus. Everybody laughs.

"Go on," says Vincent. "And the next person that interrupts can get the fuck out. Go on, Tyrone. We're listening..."

"Okay," says Tyrone. "So this dog, his name is Redrum. He a red nose pit. Redrum is murder spelled backwards. Redrum, he had a lot of shit happen to him but he just be comin' back stronger each time. Like when he had his first big money roll against Coffee. Rum had the life near shaken out of him by Coffee. It looked like it was no match, 'specially when Coffee nearly teared Rum's leg right off his ass. But Rum, he come back at Coffee with just his three legs left. He let Coffee think he givin' up, even lets Coffee tear into his ripped up leg. But then, while Coffee be all up in that leg, Rum come round under Coffee and take out his neck and he wins. Peoples can't believe it. Still talk about that fight today. After that, Rum just keep on winnin' with only three legs. There was no dog like Redrum. Then, one day, during the scratch, Rum got fucked up by the shot Rosco give him and because of this, he couldn't fight no more. You see, it wasn't Rum's fault that he lost but it don't matter 'cause he lost anyway. So if you lose you gotta pay, 'specially if you lost the kind of paper Rum lost that night. So Rum sees his last night on earth hangin' from the Losing Tree until he dead. But here the thing: Rum, he come back from the dead. Like a dog world miracle. Three days after he was hangin' on the tree, he be seen back alive, huntin' down a white man in Morningside."

"Dat's the dumbest thing I ever heard," says Shakia. "You sayin' the dog rose up from the dead?"

"I do believe so," says Tyrone.

"Dogs don't raise theyselves up from the dead," says Drevone. "Nuthin' in the Bible say nothin' 'bout that."

"Nigga, please,' says Tyrone. "You don't know shit."

"I know the Bible," says Drevone. "And I know there's no such thing as a dog raising his self up from the dead."

"The dog did come back," says Antoine. "Maybe he wasn't all dead in the first place. But he did come back."

"You saw it yourself," says Tyrone. "We both took him down from the tree together. Tell me Rum wasn't dead when you cut him down."

"He seemed dead," says Antoine. "But sometimes things ain't what they seem."

"Maybe he was in a coma," says Aisha.

"He wasn't in no coma," says Tyrone. "The dog was dead. No moving, no breathing. Dead. You all just afraid to see it for what it is. Me, I believe my eyes. I saw that dog dead."

"Ty be talkin' junk," says Shakia.

"Maybe not," says Vincent.

"Yeah, right," says Shakia. "What you know about some pit bull from the 'hood?"

"I was the white man who was attacked."

"Get the fuck outta here," says Tyrone. "Really? You?"

Vincent puts his foot up on his desk. He pulls up his pants to reveal the purple, jagged scars from the attack. He says, "I was on my way here to see about a teaching job. I was crossing through Morningside Park when this three-leg dog comes running out of nowhere. But he wasn't after me. Not at first. He was after this little kid... Somehow I found myself between the dog and the kid and I ended up at St. Lukes'."

Tyrone gets up from his chair. He approaches Vincent. He looks at the scars. Other kids follow Tyrone. A small crowd forms at the front of the room, mumbling and pointing and staring at the scar tissue.

"You think it made you stronger?" asks Aisha.

CHAPTER FOURTEEN

"The guy who first wrote that line was Friedrich Nietzsche. He was a midget and a cripple who ended up dying in a mad house. But he also was a man of history who's most famous line was, "God is dead.""

"That's a sin," calls out Drevone. "He in hell."

"Maybe so," says Vincent. "But he still might be worth thinking about."

"I don't want to think on no sinner," says Drevone.

"Alright, then don't," says Vincent. "Anyway, this Nietzsche was a philosopher who believed that since God is dead, the world has no real meaning."

"Why not?" says Antoine.

"I'm not exactly sure myself," says Vincent. "But I think he figured that without a God running things, then people are free to do whatever they want without fear of being punished in the afterlife, of being sent to hell after they die."

"So even if he did go to hell, he wasn't afraid of going there because he didn't believe in it," says Aisha.

"That's right."

"I don't believe in hell either," says Aisha.

"Then you going there too," says Drevone.

"Nigga, shut the fuck up 'fore I jap you in the eye!"

"Alright," says Vincent, smiling. "So this Nietzsche said that since there's no meaning in the world, a person has to create his own meaning and impose it on others. He called this, 'the will to power.' Nietzsche said that the 'Superman' would use his will to power to control others for his benefit."

"That's bugged," says Rowland. "No such thing as Superman. This Neetzee believe in Santa Claus too?"

The class laughs. Vincent smiles. He says, "It's not like the TV Superman. Nietzsche's Superman is a man who is stronger, smarter and more dominating than all those around him."

"Like Shaq," says Tyrone.   "He got a Superman tattoo too!"

"Yeah, sorta," says Vincent.   "Shaq is a superman when it comes to basketball."

"Shaq ain't shit," says Rowland.

"Stop hatin'," says Tyrone.   "Ain't nobody can mess with Shaq."

"Didn't Superman get crippled?" says Antoine.

"The actor who played Superman is crippled.   Yes, that's right," says Vincent.

"And his Pops, he was the first Superman, the one from the old TV show.   He kilt himself.   Went crazy thinking he really was Superman and jumped off a building, thinking he could fly," says Antoine.

The class laughs.

"Get the fuck outta here, really?" says Rowland.   "Is that true?"

"Yeah, that's what I heard," says Antoine.

"Then he be goin' to hell too," says Drevone.   "Suicide is a mortal sin."

"Nigga, shut the fuck up," says Aisha.   "Dumb ass think he be knowin' who goin' to hell, who goin' to heaven. Dumb ass don't even know how to match his own clothes. Look at you nigga, with your tight ass pants and your old man shoes."

Laughter and finger pointing at Drevone's wardrobe.

"Actually," says Vincent.   "The old Superman, George Reeves, was not related to the crippled Superman, Christopher Reeve.   It's just that their last names are almost the same...   But George Reeves did die under unusual circumstances.   Although he didn't jump off any buildings, he was shot in the head.   Yet nobody knows for sure whether it was a suicide or if he taken out by somebody else."

"Either way, they both Superman and they both got all fucked up," says Tyrone.

"True that," says Antoine.

"Well, anyway," says Vincent. "Let's get back to the topic... So Nietzsche says that to be 'The' Superman you have to have self-discipline. You have to work on your strengths and eliminate your weaknesses. You have to be hard on yourself so that you will be hard enough to smash down those around you."

"Like Scarface?" says Tyrone.

"Who?"

"Scarface. You know, that movie about the Cuban nigga who comes over here with nothin and ends up king of Miami."

"Oh, yeah, right," says Vincent. "I saw that. Yeah, sure... Scarface was a kind of Superman."

"Nigga was 'The Man,'" says Tyrone. "'Say 'ello to my little friend!' I love dat nigga."

Antoine turns to Tyrone. He quotes, "'Why don't you try stickin' jou head up jour ass—see if it fits!'"

The class roars with laughter.

Tyrone stands up on his chair. He looks about the room. Everybody goes quiet. He says, "'Whattaya lookin' at? You all a bunch of fucking assholes. You know why? 'Cause you don't have the guts to be what you wanna be. You need people like me. You need people like me so you can point your fucking fingers, and say, 'that's the bad guy.' So, what dat make you? Good? You're not good; you just know how to hide. Howda lie. Me, I don't have that problem. Me, I always tell the truth—even when I lie. So say goodnight to the bad guy.'" Tyrone jumps down off his chair, heading towards the door. "'Make way for the bad guy. There's a bad guy comin' through; you better get outta his way!'" Tyrone exits from the classroom. The entire class (except for Drevone) starts clapping and hollering and hooting. Tyrone comes back inside. Vincent whistles loudly with his fingers. The class continues to hoot and applaud. Tyrone takes a bow at the front of the room.

"That was fantastic," says Vincent.

"Thanks," says Tyrone.

"Look at the nigga," says Aisha. "He all gassed."

Tyrone heads back to his seat, giving a number of high-fives on the way.

"You guys really like Scarface, huh?" says Vincent.

"He took everybody out," says Rowland. "He didn't give a fuck 'bout nuthin'."

"Except being the best, the most powerful." says Vincent.

"Dat's right," says Tyrone.

"Word up," says Rowland.

"Nigga died in the end," says Antoine.

"So?" says Tyrone. "He went out blazin'. Nobody ever gonna eat his food."

"True dat," says Rowland.

Although he hadn't seen it in a long while, Vincent remembers the movie well. Pacino was secretly one of his idols as a young actor. "Okay, I gotta question," says Vincent. "In the movie, there's this scene... Scarface is looking out from his glass house. It's night time and up in the sky he sees a blimp and on the blimp there's some words flashing. Does anybody—"

"I know! I know!" shouts Tyrone.

"Dag," says Antoine. "Then just say it, nigga."

"It says, 'The World is Yours!'"

"Right," says Vincent. "And that's exactly what Nietzsche is talking about. Scarface is a perfect example of a Nietzsche Superman. He came from nothing, without money, without power. But he created himself, he willed himself to power being ruthless and relentless until he was a kinda king. You see?"

"Yeah, but the nigga also smacked around his woman and snuffed his best friend," says Aisha.

"That's true too," says Vincent. "And that's the dark side of the whole Superman idea. In his ruthless struggle for power, there's no room for sympathy or love. Those in the way, the weak, are destroyed without guilt."

"That's how you gotta be to be on top," says Tyrone. "That why he Scarface."

"Yeah," says Vincent. "But the Nazis, they believed in the Superman idea too. And look what happened because of them."

"Who the Nazis?" asks Tyrone.

"You one dumb ass, nigga," says Aisha. "They the ones who tried to kill all the Jews. Burnt them up in ovens."

"Oh, yeah," says Tyrone. "I knew that."

"Nigga be frontin'," says Aisha. "You don't know shit 'bout the Nazis."

"Yeah, and you don't know shit 'bout soap and water. Your bitch ass be stinkin' from here to da Bronx."

"Fuck you, nigga," says Aisha, getting up from her chair. "I ain't scared of you."

Shakia grabs Aisha's arm. "Chill," says Shakia. "Nigga just be stupid."

"Aisha, please. And Tyrone no more outta you either," says Vincent. "Some times you guys are so smart and then you gotta ruin it by acting retarded."

The class laughs. Except for Shakia. Shakia stands up, her hand on her hip. "My little brother is retarded!"

"Oh, I'm sorry, Shakia. I shouldn't have said that. Please forgive me."

"It's alright," says Shakia. "But it's not his fault. He borned that way."

"Of course," says Vincent. "I think we all gotta chill a minute here. Alright then... So, getting back to Mr. Nietzsche... We can look at what he said and think about what he said and if you think some of it rings true, then maybe someday you'll think about it again and use it as you see fit."

"Like how?" says Antoine.

"Oh, I don't know. Maybe using the idea of self creation to make yourself the best at what you wanna do. It doesn't have to be like Scarface. A person can also be the best doctor or scientist or whatever."

"Hey," says Tyrone. "Why don't we watch the movie in class? Other teachers be bringin' movies to watch. We could watch Scarface."

"Yeah, right," says Aisha. "Teacher can't be showin' Scarface. Movie gotta be educational. Like 'Gandhi' or 'Malcolm X.' Isn't that right?"

"Yeah," says Vincent. "But I don't see why Scarface can't be educational either."

"You gonna show Scarface?" says Aisha.

"Sure. Why not?"

"My brother got the tape!" shouts Rowland.

"Then bring it in, nigga," shouts Tyrone.

CHAPTER FIFTEEN

In October of that year, Vincent leaves his parent's home to move into a small studio apartment above the Lennox Lounge on 125th Street. Located on the second floor over the bar, Vincent's flat has a window facing an alley and the bathroom down the hall. The rest of the floor is taken up by two other "apartments." One used as an extra storeroom and the other as a fuck room by the manager of the lounge. In Vincent's room, there is a futon couch/bed, a desk, reading chair, small bookcase and chest of drawers. He either cooks frozen dinners in a microwave or eats out. There is a small sink by the window that he can piss into when he doesn't feel like making the walk down the hall. He has a radio but no TV. Vincent's parents were not happy about his choice of neighborhood.

"Why don't you stay here," said his Mom. "At least until you get back on your feet."

"I am back on my feet, Ma. I've got a job with regular paychecks and benefits too."

"That's fine," said his father. "I can understand you wanting to get out on your own. Hell, I was on my own at sixteen. My mother died and my father—"

"We heard the story a million times, Dad."

"Yeah, okay. But getting out on your own don't mean you lose your common sense. There's plenty of nice flats out here in Hoboken or even Jersey City. You should see the way they cleaned it up over there."

"You mean got rid of all the minorities."

"I mean getting rid of all the whores and the junkies and the thugs. I didn't say nothin' 'bout the spades and the spics. Plenty of white hookers and junkies to go around."

"You're a racist, Dad. So why not just say it like you feel it. You don't have to pretend otherwise around me."

"Pretend? What the hell are you talking about? When I say nigger or spic or chink or mick or even wop, I'm talkin' about a particular type of individual. But there's a difference, for instance, between a nigger and a black man, a spic and a Puerto Rican. I hate niggers but I sure as hell don't have anything against a black man. I worked for eighteen years, side by side, with the best damn black man I ever knew. Me and Earl—"

"Earl Starks. Yeah, Dad, we all know about what a 'good negro' Earl was... How you and him worked side by side for eighteen years."

"That's right. No reason for you to try and tear it down with your smart mouth."

"Okay, so let me ask you something. How come in all those eighteen years did Earl never come over here? You had other guys from work come by. I remember bringing them beers out in the backyard. There was Uncle George and Uncle Billy and Uncle Frank... Lot's of drinking uncles out in the back. They were real nice too. Some of them used to slip me dollar bills and then sips of beer and cigarettes when I got older."

"They were all good men. Now you wanna bad mouth them too?"

"No. Not at all. I didn't see nuthin' wrong with them. I'm just wondering why we never saw 'Uncle Earl' out back with all those other uncles. Huh? Why was that? Had nothing to do with him being a 'negro' did it?"

"There you go. Twistin' up the past so it suits your pea-headed argument."

"I'm not arguing. I'm just wondering."

"Okay, smart mouth. The truth of the matter is that I invited Earl out here many, many times."

"Many times?"

"That's right. As God as my judge. Ask your mother. Go on."

Vincent looked at his mom. She said, "Your father did invite him, Vincent. It's true."

"And?"

She shrugged.

"He always had some sort of excuse," said Vincent's father. "Either his wife was sick or one of his kids was sick or a relative was sick. Somebody always got sick so after awhile, I just stopped asking him because I realized it was him who didn't want to be here with me. And I don't hold that against him either. I respected the man so I just let it go. Something you still gotta learn."

"So why you got a problem with me moving to a place near my job?"

"For a smart kid, you sure are dumb. Your job is in goddamn Harlem: Zulu City, Jungleland! You're just walkin' white meat to those spearchuckers. But what can I say? What can I do? You're a man now. I'm not gonna hold your ass. You wanna hop with the jungle bunnies, then just make sure you look before you leap. You would think that incident with the dog woulda taught you something."

"Like what?"

"Like how dangerous it is."

"Jesus, Joseph and Mary," said his mother.

"It's not that dangerous, Ma."

"Yeah, sure. And that was just a dog. There's plenty more animals in the jungle. Most of 'em armed to the teeth, better than the cops. But why am I wasting my breath? We should be at least happy he's got a job and he's off the dope. I hope and pray..."

"I'm clean. No hard drugs. Maybe a beer now and then but that's it."

"You're not supposed to be drinking at all," said his mother. "That's what they told us."

"They don't know everything either," said his father. "A beer now and then ain't gonna kill him."

"Thanks, Dad."

"Just watch yourself, Son. I mean it."

"I will."

"And you always have a home to come home too here," said his Mom.

"I know it, thanks, Ma," says Vincent.

CHAPTER SIXTEEN

By the time Vincent maneuvers the TV cart to his classroom, all his students are sitting in their seats, waiting for him.

"Yo, you late," says Aisha.

"Sorry," says Vincent, plugging in the TV and VCR.

Rowland gets up from his seat. In his hand is a copy of "Scarface." He goes to hand it to Vincent.

"Oh, thanks, Rowland. But I've got my own copy."

Rowland shrugs, sits back down at his desk. The shades have already been pulled down in anticipation of Vincent's arrival.

"Somebody get the lights please," says Vincent.

The lights are flicked off. Vincent presses the button on the VCR. The movie begins...

"Hey, what's this?"

"This ain't 'Scarface'!"

"You said we gonna watch 'Scarface!'"

"What the fuck?"

"I knew the nigga be frontin'."

Vincent hits the "pause" button. He says, "Before they made "Scarface" with Al Pacino, there was an original version made over forty years before that. That's the movie I'm gonna show you now."

"But we wanna see, 'Scarface,'" says Tyrone. "The real one."

"There is no 'real' Scarface," says Vincent. "Scarface is just an idea. Scarface is an actor pretending to be what the writer had in his mind about a guy in his mind. Scarface is no more real than Bugs Bunny."

"That's that bullshit," says Antoine.

"It's not bullshit," says Vincent. "I told you the first day, I will not bullshit you and—"

"Yeah, whatever," says Antoine. "You can try to talk your way out of it any way you want but you know we all was 'spectin to see the Scarface we seen before. Not some 'original' joint. You never said nothin' about that 'till just now."

"You're right," says Vincent. "I'm sorry. I didn't think of it until I got home. But I was in no way trying to pull any bullshit. Look, after we watch this, we'll watch the 'real' one and then compare the two. Okay?"

"We wanna watch this one!" says Rowland, holding up the video.

"Okay, fine. We'll watch, I promise you. We'll watch them both, back to back for the rest of this week, how ever long it takes. You watch my tape and then we'll watch Rowland's."

"Why?" says Tyrone.

"Because I want you to see, to understand that there's a history here. A history to Scarface. I want you to see that the Scarface that you all know and love is a remake, a kind of copy."

"So? So what? It's still good," says Tyrone.

"Sure it is. I'm not saying it's not. What I'm saying is that to reach the top, to be the best, you gotta know the history of your game. Without the original version of Scarface, there's no movie in Rowland's hand. It wouldn't exist. Al Pacino? The actor who plays Scarface? He only decided to do the movie after he saw the original one... And you'll understand this after you see the original. In all great art, an artist has to be aware of what went before. I don't care whether it's movies or books or music. It doesn't matter. You think Mary J. Blige never listened to Billie Holiday?"

"Who Billie Holiday?"

"She was a singer," says Vincent.

"I know her," says Aisha. "My Moms listen to her. She alright. But she don't sound nuthin' like Mary J."

"No, she doesn't," says Vincent. "But you can be sure that Mary J listened to everything Billie Holiday ever recorded. Why? Because that's what came before her. Same thing with rap. Especially with rap."

"We don't wanna hear nuthin' about Eminem," says Marcus.

"Eminem alright," says Shakia.

"For a white boy," says Rowland.

"I'm talkin' about any rapper who's got skills," says Vincent. "You think Biggie or Tupac never heard of Grandmaster Flash? I don't think so. And it's the same with movies, basketball, whatever art form you're talking about. You gotta know the game, the roots of the game, to rise to the top of the game. If you look at any famous person, it's pretty easy to see what they were influenced by, where they were coming from. Take Martin Luther King, for instance. Nonviolent protest did not start with him. Before King you had Gandhi."

"Who that?"

"Gandhi was from India. We'll talk about him soon."

"I heard Martin Luther King was a playa," says Aisha.

"A playa?"

"Somebody who always be messin' around."

"Well, that may be true," says Vincent. "But that don't take away from the other things he did, the other things he said and stood for. The things he ended up dying for."

"Martin Luther King was a playa?" says Rowland. "You be buggin'."

"President Kennedy was a playa too," says Vincent. "But a lot of people say he's one of the best presidents we ever had."

"Wasn't he shot too?"

"Yep," says Vincent.

"My grandma has a picture of him up on the wall," says Shakia. "The only white nigga I ever heard her spoke good about."

"I'll bet you didn't know that his father was a big time bootlegger."

"Bootlegger? You mean like bootleg jeans?"

"No. Back in the 1920's, liquor was illegal. They called it 'Prohibition.' But people still wanted to drink so bootleggers made and sold whiskey illegally. John F. Kennedy's father, Joe Kennedy, was a big time bootlegger. Back then, bootlegging was same thing as drug dealing today."

"Was he like Scarface?"

"In a way, yeah. But he was a bit more crafty than Scarface. And he was real. Joe Kennedy was not from some movie. The man walked the earth like you and me. And he knew enough to take the money he made from bootlegging and parley it into legitimate businesses, politics and power. Unlike Scarface who ends up getting blown away, Kennedy ends up starting an empire of his own and fathering a son who becomes president of the United States."

"We gonna watch the movie or what?"

CHAPTER SEVENTEEN

Bert Steinberg is a big and imposing Jew. Standing six foot six, he has a shaved head, thick lips and a long, broad nose.

Steinberg played power forward for City College. Not quite fast enough to make it in the NBA, Steinberg ended up coaching varsity basketball with one of the top winning records in the city. Over the years, people often wondered why he never tried moving up—coaching college or the pros. Those close to him knew. Steinberg, a true rabbi of the sport, could never play the politics necessary to advance in the college ranks, much less so for the NBA.

Last year, Steinberg's team, the Wadleigh Tigers, went all the way to the semi-finals, losing to Kennedy High in an overtime heartbreaker. Kennedy in turn, lost to Lincoln in the finals at Madison Square Garden. Today, the Tigers, play Lincoln at home. It is very early in the season but a very big game, possibly a preliminary run for a later showdown in the Garden.

Lincoln, like Kennedy, is a large population school, with thousands of kids. Wadleigh is much smaller with less than four hundred kids attending (on a good day). But this disparity in potential talent pools never discourages Steinberg. It is not beyond him to walk the streets of Harlem, enter unannounced through a rip in the chain link fence, and stand with his arms crossed watching a pick up game, maybe even joining in himself, before pulling one or two of the most talented players aside.

"Follow me and I'll change your life."

Many kids who meet him like this think he's crazy. But others see this white man as their savior, following him out of the run down parks and playgrounds to Wadleigh where he gets them enrolled and going to classes and playing a type of ball unlike anything they ever saw or played in the streets.

Vincent has mixed feelings about sports. As a kid in Hoboken, he was considered an excellent athlete. But as he got older, he became what coaches called "wasted talent." Despite his brilliance on the field, Vincent was often late to practice, or missing from practice, or showing up drunk or high to practice. For Vincent, practice was boring. As a little kid, there was no such thing as practice. In the street or in the schoolyard, there were only games. Contests that you either won or lost. That was fun. As he got older, Vincent began to question the whole competitive thing. Those kids and coaches screaming and yelling and sometimes even crying—over what? A game?

Vincent's father was a big sports fan. His sainted heroes—Ruth, DiMaggio, Mantel. He encouraged Vincent early on to play all the sports: football in the fall, basketball in winter and baseball in spring and summer. When it was discovered that Vincent had exceptional ability in all three, his father pushed him all the more. Never were Vincent and his Dad so close as when Vincent made varsity baseball and basketball in his sophomore year of high school.

In his senior year, however, Vincent quit all his teams to join the drama club. Short of calling his son a faggot, Vincent's father made no attempt to disguise his contempt for Vincent's desire to become an actor.

At the time, Vincent had fallen in love with Janelle Capello, the shining star of Hoboken High's drama club. Vincent's pursuit of acting was basically a pursuit for that star. The acting part only a means to an end, a pretending to be a pretender. Vincent was relentless and successful, securing the male lead opposite Janelle for the spring production of, "Look Back in Anger."

Janelle managed to get into Yale on the strength of her performance. But Vincent did not get into Yale. His grades put him out of contention. The love affair ending the day Janelle went away to college.

Vincent sits in the stands across from the home team bench. The cheerleaders are not really cheering, but dancing and shaking to the beat blasting from two speaker towers on each side of the scorer's table. They are not anything like the cheerleaders from Vincent's memory.

The gymnasium is packed with more people still streaming inside. There are many students in attendance but plenty of other humans too. Parents, and aunts and uncles and brothers and sisters and friends. Grandmas pushing baby carriages and mothers pushing baby carriages and teenagers pushing baby carriages. Lots of babies. Also, drug dealers, pimps and gang bangers. Cops at the exits and cops in the aisles. Not far from Vincent are the two cops who saved him from the pit bull—York and Colon. A hot dog cart selling meats and soft drinks. The momentary whiff of reefer along with the wavering scent trails of clandestine malt liquor and booze.

The rap song stops. The cheerleaders run off in the wake of whistles and barks of appreciation.

The visiting team's locker room door bursts open. The Lincoln Railsplitters take the court for their warm-ups. The enemy has arrived. Although this is the team that won last year's championship, they seem nervous to be here. As they line up to take their pre-game lay-ups, many of them bungle and miss, much to the raucous amusement of the crowd. Looking at their faces, their postures, Vincent can see that these guys are losers. He knows that look. He saw it countless times when he was a player himself. The look of unmitigated fear mixed with the unholy desire that this whole thing will be over soon, the wish for today to become yesterday.

Just before the start of the game, Vincent watches Antoine sit down beside Tyrone at the end of the bench. A shade darker than Antoine, Tyrone is similarly long and strong and maybe even more handsome in the face if it weren't for those pervading pockmarks, a Maori-like tattoo that Vincent can spot clear across the gymnasium floor.

Vincent considers the pockmarks, wondering just how such an affliction can shape or deform a personality. He thinks fleetingly of Charles Bukowski who was not only pimple stamped but transcendently ugly too. Maybe he should read some of his stories to the class... Or maybe not... In the last minutes before the opening tip, late arrivers pass by the bench to pound fists with Antoine. For the most part, Tyrone is completely ignored, the shadow friend of the blazing star. Unlike Antoine, Tyrone is anything but stellar. Tyrone is a scrub, the guy who only gets to play at the end of a game when your team is so far ahead or so far behind that the outcome is definite with no chance of reversal.

The game begins. Another massacre in the making. The Tigers are pressing full court, stealing the ball and dunking it with outrageous abandon. In a matter of minutes, they are up by twenty. Vincent is impressed.

By half time, the Tigers are up by thirty. They stretch the lead to forty-one by the end of the third. It looks like the fourth quarter is destined to be garbage time, when the scrubs from both sides get their chance to play. Sensing this, Antoine puts on a show for the crowd. A wild dervish, he spins in mad circles, the ball like a magician's dove, disappearing and reappearing in the flash of his black arms and legs and hands. Antoine shooting the three, hitting the three. Antoine tossing the no-look alley-oop. Antoine dunking it himself after passing it to himself off the backboard. Vincent has never seen anything like it. The closest comparison that comes to his mind is a higher jumping, Pistol Pete Maravich.

With the Tigers up by forty-five, Steinberg puts in the second unit. They are a bit embarrassed and a bit awkward but they do what they can against the Lincoln starters who have not been pulled by the other coach.

With five minutes to go, the Railsplitters have cut the lead to twenty-four. But Steinberg sticks with his scrubs, calling a time out, giving them careful instructions and sending them out again. Emboldened by their success in the fourth, it's Lincoln who's pressing the Tigers now, making steals, running the fast break and scoring without answer until the lead is down to sixteen with three minutes left. Steinberg sticks with the scrubs. He holds up four fingers to designate a play. The Tigers fan out to the four corners of their half court with one player at the top of the key. The Tigers play a passing game with no attempt to score. They just dribble and pass and dribble and pass to each of the four corners or into their man at the key, running down the clock with no chance of the Railsplitters to get the ball back and score themselves. The strategy works well. The Railsplitters are forced to foul in order to regain possession of the ball.

With a minute to go, the Harlem crowd is on their feet, screaming, dancing and pushing up their hands in the classic "raise the roof" gesture. As the last sixty seconds tick by, the collective noise of appreciation makes all other communication impossible. The crowd counts down: "Ten, nine, eight, seven, six, five, four, three—" The whistle blows. Tyrone is fouled hard across the forearm. It is an unnecessary foul. A stupid foul. A foul of frustration.

The Tigers are up by sixteen. Three seconds left. Tyrone's two free throws are meaningless in terms of winning and losing. But unlike most situations like this, the fans have not begun to file out. They stay, standing on their feet as if these two shots are of critical importance—in part to show support for the poor scrub destined to shoot them and in part to indulge in the final seconds of victorious pleasure.

Tyrone bounces the ball before him. He closes his eyes to clear his head. It's a tough position to be in. You're supposed to be happy, your team is about to beat one of the best teams in the city but you cannot be truly happy because you are a scrub and everybody knows it. You remember Antoine telling you that you are not a scrub because you made the team. "The scrubs are all those niggas in the stands watching. You made the team. Those niggas got cut." You open your eyes. You line up your shot. You follow through just like coach Berg taught you. You miss. A tremendous, collective groan...

Although never a scrub himself, Vincent knows how Tyrone feels and without thinking, he shouts out: "C'mon, Tyrone! You can do it. Nail that shit!"

The fans near Vincent stare at him. Some point and some snigger before focusing back on Tyrone who's ready for his next and final shot of the game.

Taking aim, Tyrone shoots and misses, the ball clanging off the front of the rim, whirling back towards the free throw line.   Instinctively, bodies from both teams converge on the ball. As two seconds become one second, the ball is deflected into Tyrone's surprised face. Knocked off balance by a leaping opponent, Tyrone falls on his ass, but with the ball held firmly in his hands. As the buzzer sounds, Tyrone pushes the ball away like a hot potato and, this time, the rock finds its mark, sailing up and down through the rim for two points. All net.

For a split second, the entire congregation is struck mute by the image: Tyrone on his ass and scoring at the buzzer. It is a hole in one, a grand slam, a touchdown bomb, Neil Armstrong stepping on the moon...   The silence combusts into an explosion of applause.   People are going nuts, acting like the kid just hit the buzzerbeater in the NBA Finals.   The stands empty, bodies rushing onto the court. Tyrone is mobbed and heaved into the air, the newly crowned hero, carried up and down the length of the court.   The music is blaring again and everybody (except the losers who flee to their locker room) is laughing and celebrating.

Tyrone's last second shot is the highlight of the contest.   There is even a mention of it in the "Daily News" coverage of the game.   It is the shot heard around the 'hood. The shot everybody is talking about for days and weeks to come.   More than any other single play, more than the great dunks and passes and scores, it is Tyrone's shot, the shot that he "pulled out of his ass," that will not be forgotten.

Vincent watches as they parade Tyrone about the court. Although Tyrone is doing his best to go along with the fun, his smile is a twisted, painful grin that nobody seems to notice.   As Vincent makes his way down the bleachers,

Tyrone catches Vincent's eye for a brief instant and both are equally embarrassed. Lucky for both, the instant is only an instant due to the fast pace of the revelers.

When Vincent reaches the gym floor, he is confronted by yet another sudden vision. Seeing her so suddenly takes his breath away. But she is instantly gone, blocked by the mass of moving bodies between them. Struggling forward, stretching his neck, he catches sight of her again. There she is! It's definitely her, the woman from the park, her small son on his toes and holding her hand. But she does not see Vincent. She is talking to another young woman and heading for the exit at the far side of the gym.

Vincent tries to make his way to her, cutting and weaving as fast as possible without having somebody "jap" him for pushing too fast or too hard. Vincent does not think about what he's going to say once he reaches her. He is just intent on getting there, on seeing her once more. As Vincent squirms his way through the meandering spectators, he loses sight of her, gains it again, and loses it again. Forging ahead, all desire and hope, Vincent finally makes it to the exit only to be blocked and then knocked into the bosom of a mountainous black woman.

CHAPTER EIGHTEEN

Desiree holds Clyde by the hand while speaking to Marisol, "Can't you just hold it?"

"I can't. I'll be just a minute."

"Damn... Okay. But hurry up."

"Okay," says Marisol, running back inside.

Salmon-like, Marisol rushes against the crowd streaming from the exit. Crossing inside, she is momentarily blocked by the white man heading out. Marisol steps to her right but the white man steps to his left, causing them both to end up face-to-face again. Without thinking, they repeat the procedure in opposite directions, ending up face-to-face a third time.

"We gotta stop meeting like this," he says with a smile.

Marisol is in no mood for games. With her bladder ready to burst, she shoves the white man out of her way, causing him to crash into Crystal Ferguson.

"I'm sorry," he says, trying not to stare at the woman's outstanding largeness.

"You alright?" she says, helping him back to an upright position.

"I'm fine," he says, thinking she's gotta weigh at least three hundred pounds.

"You a teacher here? What you teach?"

"History."

"Oh, I love history."

Outside, Desiree shakes loose a Newport from its box. She lets go of Clyde's hand to spark the flame. Desiree smokes her cigarette. She smokes below the streetlight, watching people leave the gym, hoping Marisol doesn't take forever. She smokes and watches the faces coming out, turning right and left into their separate lives. Some of the people she knows. Some of the people she never saw before in her life.

"Oh, shit!" says Desiree.

"What Mommy?"

Desire sees Crystal Ferguson, a girl she used to go to school with until Crystal dropped out in ninth grade to have her baby. But Desiree's surprise isn't in seeing fat Crystal, now even fatter than ever. Her shock is in seeing the white man. The white man from the park. She watches in amazement as he talks to Crystal Ferguson just outside the exit door. As he talks to Crystal, Desiree can see his eyes scanning the block. What is he looking for?

Desiree smokes and waits. The white man shakes hands with Crystal Ferguson. He watches Crystal walk away, up the block. He turns towards Desiree. He walks to her.

Desiree drops her cigarette to the ground. She smiles. But she feels strange. It's like she's suddenly face to face with some kind of celebrity, a famous movie actor or sports star.

"Hello," he says.

"Hi," she says.

"I don't know if you remember me but—"

"I remember you."

"My name's Vincent," he says, extending his hand.

"I'm Desiree and this is Clyde," she says.

"Hello, Clyde," says Vincent.

"Say hi," says Desiree. "And say thank you too. He's the man who saved you from the dog."

"You did?" says Clyde.

"Yeah, I guess," says Vincent.

"Thank you," says Clyde.

"You're welcome," says Vincent.

"Are you okay?" says Desiree.

"Me? Yeah, I'm fine. Just some stitches. Nothing too serious."

"I got stitches," says Clyde. "You wanna see 'em?"

"Sure."

"Look," says Clyde, pulling up his shirtsleeve to show a small scar on his right forearm. "I fell off the monkey bars on a piece of glass."

"Wow," says Vincent. "That's a nice one. You wanna see mine?"

"Okay."

Vincent pulls up his pants leg. "What do you think?"

"Dag," says Clyde. "It's better than mines."

Vincent smiles, lowers his pants leg back down. "That was some game, huh?"

"Yeah," says Desiree.

"You know anybody on the team?"

"I know most all of them," says Desiree. "I used to go to school here. We live a few blocks away."

"Really?"

"Hm-m. My cousin's on the team."

"Which one is that?"

"Antoine."

"Antoine? I know Antoine. He's in my class. Him and Tyrone."

"So you a teacher?"

"I'm tryin'. This is my first year."

"Hey, yo! Yo, Dee Dee!"

Horrified, Desiree turns to face the voice. She says, "I got no time for you, Rosco."

"Daddy," says Clyde.

"What up, little man?" says Rosco.

"Well," says Vincent. "It was nice—"

"Wait," says Desiree. "Just a minute, okay?"

"Sure," says Vincent, drifting off, putting the sidewalk traffic between himself and Desiree.

Vincent pulls out his pack of Marlboros. He shakes out a cigarette. He leans against the brick wall of the gym. He lights the cigarette. He smokes...

Desiree speaks to Rosco in a low but firm voice. She says, "You better go. You better go 'cause I can't and I won't talk to you right now."

Rosco smiles, looking over his shoulder at Vincent and back to Desiree. "Who the cracker?"

"That's the man who saved Clyde from your dog," says Desiree. "But you better go now before I call that cop. See him? He right over there."

Rosco sees the cop standing near the exit. He smiles again. "Okay, but I need to talk to you, alright? I'll call you."

Desiree doesn't answer him, just glances at the cop again.

"Bye-bye, little man," says Rosco, giving Clyde a fake punch to the jaw. He crosses to Vincent, "Hey, Mister Man."

"Excuse me?" says Vincent, blowing smoke out the side of his mouth.

"I hear you the one who saved my kid."

"It was nothing," says Vincent, dropping his cigarette, stepping it out.

"It wasn't nothing. That's my son," says Rosco, reaching into his pocket. "I want you to take this."

Vincent looks at the roll of money. "I can't," says Vincent. "Thanks, though."

"Why not?'

"Because it wouldn't be right. I did it because I wanted to do it."

"I know that," says Rosco. "But now I wanna thank you and I want you to have it."

"Well, thank you again. No disrespect intended, but I really can't."

"You think you better than me?"

"No," says Vincent. "I'm just not gonna take money for something I should have done, something anybody should have done in those circumstances."

"White people sure is crazy," says Rosco, pocketing his roll. Rosco smiles. He looks at Desiree and back to Vincent. "You tryin' to get wif her?"

"Excuse me?"

"Excuse me?" mimics Rosco. "You heard me."

"Yeah, I guess I did," says Vincent. "I don't think that's anybody's business."

"Do you know who I am?" says Rosco.

"Not really," says Vincent. "Not anymore than what you told me."

"Fair enough," says Rosco. "We cool. It's all alright."

"Sure," says Vincent.

Rosco smiles and heads up the block.

"Hey, I'm sorry about that," says Desiree, coming over to where Vincent is standing.

"Not a problem," says Vincent. "He just wanted to thank me."

Desiree glances up the block. Rosco is gone in the flux of people meandering towards Seventh Avenue. Desiree says, "I really don't know how to thank you."

"Unlike your friend," says Vincent.

"He's not my friend... But I really can't speak on that right now."

"Sure, sure," says Vincent. "I was just kidding around."

"I know it."

"Hey, uh... You know, maybe we can have a cup of coffee or something sometime? Is that okay for me to ask?"

"Yeah. Sure," she says. "We can have some coffee."

"Can I call you then?"

"You gotta pen?'

Vincent checks through his pockets. "Sorry, no."

"Wait a minute,' she says, rummaging through her pockets and then her purse.

"Huh?" says Marisol just now coming into the picture.

"Hello again," says Vincent.

"Do I know you? I don't know you!"

"Marisol," says Desiree. "This is Vincent. He's the one I told you about. The one who saved Clyde in the park."

"You him? You the white man?"

"I suppose so."

"You gotta pen?" says Desiree.

"I don't know."

"Can you look? Thank you."

Marisol looks in her bag. "I gotta pencil."

"That's fine," says Desiree.

"Don't snatch," says Marisol.

Desiree pulls a scrap of paper from her purse. She writes down her phone number, handing it to Vincent.

"Thanks," says Vincent, glancing at the number.

"I gotta pee," says Clyde.

"Alright, baby," says Desiree. "We gonna be home in a minute. Can you hold it?"

Clyde nods.

"We gotta get going," says Desiree.

"It was great meeting you. All of you," says Vincent.

"Yeah, and thanks again," says Desiree.

As Vincent crosses the street, Marisol says, "What was that all about?"

"We goin' out for coffee."

"What? You and that cracker?"

"That's right."

"You must be buggin'. That cracker's crazy. Nearly knocked me over back inside."

"What you talking about?"

"The damn fool wasn't watchin' where he was going and nearly knocked me down."

"Or maybe it was the other way around. As I recall, you was the one all in a rush to go and pee."

"Are we gonna stand here all night or what?"

CHAPTER NINETEEN

Vincent is walking happy. It seems like Desiree genuinely likes him. Or else why would she give him her number? Simple logic. But logic has a way of betraying you, especially when it comes to women... She sure is gorgeous though. What would it be like to kiss her? To fuck her? To really get to know her? She's obviously not just some no-brain, ghetto chick. She's got a depth to her, that's for sure. And a history... What, with the kid and that smiley guy... What the hell was he all about? Alright, enough. Calm down, one step after the next step. Move forward. Just relax. Take it easy. One day at a time...

Vincent turns the corner. He sees the basketball coach, Bert Steinberg, going towards his car. Vincent says, "Good game, coach."

Stenberg turns, car keys in hand. "Thanks." He squints. He recognizes Vincent. He says, "You're a history teacher, right?"

"Yeah. Vincent. Vincent DeRosa."

"That's right. We met at the beginning of the year. You're new."

"Yep."

"I've been meaning to talk to you."

"Oh, yeah?"

"Uh-huh. Can I give you a lift?"

"I don't live far," says Vincent. "I usually walk."

"C'mon, hop in. I'll drop you off."

"Okay. Thanks."

Steinberg drives a 1968, powder blue Cadillac. The car is kept in tip-top condition. Steinberg starts the engine.

"Nice ride," says Vincent.

"Thanks," says Steinberg. "Where you headed?"

"125th."

Steinberg gives him a sidelong glance. "And what?"

"Lenox."

"Near the Lenox Lounge?"

"Right above it."

"Been living there long?"

"Not really."

"Hm-m."

Vincent is not sure whether he likes this Steinberg. "So what you want to talk to me about?"

"Do you drink?"

"On occasion."

"How 'bout we stop for a quick one. I like talking with a drink in my hand."

"Alright," says Vincent.

Steinberg nods, continues driving uptown. At 118th Street, he stops the car at a red light. Two male teens cross the street in front of them. Steinberg pushes on the horn. The teens flinch, stop, stare. But Vincent and Steinberg know who they are. It's Antoine and Tyrone. When Antoine realizes it's his coach, he smiles and gives the finger. Steinberg presses the button, the window sliding into the doorframe, his bald head out the window. "Hey, get the hell outta the way!"

"White man, you in the wrong part of town," says Antoine.

"Where you two clowns headin'?"

"Chill, coach. We won. Right? We just gonna see some friends."

The light changes to green. Cars blow their horns behind the Cadillac. Steinberg pulls to the curb. Antoine and Tyrone step back out of the traffic. Steinberg says, "Just watch yourself. Both of you. Remember what we talked about."

"I got you, coach," says Antoine. "Don't worry. We fine. Hey, who that with you? Oh, snap! Yo, Ty, look who's with coach! Hey, what up?"

"Hey," says Vincent, bending his head to talk across the front seat. "Great game tonight. You guys were fantastic."

Antoine smiles. "Thanks."

Tyrone looks away, looking towards the tenements on the far side of Lennox.

"I'll see you at practice," says Steinberg. "Behave yourselves, hear?"

"Bet," says Antoine.

Steinberg pulls away from the curb, watching Antoine and Tyrone cross the street in his rearview mirror.

Vincent says, "Tyrone seemed pretty upset." When Steinberg doesn't answer, Vincent says, "I'd be upset too."

"Oh, yeah?"

"Sure. You won. The team won. But Tyrone ends up playing the fool. That's gotta be hard on him."

Steinberg parks the car on the corner of 124th Street. He says, "That which does not kill you, only makes you stronger."

Vincent tilts his head, unsure how to take this comment.

Steinberg cuts the ignition. "C'mon, let's go."

They find two stools at the bar. "I haven't been here in years," says Steinberg. "Hasn't changed much..."

The Lennox Lounge is divided into two parts. Out front there's the bar area with an old jukebox and mostly regular customers and then there's the backroom, the lounge proper, a place specifically set up for jazz concerts with low lights, fancy tables, cocktail waitresses and foreign tourists.

Steinberg drinks whiskey over ice. Vincent drinks from a bottle of Bud. They are the only two white men sitting at the bar. But nobody pays them any mind except for a guy who suddenly recognizes Steinberg. He snaps his fingers. He taps Steinberg on the shoulder. "Hey! Hey, how you doing?"

"I'm fine," says Steinberg, half turning to see who it is.

"Can I buy you a drink?"

"Nah, I'm okay," says Steinberg. "But thanks."

"How 'bout you buy me a drink?"

Steinberg smiles at this.

"You don't remember me, do you?"

Steinberg looks at the man. He is dark skinned and disheveled with a long skinny head. The man says, "King. I used to play for King."

Steinberg remembers, recognizes him. He smiles. "Dwight. Dwight Davidson. 'Davidson the Destroyer.' You were first team, All City, two years in a row."

"Right! That's me!"

"So how you doin'?"

"I'm alright."

"You had that mean cross-over. Man, you were really good. I hear you got a full ride at Providence. But that must be goin' on ten years now..."

"That's right."

"How'd it go there?"

"Ah... Alright. I busted up my knee though... Never could play the same after that..."

"Sorry to hear that," says Steinberg.

"Yeah, well... Shit happens..."

"But it's great to see you again. What you drinking?"

Dwight lifts his glass, looks in it. "Rum and coke."

Steinberg motions the bartender to refill Dwight. Vincent sips his beer. Steinberg sips his whiskey. Marvin Gaye sings from the jukebox. The bartender hands Dwight his rum and coke. Dwight says, "Thanks."

Steinberg says, "Cheers."

"Cheers," says Dwight. "Thanks."

Dwight drinks some and shuffles towards the door. Vincent watches him finish the rest in a single gulp. Vincent says, "He left."

Steinberg nods. "He was pretty good."

"You think he ever finished school?"

"I don't know," says Steinberg. "Probably not."

"And what do you think about that?"

"It's a shame."

"You think Tyrone will end up like him?"

"Huh? Tyrone? I don't know. That's up to Tyrone."

"So what do you think happened with Dwight?"

"What are you getting at?"

"I don't know exactly. I'm just thinking about Tyrone," says Vincent. "That's a hard thing for a kid to swallow."

"What's that?"

"You saw it. Everybody saw it. They were parading him up and down the court on their shoulders."

"And that's bad?"

"They were making fun of him. It was just a big joke. With Tyrone as the punch line."

"Yeah, okay... But what am I supposed to do? What can anyone do? It's over now. Tyrone has to move on. Get over it and move on."

"And what if he doesn't get over it?"

"I don't know."

"Maybe he'll end up like that guy who just walked out. Or maybe somebody worse."

"Maybe. Or maybe he'll get stronger by it. It didn't kill him, did it?"

Vincent offers Steinberg a cigarette. Steinberg declines. Vincent lights up. He puffs smoke. He says, "So what did you want to talk to me about?"

Steinberg motions the bartender for another round, draining his glass and chewing on the leftover ice cubes. "I wanted to talk about your class. I heard some of my boys talking about it. It's not too often you hear kids talking about school in the locker room."

"What were they saying?'

"They were saying a lot of things. Stuff about you and Scarface and that Nietzsche quote about getting stronger."

"I see. And?"

"And then I asked them about it. I asked them about you and about Scarface and some of the things you've been teaching them."

"And?"

"And I don't know. I don't really know what to think. I mean, you seem like a decent enough guy. I can tell that you care about them. But, then again, and I'm going to be straight now."

"Please."

"I believe you may be doing more harm than good. I think you're really fucking them up."

"What?"

"I think you're fucking with their brains. Most of them are living very close to the edge. Some of them, right on the edge. And it doesn't take much to knock them off."

"I'm telling them the truth. I give them nothing but the truth."

"What's the truth about Scarface? Scarface is a goddamn hero to those kids."

"I know that."

"And you think that's good?"

"It's something. Something that they relate to. So I figure I'd try and use that connection to make other connections. Listen, I did not in any way try to glorify the man, I just—"

"You just compared him to President Kennedy."

"What? No. I compared him to Joe Kennedy, the father."

"Whatever."

"It's not, 'whatever.' There's a difference."

"Yeah, okay. And what about Nietzsche? You were talking about him too. Right?"

"Yeah. Why?"

"He was a Nazi philosopher, wasn't he?"

"The Nazis used him, used some of his ideas for their own ends. But Nietzsche wasn't a Nazi himself. But why—"

"The 'will to power.' The 'Superman.' I know a bit about that kind of philosophy."

"So what's your point?"

"My point is that I think you're fucking with their minds. You're misleading them with your truth. Stuff like Scarface and Nietzsche and the will to power can put the wrong idea in a kid's head. Especially these kids. Look, I know you're new. I know you're trying to do the right thing. But do you know what they say about the road to hell?"

"It's paved with good intentions. You sound just like my father."

"I'll take that as a compliment."

"I gotta get going."

"Look, kid," says Steinberg. "I'm not trying to insult you or anything. Hell, you're the first teacher I ever heard any of my players speak so much about. You're an original. And I respect that. And that's why I felt I had to talk to you. Because I think you can really help them. They respect you and they trust you and I've found if you got those two things, they'll follow you anywhere, they'll do anything for you. But with that comes the responsibility of taking them in the right direction."

Vincent nods, "I hear what you're saying. And I'm gonna think about it."

"That's fine," says Steinberg. "That's all I ask. Hey, drink up. It's still early."

"Na," says Vincent. "I gotta get going. That's one hell of a team you've got."

"They're pretty good this year. Tough too."

CHAPTER TWENTY

Yummy turned eighteen two weeks ago. But he is celebrating his party tonight because he had to wait for the settlement money to clear. When Yummy was a little boy, he used to eat paint chips off the wall. Yummy's grandmother used to watch him while his moms was at work. But because Yummy's grandmother drank and watched TV while she watched him, she never noticed Yummy consuming all those paint chips. Although nobody knew it at the time, Yummy's paint intake was messing with Yummy's brain. Yummy never did well in school. He's what they call a "slow learner." But Yummy is not dumb, at least not to his friends. Yummy is funny. Yummy is a master at the art of "snapping." Snapping is a modern form of "the dozens," whereby the snapper snaps various insults about a person, usually (but not always) concerning their mother.

Yummy got left back in second and fourth grade. Yummy's second time, fourth grade teacher, Mrs. Seltzer, took a special interest in Yummy. Mrs. Seltzer introduced Yummy's mom to her husband, the attorney. It was Mr. Seltzer who got Yummy a settlement of $137,000 from the landlord, the money held in a trust fund until Yummy turned eighteen.

Tyrone and Antoine have known Yummy since they were little. They are looking forward to this "invitation only" party because everybody is going to get a gift like it was their birthday instead of Yummy's. It was Yummy's idea to give presents on his birthday. He said he was gonna bless his dawgs like they never been blessed before.

Yummy's apartment is on the fourth floor. The elevator is broke, as usual. Tyrone and Antoine take the steps, two at a time. Outside Yummy's door stands Ivory White. In Ivory White's pocket is a list of people invited to the party.

"Waz up?" says Antoine.

Ivory White looks at Antoine and Tyrone. Rather, Ivory White looks down at Antoine and Tyrone. Ivory White stands six feet six. He is muscle-bound yet surprisingly agile. Ivory was once a member of Rosco's high school basketball team until he got expelled for pimp-slapping a referee. Ivory White has a particular kind of bad temper. It's the kind that suddenly lashes out when least expected. When Ivory White slapped the referee, his team had already won the game. To this day, nobody knows why he slapped that ref. Some say it was a bad call made earlier in the season. Others claim the ref looked at Ivory the wrong way. Rosco thinks the ref may have once gone out with Ivory's mother. In any case, only Ivory knows and Ivory doesn't like questions.

"We on the list," says Antoine.

Ivory checks his list. He puts a check beside Antoine and Tyrone's names. "Okay," he says, standing to the side of the door. "It's open."

Antoine looks at Ivory's dark-skinned hand, thinking, "You gotta be the blackest nigga on the planet."

"Excuse me?" says Ivory.

"I didn't say nothin," says Antoine.

Ivory White nods. Antoine and Tyrone pass into Yummy's apartment. On the far side of the living room, two red-faced cops handcuff a crackhead, the crackhead's face pressed hard to the floor. Watching the scene is Rosco and Yummy's mom. Yummy's mom sits in a wheelchair. She has diabetes and no legs. For a number of years, Yummy promised to buy her a new car with the settlement money but then, like her own mom before her, she developed diabetes, losing herself in increments: the toe to the foot to the knee to the hip. So Yummy bought her the giant projection TV instead of the car. Yummy's mom watches TV for most of her waking hours. "Cops," is her favorite program. Rosco enjoys the show too. In Rosco's hand is a forty ounce bottle of malt liquor. Yummy's mom sips vodka and coke through a straw from a red plastic cup.

Rosco used to be tight with Yummy's older brother, Cheezy. They called him Cheezy because he always had a smile on his face. But unlike Rosco's, Cheezy's smile was a happy smile because Cheezy was a naturally happy kind of a guy. Cheezy named his younger brother Yummy not because Yummy ate paint but because Yummy ate everything. Yummy was and is always hungry. Yummy can eat and eat and he never gets fat. Unlike Yummy, Cheezy was "gifted" in school. Cheezy used to let Rosco cheat off him during tests. Rosco never forgot his friend. When Cheezy died while riding his motorcycle into the side of a garbage truck, Rosco took it on himself to help out Yummy's mom. In addition to giving her money, Rosco made it his business to comfort and spend time with her.

The theme music to "Cops" blares from the projection screen TV:

> *Bad boys, bad boys watcha*
> *gonna do? Watcha gonna*
> *do when they come for*
> *you... Bad boys, bad boys,*
> *watcha gonna do...*

Antoine and Tyrone give Yummy's mom a kiss and a pound to Rosco.

"Good game, tonight," says Rosco to Antoine. "You remind me of me."

Antoine smiles.

"You did good too," says Rosco to Tyrone. "Nigga, don't frown. I'm talkin' about your 'D.' You had that other nigga on lock."

Tyrone shrugs.

Antoine says, "Where Yummy?"

"He inside with the other knuckleheads," says Rosco. "Alright, go on, you standin' in my way."

Tyrone and Antoine head down the hall to Yummy's room. Inside are Yummy, Roland, Corey and Marcus. When Tyrone and Antoine enter, the other boys take no notice because they are focused on the TV. Although not as big as the one in the living room, it is still quite large and very loud. Marcus is going up against Yummy. Each one jerking the joystick. Marcus is a giant koala bear with razor claws. Yummy is a half man, half robot, with a long samurai sword. They are fighting to the death in a parking lot.

The koala bear jumps behind the samurai, slashing his back. Blood spurts and temporarily blinds the koala bear. Feverishly working his joystick, Yummy chops off the koala bear's feet. As the koala bear hobbles backwards, the samurai stabs him through the mouth.

"Game over, nigga!" says Yummy. "You can't beat me. Nobody can beat me."

"I can beat you," says Antoine.

Yummy sees Antoine and Tyrone by the door. "Yo, look who here?" says Yummy. "What's poppin', dawgs?"

Tyrone and Antoine exchange pounds with Yummy and the other boys. "Yo, Tyrone," says Yummy. "You was killin' those Lincoln niggas tonight."

"Whatever," says Tyrone.

"Yo, dawgs," says Yummy, putting his arm around Tyrone. "You niggas see my man Tyrone out there? This is my nigga!"

Tyrone steps out of Yummy's arm.

"Dawgs? What's wrong?" says Yummy, grinning. "You not my nigga?"

Tyrone tries to smile.

"Yo, Ty. Like, did you plan that shit? Tell me the truth," says Yummy. "You planded it, right?"

"I don't know what you're talking about," mutters Tyrone.

"What? Nigga, please!" says Yummy, turning to the others. "You all seen it, right? I wasn't that high. I know what I saw. What every nigga in the gym saw. And what I wanna know is: did you plan that shit or what?"

"Lay off," says Antoine.

"Lay off? Lay off? This nigga here should be getting a got-damn medal. Some kinda trophy or plaque or somethin'! I mean, you good Antoine, you real good, but I don't ever remember you makin' no shots out yo ass. You ever make a shot out yo ass? I don't think so. I don't even think Michael J ever made no shot out his ass. No nigga in history ever known for shootin' out they ass. Shit... Ty here, has done tonight what no nigga has ever done before: the nigga has hit the buzzerbeater straight out his ass! Straight from his ass, outta his ass. And that is truly an original feat. Damn Ty, you right up there with Rosa Parks. She made history by sittin' on her ass and you be makin' shots straight outta yo ass. Rosa and Ty—two African-American heroes!"

Everybody is breaking up except for Tyrone. Normally, Tyrone would have tried to snap back. But Tyrone checks himself tonight because he needs Yummy's help. For months, Tyrone has been talking about buying a pit. But not just any old pit. Tyrone was able to get Rosco to promise that he would help him get a pit from "The Breeder." Yummy agreed to give Tyrone the money as soon as the settlement money came through. Yummy would put up the $9,000 to buy the pup and Tyrone would do all the caring and training. Once it was ready to roll, they would split the winnings after the first 9,000 went back to Yummy for his original investment.

Yummy clicks off the TV. "Alright, dawgs," he says. "Everybody take a seat. Yo, Twan, holla at Rosco for me? Thanks."

Antoine heads back to the living room. "Yo, Rosco," he says. "Yummy wants you."

"In a minute," says Rosco.

When Antoine returns to Yummy's room, a waft of smoke greets him at the door. Not one, but five blunts are burning. Yummy hands Antoine a blunt. The stereo is turned on—"Gin and Juice," by Snoop. The weed is sweet and strong. Antoine stares at the pile of giftwrapped boxes on the floor.

"My niggas!" says Yummy. "You all been wif me thick and thin and I wanna say I love ya all and I appreciate all our times together. Good times and bad times..."

"Stop talkin' junk," says Rosco, appearing in the doorway. "They here."

"They here?" asks Yummy.

"Is there an echo?"

"Where they at?"

"They out in the hall with Ivory."

"What they doin' in the hall? Tell 'em to get they asses in here."

"Chill," says Rosco. "I first wanna let all you niggas know about the rules."

"Rules?" says Antoine. "What you talkin' about?"

"It's part of the surprise," says Yummy.

"Okay, look," says Rosco. "Yummy has a little somethin', somethin' for you all."

"What up?" says Antoine.

"You gonna see in a minute," says Rosco. "And you all can have yourselves some fun. Alright? But you gotta understand you gotta stay inside the rules."

"What rules?" says Roland.

"The rules about what you can and cannot do. Now, you all know Ivory White... He's gonna tell you the rules. And you especially don't wanna break any rules that Ivory takes the time to tell you. Okay? Good. I'll be right back."

"Yo, Yum, what up?" says Antoine.

"Don't worry, you'll see in a minute. Anyway, here," says Yummy, handing Antoine a present. "And that's yours Ty, over there."

Antoine and Tyrone begin tearing at the gift wrapping.

"And for the rest of you niggas, your name is on your presents. Go on, check it out."

Antoine pulls out a custom painted leather jacket by Easy Eric from the Foster Projects. On the front is Antoine's name and on the back is a painting of Antoine dunking the ball in Madison Square Garden.

"Is that phat or what?" says Yummy.

"Damn... Thanks, Yum," says Antoine, giving Yummy a bear hug.

Tyrone also receives a leather jacket. But on the back of his is a snarling pit bull with a giant head. "It's beautiful," says Tyrone. "Thanks, Yum."

The other boys attack their presents. Instead of jackets, they get XXXL Gucci sweat suits.

"This the best Christmas I ever had," says Marcus. "And it ain't even Christmas. Thanks, Yum."

"It ain't nuthin'," says Yummy. "The best part still is comin'... Now, where the fuck are they? Hold on. I be right back."

Yummy goes off inside. Antoine and Tyrone put on their jackets. The others try on their sweat suits. Marcus turns up the music, puffs his blunt, and begins to moonwalk across the floor.

"Turn that shit off," says Ivory White, filling the doorframe.

Corey shuts the stereo. Ivory White comes into the room followed by Yummy and two girls wearing long coats.

"This is Yahira and Shatique," says Yummy. "They here for the party."

The boys stare at the two girls. Both are very tall but Yahira is the taller by about an inch. Yahira has on a blond wig and Shatique has box braids dyed red.

"You all don't know how to talk?" says Yahira.

"What up," says Antoine.

"He cute," says Shatique.

"Yummy," says Ivory. "Why don't you show them they room."

"Right," says Yummy. "C'mon girls." Yummy leads Yahira and Shatique to the next bedroom down the hall.

Ivory White says, "These are the rules. They is five of them so pay attention. Number One: No rough stuff. Any rough stuff, you gotta answer to me. Number Two: No biting, no pullin' hair. Any bitin' or pullin' of the hair, you gotta answer to me. Number Three: Nothin' up the ass. You try to go up the ass, you gotta answer to me. Number Four: If you wanna get sucked, you can get sucked but no holdin' the head down on yo dick. Anybody tries holdin' the head down, they gotta answer to me. Number Five: Once you bust yo nut, it's the next man's turn. No double-dippin', no extra sucks after you bust a nut. Anybody tries double-dippin' or getting' an extra suckin', they gotta answer to me. Those are the rules. You all understand them? Good. I'll be inside if you have any questions."

Ivory White walks out. Rosco says, "Now you all heard the rules. Just make sure you don't forget 'em."

"Damn," says Marcus. "I can't believe it."

"Believe it, nigga," says Rosco. "Yummy done bought you the two finest hoes in Harlem."

"Anybody got an extra condom?" says Corey. "I don't have a condom."

"Me neither," says Marcus. "I ain't hittin' nuthin' without no bag. I don't care how fine they look."

"They professional hoes," says Rosco. "They got they own condoms."

"Yo, where Yummy at?" says Corey.

"Where you think he at, nigga?" says Antoine. "You know he gotta be the first car on this train."

"True that," says Marcus. "It's his birthday. And he payin' too."

"Well, who next," says Corey, quickly checking himself. "I mean, who next after Rosco."

"I don't do trains," says Rosco.

"Then I'm next," says Antoine.

"Fuck that," says Corey. "I'm goin' next."

"You think so?" says Antoine.

Rosco smiles. "You both better chill. Yummy's moms is inside with her legs cut off. Show some respect. Ain't gonna be no niggas carryin' on while I'm here."

"What up?" says Yummy at the doorway. "What wrong with you niggas? Why you be lookin' like that?"

"Niggas be bitchin' about who next," says Roland. "First car, last car, don't make no difference to me."

"Only one nigga here that truly deserves next," says Yummy.

"Rosco say he don't do trains," says Corey.

"I know that," says Yummy. "I ain't talkin' about Rosco."

"Who then?"

"Who?" says Yummy, grinning and shaking his head. "You niggas got no respect for nuthin'. I'm ashamed of you. I mean, here we are, a room full of niggas lucky enough to be in the company of a genuine African-American hero. Shit... What if Martin Luther King was here? Or Mohammed Ali? You'd all let the famous nigga go next. Right? 'Course you would. So why you gotta ask me who go next? I shouldn't have to answer that 'cause you should never have asked it. Unless one of you know how to score from yo ass. Anybody here got skills like dat? I don't think so. Not even you, Twan, got skills like dat. So Tyrone, they all yours. Go on now, nigga, go tear up some ass!"

"Yo, Yum," says Tyrone. "I gotta talk to you."

"Talk about what?" says Yummy. "I just be playin'."

"I know it," says Tyrone. "It's not about that."

"What then?"

"The pit... The pit we been talkin' about. I was wonderin' when we can do it."

"The pit?"

"Yeah, the pit Rosco gonna hook us up with. Right Rosco?"

"It's not up to me," says Rosco. "Kinda dog you want gonna cost mad paper."

"Yo, Ty," says Yummy. "Check it, there's two fine bitches down that hall just waitin' on you. Waitin' on you to tear 'em up. And when I say fine, I'm talkin' 'bout top of the line, prime beef, USDA choice. I'm talkin' about rib eye and T-bone."

"Yeah, that's cool," says Tyrone. "That's mad cool. But what about the pit? We gotta get goin' on this thing. That's what Rosco says. Right Rosco?"

"What business you two got is not my business. But my connect has a top dog ready to go. He'll hold it over the weekend, maybe another week, if I ask him. After that, he's gonna sell it to somebody else. Nothing I can do about that."

"See?" says Tyrone. "We gotta move on this thing or we gonna lose it."

"Nigga, you must be crazy. Crazy and ungrateful. Will you look at this nigga here... I buy him a new leather and he got his hand stretched out for mo! You nuthin but a black ass Oliver Twist."

"Who Oliver Twist?" says Corey.

"Yo, Yum," says Antoine. "You did say you was goin' in on the pit with Ty. I was there when you said it."

"Damn! Yet another ungrateful nigga! I got a notion to throw you both off the train."

"Don't be talkin' to me like that," says Antoine.

"Then get off Ty's dick and outta my grill."

"Chill. Both of you," says Rosco. "All of you just chill the fuck out."

"Yo, dawgs," says Yummy. "This is supposed to be a party. We supposed to be havin' fun. I got two bangin' hoes waitin' on us in the next room and we arguin' over bullshit."

"It's not bullshit," says Tyrone.

"Nigga, please. Why don't you take your ungrateful ass self the hell outta here then."

"Yo, Ty," says Antoine. "That's that bullshit. C'mon, we outta here."

CHAPTER TWENTY-ONE

Back on the street, Tyrone and Antoine are wet and getting wetter. Antoine tries to flag down a series of gypsy cabs. But the taxis are either taken or unwilling to stop for large black males. Although they have no intention of going back upstairs to Yummy's, they do retreat to the tenement's vestibule for shelter. Not a moment later, Rosco appears behind them.

"At least you have the sense to come in out of the rain," says Rosco.

"What up?" says Antoine.

"You left quick," says Rosco.

"Nigga be frontin'," says Tyrone.

"Fuck him," says Antoine.

Rosco says, "My grandmother used to tell me: 'When God closes a door, the devil opens a window somewhere else.' You know what that means?"

Tyrone shrugs.

"I know what it means," says Antoine. "But it ain't always true."

"Maybe not. But this time it is. I'm gonna give you the money."

Tyrone looks at Antoine and back to Rosco.

"Well, nigga?" says Rosco. "A 'thank you' would be correct right about now."

"Thanks Rosco," says Tyrone. "But... I mean, that's a lot of paper. What if the dog gets hurt or somethin' and I can't—"

"You don't have to pay me back. It's not a loan. But if it makes you feel better, if the dog starts earning big time, you can hit me off some. That would be fine."

"Damn," says Tyrone. "I can't believe it. Thanks, Rosco. And bet: as soon as I win back enough to pay you, I'm gonna pay you."

"Nigga, don't be makin' no promises. Just leave it alone."

Tyrone nods. He says, "Yo, Rosco? What about Twan? Would it be alright for him to be in on it too?"

"I gotta concentrate on my game," says Antoine. "I don't have time to be workin' on no pit. Especially not during the season."

"Well, then after the season," says Tyrone.

"This is your thing, Ty."

"Alright, then," says Tyrone. "But you let me know if you change your mind after the season."

"Bet," says Antoine.

"So Rosco?" says Tyrone. "When you think we can do this? I mean—"

"How about right now?"

"Now?"

"Yeah. Let's go."

"Where we goin'?"

"To see the Breeder," says Rosco.

"Where he at?" says Antoine.

"On top of a mountain," says Rosco.

"Huh?"

"The Breeder lives up in the mountains."

"Mountains?"

"That's right," says Rosco. "They ain't so far. We can go there now, spend the night and meet with the Breeder first thing in the morning. Be back by Saturday night."

"I can't go to no mountain," says Antoine. "I got practice in the morning. Ty do too."

"Fuck practice," says Tyrone. "Did you just hear what Rosco said? He gonna take us to meet the Breeder. How many niggas you know get a chance like that?"

Antoine shrugs. "You do what you gotta do. I can tell the coach you sick or somethin'."

"Why don't you come, Twan?" says Tyrone. "What he gonna do if you don't show? Cut you? I don't think so."

"That not it."

"Then what?"

"I gotta keep everything focused on my game. Just like a pit. Everything I do, everything I think, has to be about my game. No disrespect Rosco... I appreciate the offer. But I think you know what I'm talkin' about."

Rosco nods. "Yeah, I know. We all here know."

CHAPTER TWENTY-TWO

Clyde is asleep on the couch. Aunt Gloria is babysitting. In her hand is a set of rosary beads. She pinches each bead for the duration of the Hail Mary.

Marisol knocks on the door. Aunt Gloria goes to the peephole. She lets Marisol in. Aunt Gloria puts her finger to her lips, nodding towards Clyde. Marisol looks, nods and walks inside. Aunt Gloria shuts the door behind her.

In a low voice, Marisol says, "Where Desiree?"

"She went shoppin'. She be back soon."

"Okay," says Marisol, sitting at the table. "I'll wait for her."

Aunt Gloria goes back to the couch. She holds up her beads. "You mind?"

"No, no," says Marisol. "Go on. Say some for me too..."

Aunt Gloria smiles, pinching and muttering and bobbing her head...

A few moments later, the telephone rings. Marisol grabs it on the first ring.

"Hello?" says Marisol, her voice hushed.

"Desiree?"

"No, this her cousin."

"Oh, hi. I think we may have already met. The other day, the other day after the basketball game?"

"Who this?"

"It's Vincent."

"I don't know any Vincent."

"I'm a friend of Desiree. I'm a teacher at the high school. Is Desiree around?"

"No, she not."

"Well, could you tell her I called?"

"Okay. Bye."

"Wait! Can you give her my number?"

"Yeah. Okay, what is it?"

"634-2503. That's 212 first."

"Yeah, yeah... Okay. I'll give it to her."

"Thanks."

Marisol hangs up the phone. Aunt Gloria looks up. "Who was that?"

"I don't know," says Marisol. "Somebody askin' for Dee Dee."

Aunt Gloria nods and goes back to praying. After she's done, she puts the beads away in her pocket. Clyde mumbles in his sleep. Aunt Gloria rubs his head and the boy wakes with a start.

"Can I watch TV now?"

"Your Momma said no TV 'till she gets back."

"When she comin' back?"

"Soon child. Very soon."

"What I gonna do then?"

"You gonna be good," says Marisol. "That's what you gonna do."

"I am good," says Clyde. "Right, Auntie?"

"Sure you are," says Aunt Gloria.

The key turns in the lock of the front door. As Desiree enters the apartment, Clyde jumps from the couch to greet her.

"Can I watch TV now?" says Clyde.

Desiree looks to Aunt Gloria. "Was he good?"

"An angel."

Marisol rolls her eyes.

"In a minute," says Desiree.

"You be spoiling him," says Marisol.

"Hey, anybody call?" asks Desiree.

Aunt Gloria looks to Marisol. Marisol says, "Some guy called. Victor or Viceroy or somethin' like that."

"What? You mean Vincent? They guy we saw after the game?"

"I coulda been. He sounded white."

"What did he say?"

"He didn't say nuthin'. He just asked for you."

"Is he calling back?"

"How should I know?"

"Did he leave a number?"

"Damn, girl! You too thirsty. What is it with you and this cracker?"

"Did he leave his number or not?"

"I don't think so. I don't really remember."

"How could you not remember?"

"I don't. Okay? Damn... You too thirsty..."

"You shoulda asked for it."

"He hung up first."

"Next time, just let the machine answer it."

"I can't believe it," says Marisol. "It's like... It's like you like him."

"I do like him."

"You trippin'."

"You hatin'."

"Oh, please."

"You are," says Desiree. "You don't even know him."

"Neither do you."

"I know he risked his own life to save my child."

"Whatever..."

"And he cute."

"Whatever."

"Yeah, whatever—whatever. You just don't like him 'cause he white. It's as simple as that."

"Oh, really?"

"Yes, really. So why don't you just admit it? You don't like white people."

"Alright. I do not like white people. Alright? I said it. Now what?"

"I used to be the same way," says Aunt Gloria. "Maybe worse."

"Maybe we should talk about this another time," says Marisol, cocking her head towards Clyde.

"No, that's alright," says Desiree. "Clyde knows all about it. Right Clyde?"

"Hm-m," says Clyde. "Until she got her miracle."

Marisol rolls her eyes.

"Everybody gets at least one miracle in they life," says Clyde. "But sometimes people don't want to believe in it and then they get no more. Right, Auntie?"

"That's right," says Aunt Gloria.

"Go on, Auntie," says Desiree.

"Do you have any beer?" says Aunt Gloria. "I'm a bit dry."

"Sure," says Desiree, going to the fridge. "Marisol?"

"You don't have to ask me," says Marisol.

"Gimme a hand Clyde," says Desiree.

Clyde returns holding a glass of juice and a glass of beer. He hands the beer to Aunt Gloria and sits down next to her on the couch. Desiree hands Marisol a bottle of beer and sits with her at the Formica top table.

Aunt Gloria takes a few long swallows. She says, "Hate was once my daily bread... That's right. I know it... You see this smiling old lady and you thinkin' how could somebody like her possibly be so hateful? But I was. I hated the white man. I hated him as soon as I woke up. I hated him all the day long. I cursed him before going to sleep. And I hated him in my dreams. But I wasn't always this way. Only after I lost Clyde. After I lost him there was nothing but a big empty hole inside of me. A hole I tried to fill up with hate."

"Clyde?" says Marisol.

"Her husband," says Desiree. "I named my Clyde after him. I told you that."

"Oh, yeah," says Marisol. "That's right... He died young, right?"

"He was just twenty-five," says Aunt Gloria. "Clyde was the sun and the moon, the sky and the sea. I never loved a man again like I loved my Clyde..."

"You okay?" says Marisol.

"Oh, I'm fine," says Aunt Gloria, drinking more beer. "They never found the man who killed him, who ran him down in the street. But for many, many years, I held the white man responsible. You see, it was a limousine that hit

Clyde and just kept right on going. It happened so fast and nobody got a good look at the driver or the plate. One woman claimed she saw a black man behind the wheel. But when the police questioned her, she couldn't be sure if he was black or Spanish or even Italian... But that didn't really matter because no matter who was doin' the driving, there had to be somebody in the back who was being driven. The Boss Man. The man who gave the order to keep on going. 'Nigga, don't you dare stop this car!' Just had to be a white man. Right? Who else but a white man? A rich, hateful white man who ordered his nigga to keep on driving."

"Makes sense," says Marisol.

"And, over time, that white man became all white men. The hate feeding on itself, getting stronger and stronger by the day, the months and the years gone by."

"And then came the miracle," says Clyde.

"Hush," says Desiree.

Aunt Gloria smiles at Clyde. She drinks beer. She says, "It was a beautiful sunny Sunday morning in April. The cherry blossoms were blooming. And because they were blooming, I set out to walk to where they were in Central Park. Every year since Clyde passed I would do this. It was Clyde who first took me to see them... We even had us a favorite bench that we'd sit on... Some folks, they like to go and visit the grave. But me, I preferred our old bench. Each and every year I'd go back there to sit and think about the times we used to have... Now, as it turned out, on this one particular day, the bench was taken by this white man wearing sunglasses. First, I just walked on by, hoping that he'd be gone soon enough. But this white man, he wasn't going nowheres. I walked all up and down those cherry blossoms and each time I passed by, wouldn't you know it, he'd be right there on my bench, grinnin' to beat the band. Of course, it didn't take me long to figure out that he was grinning at me. He musta known I wanted that bench. He had somehow figured this out and there was no way he was gonna give it up to some little black girl like me. So finally, I just went right up to him. I went right up to that white man and I said, 'What you grinnin' at?' But the white man? He didn't say not a word... Not a word come out of him. He just sat there with the sun on his face, grinnin' and staring at me through them sunglasses. 'You hear me?' I said. 'Somethin' funny to you?' But nuthin'. He just kept right on with his grinnin'. I don't know what came over me, but I do know that it was made strong by years of hate, an evil that told me that this white man was thinking things about me that no man ought to be thinking. Without thinking, I slapped him right across the face. Knocked those glasses flyin'. But, you know what? The white man? He didn't fight back. He didn't make no moves to fight back or get up or even say a word. And I do believe it was the fact that he didn't fight back that made me stop and look and see and realize that the white man was blind."

"What about the bells?" says Clyde.

"I'm comin' to it," says Aunt Gloria. "So, like I said, it was a Sunday morning. But I forgot it was a Sunday until I heard the church bells. They had been ringing for a while but I took no notice until I was standing there looking at the white man's dead eyes. It was like the whole world had gone quiet except for them bells. I felt real bad then, real ashamed, for what I had done. And I suppose I should have apologized. But I didn't apologize. Instead, I turned and I run. I run all the way back uptown, the church bells still ringing away, all through the park, all the way home."

"It was a miracle," says Clyde.

"A Jesus miracle," says Aunt Gloria. "When I got home, when I got upstairs and locked the door, it suddenly struck me that that white man was Jesus. Of course, there's no real proof to this fact. I can't prove it. How could I? Nobody can. Maybe it was those church bells that got me thinking in that direction. Maybe all I saw that day was a regular ol' white man. Maybe so... But who he was or who he was not, isn't what really matters. What matters is that I finally saw my hate for what it was. By slapping him, I was in turn struck with the knowledge of my own ignorance, my own blindness. Like Saul on the road to Damascus, I was knocked blind by the hand of God.   My life, like Saul's, forever changed because for the first time it occurred to me that maybe there was no white man in the back of that limo giving orders. Maybe the limo was empty back there. Maybe the driver was all by himself and got scared and just kept running. Just like I did. Who knows? But whoever it was, it really don't matter. What matters is the revelation."

"And you don't hate white people no more," says Clyde.

"That's right," says Aunt Gloria, finishing her beer and turning to Marisol, "So don't you ever think that a person can't change. People be changing all the time. Some from the good to the bad. Some from the bad to the good. Sometimes they change with the help of friends or family. Sometimes it takes a miracle."

CHAPTER TWENTY-THREE

Rosco's BMW is parked at the curb. Rosco presses a button on his keychain. The BMW chirps. "C'mon," he says.

Tyrone and Antoine run through the rain to the car.

"Go ahead," says Antoine. "I'm getting out first."

Tyrone nods and takes the front seat. Antoine gets in the back. Rosco starts the car. But he does not pull away from the curb. He looks across to the other side of the street. He makes a signal with his fingers. The headlights of a black, Lincoln Navigator flash on. The Navigator pulls out, making a left at the next light.

"What we waitin' for?" says Antoine.

"We be goin' in a minute," says Rosco.

The Navigator rolls up next to Rosco's BMW. The tinted window on the Navigator slides down. A white man's head appears.

"Shit," says Antoine. "Five-O."

"Chill," says Rosco, his own window going down.

The white man says, "Rainin' like a motherfucker."

Rosco nods. He pulls out two pistols from his person. Tyrone's eyeballs are popping.

"Chill," says Rosco. "Everything's cool."

Antoine considers running out of the car. He reconsiders. He is only accepting a ride home in the rain. He has nothing on him. He knows nothing of guns or drugs. He will stick to this truth because it is the truth. If he runs, the truth runs too.

Rosco puts the two guns inside a black plastic bag. He says, "All clear?"

"Yeah, it's clear," says the white man.

"After the bridge, I'm alright 'till Saturday night the earliest," says Rosco. "I'll call you."

"Fine," says the white man. "Have a nice trip."

Rosco hands across the plastic bag, pulling out as the light turns green.

"They was cops?" says Tyrone.

"Yeah," says Rosco. "They was. But not no more. They retired. Retired and in business for themselves now."

Antoine looks out the back window. He says, "They comin' up behind us."

"Chill," says Rosco. "They work for me."

"They collectin'?" says Tyrone.

"Na, nothing like that," says Rosco. "They their own private security company. I'm their client."

"I never saw them before," says Antoine.

"You not supposed to," says Rosco. "You only saw them 'cause I let you. And 'cause I know you know how to keep your mouth shut."

"Dag," says Tyrone. "That's deep."

"You trust them?" says Antoine.

"As much as I need to," says Rosco. "They makin' mad paper on me. And they not breakin' no laws. They just doin' they job. They no different than the security niggas guarding Puff or Michael J."

"Biggie and Pac coulda used some niggas like them," says Antoine.

"True dat," says Tyrone.

Rosco double-parks in front of Antoine's project. "You sure you don't want to come?" says Rosco.

"Yeah, I'm sure.

"When you playin' King?"

"Thursday comin' up."

"Bet, I'll be there."

"Alright, then," says Antoine, opening his door.

"Alright, dawgs," says Tyrone.

Antoine gets out, closes the door and runs through the rain into his project. Rosco heads back uptown, taking the West Side Highway to the George Washington Bridge. The Navigator follows Rosco across the upper roadway. As Rosco goes right for the Palisades Parkway, the Navigator continues on into New Jersey.

Tyrone sees the Navigator when Rosco points a finger up from the steering wheel.

"That them?" says Tyrone.

"Yeah, they live in Jersey," says Rosco. "City cops always end up living outside the city. Places like Jersey and Long Island. Places without niggas like me and you."

Tyrone nods. He thinks some. He says, "Hey, Rosco?"

"What?"

"Can I ask you a question?"

"Nigga, listen... You can ask me whatever the fuck you want. And maybe I won't always answer you. But I won't be mad for you askin'. Alright?"

"Yeah."

"You my nigga, right? You think I be letting any nigga roll with me? Roll with me to see the Breeder?"

"No. I know it. And I appreciate it."

"I know you do. So don't be worrying about what you should say or not say. I know what people be poppin' about me. But that don't mean all of it's true."

"You always done right by me," says Tyrone.

"That's not what I'm talkin' about. I'm talkin' about you being afraid that I might start wildin' out on you."

"I don't be thinkin' that."

"Then why you gotta ask me to ask a question? You ask Antoine if it's alright to ask him something?"

"No. But me and Twan..."

"Chill," says Rosco. "It's alright. You'd be crazy not to be wonderin'. But you'll see. The more you be around me, you'll see I ain't crazy, not one bit. What I am is real. Maybe too fuckin' real. But real. And sometimes people mistake that for crazy."

"Oh... Okay, then..."

"So what you wanna ask me?"

"Oh... Yeah, so ah... So how come you gave them your guns back outside Yummy's?"

"DWB."

"What?"

"Driving While Black. Once a nigga leaves the city, it don't take nothin' for some redneck trooper to pull you over 'cause you black."

"Oh," says Tyrone.

"Which don't mean I still can't protect myself."

Tyrone nods without clear understanding.

"Turn the radio on," says Rosco. "Hit the button that says AM."

Tyrone switches on the radio, hits the button.

"Now, dial the station to 99. Good. Now, push in the cigarette lighter."

After pushing in the lighter, the radio console flips open to reveal the stash box.

"Dag!" says Tyrone.

"Check it out," says Rosco.

Tyrone looks inside the steel lined box. He sees a roll of cash and two .38 snub-nose revolvers.

Rosco says, "When that's locked closed, they'd have to tear the car piece by piece to find it. Now, hit the lighter and switch off from 99."

Tyrone complies. The stash box closes, locking back into place.

"I never seen anything like that before."

"They been around for a while," says Rosco. "But they custom built and they ain't cheap."

"Dag..."

"You don't got anything on you? Weed or anything else?"

"Naw. Nuthin' on me."

"Good. So now I'm gonna ask you somethin'. Why you think I decided to take you with me to meet the Breeder?"

"I dunno... I didn't really think on it."

"Well, think on it."

Tyrone attempts to think. He says, "I dunno, Rosco."

"Alright. Fair enough. I'm gonna tell you. I had a dream tellin' me to. It was both you and Antoine in the dream."

"A dream?"

"Yeah. And, on top of that, you the only nigga outside myself that I can trust with my dogs. Antoine, he has the feel too, but he on another mission right now."

"No doubt," says Tyrone. "When it comes to ballin', he got the whole package."

"He for real. That's for damn sure."

"I heard you was just as good. Back in the day..."

Rosco smiles. "Yeah, but that's dead."

"Oh, okay..."

"So I'm plannin' on rollin' in the Big Time. You know what that is?"

"The Circuit?"

"You know about that?"

"I heard about it. It's like the NBA of dog fighting."

"That's right. They got spots all over the country. But not just any nigga can show up with his dog and roll."

"They let brothers in?"

"As long as you got the right credentials and references."

"And you got 'em?"

"I'm about to. That's why we goin' to see the Breeder. He's gonna hook me up."

"Dag..."

"And I gonna need a 'Second.' That's you. Nigga can't be goin' into the Circuit solo. Every top dog man's gotta have him at least one Second."

"I gonna be your Second?"

"That's right."

"What I gotta do?"

"Don't worry. I'll let you know."

The BMW continues its roll through the night. The Palisades Parkway is empty and lonely but Rosco keeps the speed just under 60. He turns on the radio to a jazz station. He says, "You like this?"

"I dunno... I don't listen to it much."

"I like it sometimes."

The set is a long one, off the album, "Charlie Parker and Strings." Tyrone watches the trees blur on the roadside. Closing his eyes, he rests his head against the cool of the window.

The rain continues. Falling hard and then, even harder. When Tyrone opens his eyes again, he's back in Harlem, outside Morningside Park. Rosco is mad about something. But Tyrone has the sense not to ask what it is. He gets out of the car. The rain blows in a roaring wind that consumes all other sounds, the water rising and rushing through the street and over the sidewalks. Up on the hill, Tyrone sees a bright light from on top of the church. Like a prison yard spotlight, it shines down into the park searching along the trees and the outfield. It is a powerful light, a beam that cuts through the dark and the storm and everywhere it hits is suddenly illuminated and highly defined. Transfixed, Tyrone sees the light stop, dart back, and fix itself upon something on the far side of the basketball courts. A sudden chill shudders through Tyrone. The rain slows and stops. The wind relents. The air is calm but heavy. A sheen of water covers the ground. Across this sheen, running in the light, is the three legged dog, Redrum. Tyrone is afraid. He knows the dog is dead so maybe he is dead too. Redrum crosses the watery surface in a blaze of light. Tyrone does not run, does not move. The dog stops before Tyrone. A sharp circle of light holds steady on Redrum facing Tyrone. Tyrone sees the dog more clearly than ever before—the tremendous head and muscled neck and those black eyes fixed on his own—the light so strong now that his fur seems to stand on end, glowing from within. But Tyrone is no longer afraid. Like the rain and the wind, his fear has transformed into a deep and heavy calm. A calmness so strong that he cannot move, cannot speak, cannot do anything but witness. For an instant, it seems like Redrum is about to say something. But instead, the dog begins to cough, coughing up a series of coins that sparkle in the light.

CHAPTER TWENTY-FOUR

Rosco grabs his arm, shakes him. "Wake up, nigga. We here."

Tyrone opens his eyes in confusion. He looks at Rosco but he's still not all awake. He rubs his face. "What up?" he says.

"We here."

Tyrone looks out the window into the dark.

"What the fuck wrong with you?"

"I guess I was dreamin'," Tyrone answers.

"Was Rum in it?"

"How'd you know."

"Did he say anything?"

"No. I thought he was gonna say somethin'... I felt like he was... But he just choked up some money."

"Money?"

"Yeah. But not paper. Just a bunch of coins... It was totally bugged... What you think it means?"

"Fuck if I know. But Mab might know. We'll ask her."

"Who Mab?"

"My grandmother."

Rosco turns off the main road. He puts on the high beams. The rain has stopped. The headlights shine on an empty road bounded by fields and trees.

"Where are we?"

"Right now, we in the Wanaque Valley," says Rosco, turning right onto a smaller, unmarked roadway. "But you see that turn up there? That's gonna take us straight up the mountain."

Rosco rolls slowly to the turn-off. He stops the car. The way is blocked by a heavy chain. "Go move the chain. The lock don't work. Just pull it open and after I drive through, hook it back up again."

Tyrone gets out of the car. He sniffs the night air. Tyrone has never been this far out of the city. The absence of car sounds and street sounds irks him. The chain is bolted to a tree on one side and padlocked to the skeleton of a burned out pick-up truck on the other side. Tyrone pulls on the padlock and it opens just like Rosco said it would. Tyrone twists the padlock, letting the heavy chain drop to the ground. As Rosco rides over the links, Tyrone finds himself in the dark. Tyrone does not like this dark. It feels like there's somebody watching him.

There is somebody watching him. Tyrone croaks with surprise and fear. Across the road stands a figure. In the instant before he sprints to the car, Tyrone realizes that it's not one but two or three figures watching.

"I just saw somethin, somebody," says Tyrone, locking the door. "A group of 'em over by that tree!"

"Chill. It's alright."

"You saw 'em?"

"Yeah, I saw 'em. Not at first. Otherwise I woulda warned ya."

"Who are they?"

"They the mountain people."

"Mountain people..."

"Yeah. They called the Jackson Whites. But don't you ever call them that. They don't like it."

"I ain't gonna say nothin' to nobody."

Rosco puts the car into gear. He drives slowly up the steep incline of the unpaved road. As they make their way up, they pass wreck after wreck of car and truck. Some of them are burnt out, all of them rusted and sunk into the earth in varying degrees by gravity and time. There are also rusted refrigerators, bedsprings, hot-water heaters. Set back off the road stand shanties and shotgun shacks—some with rotting roofs and timbers, others in fairly decent shape with glass windows and intact doors.

The road winds steadily upwards. It is dark except for Rosco's headlights. Up ahead, in the middle of the road, is an upside-down Good Humor ice cream truck. As they ride closer, they see that it's not in the middle, but marks a fork in the road. Rosco veers right, driving even slower to avoid the numerous rain filled ditches and holes. Up ahead, faint flickering light illuminates an old man working a broom over packed earth in front of a broke-back shanty. Strung from the shanty to a tree, a line of naked light bulbs burns dimly. The old man stops pushing his broom to stare at the BMW.

Tyrone sees the old man's face by the light of a flickering light bulb. He is an albino with a wide nose and full lips, his hair kinky and bald at the crown. The old albino stands motionless, staring without expression.

"Yo, Rosco."

"What?"

"I feel like I'm in a horror movie and we them white people too stupid to turn back before it too late."

"Ah, don't worry... That old Mousy Mulligan. He harmless."

"He looked completely bugged. You see the way he was lookin' at us?"

"Mousy be broomin' that yard for years. Since before I was born. He just don't like to be distracted. That's why he brooms only at night."

"Yo... I'm not really scared or nuthin'... But this place? Every since we crossed that chain? The vibe is completely bugged out. Like, where the hell are we?"

"We in the Ramapo Mountains. Mousy Mulligan and those niggas down by the chain? They mountain people. They live up here."

"The Jackson Whites."

"Yeah, but—"

"I know. Don't call 'em that."

"They don't like it."

"So who are they then? What's up with them?"

"Alright... I'll tell you. I'll tell you as best I know... The outsiders, people off the mountain in the regular towns and such, they all call the people up here the Jackson Whites. Most people don't even know why they called that other than they been callin' them that for hundreds of years now. But supposedly, there's a story behind it, a legend of how they come to be the Jackson Whites."

"So it's not true then."

"I didn't say that. Maybe it's not but maybe it is or maybe just pieces of it is. Like Michael Jackson owning the skeleton of the Elephant Man. Maybe it's made up but it could be true even though it sounds made up."

"I heard about that," says Tyrone. "So he related to these niggas up here?"

"What? No. The Jacksons I'm talkin' about here lived back in the olden days, back during the Revolution and the original Jackson I'm talkin' about was this big time pimp. You could say, the father of all American pimps."

"The George Washington of pimps."

"Exactly. He was the man. And during the revolution, when the British had control of New York, it was Jackson who tried to hook up the whole British army with hoes... But there just wasn't enough hoes in New York to go around. So Jackson, he got right on it, setting sail for England in twenty ships to bring back three thousand bitches."

"That's a lot of hoes."

"No doubt. But the thing of it was, on the way back, some of the ships got sunk in a storm. So Jackson, he took a quick side trip to the Bahamas and picked up a mess of black hoes to replace the ones he lost in the storm. And when he got back to New York, his bitches got to be known as Jackson's whites and Jackson's blacks. He kept them locked up in a stockade, pimpin' 'em out to the British soldiers. Jackson made mad paper on them hoes. Until George Washington and his crew attacked. As soon as the shootin' started, them hoes broke the hell out of the city, walking by night up the shore of the Hudson River."

"Up to where we at now?"

"That's right."

"They walked it?"

"People did a lot of walkin' back in the day. Especially if you a hoe during wartime."

"Dag. Then what happened?"

"Then, the story gets a little fuzzy. Some say they hooked up with runaway slaves. Others tell of them hookin' up with the local Indian tribes and outlaws. Nobody knows for sure, not even the mountain people themselves. But the name, the Jackson Whites, is supposed to come from those hoes and the people they hooked up with along the way."

"So these Jackson Whites, they black then?"

"They most definitely mixed. You can tell that just by lookin' at 'em. But they don't consider themselves black. They'll say they part Indian or Dutch or Italian. They'll admit to being a mix of just about anything but black."

"I know peoples like that."

"Yeah, but these peoples are different. It's like they they own race now. They been living up in these mountains for hundreds of years, marrying only each other so that just about everybody's at least a cousin or an uncle and aunt."

"And you grandmother's one of them?"

"Yeah, she one of them."

"Oh, okay..."

"I'm one of 'em too. Well, at least in part."

"And the Breeder, he's one of them I guess."

"Of course."

"When we gonna see him?"

"Tomorrow morning. Tonight we gonna stay with Black Mab. That's what people call her but don't you call her that."

"I won't."

"Yeah, she almost as dark as me. A shade somewhere between me and you."

"But she don't consider herself black."

"No. So don't be saying' or even thinkin' along those lines."

"Okay."

"There it is right up there."

Rosco pulls the car up onto the side of the road. A rock path leads to the front door of a small cottage. To the right of the front door is a window. Behind the glass, Black Mab is looking out. As Rosco and Tyrone approach, the head retreats.

Rosco knocks and the door is opened. Black Mab has long white hair, braided and pinned in a bun. Her features are small and sharp. Her skin, dark. Eyes a dull yellow. The cottage consists of one big room. The furniture is old but solid and in good condition. Rosco holds his grandmother's hands. But they do not hug and they do not kiss. Rosco introduces Tyrone. When Tyrone shakes her hand, he realizes that something is strange. Looking down, he sees that she has an extra finger after the pinky. But it's longer than the pinky and sticking out at an odd angle. Tyrone tries not to stare at her extra finger. He says, "Do you mind if I use the bathroom?"

"Not at all," says Mab. "Rosco will show ya."

Rosco says, "You gotta go number one or two?"

"Huh? Oh, one," says Tyrone.

"C'mon," says Rosco, leading Tyrone out the front door. "There's no regular bathroom, just an outhouse. But you can pee anywhere over there. Just not too close to the house."

"No bathroom?"

"No. That's why I try not to shit unless I really have to. See that little shack? That's the outhouse. But it's real nasty in there. Can't help it. You alright?"

"I'm good."

"Alright. I'll meet you back inside."

Tyrone does not venture far from the front door. He does not have a good feeling about this place. He does not like the trees and the smells and he especially doesn't like these Jackson White niggas. But if this is what it takes to get that pit, then this is what he'll do, even if he ends up having to take a shit in that outhouse. As Tyrone pisses, he looks up at the moon made fuzzy by the overcasting clouds.

CHAPTER TWENTY-FIVE

Tyrone wakes on the couch but does not stir. He's had many dreams but they were all fast flowing images of places and things he couldn't quite focus on. They were the "racing" dreams he has from time to time. Dreams that fleet and blend so fast that they can be considered one single dream, an abstract painting of the mind, the whole less than the sum of the parts, all forgotten upon the waking. Tyrone does not like these racing dreams. They leave him uneasy and unrefreshed, almost as if he didn't sleep at all.

Across the room, Rosco sleeps on a cot beside his grandmother's bed. But the grandmother's bed is empty. The grandmother, Black Mab, is standing at the window, looking out. She stands on her tiptoes. She walks on her tiptoes. Tyrone was glad when Rosco gave him the couch. Rosco wanted to sleep on the cot because that's where he slept when he was a little kid. Black Mab took care of Rosco for three years after his father died. Last night, Black Mab seemed happy to tell it. How Rosco's daddy dropped him off while he hunted Rosco's mom. Black Mab called Rosco's Mom a little nigger girl.

"He should have never messed with that little nigger girl," she said. "I knew she was trouble from the get go."

Rosco smiled at this but he did not say any words. Instead, he just let her go on until she was done.

"Rosco's Daddy, he had a special gift. Ever since he was a child... I remember the first snake he ever caught. It was one of them black racers. A long, lightning fast snake. Not even seven yet and he come right in that door holdin' it by the back of the head. That boy was a regular snake catchin' fool. He musta caught thousands of 'em, all kinds of snakes, thick and thin, long and short, harmless and poisonous. He got 'em all. Hands quick as lightning. Quicker than a snake, that's for damn sure... When he got older, he started making money by them snakes, sellin' 'em to the Pfizer man down the mountain in Mahwah. And that's how he met him his little nigger girl. A little nigger girl who sucked him dry for everything he had and then some... I knew it. I knew her kind as soon as I laid eyes on her. But Rosco's daddy, he was hard headed just like his son here. That little nigger girl musta ran away on him a dozen and half times before the last time. Before the time that he didn't come back here to pick up his boy."

Tyrone listened uncomfortably as she went on about how Rosco's father was shot by the man who was sexing Rosco's mother. After the shooting, she disappeared for close to three years.

"But like a bad dream, she come back again, come back here for the little boy. What could I do? I couldn't stop her. She was his momma. Took him down the mountain to the big city and there you have it. Look at him. Smilin' to beat the band but burnin' up on the insides."

Black Mab turns from the window. She stares at Tyrone and Tyrone tries to smile at her. But she does not smile back. She tiptoes across the room to the front door. She goes out the door. Tyrone looks over at Rosco.

"Yo, Rosco," he says. "You up?"

Rosco opens his eyes. "Yeah, I'm up. I've been up."

"We goin' to see the Breeder now?"

"Yeah. Where's Mab?"

"She went out the door. Just a minute ago."

"She say anything?"

"No."

The front door opens. Black Mab has a half dozen eggs. She holds the eggs by holding her dress out, the eggs resting in the hammock made by the cloth. Black Mab cooks the eggs on the wood burning stove. Tyrone and Rosco eat bread and eggs and they drink coffee. When they are done eating, Rosco has Tyrone tell Black Mab about his dream with Redrum. When Tyrone's done recounting the dream, Black Mab says, "I wish you woulda told it to me last night."

"How come?" says Rosco.

"It's just a feeling," she says. "But it's a feeling that I don't rightly like. Especially him sleepin' in the couch and you sleepin' on the flo by me. It's the mixin' that don't set right."

"What mixin'."

"What was and what is. How they mixed. The mix makin' a foul smellin' feeling."

"Alright then," says Rosco.

"Well, boy, you got me started and do I look like a faucet? You can't just shut down a feelin'. It don't work that way."

"I know it."

"Your daddy, he slept on that same couch the night he left you, the night he never come back to the living. I had the feelin' then too. It was the same kinda feelin' but more powerful. I told him to watch out. I told him to be careful 'cause death is right 'round the corner. You remember? You was little but I know you remember. I tole your daddy he better change his direction 'cause speed just ain't gonna be enough no more. And what happened? He got caught."

"You saying I'm gonna die?" says Tyrone.

"Boy, we all gonna die. In the end, death gonna find you, gonna find us all. No matter how fast you run, how good you try and hide. With that said, I'd be a bit more careful than normal."

"Dag..."

"What about the dream?" says Rosco. "Aside from the feelin'."

"The dream pretty much mean just what it say. Your little nigger friend here lookin' to make a mess of money off that dog in the dream. But the mammon only come off the sufferin' of the animal. That's why you here, ain't it? You didn't come up here just to visit me, did you?"

"But the dog in the dream is dead," says Tyrone.

"That's not my concern," says Mab.

CHAPTER TWENTY-SIX

Tyrone is glad to get the hell out of there. Once inside Rosco's car, he looks back at Black Mab in the window. Black Mab has the same dead expression as the guy who was brooming his yard. As they pull away, Rosco says, "What's wrong?"

"I dunno," says Tyrone. "I'm feelin' a bit bugged..."

"Mab always been like that. I seen her say stuff like that to plenty of people and most of 'em healthy and still walking around today."

"What about the others?"

"Dead."

"Damn..."

"At least she didn't say you gonna die specifically. She said for you to be careful."

"Don't worry 'bout that."

"Mab gotta nose for death. Like a dog can smell things we can't, Mab can sense when death is near. She was born with a caul."

"A caul? What's that?"

"A caul is like a web, a web of skin. Some people are born covered with a caul. In the olden days, if you was born with a caul, that meant you was a witch." Rosco drives slow around the ruts and holes. Tyrone takes in the daylight landscape of upside-down cars and rusted debris. Rosco stops the car. Up ahead, three boys, maybe a year or two younger than Tyrone, stand in the road. They hold large stones in each of their hands.

"Now what?"

"Rock boys," says Rosco. "Just chill."

Flanking the car and then behind the car come more Rock Boys, all holding rocks.

"Motherfuckas need a cap busted in they ass," says Tyrone.

"Chill, I got this," says Rosco.

"Chill? Niggas holdin' rocks. You want me to open the box?"

"Not necessary," says Rosco, opening his door.

"Yo, Rosco!"

Rosco pays Tyrone no mind. He gets out of the car. He opens his arms wide. The three in the road are light-skinned and squinty eyed. They look like triplets except for the variance in height.

"What up, cousin?" says Rosco. "It's me, Rosco. Don't you recognize me? We just come from Black Mab. I believe you seen us drive up last night."

The shortest of the three takes a number of steps forward. He stares at Rosco. After a moment, he says, "Yeah, alright... But what about that nigger you got in there with you?"

"Who the fuck he think he's talkin' to? I will fuck him up, rock or no rock!"

Rosco motions to Tyrone with his hand. Rosco says, "That be Tyrone. He a cousin of mine."

The boy looks at Tyrone, frowning. "Yeah, alright. But I still feest of it."

Rosco smiles. "We on our way to see Jesse Munch."

"That be your business, not mine."

Rosco gets back in the car. The Rock Boys fade from the road.

"What the fuck was that?"

"They not happy. But I'm still one of 'em by blood so they gotta let me pass."

"What if you wasn't?"

"You see that car?"

Tyrone looks at the overturned wreck, the rusted skeleton of somebody's station wagon.

"They don't take to outsiders," says Rosco.

"They sure as hell didn't take to me."

"Don't take it personally."

"What was that cross-eyed, yellow face nigga trying to say about me?"

"When?"

"He pointed at me and said somethin' I couldn't make out."

"He said he was 'feest' of it. That means disgusted. You make him sick just looking at you."

"Motherfucka best not come near me."

"He gone."

"These gotta be the most fucked up niggas I ever did see."

"No doubt."

"So Uncle Jesse, he the Breeder?"

"Yeah, that's him. Uncle Jesse Munch."

"He your uncle?"

"He's everybody's uncle. Everybody here either an uncle or an aunt or a cousin."

Rosco makes a right turn down a narrow road, so narrow that the trees touch their limb tips along the side of the car.

"What if somebody comin' out this way?"

"We'd have to stop and back up," says Rosco.

The road opens up to a small, unpaved lot. A hand painted sign reads: "Munch Chickens and Eggs." Rosco and Tyrone take the footpath beside the sign.

"No need for you to be shy around Uncle Jesse," says Rosco. "Ask him whatever you want. Uncle Jesse loves to hear himself talk."

The path goes down a small incline before running into a series of chicken coops surrounded by a chain link fence. The chickens make chicken noises. A rooster crows.

"Ain't he a little late?" says Tyrone. "Dawn come and went hours ago."

"That's not true," says Rosco. "Damn things crow whenever they feel like it." Rosco stops to look at the coops. There are four large coops and two smaller ones. Rosco and Tyrone watch the chickens peck and poke. Rosco says, "When I was a kid, I used to steal 'em. The best way is to sneak in at night with a warm stick. The chickens, they'll leave their roosts to get on the stick. If you're fast and quiet, you can get a mess of chickens in no time at all."

"A warm stick... That's a good idea."

"Yeah. But that's not the hard part. The hard part is getting by Jesse's brother. He the chicken man. Martin Munch."

"Can I help you with somethin'?"

Tyrone and Rosco turn from the fence. Martin Munch is a lanky old man with long, dirty hair falling from beneath a straw cowboy hat. Another notable detail is Martin's bright red hand—the thumb and fingers fused—with his palm at a right angle and facing the ground like he's dribbling a basketball or working a yo-yo. Tyrone does his best not to stare at the red hand.

Rosco says, "We here to see Uncle Jesse."

"I seen you lookin'."

"We was just lookin'," says Rosco.

"Alright then. But remember: Next time I'm gonna stick that stick right up your asshole."

"I know it."

"I may be old but I don't forget and I don't forgive."

"I know it... Uncle Jesse around?"

"Yeah, he around. Where else he'd be?"

"Nice seein' you again, uncle."

Martin Munch snorts and spits. "You 'member what I said now."

"I will," says Rosco, turning to Tyrone. "C'mon."

Tyrone follows Rosco down a second path, away from the chickens and Martin Munch. They approach a chest-high, wood picket fence. They stop at the gate. Just beyond the gate, a length of heavy chain forks to the collars of two mule-sized dogs. The beasts lay side by side, their chain running to a cement pillar. They look at Tyrone and Rosco but they do not rise from the ground.

"What kind of dogs are they?" says Tyrone.

"They called Tossas," says Rosco. "They from Japan."

"They look like giant pits."

"They just as tough too. Maybe even tougher. Not as quick though."

"They mad diesel. I never heard of no Tossa before."

"They hard to get a hold of. Got to go to Japan to get one. And they rare over there too. Even harder to breed right. But Uncle Jesse, he been workin' with them for years. They strange dogs. The Japs, they breed them so that they don't make a sound when they fight. Whether winnin' or losin', they always silent. Silent but deadly."

"Dag."

"Why don't you go on over there and pet one. Say hello."

"I ain't goin' nowhere near them things."

"They chained."

"Chain or no chain. I followin' you. I'm your second, right?"

"Yeah, that's right. C'mon."

Rosco walks forward, Tyrone a step behind. The dogs don't move anything but their eyes. Rosco unlatches the gate. He swings open the gate. One of the Tossas cocks his head, ever so slightly, to the side. Rosco turns to Tyrone who's keeping his eyes trained on the dogs. Rosco grabs Tyrone, yanking him over and back past the threshold of the gate. In Tyrone's wake, the monsters spring into flight, their tremendous jaws snapping without a growl or a bark. Instinctively, Tyrone breaks from Rosco, dashing a good ten yards behind the nearest tree. He watches Rosco watching the great dogs at the open gate, giant heads biting air, the cement pillar rocking. Rosco walks over to Tyrone. He picks up a fallen branch from the ground.

"Damn Rosco, you shouldn't be playin' like that."

"C'mon, Second. Watch this."

Tyrone follows a few paces behind Rosco. The Tossas are still straining against their chain, jaws snapping, great froths of drool falling from their maws and soaking the ground beneath them. Rosco reaches out with the stick. The Tossas snap it into splinters.

"Dag."

A whistle. The Tossas fall back and sit down. Jesse Munch looks much like his brother except without the hat and without the frozen red hand. Jesse Munch is proud of his long, yellow hair. He washes it each and every day. Brushes it too: a hundred times at sunup and another hundred at sundown.

"Stop fuckin' with my dogs."

"Hello, uncle," says Rosco.

"Who he?"

"He my cousin, Tyrone. He my Second."

"That so?"

"Yes it is."

"Well, c'mon then," says Jesse Munch.

Rosco walks through the gate past the sitting Tossas. "C'mon, Ty," says Rosco.

Tyrone moves slow and wary past the gazing dogs. Then, when he's sure he's beyond the limit of their chain, he sprints to catch up with Rosco and Jesse Munch. A wellkept lawn fronts the wood porch of an old stone farm house. A more modern garage is tacked on next to the house. On the porch are a number of ladder-back chairs. Jesse Munch sits down in a chair. Rosco and Tyrone do the same. Jesse Munch pulls a pouch of tobacco and some papers from his pocket. He rolls a cigarette and lights it up. He smokes. Nobody is talking. When the cigarette is near to burning his fingers, Jesse Munch tosses it off the porch, the red coal turning to ash.

"You see Martin?"

"I saw him," says Rosco.

"He ain't never gonna forget you stealin' his chickens."

"I know it."

"He all fucked up," says Jesse. "He my brother, but he all fucked up."

"How's Cremator?"

"He ready. But I suppose you figured that since you here."

"And Tnuc ready too?"

"They both of 'em ready. Question is: is you ready?"

"I am."

"The Circuit is not for fools. You only goin' into it on my say so."

"I know it and I appreciate it, Uncle Jesse," says Rosco pulling out two thick envelopes. "The fat one's for Cremator."

Uncle Jesse thumbs through the two envelopes of hundred dollar bills. "Fifty and nine, right?"

"It's all there," says Rosco.

"Yeah... Well, c'mon then," says Uncle Jesse, leading them to the garage.

Uncle Jesse turns the handle. He reaches down and pulls up the garage door. He flicks a light switch. He closes the door. There is no car or tools or anything you would normally expect inside a garage. Instead, the space serves as a gallery of fighting dogs, the walls filled with framed photos, old dog collars, breaking sticks, and various mementos of fighting days gone by.

"Somethin' huh?" says Rosco.

"This is the shit," says Tyrone.

"That's the wall of fame," says Rosco. "All them famous people."

Tyrone looks first at the framed photo of Thomas Edison. Below his nameplate is the quote: "There is nothing cruel about pit fights." On either side of Edison are Helen Keller and Teddy Roosevelt. Rosco points to Roosevelt, saying, "He was a president."

"He don't look like no president," says Tyrone.

"Back in the day, they dressed different."

"Oh."

Tyrone quickly glances at faces and names... Sir Walter Scott, Fred Astaire, James Caan... He pauses at Michael J. Fox. "I know this guy. I seen him in those 'Back to the Future' movies."

"That's right," says Uncle Jesse.

"You know him?" says Tyrone.

"We've met," says Uncle Jesse.

"Hey, who that?" says Tyrone.

"That's Jack Dempsey," says Uncle Jesse. "One of the great heavyweights of all time."

"He's one of Tyson's favorites," says Rosco.

"What about those guys?"

"That be Jack Johnson, the best of the early, colored boxers. The other is John L. Sullivan. Each great champions. Great dog men too."

"Look over here," says Rosco.

"The Little Rascals!" says Tyrone. "Yo, Petee! Yeah, that's right, he was a pit."

"And Buster Brown's dog too," says Rosco. "See?"

"And that one's Nipper," says Uncle Jesse. "He was the RCA Victrola dog. They say he only listened to classical music."

"I never heard of him before," says Tyrone. "And what about this wall?"

"Those are all the famous pits from back in the day," says Rosco. "But Uncle Jesse, he knows more about them than me."

Uncle Jesse runs a hand through his yellow hair. He takes a moment to gaze at the photos. Pointing a finger to the nearest frame, he says, "That be Blind Billy. He located his opponent by smell. He was a great champion. Lost only one match because his nose was chewed on. Poor bastard was counted out while searching the pit for his opponent. 'Course, he couldn't find him, nose all clogged up... I was there boys... He was one game dog. Not a drop of cur in him."

"I never did hear of no blind fighting dog," says Tyrone. "Musta been hard to train."

"Naw... Blind Billy wasn't blind from birth. He went blind. His owner was a welder and didn't realize how close the dog was watchin' him 'till it was too late."

"Dag..."

"Now there's Jeep and Homer. Two of the most game dogs ever to look through a collar. Homer ended up losing to Jeep in the early days of the Circuit. Yeah... All magnificent animals. There's Boots... Gator... Hope... Hurt and Tinker. Mister Juan and Garbo. That there's Tudor's Dibo. Now that's a dog who figures in the pedigree of just about every purebred pit today. That's right. See, and there's Centipede. He was one of the first in the old red nose line... Honeybunch... Wallace's Dude and Fancy... Hammond's Bruno and Macho... Carver's Black Widow... Dogs bred by real dog men..."

"Look at the head on this one!"

"That be Tugger. A hard biting dog if ever there was one."

"Who's that guy?"

"That's Richard Stratton," says Uncle Jesse. "He's the Hemingway of the Pit World. He wrote a number of very knowledgeable books on the subject."

"Look at those guys," says Tyrone. "They all dressed up."

"Back in them days, you had to wear a jacket and a tie," says Rosco, looking close at an old black and white print from the 1930's. In it, two dogs, Smiling Jack and Thunder, are ripping into each other's throat while up on their hind legs. Behind them, the men of the Circuit are all nattily dressed in jacket, ties and hats.

"Them days are long gone," says Uncle Jesse. "But the Circuit's still here... Speakin' of which, you gonna be needin' your pins."

Uncle Jesse crosses the room to a roll top desk. He opens a cabinet with a key. He puts the cash envelopes inside. He takes out an old Maxwell House coffee can. He holds the can out to Rosco and then Tyrone who reach in for their pins. They look at the pins: The head of a pit bull clenching a rooster by the neck. Inscribed at the top: "CIRCUIT - ACTIVE MEMBER 1274." Inscribed at the bottom: "MUNCH MOUNTAIN GAME DOGS."

"Beautiful," says Tyrone.

"Go on, take a few more," says Uncle Jesse to Rosco. "They can be your spares or if you be needin' some handlers.

But don't lose 'em now. You lose 'em there ain't no more for ya."

"Thank you," says Rosco.

"Thank you," says Tyrone.

"I know you won't let me down. Hell, you gonna be workin' two of the gamest dogs that ever came down the pike. Especially Cremator. They ain't never seen a dog like him since the original Cremator, and boys, I ain't one to boast... C'mon, you'll see yourself."

Tyrone and Rosco follow Uncle Jesse out the back door leading directly to the kennel.

The kennel houses close to one hundred and fifty dogs. It is a narrow but long structure topped with a slanting, corrugated roof. Loud. Individual pens line each side of the cement walkway. Each pen has cinder block walls and a chain link door facing the walkway. Some of the pens are empty, the dogs training in the yard. As the humans pass by, many of the dogs bark and gnash their teeth.

"That ain't no pit," says Tyrone, stopping at the pen of a large boned dog.

"No. That's a Presa Canario," says Uncle Jesse.

"They can jump an eight foot fence," says Rosco. "They real hard biting dogs, right Uncle?"

"Yep. Your Cremator got a flavoring of the Presa in him. And the Tossa too."

"Those dogs out by the gate?" says Tyrone.

"That's right," says Uncle Jesse.

"What about Tnuc?"

"Tnuc's a pure pit. But she all game. No cur in that bitch."

"A hard biter?"

"I suppose. But don't put all your stock in hard biting. I seen many a hard biting dog go down to the more game dog who's a little quicker and smarter. In any case, a pure hard biter is rare. I'm talkin' 'bout a dog that can kill an opponent by biting him in the chest."

"Rum was like that," says Rosco.

"Hm-m," says Tyrone.

"It's awful hard to breed a hard biter. You can breed gameness over time, but hard biting is much more elusive."

"What exactly makes a dog a hard biter?" says Tyrone.

Uncle Jesse stops his walk. He looks at Tyrone. He says, "The mechanics of it are straight forward. It's how the length of the jaw relates with the temporal fossa muscle. The farther the temporal fossa muscle is attached from the pivot point of the lower jaw, the greater the leverage that can be applied in closing the jaws. But for some reason, breeders can't seem to get a firm handle on hard biting. The way I see it, don't matter how hard a dog bites if he's not game. Your best breeders, they'll all tell you that a pit without gameness is a like a cock without balls. C'mon, let's see what's doin' outside..."

Uncle Jesse pushes open the back door. A flood of bright sun temporarily blinds them. As Tyrone's eyes adjust, he first sees the fighting pit. It is a sixteen-foot square with wood sides and a red cement floor. Scratch lines in white are fixed four feet from two opposite corners. Around the fighting pit are long benches made from planks of wood and cinder blocks. The benches are not empty. They are occupied by the Rock Boys. A number of them hold faded copies of porno newspapers and magazines. Lying beside them, or in their laps, are heavy stones. Tyrone sees the one who called him a nigger. But he looks almost normal compared to the rest. With distorted features and expressions, they remind Tyrone of the retards who wear helmets and ride the mini-bus. Looking up from their porn, more than a few fondle a stone. They remain silent. They stare.

"I know what you thinkin'," says Uncle Jesse, moving away from the fighting pit. "How'd they get to be like that? Right?'

"Kinda," says Tyrone.

"They like that 'cause they born to be like that. We all born to be what we have to become. It's a matter of scientifics. People like to think they got a choice in what they do, what they become. That's because we like to think we different than the animal world. But we not. If you a scientist or a breeder like me, it's not hard to figure out that an animal is only what his genes say he's gonna be. Now, of course, here on the mountain, it's peculiar. It's peculiar because you got, for the most part, a limited gene pool. Which is not bad in itself if you got somebody who's breedin' towards what you want and don't want... Nothin' wrong with inbreedin' if you makin' the right calculations. But with those boys over there? There's no selecting hand in the mix. And that's your problem. A problem that only gets worse over time."

They approach yet another chain link fence. Growing up over either side is a thorny hedge. They pass through the gate. The thorny hedge makes a bright green border the size of a basketball court. This is the work area, the place where the dogs are conditioned for the fighting pit. In the center is the cat mill, a medieval looking apparatus that starts with an eight-foot iron pole set in cement. Three feet up and parallel to the ground, a ten foot steel arm is counterbalanced by another arm in the opposite direction. Harnessed to the first arm is a pit bull dog. A short, third arm juts out just ahead of the dog, supporting a cage with a cat inside. Around and around, the dog "chases" the cat to build up his endurance.

Flanking the cat mill are a number of treadmills. Like the cat mill, the treadmills also have a cage of cat for the dog to chase after. But on the treadmill, the dogs have the added burden of a steel dumbbell tied to either their lower jaw or neck. In the hot sun, the dogs froth at the mouth. One dog, clearly exhausted, labors forward, his jaw stretched to the limit by the dumbbell, his tongue bloated to three times its normal size and coated with foam.

"Gotta get them used to being dehydrated," says Uncle Jesse. "You gotta deprive them of water before any big match. It reduces bleeding."

"Where's Cremator?" says Rosco.

"Both your dogs over there, by the spring pole," says Uncle Jesse. "That's Tnuc now. Cremator's waiting his turn."

"Dag," says Tyrone.

The spring pole consists of a pole set in cement like the cat mill. But the spring pole only has one arm to which a steel mesh bag is attached by a heavy spring. The bag hangs six feet from the ground. To taste the prize, the dog has to jump and hang on with his teeth. Tyrone's pit, Tnuc, hangs by his grinding jaws, swinging in a slow circle, shaking his head and growling loudly.

"What's in the bag?" says Tyrone.

"It was a couple of cats," says Uncle Jesse. "You put two of 'em in the bag and when they go at it, you let your dog lose. The action in the bag will get most any dog excited. I've found it's the best way to blood your pups and younger dogs. Okay, Slim, why don't you give Cremator a turn."

Standing at the ready is a young man: Slim. Slim holds a breaking stick. The breaking stick is most often used to separate two dogs for a scratch. The breaking stick looks like the oar of a boat, except smaller, the length of a tennis racket. The breaking stick is used to break a jaw lock. You first work it in with the flat part between the teeth. Then, you turn it, forcing open the jaws.

Slim clips a leash to Tnuc's choke collar. He deftly inserts the breaking stick. He works it until the jaws are pried open. The mesh bag jerks skyward on its spring, spraying Slim with blood and bits of cat meat. Slim yanks the leash. The choke collar chokes Tnuc into submission. Slim pulls the dog away. He clips the leash to a ring in the ground. Slim goes back to the spring pole. He unhooks the mesh bag and dumps the bloodied remains into a bucket. He rerigs the mesh bag, its mouth open. Slim walks to a small shed. Inside, cats and kittens are kept in wire cages. Slim carries out two cats by the back of their necks. He brings them to the open mesh bag. He drops them in, clipping it closed. The cats commence to screeching and clawing, the mesh bag bouncing and circling about the spring pole. Tnuc and Cremator strain the limits of their leashes, jaws snapping and frothing. Tnuc is a brindle bitch, forty pounds of muscle, bone and fury. But Tnuc looks like a toy dog compared to Cremator. Rosco and Tyrone never saw any dog like Cremator. Although Cremator looks like a pit bull, he is not a pure pit bull. Cremator is close to ninety pounds. Uncle Jesse has bred in the speed and agility of a pit with the strength and power of the Tossa and the Pressa. Cremator has a white body and a perversely gigantic, black head.

"He's a goddamn monster," says Tyrone.

"Usually, smaller dogs are more game," says Uncle Jesse. "But this here Cremator is the gamest bastard I've seen in many, many years... Go on, Slim."

Slim unleashes Cremator. The beast takes two bounds before soaring to the bag of felines. In one bone-crunching snap, both cats are pulverized out of misery. It is a sickening sound that makes Tyrone close his eyes and gag. When Tyrone opens his eyes again, Cremator is bouncing and spinning around the spring pole, grunting with satisfaction.

"Let go," says Uncle Jesse.

Cremator drops to the earth. He sits staring at Uncle Jesse, licking the blood off his chops.

"Dag," says Tyrone.

"Wash 'em up for these two boys," says Uncle Jesse. "They takin' 'em today."

Slim looks at Uncle Jesse. Slim is dark skinned with yellowy eyes. Tears run down his face.

"That's business, Slim," says Uncle Jesse. "I know you sad, but cryin's not gonna help none. Go on, now. You boys can come with me while Slim readies your dogs."

Tyrone and Rosco follow Uncle Jesse across the yard, images of Tnuc and Cremator hanging from the spring pole, still stuck in their brains.

"You boys interested in watchin' the Battle Royal?"

"What's that?" says Tyrone.

"That's how I cull the curs from the game dogs."

They walk through the yard back to the fighting pit. The Rock Boys have put aside their rocks and porn. The Rock Boys are inside the pit now, their backs to the boards, a young pit bull between each of their legs. Uncle Jesse, Rosco and Tyrone sit on the benches. Uncle Jesse makes and lights another cigarette.

Tyrone notices the duct tape. "How come you got their eyes taped?" he says.

"I got the idea from Blind Billy," says Uncle Jesse. "Blindness is an equalizer."

"True that," says Rosco.

"He was some dog though," says Uncle Jesse. "Even in losing, he was still one game dog."

"Just like Rum," says Tyrone.

"Your dog, Tnuc, she got some Redrum in her too," says Uncle Jesse.

"She related to Rum?"

"Tnuc is Redrum's great, great granddaughter."

"What kinda name is Tnuc?" says Rosco. "That an Indian name?"

Uncle Jesse smiles, "Naw. Slim named the bitch. Named her not long after I told him you was gonna buy her. Slim wanted Tnuc for himself. Of course, Slim don't have the kinda money that you got. So Slim started calling her Tnuc in the same way that you called Redrum, Redrum. Get it?"

Tyrone thinks... "Oh, I get it. That's messed up."

"It's fine," says Rosco. "Don't matter. A killer is a killer no matter what name you call it."

"Word," says Tyrone.

"How old are they?" says Rosco, nodding towards the pit.

"They all about nine months. None more than a year," says Uncle Jesse.

"You would think you wouldn't have any curs left," says Tyrone. "I mean, you been breeding them for so long."

"Yeah, that's the thing," says Uncle Jesse. "That's what you would think. But gameness is not hooked on a single gene. There's a combination of genes that make a dog game or a cur. And these same genes affect other aspects of a dog's makeup at the same time. It can be tricky. Inbreeding lets you overcome filial degeneration by reducing the variety. Selectivity is the key."

"What's filled generation?" says Tyrone.

"Filial degeneration. That's a scientific word that says that the tendency of the offspring is to revert back to the average of the race."

"Huh?"

"Say you have two champion dogs and you breed them. Their offspring have only a small chance of being as good as either parent. It's possible, of course. But not probable. When you breed any two dogs, you most often get an average of the two which most often ends up being just that, average. Same with people. Is it possible to get a pretty girl from ugly parents? Sure. It may not be probable. But it is possible. But now, you take that same pretty girl? She may well end up with a mess of ugly kids. That's filial degeneration. What they call, 'the drag on the race.' What I try to do is weed out the curs as they crop up in each generation. Here comes Slim. You boys in for a real treat."

Slim approaches holding a large tomcat by the scruff of the neck. The cat's hind legs are lashed together. The blinded dogs start yowling and barking. They sense the cat. They have been blooded on cats for weeks. Slim stops at the edge of the pit. He looks up at Uncle Jesse. Uncle Jesse nods. Slim tosses the cat into the center of the pit. The Rock Boys loose the dogs and step out of the pit. As the cat scrambles and flits, the dogs bump and bash and snap away at anything alive—including each other.

"They all goin' nut," says Tyrone. "How you gonna tell who game and who's a cur?"

"The signs. You gotta look for the signs."

"Signs?"

"That's right. See, see that little black bitch over there? She got a hold on that big one's ear. Now if she keeps that hold... If she keeps it no matter what the big dog does, no matter if she gets bit by some other dog, then she's a keeper, she's game. The surest sign is a holdin' dog. If a dog takes a hold and keeps it, then sure as shootin', you better keep that dog. You want a dog that makes a hold and don't let go no matter what."

"What if the dog goes down while he holdin'?"

"Don't matter," says Uncle Jesse. "A game dog will keep his hold and try to wrestle his way back up. A true game dog will not let go, top or bottom. 'Course, they sometimes get themselves killed by doing it..."

The cat is caught in the ass. It is one of the larger pits who's got him and he's shaking that cat hard, back and forth, until another dog manages to lock on to the cat's face. In a blind fury, the two pits tug via the cat. The larger pit is bumped by a third dog, causing him to lose his footing and roll on his back. But the pit does not let go. A good sign. Alligator style, the pit retains his grip while continuing to roll which in turn twists the cat's middle like a rubber band. Seconds later, the cat is torn in two.

Uncle Jesse points to the far corner of the pit. "See those two in the corner? There, you see that one turn away? That's a tell tale sign too. That dog is a cur."

"What, where?" says Tyrone.

Uncle Jesse motions to Slim. Slim moves about the perimeter of the pit.

"Slim's gonna get him," says Uncle Jesse.

Slim yanks out a chocolate colored pit. The dog is strong and powerful and Slim is careful to avoid being bit by his gnashing teeth.

"He turned," says Uncle Jesse. "If a dog turns his head and shoulders away from an attack, it's a sure sign of a cur. Dog like that won't never make his first scratch."

The Rock Boys no longer look to the action in the pit. They are picking up their stones. Uncle Jesse nods and Slim tosses the dog across the yard. Confused by being airborne, the blindfolded pit shakes his head and skits in a disjointed circle. Uncle Jesse whistles with his fingers. The Rock Boys race in a pack. They hurl their stones at the chocolate colored pit. Despite the onslaught, the pit keeps moving, snapping at the empty air, until he is knocked senseless and broken and finally dead. But the Rock Boys don't stop. Over and over, they pick up their stones, continuing to decimate the dead cur until Uncle Jesse whistles to stop the frenzy.

"Them niggas straight up crazy," mutters Tyrone.

The Rock Boys retrieve their stones. They return to the perimeter of the pit. The Battle Royal continues...

A dog fuzzes up at the base of his tail after being bit in the nose. This is a sign. The dog is tossed by Slim to be rocked by the Rock Boys. Another dog howls when bit and another whimpers in pain. Again, both tossed by Slim and rocked by the Rock Boys. In under twenty minutes, eight dogs are tossed and stoned to death. Five are still in the pit, jaws locked and holding onto pieces of each other.

"Maybe you boys can give Slim a hand. I do believe we've found our game dogs."

Tyrone and Rosco work the breaking sticks. Slim pulls the dogs out of the pit to Uncle Jesse who rips off the duct tape. Seeing their master, the dogs relax despite any loss of blood or meat. Uncle Jesse chains each dog along the side of the benches.

With a snow shovel, Slim scoops up the remains of the cat. Uncle Jesse unspools a garden hose to the pit. Tyrone and Rosco wash their hands. Uncle Jesse hoses all the blood and gore down a drain in the corner of the pit.

The Battle Royal over, the Rock Boys are allowed to carry away the dead curs in burlap bags.

PART TWO

CHAPTER ONE

Vincent hasn't seen Tyrone all week. This is unusual because Tyrone has never missed his class before. Like Antoine, Tyrone is forced to go to class during the basketball season. It is one of coach Steinberg's rules. When Vincent asks Antoine what happened to Tyrone, Antoine shrugs.

"Have you seen him?"

"He be around," says Antoine.

"He just doesn't come to school anymore."

"That's right," says Antoine.

"What about the team?"

"He off the team. He quit."

Vincent doesn't push Antoine any further. Not yet. Especially not in front of the class. Hopefully later, he'll catch Antoine alone and find out what's what.

Vincent doesn't have to wait long. As the class lets out following the bell, Antoine stays behind. He tells Vincent that Tyrone quit the team and quit school because of Vincent.

"Because of me?"

"Yeah. He say he don't need school. Same for ball. He say they only getting in the way for what he gotta do."

"And what's that?"

"Being on top."

"On top? On top of what?"

Antoine shrugs, "You know, like Scarface. Only without getting killed. Like that other guy. The president's pops."

"He told you that?"

"Yeah."

"What do you think?"

"About what?"

"About Tyrone quitting school?"

"It makes sense to me. He's got a plan. It could work."

"Selling drugs?"

"Man, you white people always be thinking that."

"I was just asking."

"You was asking 'cause that's what you be thinkin'. And you wrong too."

"Well, I'm glad I'm wrong."

"Nigga wanna make something for himself and the only way you think he gonna do it is by selling drugs."

"So then how?"

"He got himself a new pit. He gonna roll it and with the money he gonna start up his own breeding business. He gonna be a breeder. He say he gonna be the best. He gonna be the Scarface of the breedin' world."

"I don't know much about dog breeding. But I guess there's money to be made on it."

"Hell, yes. A top pit from a top breeder can sell for mad paper. Ten, twenty, even thirty thousand or more."

"For a dog?"

"Hell, yes."

"Maybe I should see if he needs a partner."

Antoine smiles. "Yeah, you should ask him."

"Maybe I will."

"Yeah, okay… I gotta get going…"

"Thanks, Antoine."

"Whatever."

"No, but thanks, really. You didn't have to say anything and I appreciate it."

"I know you be wonderin'. And Ty, he really likes you."

"Tyrone would like any teacher who shows Scarface in class."

"True that."

CHAPTER TWO

When Vincent tries to call Tyrone, he's told that the phone has been disconnected: "No further information is available..." Tyrone doesn't live far from the school. He lives in the Schomburg Towers on the corner of 110th Street, across from Central Park. When Vincent sees the address on Tyrone's Contact Card, he recalls something about the Towers, but can't quite place exactly what it is.

As Vincent leaves the school, walking east, he remembers: the Schomburg Towers were the home of the Harlem Wolf Pack, the gang of teens falsely accused of raping the Central Park Jogger. The story was all over the papers and the TV. It told of a young white woman taking her daily run through the park only to be waylaid, beaten, and gang raped by a band of marauding black youths. Video footage of the scene of the crime, along with shots of the Schomburg Towers, was endlessly broadcast along with sound bites from either side of the color line.

The Towers are a ten minute walk from the school. Vincent can see them clearly now, rising high over the tenements and projects. Up ahead, a group of teens play Cee-Lo against the wall of the building. One of them notices Vincent. He shouts, "Five-O!" The dice and the cash quickly disappear into pockets. The group scatters up the sidewalk and around the corner. Vincent smiles. He enjoys the irony of himself being mistaken for a cop.

At the base of the two towers is a large courtyard facing a traffic circle. On nice days, like today, the entire courtyard is bursting with people. Young teens and older teens burn blunts while hoisting 40 ounce bottles of beer. Four girls jump double-dutch. Like metronomes, the turners tick their heads back and forth in time to the beat of the wire rope as it strikes the pavement. One jumper and now two skip faster and faster.

Vincent crosses the traffic circle and into the courtyard. People stop talking. Some look away and others stare. The double-dutch game stops. Either he's some lost tourist or a cop pretending to be a lost tourist. Vincent walks towards the tower on the right. In his wake, the courtyard goes back into motion.

Tyrone lives on the thirty-third floor. Tyrone lives there alone ever since his grandmother died. After she passed, Tyrone kept the place for himself, paying the bill himself with a money order, just like his grandmother did. The rent is cheap, Section 8, and Tyrone is never late.

Vincent knocks on the door. A loud barking from within. The peephole is used and the locks are turned. Tyrone opens the door, holding Tnuc by the collar. Tyrone smiles. "Yo, is that you? What you doin' here?"

"Hey, Tyrone," says Vincent, looking at Tnuc.

"You wanna come in? Don't worry, she don't bite. Not unless I say so."

"Can you maybe put it in another room?"

"Yeah, sure. Hold on... C'mon, Tnuc."

Tyrone takes Tnuc down the hall. Vincent smells the dog smells. He sees an old tire, pocked and torn, in the middle of the room. A door is closed and Tyrone returns. "Come on in," he says.

Vincent follows Tyrone inside. He steps over the tire. The picture window shows a view of Central Park. It is a magnificent view, the shining skyscrapers rising up from the far edge of the trees like a modern day Oz. "What a view," says Vincent.

"Yeah, it's alright," says Tyrone. "But I don't like being so high up."

"Why not?"

"While back, they had a fire in the apartment below and the whole family had to jump or be burned. They jumped. The mother and all her kids. Father, he was out working."

"That's terrible," says Vincent.

"Shit happens," says Tyrone.

Gazing across the park, Vincent thinks how much this place would be worth if it were only a few blocks south... He turns away from the window. There is a ripped up couch, and some chairs and a TV set on top of a pink milk crate. The sound is off. On the screen, two pit bulls are fighting. But it must be late in the match since both dogs are clearly exhausted and not doing much but holding their locks on each other's shoulders.

Tyrone sees Vincent staring at the screen. He picks up the VCR remote. He fast-forwards. The dogs are separated for a scratch.

"Watch this," says Tyrone, pressing the remote for normal speed.

The one pit stays his ground, not moving, while the second dog charges in a final burst of energy. At the last possible instant, the motionless pit makes his move, sidestepping the charge and then pouncing with a death lock to the neck. Two headshakes and it's over. The dead dog held until the victor's jaws are pried open with a breaking stick. Tyrone clicks off the TV.

"You like dog fights?"

"I never saw one before," says Vincent. "That was real? That was your dog?"

"Na. That fight was from last summer," says Tyrone. "I just got mines last week. So, yo... Waz up? I can't believe it! You being here. In my crib. Out here in the 'hood."

"I wanted to talk to you. Your phone wasn't working."

"I hope you not gonna be tellin' me to come back to school. It's not happening Teach. Not a chance. No disrespect, I appreciate you tryin'. I appreciate you thinkin' about me and all... But there's no way. No way."

"That's not it," says Vincent. "I guess I feel guilty or responsible in some way."

"Antoine musta told you somethin'. Right?"

"We spoke."

"And he told you it was your fault I dropped out?"

"Is it?"

"Yeah, kinda."

"That's just great," says Vincent.

"It is great."

"No, it's not. A teacher is not supposed to teach you to drop out."

"A teacher is supposed to teach. And that's exactly what you did. I may not be the smartest nigga around but me droppin' out has nothin' to do with me being dumb."

"What are you talking about?"

"I'm talking about Superman and Scarface and that President's daddy. I'm talkin' about makin' a plan and rising to the top no matter what stands in my way."

"The dog fighting."

"Yeah. That and breeding them. There's a lot of money to be made if you know what you're doing."

"So I've heard."

"Maybe I'm not so fly when it comes to studying and test takin' but when it comes to dogs, I'm the bomb. That pit inside? That pit is gonna be my first step outta here. And you the one who opened my eyes. You the one who helped me see things clear for the first time. You one hell of a teacher and I ain't gonna forget it. So, for that, I say, 'thank you.' I'm serious. Thanks man."

"You know what Nietzsche says about gratitude?"

"What?"

"He says gratitude is the flip side of revenge."

CHAPTER THREE

Like all home games, this one is packed, so Desiree and Marisol have to sit at the very top of the bleachers to find seats. The game itself proves rather boring, another lopsided affair with the Tigers jumping to an early and insurmountable lead. By the end of the third quarter, Antoine has scored forty-five of his team's ninety points. But he remains on the bench for the start of the fourth. Coach Steinberg will keep him there for the rest of the game to give the scrubs their chance to play. Sensing this fact, many people start to file out. It's garbage time now and Tyrone, the crowd's scrub favorite, is no longer on the team, no longer ready and able to pull another legendary shot from his ass.

"I hate when he does that," says Marisol.

"What's that?" says Desiree.

"Fuckin' coach be sittin' Antoine every time he on a roll."

"That's what coaches do," says Desiree. "To give the other niggas a chance to play.'"

"That's what white coaches do," says Marisol. "Put a real nigga in there coachin' and Antoine be free to keep on killin' them."

"Yeah, whatever," says Desiree. "I'm gonna go get me a hot dog. You want one?"

"Na."

"Ok, I'll be right back then."

Since the first hot dog tasted so good, Desiree treats herself to a second, knocking it off in five bites, just like the first.

"Damn, you must be hungry."

Desiree turns to the voice behind her. It's him. "Vincent?"

"At least you remember my name. I guess I should be glad for that."

"What?"

"It's alright," he says. "It's nice seeing you again."

"Hey, how come you never called me back?"

"Excuse me?" he says.

"How come you never called me back?"

"I called you once and you didn't return my call so—"

"I didn't have your number."

"I gave it to your cousin."

"To Marisol?"

"Yeah. I think so. I called and she said you weren't home so I gave her my number for you to call me back."

"She never gave it to me."

"Really?"

"Yeah," says Desiree. "Sorry."

"I don't think she likes me."

"But I do," says Desiree.

Vincent smiles. "So you still up for that cup of coffee?"

"Forget the coffee. How about a drink or two?"

"Sure. When?"

"How about right now? You free?"

"I am. Yes. Great. Let's go. Where should we go?"

"It doesn't matter. But first I gotta tell Marisol. I came here with her. She's sittin' somewheres over there."

"Oh, okay."

"Don't worry. I'll ask her if she wants to join us but she'll say no and then we can go. C'mon," she says, grabbing Vincent's hand.

Vincent is acutely aware that he is not only holding her hand, but that everybody else is aware of it too.

"Wait," says Desiree, stopping and scanning the area where she last sat. "She's gone."

"You think she left?"

"Maybe," says Desiree. "She coulda saw you with me and left or maybe she's in the ladies room. Most likely she left though."

"So what do you wanna do?"

"Just let me check the bathroom first. She's probably not there but I should check just in case. And then we'll go."

Desiree leads Vincent by the hand around the court and to the bathrooms. Once again, they stick out and are noticed by many. Although Desiree clearly hears every sucked tooth and grumble, she pays them no mind.

"I'll wait over here," says Vincent.

"I'll be just a minute."

Vincent leans against the wall in the corridor leading to the bathrooms. He is nervous but happy. He had been thinking about Desiree for the past few days. Like the fisherman who's lost the biggest catch of his life, he couldn't get "the one that got away" out of his mind. But now, here he is in a place beyond his imagining, the great fish miraculously dropping into his lap from a clear blue sky.

"Hey, Vincent! What up?"

Vincent looks around. "Tyrone!"

"What you doin' here?"

"I came to see the game," says Vincent. "What about you?

"I was taking a piss."

"How you doing?"

"I'm fine. I got my first big fight coming up next week."

"Good luck."

"Thanks," says Tyrone. "You wanna come see it?"

"You think it would be okay? They might think I'm a cop or something."

Tyrone smiles. "They might. But don't worry. You'll be with me. It won't be a problem."

"Well, let me think about it, okay? Thanks for asking. I'm honored."

"Stop talkin' junk," says Tyrone.

"I'm serious," says Vincent. "I am."

"Alright, then."

"Yo! Tyrone!"

Tyrone and Vincent turn. They see Rosco and Ivory White. Rosco calls out again, "You comin' or what?"

"Yeah, I'm comin'," says Tyrone. "Okay, so I'll see you."

"Take it easy, Tyrone," says Vincent.

"Hey, Tyrone," says Desiree coming up from the bathrooms.

Tyrone turns. "Oh, hey. What up, Dee Dee?"

"Nothin' much," says Desiree. "What up with you?"

"Chillin'."

"Hello there," says Rosco, coming over to Desiree's side.

Desiree looks hard at Rosco but says nothing.

"You gotta problem? What's the problem? I'm just tryin' to say hi," says Rosco. "And you're Vincent, right? What up, Vincent?"

"Hi," says Vincent.

"You two enjoy the game?" says Rosco.

Vincent shrugs. "It was sorta lopsided."

"True that," says Rosco. "But sometimes even a massacre can be entertaining."

"We gotta go," says Desiree.

"We? We?" says Rosco, smiling. "Who's we? You and him? You and mister Vincent, the cracker?"

"I don't want any trouble," says Vincent.

"No, you don't," says Rosco.

"Yo, Rosco," says Tyrone. "He my teacher. He alright. He the one I tole you about. The one who showed us the two Scarface movies."

"He him?"

"Yeah. He mad cool."

Rosco stares at Vincent and Vincent returns the gaze. Rosco grins again, "C'mon, Ty, let's bounce. I'll give you a call, Dee Dee."

Desiree stares at Rosco until Rosco turns away and leaves.

CHAPTER FOUR

Vincent and Desiree are in a bar called Auggie's on Broadway near 106th Street. Luna Park, a trio of jazzmen, are expected to play later in the night according to a flyer posted beside the toilets. Vincent takes note of the burning elephant on the flyer. He wonders why the elephant is burning and why the band chose to use this image…

Vincent washes his hands and meets Desiree back at the bar. She is just now finishing her first bourbon on ice. Vincent's bottle of beer is near empty. He sits on the stool and motions the bartender for another round.

"This is a nice place," says Vincent. "You come here a lot?"

"Not a lot. I came here once before. They had a band."

"Seems kinda small for a band to fit in."

"Yeah," she says. "But they take out those tables in the corner."

"Oh."

"They gotta band coming tonight," says Desiree, nodding her head at another Luna Park flyer behind the bar.

The bartender sets down their drinks. Vincent motions to his twenty on the bar. The bartender takes the bill and they use some moments to drink their drinks.

Vincent nods towards the flyer, "Kinda strange, huh?"

Desiree looks at the burning elephant.

"Yeah," she says. "That's Topsy."

"Excuse me?"

"Topsy. That's the name of the elephant. She's being electrocuted."

"Really?"

"She was electrocuted by Thomas Edison. She was a circus elephant out on Coney Island. Way back in the day."

"And she was electrocuted by Thomas Edison?"

"Yes."

"You kidding?"

"No. Luna Park was the name of an amusement park on Coney Island. It's not there anymore. It got burnt down. But when it opened, its opening claim to fame was the electrocution of Topsy the elephant."

"Get outta here!"

"It's true."

"Really?"

"Yes, really," smiles Desiree. "Topsy was a famous elephant back in the day. Even before she was electrocuted."

"A famous elephant..."

"Yeah. Like Flipper or Lassie. Only she was an elephant."

"So why would anybody want to electrocute Flipper or Lassie or Topsy?"

"Topsy killed a man. Killed her trainer after he gave her a lighted cigarette to eat."

"That's fucked up. What was with the trainer?"

"He was a drunk," says Desiree. "Thought it was funny."

"Got what he deserved then."

"Topsy?"

"No, the fucked up trainer."

"I agree."

"But how did Edison get involved?"

"He offered his services," says the guy sitting on the other side of Desiree.

Vincent looks over at the guy. He has a tuft of gray hair just below his lower lip. A porkpie hat rests on his head.

"My name's Edwin," he says. "I'm in the band. First they tried to kill her by feeding her carrots laced with cyanide. But Topsy just wolfed them down without a problem. Then, the owners of Luna Park said they were gonna publicly hang her. Only the ASPCA protested and they had to think of something else."

"So that's where Thomas Edison came in," says Vincent.

"Correct," says Edwin. "At the time, Edison was fighting with Westinghouse for control of America's electric works. Edison was a DC man and Westinghouse was AC—alternating current. Edison had been saying that AC was dangerous and to prove it, he had been electrocuting dogs, cats, even orangutans all across the country."

"You gotta be shitting me," says Vincent.

"I shit you not," says Edwin. "Topsy gave Edison an opportunity he couldn't resist. What better way to prove AC is dangerous than to electrocute a three-ton elephant?"

"Makes sense," says Vincent.

"They set up a special platform and even a film crew. Edison showed the film all across the country."

A second and a third man, also wearing porkpie hats, come up on Edwin. Edwin turns to them and they mutter and Edwins turns back to Vincent and Desiree. "Nice meeting you guys. Maybe you can check us out. We go on soon."

"Yeah, maybe," says Desiree, turning back to Vincent. She rolls her eyes. "Asshole," she mutters.

"Edwin?"

"Yeah. He tried to hit on me. When you went to the bathroom. Tried to charm me with his elephant story. And when I told him I was with somebody, he tried to give me his number anyway."

"That fuck."

"Don't sweat it," says Desiree. "I gotta get going soon anyway."

"Oh," says Vincent.

"My son's with the babysitter. I don't want to be too late. I didn't know we were gonna meet up like this."

"I'm glad we did," says Vincent.

"Me too. What you doing tomorrow?"

"Tomorrow?"

"Yeah. All this talk about Coney Island makes me wanna see the ocean," says Desiree. "It's supposed to be nice tomorrow. You wanna go?"

"To Coney Island?"

"Yeah. We can make a day of it."

"I haven't been to Coney Island in years. Since I was a kid... But tomorrow's Friday. I gotta work."

"Oh, okay. Maybe some other time."

"No. Forget that. I'll just call in sick."

"You sure?"

"Definitely," says Vincent.

CHAPTER FIVE

Vincent waits for Desiree on a bench next to the subway at 110th and 8th Avenue. Behind him is Central Park. He spots one of his students coming up from the train who in turn, spots him.

"Hey, what up?" she says. "What you doin' here?"

"Hi, Shakia."

"Playin' hooky, huh?"

"Yeah, that's it," says Vincent. "I won't be in today."

"Oh, okay," says Shakia. "I got you. I won't snitch."

"Thanks, Shakia."

"Later."

Vincent watches Shakia cross the street in the direction of the school. Coming in the opposite direction is Desiree. Shakia and Desiree pass by one another in front of the gas station. The guy pumping gas is confused, not knowing which ass to follow.

Waiting for the light to change, Desiree sees Vincent and waves. Vincent waves back. He can't believe it. This beautiful woman waving and smiling at him. As Desiree approaches, Vincent stands up. He wonders if he should kiss her.

"Hi," she says, kissing and hugging him. "Have you been waiting long?"

"Not really."

They take the C to the D train at 59th Street. It is rush hour and the cars are crowded with people on their way to work. Vincent and Desiree stand as they travel beneath Manhattan. For Vincent, the crowded car is a blessing, forcing Desiree close and closer...

Once in Brooklyn, most of the commuters are gone and it's easy to find a seat. Climbing above ground, the train car is suddenly flooded with daylight. It is a warm and sunny day. Getting off at Coney Island, it feels like spring rather than fall.

They walk east, stopping a moment while Desiree removes her sweater, tying it around her waist by the sleeves. As she does this, she looks at the empty carousel. Skewered horses frozen in mid-stride, their worn, painted faces looking back with empty, lifeless eyes. Inside a mesh cage, a legless man stares at Desiree, saving her image for later when he will rape it in the long hours before dawn. Turning from the horses, Desiree is momentarily transfixed by his lust. She moves on. She knows the look. She has seen it countless times before.

Desiree and Vincent stroll in the shadow of the stilled Ferris wheel. They cross up the ramp to the boardwalk. A squat couple in heavy coats walk hand-in-hand towards Brighton Beach. Off to the north is the broken-down skeleton of a roller coaster, overrun with tall weeds and rot. An older black man wearing a cowboy hat and cowboy boots sits on a bench by himself, talking to himself. Beyond the black cowboy are the sand and sea.

"Ready for that drink?" she says.

"Sure," he says.

Ruby's is dark like a cave, the bats sitting on stools, blinded by the distilled spirits. The old dyke behind the bar pours without emotion, without hope, just pouring them out and ringing the register. The midget and the tattooed man sit at the corner near the front. Desiree wonders if they're gay. Not because they don't bother to look at her but by the way they look into each other's eyes.

Desiree and Vincent sit across from the cash register. On the counter, beside the register, are mini bottles of wine and cans of underarm deodorant. Desiree orders a bourbon and Vincent follows suit. "I got this," she says.

"Thanks," says Vincent, pulling out his cigarettes, offering her one.

"Thanks," she says. "But I like mine better."

Vincent lights Desiree's cigarette and then his own. They each place their packs on the bar, beside their drinks.

"This is great," says Vincent. "Smoking and drinking in the morning by the seashore."

"I like it," says Desiree.

They look at the pictures on the wall behind the bar. Old black and white photos of the sprawling masses spilling from the sand into the sea. Desiree focuses on a line of five white girls, all smiling and half bent over with their asses in the air... Five happy young tramps long dead and gone now, skulls and bones beneath the dirt...

"Look, there's Luna Park," says Vincent.

"Huh?"

"That picture there. It says Luna Park."

"Oh, yeah," she says. "I wonder if there's a picture of Topsy."

Vincent and Desiree scan the wall for the elephant. No luck. When the bartender comes over to refill their drinks, Vincent asks her about it.

"Na, none," she says. "But there's a picture of her in the book. You wanna look at the book?"

"Sure, thanks," says Vincent.

The bartender takes out a big picture book from under the counter. She places it down on the bar. Vincent and Desiree flip through the pages. They look at pictures of Luna Park and Dreamland and Steeplechase Park. Some of the pictures in the book are the same as some of the pictures on the wall. They stop for a moment to look at the pictures of Topsy being electrocuted. After Topsy, there are a number of pages devoted to premature infants.

"Are those babies?" asks Vincent.

"Looks like it," says Desiree.

"Those are premees," says the bartender. "It was a big attraction. Made a ton of money."

"They're premature?" says Vincent.

"That's right," says the bartender. "They set the poor things up in tiny crystal houses. See that? Yeah. And they would blow air in over hot water pipes to keep 'em warm."

"That's messed up," said Vincent.

"No, it's not," says the bartender. "Back in them days, hospitals didn't have incubators like they do today. Those kids would never have made it otherwise."

"But they were just another freak show," says Vincent.

"Yeah, so?"

"They were being exploited. I'm sure you couldn't see them for free."

"Somebody had to pay to keep them incubators going."

"Well maybe... But what about her?" says Vincent, pointing to the Fat Lady on the opposite page. "I suppose that's okay too."

"What?"

"Displaying her like that. Just to make a buck."

"Nothing wrong with it that I can see," says the bartender. "That's Jolly Irene. Weighed in at 689 pounds. See what it says there? She was fat all over, not just in the belly. But she was jolly. Had a sunny disposition."

"I'll bet," says Vincent.

"They say she was just 120 pounds at 21 but then she had a baby and the childbirth jolted her hormones. Poor thing couldn't help it. Just got fatter and fatter and fatter. When you're that fat, nothing much to do except join the circus. But then, she got too fat to fit in a rail car so she ended up out here in Coney."

"Lucky her."

"The freaks, they loved Coney. They still do. The one's still here. At Coney, you don't have to be on the road all the time. There's steady pay and you're treated as something special."

Vincent turns the pages: Lionel, the dogfaced boy. Zip, the pinhead. Bingo, the boy with an ear of an elephant. Rubberneck Harry...

"What's up with him?" says Desiree.

"Spider boy? Poor thing, he was born a cripple. Legs were useless and he was always being teased by the other kids. Kids can be mean like that. So he ran away into the woods, swinging through the trees like Tarzan. They say he could hang by his teeth to catch squirrels with his hands. The first time they caught him, they put him in the nut house. But he escaped pretty easy and ended up out here."

"One happy ending after another."

"You got a negative attitude," says the bartender. "You guys ready for another?"

"Sure," says Vincent.

The bartender refills their drinks before going back to her stool in the corner behind the bar. Vincent continues flipping through the pages. But Desiree stops him when he reaches the women who stretch their lips over gigantic wooden platters. Interested by their interest, the bartender comes back again.

"They had a reason for that," she says.

"For what?" says Vincent.

"Stretchin' out they lips like that."

"Oh, yeah?"

"It was a custom they had back in Africa. It started centuries earlier to protect the women from slavery by making them undesirable."

"Where does it say that?"

"It doesn't say that," says the bartender. "That's something I just know."

"Really."

"Hm-m. It's a sad story. Not at all like Jolly Irene or the Spider Boy. See, when they brought them over here, they brought their husbands too but when their husbands seen the local colored women? They fell straight in love with 'em. Especially when they tasted regular sized lips. They say a bunch of the African wives ended up throwing themselves in front of cars and trains."

Vincent closes the book. He slides it across the bar. "Thanks," he says. "I learned a lot today."

"Me too," says Desiree.

"Anytime," says the bartender, putting the book back under the bar.

When the bartender returns to her stool, Vincent turns to Desiree, "You alright?"

"Yeah, sure," says Desiree. "I'm getting real nice."

"My old man used to take me and my sister out here when we were kids."

"What about your mom?"

"She doesn't enjoy sand. She always stayed home."

"Oh."

"I haven't been out here since then, since I was a kid. I remember he used to put me and my sister on the Cyclone. I was scared to death of that thing. I hated it. But he made me go, told me to stop being a sissy."

Desiree smiles.

"He'd watch us with a can of beer in his hand, smiling and laughing like crazy as we went flyin' around the bottom turn."

"I bet you don't like roller coasters."

"Hate 'em. You couldn't pay me to get on one now. It's fucked up sometimes what a parent will do to a kid, you know?"

"Yeah."

"Don't get me wrong," says Vincent. "I know he meant well. But the road to hell?"

"Paved by good intentions."

"Exactly. He was and is the kind of a guy who will wake you up in the middle of the night to put the cap back on the toothpaste."

"Picky, huh?"

"Incredibly picky. If somebody leaves a light on, he hallucinates, thinks he sees dollar bills flyin' up through the roof. The guy is out of his mind... But he's okay, I guess."

"He loves you?"

"Yeah, sure. Of course."

"That's the most important thing," says Desiree.

"Yeah. What about you? Your father?"

"He's dead."

"Oh, I'm sorry."

"No, it's okay. He died before I was born."

"That's terrible."

"He was in Viet Nam."

"That was a fucked up war."

"Yeah..."

"And your mom?"

"She's still around. She's alright."

"She ever get married again?"

"No."

"So you grew up just with her?"

"I had kind of a step-father for a while. He used to go with my moms. It's kinda complicated. Messed up..."

"Oh, I'm sorry. I shouldn't be—"

"No, it's alright. Don't bother me none. Not anymore."

"So this step-father, what was his story?"

"Like I said, he used to go with my moms but then they broke up but then he came back again for a while. Only when he came back again? He wasn't really 'with' my moms no more. He was just basically living with us, living offa her."

"Not so nice a guy, huh?"

"Not at all."

"He still around?"

"No."

"He dead?"

"Good and dead," says Desiree. "He got what he deserved, I guess."

"Killed?"

"Yeah."

"They catch the guy who did it?"

Desiree looks away and then back at Vincent. She smiles.

"Hey, I'm sorry," says Vincent. "I'm just a nosy son of a bitch."

"No. It's just that I haven't thought about it for a long time. But it's okay. It's not something I wanna forget."

"I've always been a curious bastard," says Vincent.

Desiree laughs.

"What you laughing at?"

"You making me laugh. Because even though you're sorry for askin', you still wanna know everything."

"Oh, yeah?"

"Sure. But I don't mind."

"Alright then," says Vincent. "So what happened to the killer? He get away?"

"You've seen him."

"Me?"

"Yeah. You've even spoke to him."

"Get outta here!"

"Yeah, it's true."

CHAPTER SEVEN

When she was just a little girl, Marisol's Mom died of cancer. After that, Marisol was taken in by Desiree's mom, Delores. Although Desiree was a lot darker than Marisol, they looked enough alike for people to think them sisters or at least half-sisters. Even the girls came to believe this themselves. That is, until Raylene Sumner showed up at Morningside Park.

Raylene Sumner was a big, solid woman. Her legs and arms like giant overstuffed sausages, her belly bursting with meat but with the skin taut, not soft at all. The only thing soft about Raylene Sumner was the tone of her voice. Like Nina Simone, she spoke low and smooth, practically purring the words without sharpness or bite.

Desiree and Marisol were inside Morningside Park smoking cigarettes, just hanging out. Delores was at work, as usual. They sat on top of the picnic bench smelling the barbeque fires and idly glancing at the pick-up game over on the basketball court. Every once in a while, a few of the neighborhood boys would come sniffing around but the girls had no use for these young fools, stupid asses without money or mind.

"Hey, yo," said Desiree. "You see that fat lady over there?"

"Over where?" said Marisol.

"Sitting on them benches," said Desiree. "She keeps starin' at us."

Marisol looked over at the fat lady. She called out, "What you lookin' at?"

"Just let it go," said Desiree. "She probably just drunk or crazy."

"She gettin' up," said Marisol.

"Damn, I tole you," said Desiree. "I'm in no mood for this."

"Fuck that fat bitch. Let her come."

"Hey, just chill."

"I'm not doin' nuthin'. But she wannna bring it on, then let her bring it on."

Raylene Sumner downed the rest of her beer and slowly stood up. But she did not walk over to Desiree and Marisol. Not directly. First, she dropped the brown bag into the trashcan. Then, she went over to the playground. She called to a little boy there. The little boy slid down the slide and took her hand.

"Here she come," said Marisol. "She gotta a little kid wif her."

"Maybe she knows us from somewheres."

"I don't like the looks of her."

"You don't like the 'looks' of anybody," says Desiree.

"That ain't true. I like the way Kendal Hanover look."

"Who?"

"Kendal Hanover. The one they call Spike, over on Lennox. The tall boy."

"Oh, him... Oh shit, here she come..."

"Hello girls. My name is Raylene. Raylene Sumner? And this is Antoine. Say, 'hello,' Antoine."

"Hello," said the little boy.

"Hi," said Desiree.

"Do we know you?" said Marisol. "I think you might be thinkin' we somebody else."

"I don't think so," said Raylene.

"Well, my name's Marisol and I'm sure I don't know you but hi and good-bye."

"Marisol! Don't be so rude," said Desiree. "Don't mind her, miss."

After sucking her teeth, Marisol half-turned to watch the basketball game.

"Look, I don't want to be of any trouble. It took me a long time to find you girls and then another long time to get up the nerve to talk to you."

"Lady, what you want from us?" said Marisol, her eyes still on the game.

"I tried to talk to Delores. But she didn't want to have anything to do with me. And I can understand that. But still, I still feel I gotta talk to you no matter what anybody thinks."

"You spoke with my moms?" said Desiree.

"Yes. A couple of times. But then I gave up 'cause it wasn't ever gonna work that way."

"Watch you want from us?" said Marisol.

"I don't want anything. I just wanted to meet you and talk to you and have you meet little Antoine here."

"So you did that. Now what?"

"It's not so simple," said Raylene. "Can I sit down?"

"It's a free world," said Marisol.

"You wanna cigarette?" said Desiree.

"Thank you," said Raylene.

As Desiree lit the fat lady's cigarette, she could smell the alcohol on her breath and off her skin. Desiree lit a cigarette for herself and passed another to Marisol.

Raylene turned to Antoine, "Go on. You can go play now. I'm gonna talk some and then we be heading back home. Go on."

Antoine smiled, running for the swings. Raylene took a long drag on her cigarette. "He something, isn't he?"

"He real cute," said Desiree.

"He your cousin," said Raylene. "He your cousin and he your brother."

"Huh? What?" said Marisol.

"Antoine is your brother."

"What? You don't know what you're saying."

"It's true."

"You all messed up, lady. I'm sorry to break it to you, but I don't got any brothers. It's just me and Desiree. We sisters."

"Yeah, alright," purred Raylene, trying to smile. "Listen, I don't want to make any trouble. And after I say what I gotta say, I'll be on my way and it's up to you to do what you wanna do. The thing is this: that little boy? Antoine? He your brother. His daddy is your daddy."

"My daddy dead," said Marisol.

"No, he's not. Your daddy, Jesus Santos, is not dead. I know this because he the daddy of my little boy over there, your little brother."

"You must be trippin'."

"I'm sorry to have to tell you this way but I didn't know any other way to do it. But it's true. He's your little brother and there's nothing nobody can do about that. I know it must be hard hearing this from some stranger and all."

"Yo, lady," said Marisol. "I don't know what your tryin' to hustle here but—"

"There's no hustle. I don't want anything and I don't expect anything. I'm just trying to do the right thing by letting you all know what's what. I would have tole you before but you were too young. I figure you old enough now to know it. I'm gonna give you my address. If you ever feel you wanna come round and say hi or whatever, you always welcome. And if we never see you again, I understand that too. I won't come back here no more. You don't have to worry about that. And I'm real sorry if I upset you with all of this..."

Neither Marisol nor Desiree had anything to say.

"Well, thanks for the smoke and you all take care," said Raylene.

Marisol and Desiree watched her go to the playground to get her little boy. Taking his hand, she whispered something in his ear. The boy turned and waved at Marisol and Desiree and Marisol and Desiree waved back at him. As Raylene and her son were walking out of the park, Marisol said, "You think that lil' nigga lookded like me?"

"Yeah. Kinda."

"So you think she lyin'?"

"No. I don't think so."

Marisol looked at the paper that the fat lady gave her. She handed it to Desiree, "You hold it, I'll just lose it."

"Okay," said Desiree. "I'll hold it." Desiree looked at the paper. She said, "I never been to the Bronx."

Desiree kept the address but they didn't go to the Bronx that day or the next. And they didn't tell Delores anything about it either. Although they did talk about it to each other because they couldn't get it out of their minds. The notion of a secret little brother was mysterious and haunting.

A month or so later, Kendal Hanover, the boy they called Spike told Marisol about a Rock Steady jam up in the Bronx. Since Marisol had a heavy crush on Spike, she was careful not to let Delores know about him. Delores was very strict about them seeing boys and having boyfriends, especially before they were sixteen. Spike was tall and brown and, like all break dancers, Spike knew all about Rock Steady. The Rock Steady Crew were famous, the Chicago Bulls of the breakdancing world, and the only way to be put down with them was to battle one of their crew at a jam.

The Rock Steady Crew was notorious for hosting the best street jams in the city. A Rock Steady jam was basically an outdoor street party showcasing battles between local MCs and B-boys. Although Rock Steady was not the first group to break dance, they were the first to be recognized outside the ghetto. This happened when they were invited to perform at the Ritz with Malcolm McLaren and the punk group, Bow Wow Wow. The show was a big success, an event that for the first time united early hip-hop with punk rock.

When Spike asked Marisol to go, she agreed without hesitation. Of course, as Desiree pointed out, they would both be dead if Delores found out. But this didn't matter. No punishment could prevent such a wonderful crime. For a couple of ghetto kids, going to a Rock Steady jam was akin to a pair of flower children going to Woodstock.

They took the 4 train to 176th Street in the Bronx. It was Desiree, Marisol, Spike and Spike's friend, Leo, who hoped (in vain because he was ugly) to hook up with Desiree.

As the foursome stepped off the train and onto the platform, they flinched at the sudden barking. On a tenement rooftop, adjacent to the raised subway platform, a pack of yellow-eyed mongrels made themselves known. Moving fast from the angry dogs, they hurried through the turnstiles into a bank of urine soaked air that led to a set of stairs going down to the street.

On the sidewalk, competing sounds of salsa and rap blasted from a number of giant speakers, some stationary and others mobile in the slow stream of cars that congested beneath the steel infrastructure of the "subway" above. Outside a tiny cuchifritos joint, a group of disorderly men and women milled amongst themselves with many drinking through colored plastic straws and mumbling and cursing and laughing and sing-songing and spitting and then turning and hawking the young gang of four passing them by...

"Which way?" said Desiree.

"Follow me," said Spike.

The sun was setting and great crisscrossing shadows from the raised train tracks tagged the sidewalk. Just past the bodega, an opening on the left led to a steep set of concrete stairs going up between two tall tenements. These stairs connected Jerome and Davidson Avenues.

"C'mon," said Spike. "We gotta go up here."

"Nigga, you sure?" said Desiree. "Them steps be lookin' dicey."

"You scared?"

"I'm not scared. I just don't wanna waste my time climbin' all them steps if I don't have to."

"Don't worry, I got yo back," said Leo.

"Nigga, please," said Desiree.

Glittering in the failing light, hundreds of empty crack vials sparkled like diamonds. Broken bottles and shreds of trash were everywhere, the tenement walls covered with graffiti. One old man sat on a milk crate, his hood pulled tight about his head with his face almost in his lap, nodding and knowing nothing but his nod.

"Yo, Leo, what's yo daddy doin' here?" said Marisol.

"You got jokes?" said Leo.

"Let's just hurry," said Desiree.

Passing the old man, they started the climb up the concrete staircase. As they neared the top, two Puerto Rican girls started their way down. As the two groups passed each other, a gust of wind generated by a passing train below, surged up the crevice to blow the mini skirts of the Puerto Ricans up like inverted umbrellas. While Desiree and Marisol tried not to stare, Spike and Leo couldn't help themselves.

"Oh, snap," said Leo. "They naked under there!"

"Dag," said Spike.

The Puerto Ricans hurried down the steps, laughing and pushing down their billowing skirts.

"You think they was hoes?" asked Leo.

"Wasn't one of 'em your sista?" said Marisol.

"You still got jokes?"

The jam was located further up, on University Avenue in the schoolyard of PS 82. It did not take them long to find it. Even if they didn't know the way, they could have got there by following the heavy bass beats booming from the stacks of speakers flanking either side of the DJ's turntables.

The jam was jumpin'. Packed with mostly teens, there were also a fair number of old heads and little kids too. As they climbed in through a rip in the chain link fence, a young boy's mother was moving out, yanking her son along by his braids, barking many words in Spanish. The sun was gone and the jam in near darkness except for the sparking of lighters and the glow of burning blunts and cigarettes. Not unlike a block party, the jam had an overriding air of festivity and danger, fueled by a relentless flow of beer, booze and loud music. Scents of burning weed and sweaty body parts lingered. Oral communication was difficult. To properly understand, you had to shout in an ear.

The four from Harlem were wonderstruck. Feeling like Dorothy entering Oz, Desiree didn't know which way to turn because things seemed to be happening in all directions. Cut out squares of linoleum were surrounded by clusters of kids judging the moves of the B-Boys breakin' to the barks of the MC. Between these linoleum islands most everyone else danced freestyle or just grooved or imbibed in various drugs and sexual situations. Moving in a line with Spike at the head, the foursome made their way towards the DJ and the Rock Steady Crew.

A bald headed Spanish guy called Chico was spinning the discs, the juice to his system powered by a line tapped into a nearby utility pole. Most of the Rock Steady Crew was chilling nearby the DJ. A spotlight pointed to an empty patch of checkerboard patterned linoleum. But the light was turned off. It seemed nobody wanted to go. Not just yet.

Spike saw the guy next to the DJ. He shouted in Marisol's ear. Marisol in turn shouted in Desiree's ear: "That's JoJo."

JoJo was one of the founders of Rock Steady. The MC handed him the mike. JoJo tapped the mike. "Yo, Rick," he said, peering into the crowd. "Where you at?"

From behind Desiree was a wave of body movement. She half-turned as Slick Rick passed her by, brushing his arm against her arm. She turned to Marisol, "There go Slick Rick!"

Slick Rick and JoJo exchanged an elaborate handshake. Taking the mike, Slick Rick went straight into his rhymes, the DJ scratchin' in time. Although surrounded by darkness, Desiree could sense the collective focus on Slick Rick spittin' his rap slow and steady and hard and she thought to herself that this was the best day of her life.

When Slick Rick was through, the crowd screamed and shouted his name. Holding up a fist and a smile, Slick Rick stepped down from the DJ platform into the arms of a tall, much taller than him, Puerto Rican girl, the two moving away and into the crowd.

JoJo switched on the spotlight. The DJ dropped the needle. "The Buffalo Gals went round the outside..."

Backflipping into the center of the linoleum came Mad Mike. The crowd pushed and jostled about the perimeter of the square but never on it, never touching it. Mad Mike was all over the floor, going from headspins to hand glides to the continuous backspin called the "Windmill." Desiree never saw anybody break like that before. She cast a quick glance at Spike hawking Mad Mike's every move.

Nigga must be mad crazy or crazy nice to think he can compete with these Rock Steady niggas...

When Mad Mike was through, nobody, including Spike, would dare step out to take the challenge. So Mad Mike grabbed a younger boy, shoving him out onto the linoleum. The boy was very dark and very tall but not more than a year or so older than Desiree. His name was Rosco. It did not take Rosco much prompting to start poppin'. The kid was good, real good. Scratching the needle and setting the beat, the DJ was smiling wide now because Marisol had, without warning, pushed Spike onto the floor beside Rosco. "I believe we have a contender," said the DJ. Bewildered for but an instant, Spike quickly composed himself. Crossing his arms about his chest, he tried his best to look hard. This was what he had come for. The battle was on.

As Rosco continued breaking, he every so often glanced towards his challenger. But this glancing was without emotion. Rosco looked at Spike like a snake looks at his prey. Hyping the crowd with some fast cutting beats, the DJ segued into "Apache" from the Sugar Hill Gang.

The Rosco kid was slow, purposely slow, and silky smooth. The smoothness made the slow a marvel to look at. Desiree took in his white shell Adidas below the bell-bottom jeans with the knife sharp creases. The Rosco boy was fine to look at and dazzling to behold: from the chair freeze to the corkscrew to a totally bugged out, slow motion toe spin...

Yet Spike showed no fear. The Rosco kid was dope, but Spike was no chump either. The instant Rosco became still, Spike went into motion in an opposite style of lightning-fast kickouts and turns with a headspin and a backflip so that everybody was screaming for him one minute and then completely hushed because it looked like the kid from Harlem might just burn the young blood from Rock Steady.

Sensing the finale of Spike's routine, the DJ lowered and then cut the sound so that all you could hear was an acapella of fast and furious foot work rat-tat-tattin' across the linoleum floor.

Rosco stood unfazed. Desiree saw this. Even in defeat, this boy would not show a flicker of disappointment. In fact, it seemed like he was smiling. But what could the nigga be smiling about? It was clear that he was gonna lose. No doubt about that. Spike had him hands down. All Spike had to do was to finish him off.

Saving the best for last, Spike moved so slow to seemingly defy gravity. Arching and swinging his legs up over his head, he came down into a knee freeze that was the closest thing to perfect until it was suddenly and utterly destroyed by an explosion that took everybody (including Spike) by surprise.

In the instant following, there was a pregnant beat of pure silence, a sort of momentary implosion of acknowledgement and wonder. Not only loud and longwinded, the after-odor was deadly in the extreme. A fart to top all farts in the collective memory of everybody present.

Suddenly, bodies were stumbling backwards and away, fleeing the stench and leaving Spike alone on the linoleum island, humiliated and pickled in his own stink. With the sound system still off, word of Spike's exploit spread throughout the jam, causing those on the far periphery, the one's who had not seen or heard, to press forward to point and laugh at the stinky kid from Harlem.

Like the disciples in the courtyard, Desiree, Marisol and Leo hung back, refusing to let anybody know that they were with him.

Turning to the firm hand on her elbow, Desiree looked up at Rosco. "That your boy?" he said.

"What? He not my boy," she said, jerking her arm away.

"You was wif him."

"No, I wasn't."

"Yeah, you was."

"Nigga, who are you?"

"I'm Rosco."

"Yeah, and?"

"What's your name?"

"My name?"

"Yeah," said Rosco.

"Desiree."

The music returned. But the linoleum remained empty. Not far from the MC, Desiree could see Marisol beside Leo, but no Spike. Nigga must have bounced back to Harlem...

Above the earth, clouds swirled and the full moon punched a hole in the night. Rosco took Desiree's hand. Desiree made no move to pull away. They snaked slowly through the throng. The jam had become even more crowded than before. Movement was slow going. Desiree held fast to his hand, going where he was heading, not yet thinking which way that may be... As they passed behind the DJ, Desiree saw Marisol but she could not catch her eye because Marisol's eyes were trained on the next B-Boy. Desiree stopped. Rosco turned back. She shouted in his ear, "Where you going?"

Rosco's lips grazed her ear as he spoke and with this, words held no dominion. Desiree was awash with the heat of the feeling. He could have said anything. Understanding, thinking, was no longer important. Desiree followed Rosco to a set of stairs near the side of the school. Although the thudding beat still rocked through her bowels, the sound of music was drastically diminished as they descended to a lower lot behind PS 82. Looking about, Desiree saw a variety of couples making out and in the farthest, darkest corners, others sucking and some even fucking.

Desiree leaned against the brick wall, their bodies touching at the shoulders and the hips. She was ready for him to make a move, feeling both uneasy and excited by the prospect. Her body electric, she sought his intentions hard upon her own. But, at the same time, she also fought off the horrible flashes, the bursts of Jesus that short circuited her feelings, making her confused and afraid.

Rosco turned to her, taking her left hand in his right. They faced each other. Here it comes, she thought. Desiree closed her eyes. She waited a moment and then opened her eyes. Rosco stood looking. He said no words. Just looking.

"What?" said Desiree.

"I didn't say nothing."

"I know that," said Desiree, her mind descending back to earth. "You were staring."

"Sorry."

"It's okay," she said.

"That boy? You were with him?"

"I know him. He was trying to get with my sister."

"Oh."

"Yeah, I better be gettin' back up there. She gonna get worried."

"In a minute," says Rosco.

Desiree smiled. But he did not smile back.

"You alright?"

"I'm good," he said. "Real good."

"You had some dope moves."

"So did your friend. His were better... He had me beat."

"Then how come you were smiling? I saw you smiling when he was breakin'. Right up to the part when he lost it."

"I was mad."

"You didn't look mad."

"I smile when I'm mad."

"That's bugged. Why?"

"I don't know," he said. "I don't even know I'm smilin' when I'm smilin'."

"What about when you're happy?"

"I don't know. I'm happy now."

"You are?"

"Yes. You're beautiful."

"I'm so beautiful, how come you didn't kiss me?"

"You bold too," he said. "But you too young."

"Says who?"

He kissed her. Came blazing in, his mouth and tongue all up in it, eyes wide open. Desiree could see this because she found herself watching him also. It was strange. But wonderful. And the flashes of Jesus fading and gone like the memory of a bad dream lost on the waking.

Desiree continued to kiss him, allowing him to pull her close... But what was next? Desiree didn't know. A part of her said that she had to chill, had to slow the nigga down. While another part wanted everything he had, everything he wanted in her and through her. She could be a hoe. She knew this, had thought about it before. Niggas be lookin' down on hoes like white people be lookin' down on niggas. But who says a hoe has to be such a bad thing? A playa ain't nothin' but a male hoe and he called a playa. But a hoe ain't called nothin' but a hoe and why is that?

Rosco held held her face in his hands, "You alright?"

"I'm good," she said.

His hands slid down from her face, along her shoulders to her hips.

"I should be gettin' back," she said. "My sister's gonna be worried."

"Okay."

Marisol was still by the DJ set-up, Leo by her side. But still, no Spike. Nigga most definitely must have bounced... Also, the music was off. Something was fucked up in the system and the DJ was working hard to get it going again...

People were fast growing restless. Lots of chatter and loud talking with no music or dance to focus on as heavy clouds shrouded the moon so that all you could see was the red glow of countless cigarettes and joints.

"Where you been at?" said Marisol, not noticing Rosco a step behind Desiree.

"Around," said Desiree, looking to Rosco stepping in beside her. "This is Rosco."

Marisol looked at the tall boy holding Desiree's hand. She was both excited for Desiree and jealous.

"And this is my sister, Marisol," said Desiree. "Oh, and Leo here, too."

"What up?" said Rosco.

Marisol smiled. Leo did not. Leo tried to look hard.

Rosco in turn, smiled wide. "You gotta problem?"

"You talkin' to me?"

"Yeah, nigga," he said, still smiling. "You lookin' like you either sick or sick of lookin' my way."

"Get outta my face," muttered Leo.

Rosco reached forward, his fingers pinching Leo's forehead, his palm covering Leo's eyes and nose. With a firm and steady push, Rosco mushed him. Mushed Leo's head straight away.

Being so boldly mushed, Leo had the two basic animal options: fight or flight. The calculation did not take long.

"Why you do that?" said Marisol.

"He was irkin' me," said Rosco.

"Leo's a punk," said Desiree. "An ugly ass punk."

"True that," said Marisol. "You from around here?"

"Yeah, not far," said Rosco.

"You know where Andrews Avenue is at?"

"Yeah, it down behind University," said Rosco, pointing to the street beyond the jam.

Marisol turned to Desiree, "You still got it, right?"

"The address? Yeah."

"What's that?" said Rosco.

"We know somebody who live on Andrews Avenue. But we never been there before."

"I can take you," he said.

Suddenly, Rosco was pushed hard from behind, slamming into Marisol who held him up, preventing them both from falling. Spinning back around, Rosco could not find the culprit because there was no one culprit but a mass of bodies being shoved by other bodies in flight from what sounded like the start of a heavy beef. Immediately following, came shouts and screams and the, "pop, pop, pop," of a cheap .25 automatic.

Pandemonium. Bodies bouncing and flying and falling in all directions at once. Rosco took Marisol and Desiree by the wrists. They dashed past the DJ stand that soon collapsed in their wake. Marisol and Desiree had not choice but to be led because they didn't know the way out and to stay was to be trampled or maybe get shot. Not running, but footing it fast, they made their way down the steps to the lower lot, through the rip in the fence, and onto the street where they kept moving from the sirens getting loud and louder.

CHAPTER SEVEN

They hurried along Davidson Avenue before circling back up to University. On the opposite side of the street, heading for PS 82, a line of cop cars and another ambulance screaming. At Burnside Avenue, they saw Slick Rick again. He was no longer with the big Puerto Rican girl.

"There go Slick Rick," said Desiree. "That's him, right?"

"Yeah," said Rosco. "You wanna meet him?"

"You know him?"

"Yeah. Yo, Rick! Hey, yo, Rick!"

"What up, Money?"

"Yo, Rick. This here's Desiree and Marisol."

"Hello, ladies."

"We saw you at the jam," said Marisol. "You got some dope rhymes."

"Thanks... You two related or somethin'?"

"We sisters," said Marisol.

Rosco put his hand in Desiree's hand.

Slick Rick said, "How old are you?"

"Me?" said Marisol. "I'm eighteen."

"What year you born?"

"Um-uh... I—"

"Yeah, okay. It don't matter," said Slick Rick, turning to Rosco. "I heard it was that kid, Horse, who started bustin'."

"Word? The one with the water head. He always chilled. You sure?"

"Yeah. Mona and Boyzee, they was right there. They seen it."

"Who'd he hit?"

"I don't know. Some big nigga that was fuckin' with him."

"Dead?"

"Don't know. Maybe, yes."

"Horse... Who woulda known? They bag him?"

"I don't think so. Name ain't Horse for nuthin'. He might have a big ass water head, but the nigga can jet. I don't suspect we be seein' him for a while."

"No doubt."

"Alright then, Rosco. I be seein' you later."

As Slick Rick continued along University Avenue, Rosco said, "Andrews is the next block up. You make a right at the corner by the school there."

"Oh, okay," said Desiree.

"Let me see that address," said Rosco.

Desiree pulled the paper from her back pocket, showing it to Rosco. "You know the name?"

"Raylene Sumner? No. Maybe I know her to see her. What she look like?"

"She fat," said Marisol.

"Real big," said Desiree. "Mad healthy all over."

"Got a little kid? A little boy?"

"Yeah, only he not fat," said Desiree. "He real cute."

"Oh, okay," said Rosco. "I think I know who she is. Who she to you?"

"We related," said Desiree.

"Oh, okay," said Rosco.

"What, there somethin' wrong with her?" said Marisol.

"I don't know," said Rosco. "You know how people be talkin' sometimes."

"What they say?"

"Different stuff."

"Like what?"

"Like she a hoe. Like she type crazy."

"She didn't seem crazy," said Desiree.

"There you go then," said Rosco. "Maybe she not. Can't believe everything you hear. People be hatin'."

"You think she crazy?" said Marisol.

"Me? I don't know. She be sellin' crabs every Saturday as far as I can remember. Sets up a table right outsider her building. I don't like 'em myself but everybody say she cook 'em real good."

"Sellin' crabs ain't so crazy," said Desiree.

"True that," said Rosco. "Like I said, I don't know nuthin' other than what people be sayin'. All I know is what I see myself. Her and her little kid and her sellin' crabs on Saturdays. The other stuff, it's just talk."

"But sometimes 'just talk' can be true," said Marisol.

"Well, you wanna check it out or what?" said Desiree to Marisol.

"Whatever," said Marisol. "We here now. Might as well."

"You wanna come?" said Desiree.

"Me? Na," said Rosco. "I gotta bounce. I got practice."

"Practice?"

"Yeah, I play with the Torros."

"What's that?"

"The Torros is a basketball club."

"I heard of them," said Marisol. "You be playin' Riverside Church?"

"Sometimes," said Rosco. "We play all over. Sometimes outta state like Jersey or even Florida sometimes."

"That boy, Kelvin? From 118th?" said Marisol. "He told me he plays for Riverside Church."

"So you break and ball?" said Desiree. "I never heard a nigga do both. Or do both good. You good at ballin'?"

"Better than I break," said Rosco. "Ballin' is my priority."

"Maybe we can come watch you play," said Desiree.

"Yeah," said Rosco. "We be playin' in the Rucker Tournament next weekend. They gonna have teams there from all over. Hey, watch out! Just move outta his way. That's it. Don't worry, he harmless."

Desiree heard the sound of the broom an instant before she turned to see him. He had a wild head of matted grey hair that ran into an equally wild and matted grey beard, reminding Desiree of the ancient prophets, the holy men from the olden days that her Aunt Gloria used to tell her about when she was little.

"What up, Solobino?" said Rosco.

But the broomer kept brooming, paying Rosco and the rest of the world no mind. Desiree was fascinated, but she couldn't see his face because of all the hair and the fact that his head was down and focused on his heavy brush strokes and the growing pile of trash. As he moved into the glow of the streetlight, Desiree could see that the hairs on his head and beard were bunched into crude braids by rubber bands and shoelace. He wore no shirt. Hanging from his neck was a necklace of empty crack vials with a rainbow of different colored tops. He sported a pair of tattered, red velour sweat pants tucked into black, knee-high rubber boots. Protruding from the back of his boots were rolled up newspapers, shredded near the top and blooming like hot house flowers. Solobino did not lookup, did not look at anybody or anything but his brooming. His strokes were short, hard and efficient. Desiree, Marisol and Rosco stood a few feet back on the sidewalk to watch as he passed them by.

"What up with that nigga?" said Marisol.

"He sweepin' up," said Rosco. "That all he do."

"Now that what I call type crazy," said Marisol.

"Watch," said Rosco, pulling a dollar from his pocket and tossing it in front of Solobino's pile of trash. "See? Bugged, right?"

Solobino did not stop his flow, the dollar bill swept up along with the broken glass, candy wrappers and filth of the gutter.

"Bet you never saw a bum like that before."

"He don't take no money?" said Marisol.

"Nope," said Rosco.

"How he survive?"

"He live off the land," said Rosco. "Eats what he finds, sleeps in abandoned buildings and sweeps. That's it.

He like a caveman. But he part of the hood here and most people leave him alone."

"That all he do? Sweepin' up?" said Marisol.

"Yeah," said Rosco. "He starts early in the morning and go all day. Stays mostly around here near Burnside and a ways up and down University. He do a good job."

"And he don't talk to nobody?" said Desiree.

"Not really. He'll take food from you if he's hungry and he might nod or mumble somethin' but he don't ever conversate. Once in a while, kids will fuck with him, throw stuff at him and such but he'll ignore 'em unless they get in his way. And even then, he don't do nuthin' but quit and walk off."

They watched Solobino continue along Burnside Avenue.

"Did you ever throw stuff at him" said Desiree. "I mean, when you was a little kid."

"No. Why would I do that?"

"Why would anyone?"

"People are fucked up," said Rosco. "Specially, little kids."

"So what time is your game?"

"Three o'clock. Three o'clock next Saturday. We play some team from Long Island. You gonna come?"

"Yeah," said Desiree. "I think so."

"You think so?"

"We be there," said Marisol.

CHAPTER EIGHT

Rosco walked them to the corner of Andrews Avenue. One side of the block was taken up by PS 26, the other side a row of tenements. Rosco gave Marisol a kiss on the cheek and Desiree a kiss on the lips. Desiree watched him head towards Phelan Place, the block he lived on with his Moms.

"You gonna fuck him?"

"Gonna? I already did," said Desiree.

"What?"

"Yeah. During the jam. He found a quiet spot."

"Girl, stop lyin'."

Desiree smiled. "Na. We just did some kissin'. But I wanted to fuck him. And that ain't no lie."

"Yeah, he fly. Nigga can break too."

"You gonna come with me to his game?"

"Sure. Maybe he gotta friend for me."

"No doubt," said Desiree, looking off to where Rosco turned the corner. "So you still wanna go up?"

"We here now."

"Alright then," said Desiree, double-checking the address on the paper with the corresponding number on the building.

"Who you lookin' for?" said the lady with the shower cap crown. She held her head in her hands, fatty elbows on the pillow placed across the sill.

Desiree looked up. "We looking for Miss Raylene Sumner," she said.

"Raylene? Raylene up on five. What you want with her?"

"We just visitin'."

"Visitin'? Shew... Well, go on up then... Door's busted. Got-damn door always busted. Shew."

There were two doors leading in, both unlocked because both locks broken. No elevator. Marisol pushed aside a baby stroller blocking the stairs. They began their climb up steps worn down in the middle. At each landing, sounds of music and TVs and loud talking fading in and out and in again... A bag of garbage stinking of baby shit placed outside a doorway... Cigarette butts and scraps of trash scattered along the hallways like fallen leaves. Bold roaches marching across the wall in the harsh light of naked light bulbs. A plastic big-wheel trike turned upside-down... Graffiti in heavy black marker... Near out of breath, they finally made it to the top floor. Standing before apartment 5-C, they heard the foreign sounds of some old time jazz singer... Desiree looked at Marisol and knocked.

"Not so hard," said Marisol. "She gonna think you the police."

The needle was pulled up from the disc, "Who is it?"

"It's Desiree and Marisol," said Desiree. "We met a while back in the park... Morningside Park?"

Desiree smiled at the peephole. Locks clicked and clacked open. Raylene wore a pink flowered housedress. A waft of weed and patchouli incense emanated from within.

"Now, isn't this a surprise," said Raylene, in her deep, Nina Simone-sounding voice. "Come on in. Come in."

Raylene stepped aside and the girls entered. Raylene shut the door. The light was muted by red colored lace draping a pair of floor lamps in the corners. Raylene locked the locks, all three of them. Desiree looked around. It was like being in some kind of museum. The walls were full of pictures, some framed, some not, but of all sizes. There was a big pastel drawing of two smiling hippos bouncing up and down on a trampoline. There was another even larger painting of the Last Supper, only Jesus and his disciples were black with the exception of Judas, who was white. A number of velvet paintings showed Afro-topped men and women in various stages of lovemaking. Spear chucking cavemen attacked a woolly mammoth struggling in black mud. Dogs played poker. A sad looking white man had his head all bandaged up. Framed pictures of JFK and Martin Luther King. Malcolm holding a rifle. Picture postcards, hundreds of them, scotch-taped to all available wall space in-between the paintings and posters.

"Sit down," she said. "Have a seat."

There was no furniture to speak of. Just a glass topped cocktail table and a bunch of giant colored pillows scattered about the red shag carpet. On the cocktail table, incense burned, smoke rising from the red Buddha's ears and nose. A seashell held a half-finished joint.

Desiree and Marisol sat close together against a blue velvet cushion. Raylene crisscrossed into a Lotus position in a remarkably nimble manner.

"I'm so glad you decided to come," she said. "Antoine's asleep now. But I can wake him up."

"No, that's okay," said Desiree. "Let him rest."

"You girls like something to drink? I got some juice or I can make you some tea or I have wine and beer if you'd prefer either one of those."

"I wouldn't mind a beer," said Marisol.

"Sure. Fine. And you?"

"A beer would be good," said Desiree. "Thank you."

"Two beers comin' up!" said Raylene rolling to one side and then up into a standing position. "This is just such a wonderful surprise..."

A mermaid with naked tits on a bead curtain led to the kitchen. Raylene walked through the tits, turning on the light inside. She started humming while rustling up the beers.

Marisol whispered, "Maybe we should book right now. I think this bitch crazy."

Desiree shook her head.

Returning to the cocktail table, Raylene had each bottle wrapped with a napkin. She handed the girls a beer and one for herself.

"You two smoke?"

Desiree and Marisol looked at the ashtray and each other. "Sure," said Marisol, smiling now.

Raylene plucked the joint from the ashtray. Reaching into the pocket of her dress, she sparked a plastic lighter set on "high." Resurrecting the joint with two heavy puffs, she held her breath and passed it on. Desiree puffed followed by Marisol in turn. They continued around until it was deemed small enough for Raylene to pinch out and swallow. The weed was of the kickass variety. Although Desiree had smoked on a number of occasions before, she was never so high as she was now. The napkin on the beer bottle was wet. The cocktail table seemed a far way off. Desiree watched her hand move through space to take the bottle and pour the beer into her mouth. It was not ice cold but still quite refreshing and tasty. She didn't realize how dry she was until after the bottle was nearly done. Carefully, she placed the bottle back on the exact same spot where it rested a moment before.

Desiree was afraid to look at Marisol for fear that she might burst out laughing. It was the only negative tension, the snake in the garden she needed to avoid. Desiree looked at the red nail polish covering Raylene's toes. Looking closer, she saw tiny white daffodils painted inside the red. They were beautiful. She looked up and realized that Raylene had seen her looking.

"You've got beautiful toes," said Desiree.

"Thank you," said Raylene.

Marisol snorted in an attempt to stave off the laughter. The snort malevolently triggering a switch in Desiree's gut. Like trying to suppress a mammoth yawn, Desiree contorted her face, fighting the laughter. But it was of no use. And once it started coming, it only got worse. She laughed and laughed and her face hurt from the laughing. Marisol was no better. Although Desiree would not, could not, look at Raylene, she felt Raylene hawking her and Desiree was dismayed.

"I'm so, so s-sorry," said Desiree, struggling to speak straight. "I don't know... Ha, ha, hee," and some snorts and, "I don't know why—"

Marisol thrust her head deep into a nearby pillow.

Desiree closed her eyes. She pinched hard her forearm. The pain welcoming and sobering. She opened her eyes. She breathed. "I'm so sorry," she said, pausing, trying to ignore Marisol still shaking into the pillow. "I don't know why I'm laughing. Why we're laughing. But—" A deep breath and near under control now. "But we don't mean anything by it. I guess I'm just really fucked up…"

Raylene smiled.

Marisol came up for air. "That's some dope shit you got there," she said, giggling.

"Thank you," said Raylene.

A moment of focus, striving for control, and then, silence. Although they still did not dare look at each other, their laughter was finally in check.

"Sorry," said Desiree.

"Sorry? For what are you sorry?" said Raylene. "Nuthin' wrong with being fucked up and happy. Right?"

"I guess."

"You wannanother beer?"

"I'm alright for now. Thanks," said Desiree.

"Yeah, I'm good," said Marisol.

"But I wasn't laughing or making fun," said Desiree. "I mean, I really do love the way you got them flowers painted on your toes."

"Thank you," said Raylene. "They're daffodils. I did it myself. A hobby of mine."

"Must be hard to paint so small."

"You gotta take your time," said Raylene. "And gotta have time to do it. So I usually work at night, after Antoine's asleep, like now."

"You don't have any TV," declared Marisol.

"No," said Raylene. "A radio and my Victrola is enough for me."

"Victrola?"

"Record player. Over there."

Against the wall were a record player and a stack of records inside a milk crate. Raylene worked herself up again. She crossed the room. Using her palms to hold the edges, she removed one record and set down another. She gently placed the needle...

> *Sunday is gloomy,*
> *My hours are slumberless*
> *Dearest the shadows*
> *I live with are numberless*
> *Little white flowers*
> *Will never awaken you*
> *Not where the black coaches*
> *Sorrow has taken you*
> *Angels have no thoughts*
> *Of ever returning you*
> *Wouldn't they be angry*
> *If I thought of joining you?*

"You like Billie Holiday?" said Raylene.

"Billy who?" said Marisol.

"Billy Holiday. She's dead now but I love her. She's my favorite."

"Never heard of her," said Marisol.

"Me neither," said Desiree.

"Listen," said Raylene.

They listened. They listened to that song and the next and the next until the album was through and the needle hissing in circles. They sat quiet and still while Raylene got up to remove the needle. After that, without asking, Raylene took their empties, bringing back three fresh bottles of beer.

"Thank you," said Desiree.

"This beer is real good," said Marisol, taking a long sip. "And your weed is the bomb."

Raylene smiled. Desiree and Marisol smiled. Desiree said, "Can I use the bathroom?"

"Sure, honey, it's just down the hall. First door on the right."

Desiree got up, her legs a bit achy from sitting on the floor. The hallway was dim but she could see well enough from the light coming from the bathroom. She went inside and closed the door. She looked at herself in the mirror. She made a funny face. She bit her upper lip and then her lower lip. She went over by the toilet, pulling her pants down to pee. As she sat, she heard the clicking noises. A noise she realized she'd been hearing all along, like the hum of a refrigerator, without taking particular notice. She peed and listened carefully to the clickings. It was coming from the bathtub. A giant roach? A fucking rat! The pee was streaming hard and steady, no chance on jumping up now. Finally finished, Desiree quickly wiped, pulled up and zipped up. She brought her head close to the "tropical island" shower curtain. She pulled back the curtain. She stifled a scream. She stepped back, gazing down at the tub filled with crabs. Seemed like there was thousands of them. All on top of each other, clicking and clacking and moving around and over each other. Desiree was mesmerized by the clicking crabs. Could they see her like she saw them? Or do their eyes only work underwater? They were gonna be dead soon, that's for damn sure. And they don't even know it. Desiree pulled back the shower curtain.

In the living room, Marisol was sitting beside Raylene. They were smoking cigarettes now. On the cocktail table was a shoebox full of photographs. Raylene held a pile of them in her lap. She passed another to Marisol. Desiree sat down beside Marisol. Her heart froze at the first image passed her way. It was Jesus. He was with Raylene. Sweat started to pour from Desiree's armpits. She took a drag from Marisol's cigarette. Her hands and face were sweaty too. She felt like she might throw up.

"You alright?" said Raylene.

"I be right back," said Desiree, heading for the bathroom.

She shut the door behind her. She rushed for the bowl, spewing mostly beer and bile. She wiped her face and the seat with tissue. She flushed and washed her face. Shutting the faucet, she heard their clicking. She had the thought, a picture in her brain of lighting them on fire. The picture was so clear that it seemed more like a memory than a thought. Her hand dousing them with lighter fluid and dropping the match...

"Damn, I am so fucking high," she whispered to herself. Desiree wiped her face with the towel. She felt better for the puking. Returning inside, back beside Marisol, she managed a smile. "I'm okay," she said. "Maybe it was the cigarette."

Raylene said, "I'm so sorry, honey. I didn't know. I'm so, so sorry."

Desiree looked at Marisol and immediately knew that she had told Raylene. But for some reason, it was okay. Okay that Raylene knew. Sensing this, Raylene decided then and there to tell her own Jesus story.

"I was his Numero Uno Chancha," she said. "That was his pet name for me. Yeah... Can you believe that? More than anything else, Jesus loved fat girls. That's what he told me. But I also knew he was married. It didn't bother me. I didn't care. I was happy being Numero Uno Chancha. Fat girls were his secret passion. I was his number one. Before Jesus, I was never number one in anything... Just the fat girl. The fat hoe... He used to come creeping around midnight... Never a call or a warning. Sometimes two or three nights in a row, sometimes not for weeks at a time. I took what I could get. He satisfied me and asked nothing in return...

"And it wasn't just fucking. It was that, sure. But more than that too. When he was here, we were like a real couple. I fixed him food and we listened to music—he the one who bought me that Victrola and those records... We used to talk about things. We talked about the world, about sports, about whatever was in the newspaper that day. He often had me read to him from the Daily News... He would sit and listen with his eyes closed and whenever I finished a sad or tragic story about people getting hurt or killed or burnt out of their homes, he'd always say, 'There's a lot of sadness in the world.' Uh-huh, that's right, those were his exact words... 'There's a lot of sadness in the world...' Got-damn crazy ass nigga, at least he got that right...

"We went on like that for a number of years... They were some damn good times. I can't lie on that... But then, he just stopped comin' round. No good-bye, no nothin'. I figured he was maybe dead or in jail but I had no way of knowing. Or maybe it was something bad that had happened. Hit by a truck and paralyzed or somethin'... Not that he quit me. I knew he didn't quit me...

"And I was right. He had been fucked up. Who, how or why—I never did find out. He just showed up here one day so beat and battered that, at first, I didn't even recognize him. I took him in and I took care of him and he stayed on with me. He holed up in here, night and day. The nigga never stepped a foot outside the apartment. Like he was afraid to go out. Which was fine by me, of course. Only now, we didn't talk like we used to, hardly talked at all. But he could still fuck. Even more so than before. Nigga lived to fuck. Eat, sleep, shit and fuck. Fucked me every which way: morning, noon and night. Nigga fucked me so much that I had to sometimes tell the nigga, 'NO,' and shove his ass away.

"I knew, deep down, that our arrangement—our 'relationship,' if you could call it that, was strange. But so what? For the first time in my life, I had me my own man. He was truly my nigga and only my nigga. My plan was to make it work. You believe that? Ha! I actually believed we could make some kind of a life together.

"Shit hit the fan in my sixth month. Hm-m, I got pregnant. Yeah, that's right. Why the hell not? Why not start a family? Maybe a baby might snap him back to reality. Make him more alive. Make him care about something other than fucking.

"So yeah, I was in my sixth month... But he didn't know it. Nobody but me knew it. Being so big and fat: another ten, twenty pounds, don't make much of a difference. On the outside...

"When I told him, he just looked at me. Looked at me and looked at my belly and pushed me down in that way that said he was ready to fuck. I went with it thinking that it was his way of saying he was happy. Something he approved of.

"When he was done, I was a bit worn out and I just laid there on the floor. Usually, he would take his self a nap. But this time, he didn't do that. The crazy ass nigga, without a word of warning, he kicks me. Kicks me while I'm down. Cracks my rib. I tell you: that shit hurt like hell but I was not gonna let him hurt my baby. I covered up so he couldn't get a clean shot at my belly. He kicked me two more times. Once in the ass and once in the side of the head. I thought I might pass out. This shit was serious, dead serious, so I struggled to get up and somehow stop the nigga before he could kill me...

"When I got to my feet, he was gone. Maybe he run off. But no. He had went to the kitchen. Got himself a steak knife. Shew, I wasn't gonna fight no crazy ass nigga holdin' no steak knife. I rushed for the door but he beat me to it. He stood in front of the door, the steak knife in his hand, pointed at my belly..."

"Damn," said Marisol. "That is so fucked up! Whatcha do then?"

"I don't remember exactly. But I knew that there was no running. The nigga had the door blocked and a knife in his hand aimed at my baby. I knew I had to fight the nigga and either stop his ass somehow or die tryin'.

"I keep sharp knives. The blade went through the meat of my left hand without a problem. See?" Raylene displayed the scar across her palm. "But lucky for me, lucky for my baby, it was my hand and not my gut. When he cut me, I lost all fear. For some reason, in that second when the blood started pourin', I knew the nigga was mine. Shew, I out weighed him by a hundred pounds," she said, smiling. "But it wasn't easy. The nigga was skinny but he was strong too. And I was hurt pretty bad. My rib hurt like hell and hurt even more every time I moved. My ass and my head were on fire... But, funny thing, my hand didn't hurt. Not then, not yet. After he stuck me, he made the mistake of letting go of the knife. That was my one chance, my opportunity. With the blade still up in my palm, I backed away. I backed off and he just watched as I pulled the knife out. That's when I felt it, that's when it really hurt. I dropped it right where I stood. I suppose I coulda used it on him but the pain was just so bad that I had to drop it and scream. After that, I think he might have went for the knife again. You gotta understand, I wasn't thinking too clear at this point. All I know is that he came my way and I went right at him, screaming and punching and kicking and biting. We banged all over the apartment. It was pretty even until I was able to clobber him with that lamp stand there, see it? The heavy one. Smashed him in the foot. Smashed his damn foot and he let me go howling. I beat that nigga to hell with that lamp. Tried to kill the nigga. That's right. But being so fat like I am, and with my rib cracked like it was, I done ran outta breath. I was sucking wind and that was his salvation.

"When I got back my air, he was a pulp on the floor, curled up and beaten up and bleedin' out his mouth and nose. One good shot to the head and he'd be done."

"Whatch you do?"

"Girl, for the life of me, I don't know why... I mean, the right thing to do would have been to kill him. But I didn't do that. I had mercy. Yes... I gave the nigga mercy. Can you believe it? I let go the lamp. But even so, I wasn't through yet. I was still heated. And mad at myself too for not killing him when I should have... With that, I grabbed him by his fucked up foot. I had no plan, no rhyme or reason. I just grabbed the nigga and he started howlin' like a dog does when he hit by a car but still alive. This got me goin' again. But he didn't fight back. All the fight was beat clean outta him. Without lettin' go of that foot, I dragged his ass down the steps, all five floors, right into the street. Left the nigga right there in the gutter. 'You got-damn nigga,' I told him. 'You nuthin' but trash. That's all you is and all you ever gonna be!'

"He didn't answer me, didn't even look up, 'cause he couldn't look up. I musta broke the nigga's head bouncin' him down those five flights...

"When the ambulance took him, I was already back upstairs and nobody on the block ever told the cops nuthin'."

"Was he dead?" said Marisol.

"The nigga was beat, but he wasn't dead."

"What happened to him?"

"By and by, he come back around. But never up here, not never near me. Still must have some sense, some animal sense maybe. If you seen him now, you might think he was retarded or brain damaged. But either way, he know enough to steer clear of me."

"When you see him last?"

Raylene waved her hand. "Oh, I don't know... He comes and goes. Everywhere and nowhere. The nigga a bum. A crazy ass bum who, even if he isn't crazy, is pretendin' to be crazy which is a kind of crazy in itself."

"What about Antoine?" said Marisol. "Who you say is his father?"

"I tell him his Daddy's dead. And I appreciate you keepin' this knowledge to yourselves. Someday, I suspect, I'll tell him the whole story, or most of the story, but not now. No sense in tellin' a little boy things that don't make no sense. For now, monsters are better kept in fairytales."

CHAPTER NINE

"You wanna walk down by the water?" says Desiree.

"Sure, why not?" says Vincent, leaving four wet bills on the bar for the bartender. "Thanks," he says.

"Yeah, okay, Bub," says the bartender.

The sun is strong but hidden behind rolling storm clouds, the earth bathed in a deep, violet brilliance that seems to radiate from the sand and sea rather than from the sky above. As they cross the boardwalk, Desiree puts her arm around Vincent. This takes him by surprise, the strength and warmth of her hand on his lower back an electric pleasure. Reaching the beach, she puts her hand on his shoulder, taking off her shoes. After she's finished, Vincent does the same. The sand is cold but they pay it no mind.

Down by the water, a jetty of black rocks juts into the surf. They stand nearby, allowing the ice-cold water to hit their feet and ankles. Jumping back, Desiree shouts, "That shit is cold!"

"Yeah!"

"You wanna smoke a joint?"

"A joint? You got one?"

"Yeah," she says. "But it's okay. We don't have to. For a second, I forgot you were a teacher."

"It doesn't matter," says Vincent. "Spark it up!"

Desiree smiles, pulling the joint from her pack of Newports. Vincent cups his hand about hers while she lights it, relishing the contact...

They smoke the joint. Vincent soon feels high and wonderful... He hasn't been high like this in a long time. Now, they are laughing at something but Vincent doesn't know, has forgoten, what that something is...

Desiree grabs his arm. Vincent turns to her. They kiss and hold each other close. Vincent feels himself getting hard and harder as the sky opens up and the rain begins to fall. A second later, lightning and thunder, and Desiree pulls away. "We better get outta here."

"Okay," he says, likewise spooked by the sudden thunderclaps and streaks of lightning. Joining hands, they run across the beach and up the steps. Hurrying along the boardwalk, their shoes in their hands, they make for an open-air shelter. Under its roof, backless benches face the ocean. Over to one side, a pair of Mexicans sit drinking tall cans of malt liquor. The black cowboy is also taking advantage of the overhang, smoking a thin cigar, his hat pushed low.

Vincent and Desiree sit on the far side of the shelter. Desiree takes her sweater from her waist. She bends over and dries Vincent's feet. As she does this, Vincent looks at the black skin exposed between her waist and shirt. After getting their shoes and socks back on, they sit close and light up cigarettes as the Atlantic thrashes foam and spray and the black rock jetty disappears in and out of the crashing waves.

Not long after they are seated, their bodies touching and warming, the Mexicans start singing a Mexican song. Vincent glances over at them. "You thirsty?" he says.

"Yeah," says Desiree. "But it's pouring."

"Wait a sec. Let me try something."

Vincent walks over to the Mexicans. They stop singing. They stare at him. He says, "You guys wanna sell any of those beers?"

The Mexicans look at each other. One of them shrugs and the other says, "How much?"

Vincent says, "Whatever you think is fair."

The Mexican makes some mock calculations with his fingers. He says, "Two for five dollars. They the big cans, see? Tall boys. And it's a very long run in the rain to the bodega."

"Five? Fine. Thanks," says Vincent, handing over a five, thinking he would have given a ten if he had to.

The Mexican twists free two cans from their plastic yoke, "Here you go, homey."

Vincent returns to Desiree, handing her a tall boy. They pop their beers and they drink. The thunder booms.

"Beautiful," says Vincent.

"Yeah," says Desiree. "But Clyde would be scared."

"From the thunder?"

"Yeah."

"Well, that's natural. We should be scared too. It's a scary thing. Kids sometimes know exactly what's what."

Desiree smiles, sips.

"Look at that... Hard to imagine people sailing out on that in wooden boats, not knowing where it ends... Drowning would be terrible. That's something I've always been afraid of."

"Burning's worse," says Desiree.

"Yeah. Burning is bad."

"I heard that when you drown, that at the end it's very peaceful. Pleasurable even."

"Yeah, I heard that too," says Vincent.

"I never heard any pleasure stories on burning."

"So if it were back in the olden days... And we were out there on a big wood ship that got struck by lightning and went on fire, then I guess we'd jump in the waves."

"Maybe you would," says Desiree. "If it was the olden days, I'd be chained down below."

"Oh. Yeah. That's right."

"Just kidding," says Desiree. "I mean, I probably would be chained up but no reason for you to feel bad about it."

"Yeah... But that whole slavery thing... It was so fucked up."

"People are fucked up. People have always been fucked up... And there's no new thing under the sun..."

"What?"

Desiree closes her eyes, concentrating, "'All the rivers run into the sea; yet the sea is not full... The eye is not satisfied with seeing, nor the ear filled with hearing... And there is nothing new under the sun... All go unto one place;

all are of the dust and all turn to dust again.'" She opens her eyes. She says, "'A living dog is better than a dead lion.'"

"What was that?"

"Something I memorized. I used to know the whole thing. I forgot most of it."

"What's that from?"

"The Bible."

"Oh. Sounds like something from the Bible. You read the Bible a lot?"

"No. Not any more. When I was a little girl, I did. My aunt used to read it to me and I used to read it to her too. Some parts I memorized, like songs."

"I wish I could memorize things. That was always a problem. I bet you were real good on spelling tests."

"I was pretty good."

"I was terrible. But I was a good cheater so I got good marks."

Desiree smiles, "Some things, like the Bible and songs that I like, it isn't hard to remember."

"You still read the Bible?"

"No."

"Me neither. Well, I never really did. I was never big on religion. My Mom's religious though. Are you religious?"

"I don't know. I don't go to church or anything like that."

"Do you believe in God?"

"Yeah. But not in a church way."

"What's a church way?"

"I don't know. I'm not an expert or anything," says Desiree. "But for me it seems to be some kind of a hustle."

"Like a scam."

"Yeah, a scam. But a scam they play on themselves."

"I don't get you."

"No matter who you are or what you got, you always be dreaming for something else, something better than where you at now. Poor people be dreaming of being rich. Rich people dreamin' of being richer. And everybody dreamin' that it never gonna end, that they never gonna go out. Maybe they gonna die, but they can't help themselves from hopin' that there's still gonna be something more. That's the hustle—when the church tells them that they ain't never gonna die. They either gonna go to heaven or hell but there's no lights out."

"Lights out?"

"Yeah. Most people can't stand the idea of it. Of being somethin' one day and nothin' the next."

"What about you?"

"Me? I try not to let it bother me. Can't do nothing about it so there's no use wasting the time we do got worrying over it."

"But you still believe in God?"

"Yeah. But just because there's a God don't mean I gotta live forever. We all go to the same place. Everything turns into dust again. Says so right in the Bible but people don't wanna hear that part."

"I don't think anybody wants to end up as dust."

"No. But you can't be thinkin' on it too much either. Because that's just wasting the little time we got in the first place. My aunt used to say that everybody's life was like a song. Some songs maybe short and some maybe long and some happy and some sad and some songs are for fighting... Got songs for just about everything. But a song ain't a song until it's sung all the way through. Can't have just a piece. Each part of the song you need in order to make it a song. The ending just as important and just as unimportant as the start and all the parts in-between. When you listen to a song, all the parts, beginning to the end, are necessary and important for the song to be a song. You worry about the end, you gonna miss out on the tune."

"That's a great way of looking at the world."

"I don't know how great it is. But it's okay for me. Makes me take things as they come. And appreciate what's good."

"Like your son."

"Yeah."

"I like your song," says Vincent.

"You a part of it now," says Desiree.

There is lightning over the sea. Looking towards the horizon, Vincent imagines Clyde tip-toeing across the water and once again realizes how high he is...

"What you thinking about?"

"Me?" says Vincent. "Nuthin'."

"Oh, okay."

"Sorry. I was actually thinking about your son. I was thinking about the way he walks. I'm sorry. I'm still kinda high and—"

"That's okay. It ain't nothing. Just a phase he goin' through."

"Like suckin' your thumb? My sister used to do that."

"Yeah. Like suckin' your thumb. He gonna grow out of it. His father did the same thing."

"Rosco."

"Yeah."

"Sorry to bring it up."

"Why you always sayin' you're sorry?"

"I don't know," says Vincent.

"It kinda irks me."

"I definitely don't wanna irk you. I'll try to watch my sorrys."

"Yeah, alright then."

"Last thing I wanna do is bring up any bad memories."

"You think so? Yeah, maybe... But you definitely a nosy kinda guy. No hidin' that."

"I guess not."

"I don't mind. Sometimes it's good for me to talk about it once in a while. Makes me appreciate the fact I'm no longer with him."

Like a video on fast-rewind, Vincent starts thinking about what she told him before, images of the jam and Rosco and Raylene racing through his mind ...

"You thinkin' again," says Desiree.

"Yeah."

"C'mon, nosy. I gonna start callin' you nosy."

"When I was a kid, they used to call me Pinocchio."

"Because you lied a lot?"

"No. Because I had a big nose. Although I did lie too. Once in a while."

"It ain't so big," she says. "I like your nose."

"Well, thanks," he says.

"You don't want me callin' you nosy then?"

"Not really."

"Okay. I won't. But if something's on your mind, something you wondering about me, then just ask. And if it's something that I don't wanna talk about, I'll tell ya. Otherwise, we'll just go forward. Okay?"

"Sounds like a good plan."

"Alright then," she says.

"Okay. Alright. So, how come you two broke up?"

"Me and Rosco?"

"Yeah."

CHAPTER TEN

Desiree kept Rosco a secret from her mom. Desiree and Marisol were not allowed to have boyfriends. Delores was very strict about this. But since Delores worked long hours, it wasn't hard for Desiree and Marisol to slip out to the Bronx. In addition to seeing Rosco, they would hang out with Raylene and Antoine. Raylene was a blast. She was always drinking and always getting high. But Raylene was always under control—steady—and with smart things to say and good stories to tell. Raylene was also the one who gave Desiree the pills.

"Nothin' wrong with havin' some fun," she said. "But a child with a child is a problem children don't need. You take one of these every day and you won't have that problem."

Desiree listened to Raylene. She took the pills. But Rosco was not happy about it.

"What you need pills for if I be wearin' a condom?"

"They can break. Remember?"

"I don't know if I like you spendin' so much time with that crab lady."

"Her name's Raylene."

"Yeah, whatever. Everybody 'round here calls her the crab lady. She a bit crazy too."

"She different. Different don't have to mean crazy. That's what you said yourself."

"I know what I said."

"You don't seem to mind so much when she lets us use her place. Never heard you say anything about anybody being crazy then."

On Saturdays, Raylene would set up her table, selling crabs on the sidewalk. Often, Desiree and Marisol would help her with the cooking and setting up. Antoine too. People came from all over to buy Raylene's crabs with the homemade hot sauce. Raylene didn't mind Desiree taking Rosco upstairs. In fact, she was the one who first suggested it. "Here, Dee Dee, take my keys. You two go on up and have some private time. I know it can be hard to be alone when you young."

"Really?"

"Yes, really. Just don't be drinkin' up all my beer. You hear that, young man?"

"Yes, Mam."

When Marisol started seeing Ivory White, she too was allowed use of the apartment on crab Saturdays. Sometimes all four of them and little Antoine would hang out together, the older kids drinking and getting high and playing "Trouble" or "Sorry" with Antoine. Other times, each couple would take turns taking Antoine to the park while the other couple fucked on the red shag rug. Although Raylene never told them not to, the girls refrained from using her bed. It was nice enough she let them use her place without them messing up her bed too.

Marisol didn't go out with Ivory White for long. She liked him well enough and he definitely knew how to fuck, but Marisol was getting lots of attention from lots of other boys. She was not married to the nigga and niggas were after her ass wherever she went. If you own the candy store, no need to eat the same candy bar day in and day out. Unlike Desiree who seemed to be satisfied with Rosco, Marisol loved variety. Which was fine with Desiree, she didn't really care who Marisol fucked. But Rosco was a different story. Rosco was Ivory White's teammate and homeboy. When Rosco found out that Marisol quit Ivory, things were never the same.

"Your sista, she be actin' like a little hoe."

"She ain't no hoe."

"Oh no? Half the niggas from the Torros be hittin' it. You blind or what?"

"You just mad she quit Ivory."

"Well, I'm not happy about it but that's not it neither. She don't have to stay with anybody she don't want to. But it's kinda hard on Ivory to see his old girl runnin' through all the niggas he know. It's embarrassin'."

"What do you want me to do? I can't be tellin' her who she gotta be with. She not gonna listen to me. That's just the way she is. No changin' that."

"What way is that?"

"The way she is. The way she be kickin' it with a lot of different niggas."

"Maybe you that way too."

"Fuck you. Just—fuck you."

"Sorry. I'm sorry. I shouldn't have said that."

"I been with you and nobody else 'cause I don't want or need nobody else."

"Me too," he said.

"So then don't be sayin' otherwise."

"Alright. But she still your sista. And you want everybody thinkin' your sista a hoe?"

"I don't' care what people be thinkin'. She not a hoe."

"What she then?"

"She active. She no different than half the niggas you be hangin' with."

"Yeah, but she a girl."

"If you a girl and you fuck a lot of niggas, you a hoe. But if you a nigga and you fuck a lot of hoes, then you a playa."

"That's right."

"That's so fucked up," said Desiree.

"That's just the way it is."

Although Marisol still came to the Bronx with Desiree, she avoided Rosco. Whenever he was around, she'd either take Antoine to the zoo or out riding in a car with one of her new boyfriends. Marisol developed a lust for cars that approached her desire for boys. If you didn't have a whip, you didn't have a chance to hit it.

The only man that was constant in Marisol's life was Antoine. Marisol loved him more than anybody else. More than her dead Moms and secretly more than Dee Dee even.

Antoine returned this love too. The little man would do anything for his big sister. It went without saying that the niggas she went with had to be approved and accepted by Antoine. So Antoine was never short of games and toys and trips to the zoo or the movies over on Fordham Road. Except when Raylene put her foot down. If Raylene didn't take to the nigga, for whatever reason, than Antoine couldn't go. Which, in turn, made the nigga history to Marisol.

Some of the best times at Raylene's were when the only nigga there was the little nigga. For hours on end, the four of them would hang out, laughing and talking, drinking and smoking (except for Antoine who was too young even by Raylene's standards) and playing Spades. They could play Spades all day long. Although Raylene was the best, Antoine was pretty close. The boy was sharp as a tack, as Raylene liked to say.

"Don't be sleepin' on my little nigga," she'd say. "Boy's as sharp as a tack."

"Sharp as a tack?" said Desiree. "Now exactly what that supposed to mean?"

"It means he smart," said Marisol.

"I know that," said Desiree. "But where that come from? Tacks and being smart. Seems like a dumbass expression for smartness."

Usually, Marisol would partner up with Antoine against Raylene and Desiree. Near half of the time, they'd win.

"Damn," said Desiree as Antoine made another book. "You smart and you lucky, you one lucky little nigga."

"We wins again," said Antoine. "Sorry to be beatin' you so much. That's three in a row. It's getting' to be too easy. Too easy!"

Marisol high-fived Antoine, "That's my nigga!"

"Okay. Alright then. One more," said Raylene. "For the championship."

"We getting' tired of beatin' you guys, right Twan?"

"I never get tired of winnin'," said Antoine.

Marisol got up from the table and stretched, arching her back like she liked to do. "Well, maybe one more," she said going to the window, looking out.

"Who you lookin' for?" said Desiree, shuffling the cards. "Kirby still be in Brooklyn. They game wasn't till two. They won't be back before five at the earliest."

"Oh, yeah? Then how come I see your lova man crossin' the street?"

Desiree looks up from the cards. "Yeah, right."

"That's right. He right down there. I'm not lyin'. He right there!"

Desiree hesitated a moment, still shuffling the cards before jumping up and rushing to the window. "Stupid," she said. "You so stupid."

Moving to the window, Raylene looks over Desiree's shoulder, the three of them looking down at the street below.

"You know she be givin' him candy bars and sandwiches sometimes even," said Marisol. "Nigga don't even say thank you. Just be snatchin' it like a monkey in the zoo."

"He can't help himself," said Desiree.

"He a bum," said Marisol. "Don't nobody have to be a bum if they don't want to. He ain't crippled or nuthin'. Why don't he get a job? He could be a sweeper somewheres, I'll bet, where somebody would pay him. He damn sure know how to do that."

"Maybe he don't wanna do that," said Desiree.

"That nigga don't know what he want. He just a crazy ass nigga. A crazy ass, street sweepin' nigga who you be givin' Snickers bars to."

"And what's wrong with that?"

"Nuthin' wrong with it. It's a nice thing to do. I just don't know why you be doin' it. Do you?"

"Do I what?"

"Know why you be givin' that bum candy and what not?"

"I don't know. I guess I feel sorry for him. Somethin' wrong with that?" said Desiree. "Is there, Raylene? What you think?"

Raylene turned away from the window. She sat back down on the floor by the cocktail table. She drank the last dregs of beer in her glass.

"What's the matter?" said Marisol.

Raylene looked up at the two girls. She said, "Nothing really wrong. But I never did lie to you two, never hid nothin' from you neither. Antoine," she said, handing him a ten dollar bill. "Run down to the corner and get Momma some more cigarettes. Buy yourself something too."

Antoine snatched the ten spot and was out the door. When she heard him bounding down the stairs, Raylene looked at Marisol and said, "He ain't just a bum. He your Daddy. He you and Antoine's Daddy."

"Solobino? The sweeper?"

"That's right. That's Jesus, your Daddy. Where he got to be called Solobino, I don't know. But whether you call him Solobino or the bum or whatever name that comes, he still your Daddy. And you know me well enough to know I'm not playin' when I say this."

CHAPTER ELEVEN

"It was like a punch in the stomach," says Desiree.

"What did you do?" asks Vincent.

"Right then? Nothin'. What could I do?"

"Did you ever try to talk to him?"

"No. I thought about it. But I never did. You know, before that, before I found out, I used to give him candy and when he took it from me, he'd never look up and sometimes, I'd hold onto it, us both holding the candy bar at the same time and still, he wouldn't look up at me. And I'd say, 'C'mon, Solobino, I'm not askin' for nothin' but to look you in the eye.' But he wouldn't say nuthin' or look up so I'd give up and just give him the candy. At the time, I didn't know why I was giving him food and I sure as hell didn't know why I wanted to look at his face. But then, afterwards, it made some strange kind of sense."

"Yeah, but maybe it wasn't him. Could that be possible?"

"No. It was him. It was Jesus. For one, Raylene never did lie to us. And she was not one to bullshit either. Even if she had made a mistake about it, which she didn't, it was still true. There was other evidence."

"We don't have to talk about this anymore if it bothers you," says Vincent.

"Does it bother you?"

"No. I mean, I'm not happy what happened to you. But I'm still interested. Still nosy..."

"Yeah. You know, it's completely bugged, but I don't hate him. I never could hate him. People who know me, know about what happened, they can't never understand that."

"It was a bad thing. An evil thing. It's easy to wanna hate something that's clearly evil."

"I know it. But for me, myself, I just can't ever feel it inside. When I was still little, he wasn't always bad. He could be real nice too. Whenever we went outside, he'd tell people I was his Daddy's little girl... He'd take me places and tell me things and treat me like I was his own daughter. So there was a part of me that loved him too, crazy as that may sound..."

"It's not crazy. You were just a little girl."

"Yeah..."

"So what was the 'other evidence' you were talking about?"

"Okay... When Raylene pointed him out? I made Marisol swear not to tell Rosco because I knew that if Rosco found out, he'd end up killing him and I didn't want that. I didn't want Rosco getting locked up. Even though Rosco knew what happened when I was little, as far as he knew, Jesus was dead."

"But he found out."

"Yeah, he found out."

"Marisol tell him?'

"Not exactly. You gotta understand, Marisol and Rosco were like oil and water... Marisol couldn't stand to be in the same room with him, much less hold on some sort of a conversation. Still the same way now. But sometimes... Sometimes, that girl can be completely out her mind."

"She seems to be a bit compulsive," says Vincent. "And with a hot temper too."

"She can get heated alright," says Desiree. "Antoine too. Only it takes him a bit longer to go off. Got a longer fuse."

"I really like Antoine. He's one of my best students."

"He was always smart. He gonna go far. Especially the way he play ball. He got a shoe box full of letters from all sorts of colleges wanting him to play for them."

"I heard Rosco was pretty good himself."

"Rosco? Rosco was even better. But don't ever tell anybody I said that... The nigga was one hell of a baller. People used to talk about him going pro right out of high school. Not that he was gonna do that neither. His plan was to play for UCLA. Like Magic."

"So what happened? He ever play college ball?"

"Na. Never did. Got locked up and then fucked up his back in jail. Ball was never an option after that. But he coulda been somebody. Ask anybody from around the way back then. You can ask his coach even. He still at the school now. He Twan's coach now."

"Steinberg?"

"Yeah, him. He'll tell you. He the one that got Rosco to transfer to Wadleigh. I remember seein' him coming to all of Rosco's games out in the Bronx, back when he was playin' for Taft."

"What's Taft?"

"Taft High School. That's where he went before transferring to Wadleigh. Him and Ivory both. Steinberg got them to switch over. Steinberg was crafty. I remember him talkin' to Rosco, tellin' him how I was gonna be in ninth grade at Harlem. 'She can watch all your games without riding the train,' he said. 'And you'd be able to walk her home yourself.' Yeah, he was crafty alright. But a good coach too. Won three championships with Rosco."

"And your mom? It must have been hard to keep such a secret."

"Yeah. Eventually, she found out. But I was older then. I was sixteen and there wasn't nuthin' she could really do about it and she knew it. Although she didn't like it none. She didn't like Rosco. Couldn't stand him. Her and Marisol both."

"How come? Your Mom, I mean."

"She said he reminded her of her father. When my Moms was little, her father killed her Moms, my grandmother, with a hammer. She only told me this once. She's like that, my Moms, always keeping secrets. But that's a whole other story."

"Okay," says Vincent, drinking from his Tall Boy.

"Yeah, we had some real good times back in the day. I won't deny it. We was young and in love. He was the star of the team. The star of the city. You'd see his name in the papers practically every single day."

"Must have been something."

"It was. Then I got pregnant. Yeah. It happened. Of course, my Moms flipped though. Which was understandable, I guess. But we was maintaining, me and Rosco. We had us a plan. We had it all mapped out."

"I thought you said you were on the pill."

"I was. But I got pregnant anyway."

"I didn't know that was possible."

"Well, it is. It happened to me."

"Like a miracle, then."

"You tryin' to make jokes?"

"No, I'm serious."

"Oh, alright then."

"So what happened? What happened with you and Rosco?"

"He found out. He found out about Jesus. Ruined everything."

CHAPTER TWELVE

When Desiree told her mom, Delores held her temper. She tried to reason with Desiree. Even though it may be a sin, it would be an even bigger sin to throw her life away.

"Who says I'm throwing my life away?"

"Not going to college? Staying home, stuck with a baby? Livin' off food stamps and welfare checks? Is that what you want?"

"Rosco's gonna be rich."

"Yeah, and that don't' mean he gotta stick with you neither. You think once he goes off to college he gonna have time to be worrying about you and some kid? He's still a kid himself. You both are. Girls gonna be crawlin' out the woodwork to be with him. You think he gonna be able to fight that kind of temptation?"

"You just don't know. We gonna get married."

"Married? You ain't even eighteen yet!"

"Well, that's our plan. And when he goes pro we gonna live in a big house. He says he gonna buy you a house too."

"Girl, you must be out yo mind."

"I'm not."

"Listen. Maybe. Maybe even if what you say, what you got planned... Even if all that comes true. Well, then, you'll still have your whole life to have a child. To have a whole family together. It's just that now is not the time. You too young for that. I know it's hard. A hard thing to do. But sometimes the hard way is the right way even if it don't seem like it right at the time."

"I'm having this baby."

"Not in this house you're not."

"Fine. I'll leave then."

"I'll have you arrested."

"Yeah, right."

"Desiree! I'm your Moms. And—"

"And you just jealous is what you are. You can't stand the idea of me having a man, a real man that can take care of me and my child. You can't stand the idea of that because that's somethin' you never had. Yeah, you can stare me down all you like. I'm not afraid of you. I'm gonna have me this child no matter what you say. And nuthin' ever gonna happen to him neither. Never that!"

"What? What you say?"

"You heard me! Nobody ever gonna hurt my child. Nobody never! Never gonna be a time I be away for somethin' to happen."

"You best watch your mouth, girl."

"I'm not watchin' nuthin'. You the one should be watchin'. Shoulda been watchin'! If you was watchin' like you shoulda, nothin' never would have happened!"

Desiree said it. It was out and too late to take it back. She stood there, not moving as Delores trembled and then snatched the ashtray resting on the Formica topped table. Desiree watched the ashtray moving through space, not making a move to duck or throw up her hands, the heavy glass splitting her lip and cracking her front tooth...

Picking herself up from the floor, Desiree put her hand to her mouth, running with blood. Delores rushed over with a dishrag, trying to staunch the flow. As the dizziness subsided, Desiree remembered what had just happened. There was nothing more to say, nothing more to do but leave. Delores didn't stop her.

Although Desiree could have stayed with Rosco, she chose to stay with Raylene instead. Marisol was living there too at the time. Marisol had been living with Raylene and Antoine for close to a year. Although Marisol miraculously never got pregnant, she had to leave because she was sick and tired of having to answer to Delores every time she came in late, which was practically every single day...

Raylene took Desiree in but like Delores, she questioned the decision of keeping the baby. Yet, unlike her mom, she didn't fight her when she realized the girl's mind was made up.

By this time, Delores knew all about Raylene and Antoine. Delores did not like Raylene. She liked her even less when she found out that was where Desiree was staying. Delores smoldered and stewed with the notion of her daughter staying with that fat, crazy crab woman, until one morning, after another sleepless night, she decided to do something about it. What exactly, she didn't know for sure. But what ever it was, she was going to do it when she got there. She was going to do whatever it took to get her baby back home again. The bitch already stole away Marisol. She wasn't gonna take her only child. Not without a fight.

It was a Saturday morning. Raylene was already down on the sidewalk with Antoine and Marisol, who was waiting for Dwight to pick her up in his new jeep. Desiree was upstairs with Rosco. Although Desiree was well into her sixth month, it did not stop her from fucking despite Rosco's worries that he "might poke the kid in the head."

"That's ridiculous, Rosco."

"I don't see why that's ridiculous. The baby up the very same place. They heads are real soft, I might hit its head and make it retarded or something."

"I asked the doctor and the doctor say it's not a problem."

"Doctors don't know everything."

"C'mere," she said. "Let me see that..."

Delores rode the 4-train to Burnside Avenue. She walked up the hill, past University and past the abandoned Castle to make a left on Andrews Avenue. She saw the crab table down the block. She saw Marisol and Antoine. He was a cute little boy. Shame it had to be like this. Not the little boy's fault his Momma was a crab sellin' hoe...

"Where's my daughter?"

Raylene looked up at her. Marisol took Antoine by the shoulders. Marisol was afraid of the look in Delores's eye. It was a look she unfortunately saw on a number of occasions when she used to live with her...

"Bitch, I ain't gonna say it again," said Delores.

Raylene stood up. She towered high over Delores. But Delores had her hand in her pocket. She didn't flinch or back off. Raylene took a deep breath. She spoke slow and low and smooth. She said, "There's no need to be name callin'. I know you upset. And I'm really sorry about everything that's going on. I know you a good mother and you been tryin' your best."

"What you know about me? You don't know shit about me."

A small crowd began to form down the sidewalk and across the street in front of PS 26.

Raylene said, "She upstairs. Marisol? Why don't you go up and get Dee Dee."

"Okay," said Marisol.

"What's wrong wif her?" said Antoine.

Raylene took her son's hand. "Hush, child. You just keep your mouth hushed now."

More people stopped to watch the drama unfolding. Raylene was big and strong but the other lady obviously had something in her pocket. Unlikely a gun, unless a small gun. Most likely a regular old kitchen knife, the weapon of choice of angry Mommas...

Desiree came out into the sunlight with Rosco and Marisol. She saw her Moms facing Raylene.

When Delores saw Desiree, she removed her hand from her pocket.

Raylene sighed, "You and Desiree are welcome to go upstairs and talk things out. Might be a bit more private then out here in the street."

Delores looked from Raylene to Rosco to Desiree. Delores said, "I don't got anything to talk about. I come here to take my girl back home."

"Marisol," said Raylene. "Would you please take Antoine upstairs. Go on, Antoine."

Marisol took Antoine upstairs by the hand.

There was a long moment of silence. Desiree looked at her mom and she looked suddenly old now. Desiree loved her mom, and she wanted to run into her arms and close her eyes and let her take care of everything... But in the instant before she could do just that, there came the sweeping. The sound of the heavy bristles striking the street, each brush stroke getting louder and closer and seemingly amplified by the lack of other sounds. Up from the corner, over by PS 26, he made his way along the gutter. The slap and scrape: rhythmic and hypnotic.

As Desiree trembled, Raylene reached out a caring hand to steady her...

"Get your hands off her!"

Without removing her hand, Raylene said, "Just take it easy now. No need for—"

"Fuck you, bitch!" said Delores, reaching back into her pocket.

For somebody so fat, Raylene was surprisingly nimble and quick. With one hand, she shoved Desiree out of harm's way, putting her own body between daughter and mother. With the other hand, she grabbed the tray of crabs, tossing its contents at Delores, striking her about the head and shoulders. Undaunted, Delores pulled out her can of mace. But most of the spray hit the empty crab tray that Raylene used as a shield. With the air saturated in noxious vapor, bodies flew into sudden motion.

As Delores rushed Raylene, Rosco pulled Desiree to the wall of the building. Raylene smashed the aluminum tray across Delores's charging head. Knocked off course but not down, Delores bit hard into Raylene's thigh meat. Raylene howled. She began hammering her fists and pumping her thighs. The two tumbled into the crab table, the table and chairs crashing and spilling across the sidewalk. Everybody nearby was crying, their eyes stung by the lingering vapor of the mace. The warbling of a police siren joined the chorus of shouts and grunts. Breaking free of Rosco, Desiree jumped into the melee, trying to get in-between Raylene and her mother. As Rosco followed in kind, a police cruiser turned up Andrews, sailing up the one-way street the wrong way. The doors flew open and were left open, one of the cops yelling words into the chattering radio before joining his partner, nightsticks in hand. Seconds later, three more cop cars charged down the block and there were cops all over the place, most of them breaking up the fight while the rest were pushing the crowd down the sidewalk or to the other side of the street.

With the two women separated, it didn't take long to reestablish order. But then, a red-faced cop became irritated with Rosco, who wasn't moving fast enough down the sidewalk.

Meanwhile, Delores, her face swollen, her eyes puffed and nearly shut, was calling for her daughter while being restrained by two lady cops.

"That's my Momma," shouted Desiree.

But the cops near Desiree wouldn't let her cross the street.

"Hey, she pregnant, motherfucka!" shouted Rosco. "Watch it!"

"Watch your mouth boy!"

Raylene, her face also swollen and puffy, called out, "Everybody just calm down. Just take it easy before somebody gets hurt bad here."

"You the bitch gonna get hurt!" shouted Delores. "I'm gonna kill that hoe!"

"You the stupid bitch!" shouted Marisol. "She the one need to be locked up! She the one who started this whole thing!"

Everybody on the street looked up at Marisol shouting from the fifth floor window.

"Who you talkin' to?" shouted Delores back at her. "You nuthin' but a hoe too!"

"Fuck you!"

"Just let me go! I'll kill 'em both," screeched Delores. "I'll kill the both of 'em so help me God!"

"You dumbass bitch!" shouted Marisol. "The one you should be killin', he be right there. Look it! See him?

There he goes. The nigga with the broom. Don't you recognize him? Can't you recognize yo man? What? That's right! That's him. That's your Jesus, right there sweepin' up the trash!"

"Marisol!" shouted Desiree.

"Fuck that," shouted Marisol. "He the one who fucked everybody up. Fucked my mom. Fucked your mom. Fucked you! And she the one bitch that coulda stopped it!"

Except for the backround chatter on the police radios, all you could hear was the broom again. Desiree felt dizzy. Although she didn't completely pass out, she did have to sit down. She sat down right on the sidewalk. The last thing she remembers is looking back and seeing Rosco. She knew that he pieced it together, that he understood, and despite the pressure of the night stick across his neck, he was smiling...

CHAPTER THIRTEEN

It stops raining. The Mexicans and the black cowboy are long gone from the shelter. Just Desiree and Vincent sit here now, still looking to the sea.

"It was terrible... But that wasn't the worst of it. Although nobody got arrested because nobody pressed charges, the cops decided to drive my Moms back to Harlem. She went along without a complaint, she was completely beat. Not so much by Raylene, but by what Marisol shouted from the window. Rosco had gone off too. I didn't know where. He wasn't at his place or with any of his friends that I knew of. But he was mad. That's the one thing I did know."

"About what?"

"About what big mouth Marisol had said. Mad that I never told him. Mad that me and Marisol knew it and kept it from him."

"What about Jesus? What was his reaction?"

"Nothin'. He didn't react other than to keep broomin'. All that drama meant nuthin' to him. Or at least he never let on that it did."

"So did you find Rosco?"

"No, I didn't find him. He came back later on his own. We were hangin' out upstairs with Raylene. The window was up and we could hear somethin' was goin' down in the street. When we looked out, Rosco was pullin' him up the block by the beard."

"Jesus?"

"Yeah. Rosco was flippin'. Had on that crazy ass smile of his. He had Ivory White with him too. Ivory walked alongside, watchin' Rosco's back, like always... In one hand, Rosco held a black, plastic bag and in the other he had a fist full of his beard, yanking him up along the street in front of PS 26. I remember him dropping his broom and trying to reach back to get it and Rosco yanking him hard by the beard, not stoppin' for a second on his way up to the castle."

"The castle? What's that?"

"The castle was this abandoned building. It was called the castle because it looked like an old castle. It once was apartments. They say it was real nice, but that's long before I was even born. Back then, it was mostly just a shell, the inside used by dope addicts and kids sometimes. Rosco took me there one time before. I hated it. It stank of piss and garbage. I remember Rosco tryin' to kick it with me there and all I could do was stare at this horrible, fucked-up old mattress and the mess of chicken bones thrown on the floor... Yeah, that was one time the nigga just had to wait... Anyway, that's where Rosco was taking him. Inside the castle. We were up at the window, watchin'. A bunch of people were watchin' it down on the street. Most of them were laughing, thinking how funny it was to see a bum yanked around by his beard like that... Marisol, she was laughin' too. 'Fuck that nigga up!' she hollered. Only time she and Rosco were on the same page. But I wasn't happy about it. I knew something real bad was about to go down. With Marisol right behind me, I ran down the stairs and out into the street. We ran up Andrews to the hole in the wall where the dope heads broke through the cinder blocks. People were outside and inside and when I pushed through, I saw Ivory standing with his arms folded. Rosco had his belt off. Next to Ivory was this other boy, Byron. He was one of Rosco's friends from the Rock Steady Crew. Byron was the only one tryin' to stop it. But Ivory wouldn't let him near and Rosco wasn't listening. With one hand still grabbin' him by the beard, Rosco whipped the shit out of him. I wanted to stop it. But I didn't do nothin'. I don't think Rosco even saw me. And the more he whipped him, the more frustrated he got because Jesus was not gonna give... Rosco was tryin' to get him to confess, to admit who he was but he coulda whipped the nigga to death before he talked.

"Finally, Rosco throws down his belt. He throws down the belt and starts punching him in the head. But

Jesus don't fight back and he don't go down. Outside of a grunt here and there, he's dead silent through the whole thing. So Rosco grabs him by the hair and smashes his face with his knee. Jesus goes down and Rosco goes in the plastic bag. He takes out a can of lighter fluid. He puts it on the ground and kicks him in the face. Jesus rolls over, curling up. But Rosco just yanks him around by the beard so that he's face up again. Rosco says, 'If you tell the truth now, I'll let you go. I'm giving you the last chance to say it. Say it! Say it or else, nigga, you gonna burn.' See, Rosco didn't know for sure that it was really Jesus... I think Rosco wanted him to admit it so he could kill him and feel right about it. I don't think he was ever gonna let him go. He just needed proof and the only proof would be for Jesus to admit he was Jesus.

"As soon as Rosco soaked his head with the lighter fluid, that's when people started clearing out. But I didn't leave and Marisol didn't leave and neither did Byron. Me and Marisol, we stayed quiet. Just watching. Maybe there was a part of me that wanted him to burn. So maybe I was guilty too..."

"You shouldn't think that," says Vincent.

"Shoulda, woulda, coulda—it don't matter now. I'm just telling you the way it went down. But Byron, he was doing everything he could to stop it. He knew it was too late to run for help. He knew the only way to stop it was to get Rosco to listen to him. But Rosco he's like a pit bull. When Rosco took out the box of matches, Byron tried to rush him but Ivory just yoked him up quick. Byron was pretty tough but he was no match for Ivory. So Byron tried to reason with Rosco. He told him he was going to ruin his life if he did something so stupid. And he was right. But Rosco didn't care. He was lightin' matches and flicking them close by Jesus, still trying to get him to talk. Telling him he was gonna set his ass on fire and watch him burn. Me, I didn't know what to do. But I did know enough that when one of those matches hit, it was going to be over. Not just for Jesus. But for Rosco, for me, all of us. 'Rosco!' I screamed. He looked up at me with this totally dumb-assed expression, like he just woke up. He looked at me and he didn't know what to do at first until he got the crazy idea that I should be the one to do it. He handed me the box of matches. But Marisol, she snatched them outta my hands and tossed them right back to Rosco. 'You stupid ass nigga,' she said. 'You not gonna put this on her. Can't you see she already suffered enough by this fuckin' animal?' Rosco looked at Marisol, 'Is it him?' Without missing a beat, Marisol said, 'Yeah, it's him. Nigga, who else could it be? It's him alright!' And Rosco looked at me, 'Is it him?' I couldn't answer. But it was him. I just couldn't get the words out to say it. 'Just let it go,' said Byron. 'Nobody knows who the fuck is who. Not even Dee Dee is sure. Just let it go, man.' Rosco smiled. He looked at the box of matches like he was reading a book. Then, he tossed them on the floor. I let out a deep breath, thankful it was over. But it wasn't over. Not a second later, Jesus reached for the box. I saw him reaching and I knew what he was gonna do."

"Damn..."

"It was the most fucked up thing I ever saw. First a big ball of blue and then red fire and black smoke and he was rollin' all over the floor screaming like nothing human. Animal screams... His head, his beard and hair, blazing and burning... It all happened real quick. The garbage on the floor, the walls and that fucked-up mattress were burning fast and Ivory and Rosco pulled me and Marisol outta there quick. Smoke kept pouring out the hole in the wall and soon the whole castle was all lit up. Police and fire trucks fillin' up the block, pushing people back and away. I can still remember the heat on my face."

"That's crazy."

"It sure was."

"So who ratted out Rosco? Byron?"

"Byron was never a snitch. Nobody said nothin'."

"But didn't you say Rosco got locked up?"

"Yeah, he did. But not for that. Not exactly. He went to jail for nearly killing Byron."

"Byron?"

"I don't know, a week or two later, Byron and Rosco got into a beef about what went down at the castle. They were at the Rucker Tournament. Rosco wasn't even playing that day. First, there were words and then it was Byron who started it. Japped Rosco in the eye and Rosco went down. Went down, but he got right back up again. People tried to break it up and they did break it up. But it wasn't over. Not for Rosco. He just smiled and pretended like everything was okay just long enough for the peacemakers to back off. Walking away, Rosco stopped at the scorekeeper's table. It was half time. He spoke a minute with some people there before grabbing a chair. Bryon didn't know what hit him. Lucky for Rosco, there were enough people around to pull him off before he could kill him. Beat the poor nigga into a coma. And, wouldn't you know it, some Japanese tourist is right there, getting the whole damn thing on video. Cops took the tape for evidence. Guilty as charged."

CHAPTER FOURTEEN

After Desiree finishes her story, Vincent doesn't know what to say. So he says nothing.

Desiree speaks, "You hungry?"

"Yeah," says Vincent. "Kind of."

"I'm starved."

"You wanna get a pizza or something?"

"No. I don't want no pizza. There's a place down the boardwalk. We could go there."

"Let's go."

Vincent and Desiree walk in the direction of Brighton Beach. Although the rain has stopped, the boardwalk is still empty. Walking past the New York Aquarium on their left, Vincent thinks about the incarcerated fish behind the walls who have no notion of the sea.

"What are you thinking?" says Desiree.

"I'm thinking about the fish in there."

"Oh, yeah?"

"Yeah. They're all in there, swimmin' around. Living their little fish lives and never knowing that the whole ocean is so close by. And they'll never know. They'll just live their little fish lives and die without ever knowing. For them, the ocean never existed. It doesn't exist."

Vincent and Desiree continue their stroll. As they get closer to Brighton, the boardwalk becomes more populated. Like birds after a heavy rain, the Russian immigrants descend in small groups, walking the earth, going about their Russian business. They dress in dark colors and heavy fabrics. They mutter and move along in jagged lines. They understand Russian words. But there is one who stands out above all the rest. One lonely bird ignored by his brethren along the boardwalk. Vincent notices him. Vincent tries to stop himself from staring. It is a problem he has, especially when he's high. Mesmerized by the flecks of flying spittle, Vincent catches himself and turns away from the guy reading aloud from a small, red notebook. But it is too late. The guy has spotted Vincent. He has caught Vincent taking notice. He jumps down from the bench he has been standing on. He is a tall and lanky with dark features and exceptionally black, wavy hair. Catching the Russian's movement in his peripheral vision, Vincent tries to pick up the pace. It is no use. The lanky Galoot is beside Vincent now, pointing to a page in the notebook, babbling in Russian. Vincent looks at the page but the letters are strange, some kind of alphabet he has never seen before.

"I don't understand you," Vincent says, turning to Desiree, "He's a nut..."

Desiree shrugs. She glances at the page. The writing is thin and spidery in both blue and red inks. "It's kinda pretty, don't you think?"

"Yeah. Colorful," says Vincent.

The lanky galoot continues to babble and excitedly turn the pages forward and backward, one time even tearing the paper.

"Alright," says Vincent. "Nice to meet you. But we gotta go now." Vincent takes Desiree by the hand. They walk fast and faster. But the lanky galoot keeps right in step alongside them.

"There's the restaurant," says Desiree.

"Let's run," says Vincent.

As they start to run, an older woman appears up ahead. Like the catcher in the rye, she spreads her arms wide in a half crouch, slowly advancing. A large green pocketbook hangs from the wrist of her arm. She shouts Russian sentences. The lanky galoot shouts back at her.

Vincent attempts to veer around the woman but she shuffles crablike to cut them off, her arms still outstretched and the green pocketbook swinging.

Desiree stops and Vincent stops and the lanky galoot stops. They stand facing the Russian lady.

"She wants him," says Desiree. "Not us. So let's just chill and let them work it out."

The lanky galoot shoves his notebook up under his shirt. He crosses his arms across his chest. The lady Russian comes forward, reaching into her pocketbook. Vincent entertains the horrible notion of a Russian pistol, something straight out of a Chekhov play... But the lady Russian pulls out a greasy paper bag instead. Coming closer, she waves the bag and smiles gold and crooked teeth. The lanky galoot laughs. The lanky galoot removes his notebook from under his shirt. He trades the notebook for the greasy bag. The lady Russian makes clucking noises.

"C'mon," says Vincent. "Now's our chance."

As they move away, Desiree glances back. "There's some kind of fried fish in that bag," she says.

"Maybe we shoulda stuck around."

"Hey," says Desiree. "There it is."

Only one restaurant is open in a row of Russian restaurants along the boardwalk. The glass door is closed but not unlocked. They step inside and sit at a table facing the beach. The place is otherwise empty. On the bar stands an opened bottle of beer. Beside the beer is a boombox playing Russian rock-n-roll. Vincent looks at Desiree who is looking out the windows. She turns into his gaze. "This music sucks," she says. "What is it?"

"I don't know," says Vincent, getting up from his chair. The restaurant is rather small as most of their business is done during the summer on umbrella-topped tables outside. Vincent moves to the bar and clicks off the cassette tape. He pushes the button for the radio and slowly spins the dial, stopping at a few rock stations that are vetoed by Desiree. He pauses at a hip-hop station. Desiree shakes her head. He turns to a jazz station.

"Leave that," she says.

Vincent sits back down. "Sounds good," he says. "You like jazz?"

"I like anything that's good," she says.

Desiree closes her eyes to let the music have the full focus of her attention. But what is that in the backround? At first soft, but getting louder and more pronounced...

"You hear that?" says Vincent.

Desiree opens her eyes, her face twisted in mild confusion.

"Is that coming from the radio or—"

"No," she says. "No, that's definitely not part of the music."

The moans have now evolved into a series of high-pitched squealings. Vincent looks around the empty restaurant. The squeals and the yelps come faster and shorter and louder. Then, a final grunt and a yelp and only the jazz and wind against the windows. Vincent looks at Desiree with a smile. But his smile drops when he looks beyond her shoulders. Desiree turns to see what he's looking at.

Glaring is a short man in a chef hat and apron. He has a big, black moustache and pasty white skin the color of bacon fat.

"Are you open?" asks Vincent.

The short man does not answer. He picks at the corner of his eye and goes back into the kitchen. The sound of his voice mixes with the sound of a woman's voice. All words in Russian. Suddenly, the talking stops.

Vincent turns to Desiree, "I wonder if he was wearing that hat while they—"

The woman appears. The waitress. A Russian waitress with a big head of bee hive peroxide-blonde hair hastily shunted back into shape. Unlike the chef, the waitress is exceptionally tall. But, like the chef, she too has a moustache, although less pronounced than her lover's. She makes an attempt to smile. She looks in the direction of the boombox, crinkling her nose as if she's smelling something gone sour. She crosses to the bar, shuts the jazz, and clicks the cassette tape back into life.

Vincent stares into Desiree's eyes. Desiree does her best not to laugh. The waitress towers above them, holding a pen and a pad. She raises her dark eyebrows. "Yes, would you like to drink?" she says in a thick Russian accent.

Vincent twists his face, trying not to laugh.

Desiree says, "Two glasses of Jack Daniel's. No ice."

"No ice," repeats the waitress. "Two of the Jack Daniels. No ice."

"Thank you," says Desiree.

The waitress goes to the bar. Loudly, she gets the glasses and whiskey. Vincent can't hold it any longer. He lets go. He laughs loud and clear and with that, so too does Desiree. They laugh and cough and shake until, with great effort, they are able to control themselves.

"Do you think she thinks we're laughing at her?" says Vincent.

"Of course. That's why she's taking so long with the drinks. She doesn't want to come over here with us acting like a pair of damn fools."

"Here she comes..."

"Alright," says Desiree. "Be good now. No laughing."

The waitress carries the two glasses on a round serving tray. She puts the drinks on little napkins before Vincent and Desiree. "Would you like the menu?"

"Yes," says Desiree. "Thank you."

"I will get now," says the waitress.

With his lips tightly compressed, Vincent laughs through his nose. The waitress looks back at him. "Is there something wrong with you?" she says.

Vincent shakes his head without looking up.

The waitress brings back a pair of menus, setting them down on the table. Without further words, she goes back into the kitchen.

"You alright?" says Desiree.

"I'm okay. I'm sorry. I guess I'm still pretty stoned."

"Me too... I never got high with a teacher before."

"This is my first time," says Vincent.

"Getting high?"

"No. Being a teacher and getting high."

"How long have you been teaching?"

"This is my first year."

"Really? What did you do before that?"

"I was an actor."

"Really? Were you on TV?"

"No. Well, once, I was in a detergent commercial. But most of my acting was done on the stage."

"So what happened?"

"What do you mean?"

"Are you still acting?"

"Na. Not anymore. I'm retired."

"Retired? You're not old."

"No, but I had enough. I quit. Just couldn't do it anymore."

"Oh."

"Well, it's more like I didn't have the desire to do it. Without the desire, what's the point?"

"That's true about a lot of things... So what made you wanna be a teacher?"

"It's gonna sound corny."

"Like you wanted to help people?"

"Yeah. Something like that."

"Yeah, that's corny."

"See?"

"I'm just playin'."

"No, you're not."

"Maybe so. But corny don't have to be somethin' bad. Especially with something like that. Something where you're trying to do something good."

"Trying isn't always achieving."

"What do you mean?"

"I'm not so sure about myself these days. Like maybe I'm doing more harm than good."

"How's that?"

"This kid in my class. He says it was me who made him drop out."

"You believe him?"

"Sure."

"How'd you do it? You fail him?"

"No. Not at all. He dropped out to make money fighting dogs."

"Fighting dogs? What that got to do with you?"

"I inspired him. He said my classes helped him see things clear. Opened his eyes to the glory of dog fighting."

"Wait a minute. What's his name?"

"Tyrone."

"I know Tyrone! He's Antoine's best friend. Antoine is Marisol's brother."

"Small world."

"But I didn't know he dropped out."

"Please don't tell him I told you."

"I'm not gonna say anything."

The waitress appears. She holds her pad.

"You know what you want?" says Desiree.

Vincent shakes his head. "No, you?"

"Yeah."

"Then order the same for me too."

"We'll each have the steak. I would like mine rare," she says, turning to Vincent. "How you want yours cooked?"

"Rare's good. And another round, only doubles this time. Please."

"I think you did the right thing," says Desiree.

"Ordering rare? Or the doubles?"

"With Tyrone. Even if you didn't mean to do it."

"It's funny," says Vincent. "A year ago, I could never imagine myself being a teacher."

"Teaching is sort of like acting. Isn't it?"

"Yeah. In the sense that you're communicating to an audience. But with teaching, you're not trying to be somebody else. At least, you shouldn't be. That's what I think anyway."

"Oh, yeah?"

"For me, yes. That's one thing I can say for sure. Whatever I say, whatever I teach, I'm saying because that's what I believe. It's something I promised myself. No bullshit."

"Tyrone must have picked up on that."

"And look what happened."

"But you didn't bullshit him, right?"

"No. I didn't."

"So then it's fine. You must be doing something right. Right?"

"I don't know about, 'right.' But a least I can say I was genuine."

"You tryin' to bullshit me?"

"What?"

"I think you're saying all this stuff just to bullshit your way into my pants."

"Huh?"

"What? Huh? You gotta speaking problem now? Do you mean, you don't want to?"

"Want to what?"

"Now, you are bullshitting me. You know what I mean."

"Yeah. Sure. Yes. But that's not why... I think you're really attractive. Gorgeous. Of course... But I'm not trying—"

"Relax," smiles Desiree. "I'm just playin' with you."

Vincent smiles. "You got me. You're a pretty good actor yourself."

"You think so? I could never be an actor. But I like watching movies."

"Me too. Maybe we can go see one sometime."

"You still tryin', aren't you?"

"What?"

"To work your way into my pants."

"Yes. I am. I think it would be wonderful."

CHAPTER FIFTEEN

"Steaks rare," declares the waitress, plopping down two plates heaping with meat, French fries and creamed spinach. Tearing into the beef, they proceed to decimate all that is edible. Vincent eats fast, swallowing hunks of steak and forkfuls of fries lathered in ketchup. Desiree goes a bit slower but just as steady, the two forging ahead relentlessly with no breaks in the action.

In a short while, they are smoking cigarettes once more, the food scarred plates serving as ashtrays because the waitress has not returned. Outside, the wind sprays the rain against the windows, giving the world the muted look of an impressionist painting.

Without prompting, Vincent tells Desiree about being taken away by an ambulance after his last performance and his subsequent stay at Veritas Village.

"On the way in, this guy, his name was Borland, Jim Borland. I'll never forget him. Big Irishman with forearms like Popeye. He picked me up at the hospital and drove me straight to rehab. He didn't talk much and I was in no mood for talking so it was pretty quiet until we were almost there. Then, he pulls over and gets out. I figured he was going to take a piss. But no. He goes to the trunk and takes out a small cooler. He places it down in the seat between us. He drove this old Chrysler, a real boat. Pulling back onto the highway, we didn't say nothing until we reach the rehab parking lot. It's dark outside so he turns on the inside light and says, 'Go on, open it up.' Inside, there's an icy sixpack of Bud. 'Go on,' he says. 'Drink your fill because those are gonna be the last beers you're ever gonna have.' You believe that? Now, this Borland character, he was an alcoholic himself. Hadn't had a drop in close to twenty years. And there he was letting me get juiced up on my way into rehab."

"Were they good?"

"Delicious. Ice cold. I think they were the best damn beers I ever had."

"And the other guy didn't have any?"

"No. Definitely not. For him, it's all or nothing. That's their thing."

"AA."

"Yeah. One day at a time. And I guess it works. For some people."

"But not for you."

"No. Not me," says Vincent. "I can't imagine never being able to drink again. But then again, I don't think I'm an alcoholic. Or a drug addict."

"They why did you go to rehab?"

"It's complicated. In part, to calm down my parents. And, in part, to calm down myself. I mean, I nearly overdosed and that had to mean something. Maybe not that I was an addict but something was wrong."

"What?"

"I was full of shit. Everything was an act for me. Including being a drug addict."

"But you weren't pretending when you overdosed, were you?"

"No. That was real. Had to take me away in an ambulance. I nearly died... I guess if you wear the mask long enough you risk the mask becoming a part of yourself..."

"So being an actor was perfect for you. In a way."

"Yeah. It made it easier, that's for sure. But just plain acting wasn't enough. So I had to find other things."

"I never heard of a valium addict before."

"They got 'em. Whatever drug there is, there's somebody who's hooked on it."

"I never did valium. Is it nice?"

"Yeah, it's alright. Not so strong, not like heroin or anything like that. Unless you do twenty or more like I did," says Vincent, smiling.

"You tried heroin?"

"Yeah."

"What's that like?"

"Probably the greatest drug of 'em all. But in the beginning, it makes you sick. I never got past that part. Threw up every single time I tried it."

Desiree laughs.

"What are you laughing at?"

"It's just funny," she says. "A white boy like you getting all caught up in the hard stuff. Only dope addicts I ever knew were from back in the day, and all of them were niggas."

"You'd be surprised. Drugs know no prejudices."

"I bet you scored from a homeboy. Tell me you didn't ever score from a black man."

"Never," says Vincent. "I got all my drugs from a girl I used to go with. And she got nearly all her stuff from a white guy with a pet chicken."

"Stop."

"For real. The guy was a psycho too. Ended up killing his girlfriend and eating her. It's true, I'm not kidding. It was in the papers and everything."

CHAPTER SIXTEEN

On a last minute whim, Desiree decides to make a stop at Vincent's apartment, a decision she makes while riding the train back from Brighton Beach. With the car fairly full, Desiree sits with her back to the map while Vincent stands before her, holding the overhead rail. She has had a wonderful time. Surprisingly enough, it has been very easy to talk to this white man. He's a good listener with a lot of interesting things of his own to talk about. Although most of her buzz is ebbing, she still feels warm and nice and can't help but notice the outline of Vincent's cock gently swaying in unison with his hips and the train car on their way into Manhattan. When the lights flicker, she closes her eyes. She sees her hand caressing his balls before moving up along the thickening shaft to the head. She wants him now. She wants him hard in her mouth and hard in her pussy. Opening her eyes, she looks up at Vincent who is looking straight ahead before looking down and smiling back at her. What is he thinking?

Although Vincent seems a bit embarrassed by the meager set up of his one room flat, Desiree does her best to put him at ease. "It's simple but nice," she says. "And I love your picture."

Vincent looks at the framed print hanging on the wall. "I got it on the street," he says. "Some guy was selling a bunch of them from the back of his van. It's called 'Hail Mary.' You see? That's Mary and Jesus, right? But there, over in the corner here... See? That's an angel. You don't notice it at first. At least I didn't."

"I never saw a nonwhite Jesus and Mary. Not like them... What are they?"

"They're Tahitian. From Tahiti. It's an island in the Pacific. The painter, his name was Gauguin. He left his home, his family—his whole life behind to go paint the natives in Tahiti."

"Looks like a nice place to go." Desiree sits down on the edge of the bed. "You wanna smoke some more?"

"Sure," says Vincent. "I think I got a couple of beers in the fridge."

"Alright then," says Desiree.

As Vincent goes to the half-size refrigerator, Desiree takes out her bag and papers and begins to roll. She rolls it fat and perfect. She lights up, sending forth clouds of smoke and Vincent sits beside her. She exchanges the joint for one of the two cans of beer he is holding. She sips and watches his lips and the smoke. They continue to leisurely drink and smoke and Desiree wonders what he is thinking.

"What you thinking about?"

"Me?"

"Yes, you," she says. "Who else?"

"I was thinking about an old teacher I used to have when I was a little kid. Well, she wasn't old then, I guess she's old now though."

"Oh, yeah?"

"Yeah. She was beautiful. I had a terrible crush on her. I used to turn bright red whenever she used to come in our classroom. She used to come once a week to teach us art. Her name was Miss Woods. God, she was beautiful... I haven't thought about her in ages..."

"What made you think of her now?"

"I don't know... Well, maybe, I know. Maybe when we started talking about the painting... Also... See, she was black. The only black teacher in the whole school. Actually, the only black person in the whole school. No, there was also Mr. Hunter, the janitor. He was definitely black."

"So what did this Miss Woods look like?"

"She used to wear these colorful scarves on her head. All different colors. But sometimes, she didn't wear a scarf and she had this wild sorta afro, I guess that's what it was..."

Desiree laughs.

"What are you laughing at?"

"Nothing, nothing. Go on. So what else about Miss Woods."

"Well, she was real black. Even darker than you. Oh, I'm sorry."

"You don't have to be sorry. It's okay. It's just a fact, right?"

"Yeah. So yeah, she was really dark with deep dark eyes, kinda like yours and she was, yeah that's right, she was really, really tall. To me, she seemed like a giant but I'll bet she was probably around six feet or so which is still pretty tall."

"Six feet is tall."

"Tall and black with the face of an angel. I was in love with Miss Woods. My first love. I used to think about her all the time. I used to think up all sorts of crazy plans where I'd hide in the back of her car or find out where she lived and just show up with flowers and candy. Stupid kid kinda stuff."

"How old were you?"

"I was in fifth grade. She replaced the old art teacher that year who got pregnant. I was pretty good in art too. I could draw pretty good. During Christmas vacation, I spent most of the time drawing a picture of the city... I had all sorts of skyscrapers and bridges with a bunch of subway trains circling around underneath. It was one hell of a picture. I'm not trying to brag about it either. But it was good. The whole thing in pencil but it was sharp, I tell you."

Desiree smiles.

"I drew it out of my mind. I guess I could have gone down by the water and tried to sketch it because we lived in Hoboken, right across the river, but I did it in secret in my room. I didn't want anybody to see it before Miss Woods because that's who I was drawing it for."

"I never been to Hoboken."

"You're not missing much. Although it's close to the city, for most people there, Manhattan is from another world. I mean, it's always there, looming on the other side of the water, but at the same time, it was never real. At least not for me. I don't know if that makes sense."

"It makes sense. So what did Miss Woods think of your city?"

"She loved it. She said I had a real talent. I nearly peed in my pants I was so fucking happy. And I wanted to tell her. To tell her I drew the city because she had told us she lived in the city but I couldn't do it. I couldn't say anything. I was red as a cherry and the other kids started laughing at me but I didn't give a damn. I can still remember her putting her hand on the middle of my back. That hand on my back was one of the best feelings of my life. Better even than my first kiss."

"Right here?" says Desiree, putting her hand in the center of his spine.

"Yeah."

Desiree brings her other hand up to his face and his hair. She pulls until their lips meet and open and she moves forward, pushing him back upon the bed, her leg between his two legs, still holding him by the hair before moving down to his neck and pulling up on his shirt. Feeling his hands now, strong along her back and ass, she finds his mouth again. Tongues and hips in a slow grind and twirl. Keeping true to the train ride, she soon has him in her mouth. She takes note that the color of his cock is a shade darker than the rest of his body. But this observation soon flies away as he guides her up and guides her down quickly and accurately and very deep inside.

After Vincent comes, Desiree stays astride of him and Vincent takes notice of the way her vaginal walls take hold of his slowly shrinking cock. They lay silently, breathing each others air in-between kisses while her pussy continues to work upon his cock.

"I must have died and went to heaven," says Vincent.

Desiree smiles and Vincent smiles and although her pussy has finally let go, she is not done. Once again, she goes down to taste him. Vincent closes his eyes and touches her curly hair and she works him hard again before swinging around and mounting him in the opposite direction, her ass pounding fast and hard and Vincent is beside himself with pleasure, his mind telling him to remember this day, this exquisite moment, because it's never gonna get better than this...

They smoke their separate brands of cigarettes. Vincent takes note how Desiree's ass and tits, while dark, are a shade or two lighter than the rest of her skin. Vincent also notices how pale his arm looks alongside of hers. As they continue to smoke, Vincent thinks about Miss Woods again. He remembers what happened. How she quit before the end of the year when some kid called her a nigger. Some little prick in fourth grade who yelled it out while her back was turned to the blackboard. Although he forgets what happened to the kid, Vincent remembers feeling the shame and the sadness. He remembers that he had heard that word on a number of occasions before. He had heard it in the schoolyard and on his block and even inside his own house. But for the most part, it was just another "bad" word like any other, no different than fuck or cock or cunt. After Miss Woods, it took on a whole added dimension. Even after all these years, Vincent still felt bad about it and guilty too. It didn't matter that he didn't say it. He still felt guilty. More so now with the realization that he chose to omit that particular part of the story in his telling of it to Desiree...

"Oh, shit," says Desiree, looking at the clock radio. "I gotta get going. Clyde's at home with my aunt. I told her I'd be home hours ago."

"Oh, okay. I'm sorry."

"No, it's fine. She won't mind. I just don't like to take advantage."

Vincent watches Desiree get dressed from his bed. As she puts on her shoes, he pulls on his boxer shorts. He walks her to the door. "Hey," he says. "I should walk you home."

"That's alright. I'll catch a cab downstairs. They're all lined up this time of night outside the club."

"You sure?"

"Yeah, I'm sure. I'm a big girl, Vincent."

Vincent kisses her. They hold each other for a moment and she pulls away. "Better let me go now or I won't be going at all."

Vincent opens the locks. Desiree walks out and turns to smile at him before the stairs.

"When can I see you again," he says.

"Whenever you want."

CHAPTER SEVENTEEN

Rosco is smiling because nobody will put up a dog to roll against Cremator. Tyrone is smiling too. His dog, Tnuc, is about to roll against Madonna. This is Tnuc's first money fight. Tyrone and Antoine have five hundred dollars riding on it. Rosco has five thousand bet. Rosco would have bet more but that is all the action he can get. Madonna is owned by a light-skinned boy called Trash Can. They call him Trash Can because when he was two years old, he was nearly thrown into the trash compactor by his father who was fighting with his mother over him. Luckily for Trash Can, his mom's two sisters heard the commotion in the hallway and ran out of their apartment to thwart the crime. With the aid of a baseball bat and a strap, the two aunts managed to disable the father long enough for the mom to take back her baby and make an escape. Later, after they pressed charges and had him arrested, the little boy, whose original name was Nelson, became affectionately known as Trash Can. Some people say that Trash Can is a lot like Rosco because he always smiles when he's mad. Also, like Rosco, he's usually armed and not afraid to fire if need be. Although Trash Can is not one to look for trouble, he is ruthless when wronged, extracting his pound of flesh if that's what he thinks is due him. It is rumored that Trash Can's father was found shortly after his son turned sixteen—face down in a dumpster, a bullet to the brain.

Trash Can's Madonna is a hard biting dog with a record of eight and one. She won her last six fights in a row, killing her last two opponents in under a minute's time. Tyrone, Antoine and Rosco know these facts. But they also know that Madonna has never rolled against a dog of Tnuc's breeding.

It is a cool night, a dark night, and it seems like it will rain at any minute. Because of this, there are not as many spectators as usual. It is a night where all but the most hardcore fans and moneymen have stayed at home. Food and refreshments are only what you choose to bring yourself.

Tnuc is on her mark facing the Madonna on hers. Straddling their dogs are Trash Can and Tyrone. Trash Can stares intently at Tyrone. Tyrone is nervous but not unnerved by Trash Can or his dog. It is just a nervousness born of expectation and the thrill of venturing into the first real moment of his chosen destiny.

Outside the pit, the referee, an old head named Maurice, holds up his hand: "One, two, three—GO!"

In a blur, Tnuc rockets across the pit, becoming airborne before striking head to head with the bewildered Madonna. The two dogs crash into the boards, tumbling and rolling fast back to their feet, facing off at near opposite corners of the pit. Without hesitation, Tnuc is flying again, her jaws clenched tight, her snout scheduled to strike the flank of the turning Madonna like a dolphin into a shark. The impact sounds the crack of a rib and a yelp of pain as the momentum sweeps away their footing in a jumble of spinning legs, heads and tails. This time, however, Tnuc is fastback to her feet in the long short seconds it takes to rush in for the kill. Madonna sees it coming but is hamstrung by a busted rib and the confusion of being battered and bloodied before Tnuc even opened her mouth.

Strangely enough, Tnuc neglects the throat. Instead, she chooses to lock on the head, her mandible incisors tearing fast through Madonna's outer and middle ear, while the upper jaw, the maxilla, clamps down into the feramen magnum: the region where the brain connects to the spinal canal. Trash Can has no chance to save his dog. With a decisive crunching, Tnuc lets go and steps away while a prostrate Madonna runs fatally disabled on her side, her legs running herky-jerky like they do in a doggy dream or nightmare.

Tyrone takes Tnuc from the pit, careful not to openly rejoice in the face of a smiling Trash Can who can't pull his gaze from his dying and dead champion.

Waiting by the side of the pit are Manny and Ruben, the two new pit boys who have taken the place of Antoine and Tyrone. They look without staring, waiting for the nod to signal them in. Trash Can is inside the pit now, his head bowed, his eyes closed. He smiles while making the sign of the cross. He opens his eyes, stepping over Madonna and out of the pit. He stops a moment to look back at his dead dog, shaking his head in wonder. He sees Tyrone off to the side with Antoine and Rosco. He nods in respect and they nod back at him. Noticing the two boys standing at the ready, Trash Can reaches in his pocket, handing them each a twenty.

"Thanks," says Manny.

"Yeah, thanks," says Ruben, examining the bill.

Trash Can moves slowly towards the hole in the wall that leads back to the street. Manny and Ruben step into the pit for Madonna, lifting her over the boards and dragging the carcass to the Losing Tree.

"Look at that shit," says Manny. "Don't even look like a head no mo."

"Never mind that," says Ruben. "Just slip it around the neck and let's get it done with."

The two boys sling the rope over the nearest branch and haul Madonna up a good three feet from the earth. They tie off and head back towards the pit. Hanging limp and deformed, Madonna is the first bloom of the night. But there are still three more fights set to go and maybe two more if the Lennox Crew and the kids from the Carver Projects show up like they said they would.

Tyrone and Antoine split their share of the winnings. "Lot easier this way then that," says Tyrone, gesturing towards Manny and Ruben.

"Word," says Antoine, pocketing the cash. "But I kinda used to like it."

"Me too," says Tyrone. "I don't know why though."

"Maybe we just bugged," says Antoine.

"I'm outta here," says Rosco.   "I'm tired of this amateur game."

"Yeah, me too," says Antoine. "Let's bounce."

The two dogs and the three humans head into the hole in the wall, through the first floor of the abandoned tenement and out to the street.   They stop on the corner. Rosco looks across the street at the Navigator. Both Antoine and Tyrone also take note of the Navigator.   Cremator and Tnuc sit side by side waiting for the next command. Rosco looks down at Tnuc.   He says, "You got yourself a genuine head dog."

"You think so?" says Tyrone.

"Definitely," says Rosco.   "I haven't seen a head dog like that in years."

"I never seen one ever," says Antoine. "Until tonight. I never even knew there was such a thing."

"You think the Breeder knew she was a head dog?" asks Tyrone.

"Most definitely," says Rosco. "Nigga's like that. He likes surprising you like that."

"I bet your Cremator is a full of surprises," says Antoine.

"Hey," says Tyrone.   "There go Desiree!   Look who she with!"

Rosco smiles.

CHAPTER EIGHTEEN

Desiree suddenly stops talking. Vincent looks up and sees what she sees. But there is no way to pretend not to notice them, to veer in another direction. Vincent keeps pace with Desiree, his hand still in her hand, his eyes trained mostly on the pit bulls.

"It's alright," she says, holding his hand tighter.

"Yo, Vincent. What up?" says Antoine.

"Hey," says Vincent, keeping an eye on the two dogs.

"You missed the fight," says Tyrone.

"What fight?" asks Vincent.

"Tnuc's fight," says Tyrone. "You said you was gonna come."

"Oh, shit," says Vincent. "I'm sorry. Damn. I forgot all about it."

"It's all good," says Tyrone. "I didn't figure you comin' anyway."

"But I was gonna come," says Vincent. "I just completely forgot about it."

"Had other things on your mind," smiles Rosco.

"It was nice seein' you all," says Desiree.

"You have any more matches set up?" asks Vincent.

"Don't worry about it," says Tyrone. "It's alright. No biggie..."

"No, really. I really wanna go."

"What for?" asks Antoine.

"Because I'm interested. I've never been to a dogfight before. And because I wanna support Tyrone. I'm serious. When's the next one?"

"I don't know," says Tyrone. "I'll let you know."

"The next one's next week," says Rosco. "He can come if he wants. I don't got no problem with that."

"You mean the Circuit?" asks Tyrone.

"That's right. You don't want mister teacher here hangin' in the 'hood with a bunch of thugs and pimps. He'll be much more at home out in the sticks. Place be crawlin' with crackers. My man sure 'nuff gonna feel more at home in a place like that."

"What are you talking about?" says Vincent.

"We be goin' to Long Island for the next one."

"Long Island?"

"Yeah," says Rosco. "Place called Montauk. Nothing but official pitmen out there. The real deal. None of this ghetto rollin' bullshit."

"Montauk, huh?" says Vincent.

"You heard of it?" asks Tyrone.

"Sure," says Vincent. "I've been there before. It's a nice place. A real nice place. Near the ocean."

"Then why don't you two come out and join us?" says Rosco. "Dee Dee loves the ocean. Isn't that right?"

"I gotta get on home," says Desiree.

"How my son doin'?" asks Rosco. "I wanna see him again."

"I'm not about to talk my business with you, out here in the street."

"Yeah, sure. Okay. But I will be talkin' to you 'bout that real soon."

Desiree turns away in disgust. Vincent says to Tyrone, "I'll get the times and details from you tomorrow, okay? Is your phone working?"

"You serious?" asks Tyrone. "You really gonna come?"

"I'll be there," says Vincent.

"Word?"

"Definitely. I went to all your basketball games, right? I still go and see Antoine, right? And if I say I'm gonna watch your dog fight, then I'm gonna go and watch your dog fight."

CHAPTER NINETEEN

Vincent stays quiet because Desiree isn't talking. Silently, they start walking faster as the rain begins to fall. As they approach Desiree's building, Vincent wonders what she's thinking—if she's thinking about him and his promise to go see Tyrone's dog fight. Wondering if she's pissed off. Watching two animals attempt to kill each other is not something a teacher should be encouraging in a student. Is it? Vincent isn't sure.

As Desiree takes out her keys, she says, "You coming up?"

"Do you want me to?"

"Sure."

"Let's go," says Vincent, inwardly relieved that she doesn't seem angry.

Upstairs, Clyde and Aunt Gloria are waiting for Desiree's return. Vincent follows Desiree inside. Aunt Gloria is on the couch and Clyde runs over to his Mom.

"Were you good for Aunt Gloria?" Desiree asks.

Clyde looks at Aunt Gloria.

"An angel. As always," says Aunt Gloria.

"Yeah, right," smiles Desiree. "Did you say, 'hi' to Vincent?"

"Hi, Vincent."

"What up, Clyde?"

Clyde shrugs.

Aunt Gloria says, "I best be goin' now..."

Desiree puts the folded bills into Aunt Gloria's palm. Aunt Gloria says, "Oh. Oh, thank you, Dee Dee."

"Thank you," says Desiree, walking her to the door and out into the hallway. Returning inside, she says to Clyde, "Time for bed."

"Oh, c'mon,' says Clyde. "Can't I stay up a little bit? C'mon, please?"

"You can go inside and read a Dr. Seuss book. And then it's sleep time."

"I wanna watch TV."

"Don't push it."

"Alright..."

"Say good-night to Vincent and I'll be by in a little while to tuck you in."

"Good-night, Vincent."

"Night, Clyde."

As Clyde heads down the hallway, Desiree rises from the couch to click on the boom box. They listen to Mary J. Blige while she rolls a joint. But they do not smoke it. Not yet. They just listen to the music until Clyde returns. "I finished my book," he says.

"Which one?" says Desiree.

"Green eggs and ham."

"Would you like them in a box? Would you like them with a fox?" rhymes Vincent.

Clyde smiles.

"Alright, off to bed with you now," says Desiree.

"Fifteen more minutes?"

"No."

"Ten?"

"You better get that black ass in gear this minute or—"

"Okay, okay! You gonna tuck me in?"

"Yes. I'll be right there and now you get goin'."

Clyde tiptoes away, slowly, and is gone.

"He's a great kid," says Vincent.

Desiree smiles. She gets up. She turns down the music. "I'll be just a minute," she says, heading down the hall.

When Desiree returns, she says, "You wanna hold me?"

Vincent crosses to Desiree. He holds her tight and they kiss for a long time. But as Vincent starts to work his hands beneath her shirt, Desiree gently pulls away. "Sorry," she says.

"It's alright."

"Clyde might still be up."

"Oh. Yeah. Sure. I understand."

They sit on the couch. Desiree lights the joint. She puffs and passes and Vincent coughs as usual. They smile at this and continue smoking until the joint is too small to hold. The music clicks off. Desiree gets up to flip the tape. Returning to the couch, she asks Vincent what he's thinking about.

"How you know I'm thinking something?'

"I can tell by the way your eyebrows go," she says. "And by the way your forehead crinkles."

Vincent laughs. "I was just thinking how lucky I am. And then about a guy I used to know named Lucky. But he wasn't lucky at all. Fell asleep at the wheel and ran into a tree."

"Dead?"

"Yep."

"Being called Lucky don't mean it gonna give you good luck," she says, going back to the fridge for two more beers.

"You know a lot of Luckys?"

"Two," says Desiree, handing him a beer. "One was a friend of my Moms. A friend who became a boyfriend who ended up getting killed by his ex-wife's boyfriend over something stupid. Shot the nigga in the back. He was a nice guy though. Always seemed to be happy. Always in a good mood."

"That's sad."

"Yeah."

"What about the other one?"

"The other Lucky? Him, I knew when I was a kid. He used to live up in the Bronx. When he was little he got hit by a stray bullet. He was inside his house and the bullet took off a tiny piece of his nose before smashing the wall mirror in his mom's bedroom. They say he was real lucky because another inch over and he'd be dead. Everybody called him Lucky after that. His mom liked to say that he was lucky and whoever shot the gun was unlucky because he broke her mirror. His Moms loved to tell it like that... But this was when he was just a little nigga. When I knew him he was older."

"How old?"

"Fifteen or so," says Desiree.

"When you were with Rosco?"

Desiree looks at him. "Yeah."

"It's alright. It don't bother me none. The past is the past as far as I'm concerned. So go on. What happened with Lucky?"

Desiree drinks her beer. She recollects. "There were these handball courts over by 176th Street. In the middle of the wall they painted a genie."

"Like the guy who comes outta the lamp?"

"Something like that. It was the tag for this gang called the Javelins. So, every once in a while, a bunch of us would get high on this roof to watch the Apache line."

"What's that?"

"They had two long rows of niggas, some of 'em holdin' chains or bats and the nigga who wanted to be in the gang, he had to run between the two rows, the Apache line, and touch the genie on the wall. If he made it to the genie, he was in the Javelins and he would get this dope denim jacket with a painting of the green genie on the back. It was to see if you had heart. Most niggas got pretty fucked up runnin' that Apache line. Some of 'em never made it. We musta watched Lucky run that line ten times before he finally gave up tryin'..."

"Oh, I get it. I guess he wasn't so lucky. At least not with the Javelins."

"After the Javelins, Lucky tried to get in this other gang. The Savage Skulls."

"Great name for a gang."

"Back in the day, they used to have hundreds of gangs like that, especially in the Bronx."

"What did you have to do to get into the Skulls?"

"You had to play a game of Russian Roulette. But the odds were with you because you got a one outta six chance of not getting shot in the head."

"So what happened? Shot himself in the head?"

"Na... He made it easy. In fact, just to impress them, he did it twice without even spinnin' the barrel."

"I guess that is pretty lucky."

"It is what it is."

"What do you mean?"

"I don't believe in luck."

"No?"

"No."

"Okay. So what ever happened to Lucky?"

"You ever hear about the big blackout? Back in the seventies?"

"Yeah, I heard about it."

"Niggas went buck wild. And the cops? They didn't even bother to stop them. It was real hot and everybody was out. Niggas busted through the windows on every store and supermarket up and down the block. Niggas was wheelin' shopping carts down the streets full of groceries, TVs, radios—whatever they could grab. Some of 'em was drivin' cars right out of the dealer's lots. I never did see nothin' like that night... Over and over, all you could hear was breaking glass. Like the clapping in Yankee Stadium after a home run... The clapping going on and on and getting louder and louder... Big plates of glass smashing one after the other, all up and down the streets, all over the world, it seemed. There were fires too. It was crazy."

Vincent and Desiree think on the blackout for a moment. Then, Vincent says, "How'd we get on this? The blackout?"

"You were askin' about Lucky. Lucky got himself killed during the blackout. Got himself run over by a car. They say he was wheelin' two shopping carts full up with sneakers and shoes. Nigga drivin' didn't see him and ran him down. July 13, 1977. I still remember the date."

"Thirteen, huh? An unlucky number. Especially for Lucky."

"You got jokes now?" Desiree is smiling.

"Naw," says Vincent. "But you really don't believe in luck? Or unluck?"

"I believe things just come about 'cause that's the way things have to go."

"Things happen for a reason."

"I don't believe that either. Ever notice how you always hear that whenever something fucked up happens?"

"I guess so."

"When they not believing in luck, people like to think they either in control of what happens to them or that God or the devil or the white man is in control. Way I see it, things have been happening and are gonna keep on happening—right after the other—ever since things started out. One thing leads to the next thing right on down the line. Lucky got himself killed that night because his line of living hit with the nigga who was stealing' that car's line of living. Each one of their lines goin' back to the second and the minute and the hour and the days since the day they was born."

"That's an interesting theory."

"It's just what I be thinkin' sometimes."

"So then," reasons Vincent. "Each line of living, like you say, is affected or controlled by what happens before it. Your parent's lines and their parent's lines, all the way back as far as it goes."

"It's even more complicated because there are so many millions of lines goin' in all directions at once. But the number don't really matter. Things happen because of what happened right before."

"And we have no choice in the matter?"

"Not really. You might think that you do. You might say, I'm gonna do this instead of that. But after you did it, when you look back at it, there wasn't any way you coulda not have done it."

"But if we have no choice in what we do, then we're not responsible for what we do."

"No. We're not."

"I don't know if I agree with that."

"You don't have to agree with me."

"I'm pretty high right now," says Vincent. "I wanna think on this some more when I'm straight."

The telephone rings and the answering machine begins it's broadcast: "Dee Dee? Dee Dee, you there? It's me, Rosco. Pick up the phone, I know you home... Dee Dee? Alright, then... We gotta talk. I wanna start seeing Clyde again. I'll call you later."

CHAPTER TWENTY

It is early Friday morning.   The winter light is unusually strong with what looks like another day of record-breaking temperatures.   Vincent sits in the driver's seat of his father's car, parked outside Desiree's tenement, his jacket tossed in the back.   He told his father he was going to a teacher's conference for the weekend.   Vincent sees one of his students, Juana, walking to school.   She wears a"Triple Fat Goose" down coat.   The puffy coat is zipped up for winter despite the fact that the mercury is pushing sixty.   Vincent does not see any other students because this is the last day of Regent's week.   Those not scheduled to take tests have no classes.   Vincent called in sick last night, leaving a message on the school answering machine.

He lights a cigarette and cracks open the window. On the radio, Howard Stern jokes about OJ Simpson.   His black sidekick, Robin, is cackling at every word he says. When Desiree appears at her doorway, Vincent punches the button to a jazz station.   Vincent has another button set to hip-hop but figures jazz as a safe bet to start out their drive.

Desiree opens the back door, tossing her bag and jacket in next to Vincent's.   She gets into the front.   She says, "Nice whip."

"It's my father's."

"I love old cars.   Especially big ones like this."

"It's a boat alright.   But he takes care of it.   Still runs great."

Vincent drops his cigarette out the window and pulls away from the curb.   They travel east and then north through Spanish Harlem.   On the way, Desiree has Vincent stop so she can run in and buy "rollos" and coffee from the Dominican Bakery.   While Vincent drives, Desiree assists him with his coffee and roll.   Vincent is hungry and finishes it off in a short number of bites.

"That was good."

Desiree smiles. Vincent hands her his coffee cup while he fishes for bills to pay the toll. As they cross the Triborough Bridge, Desiree looks at Harlem spread out on her right.

"You mind if I change the station?"

"No. Go ahead," says Vincent.

Desiree doesn't stop on the hip-hop or the rock or the oldie station. But she does stop at the voice of Howard Stern. Vincent glances over at her. "You listen to Howard?"

"Sometimes. Is that okay?"

"Sure."

Howard continues to riff about OJ while various callers call in with their own opinions and racist remarks, including a bleeped but clearly understood mention of nigger and niggers. Vincent cringes but Desiree is seemingly not offended. When the commercials come on, Desiree punches the hip-hop button.

"Only thing about Howard," she says, "is his commercials last forever."

"That's 'cause he talks so much."

"Nigga sure can go on," she says.

Vincent loves when Desiree uses the word nigga—especially regarding himself. It's like he's got some sort of free pass into her world. When she uses it for Howard Stern, he is likewise pleased. Vincent wonders why this is so... Maybe because he is secretly happy for Howard in that he too can be an honorary "nigga" like himself.

"You feel like smoking?" asks Desiree.

"Weed?"

"Yeah. You think it's okay?"

"Sure," says Vincent.

Desiree twists around over the front seat, reaching into her bag in the back. Vincent glances appreciatively at the curve of her spine and ass. Desiree twists back with a lighter and a pack of Newports in hand. She selects a joint from the pack of cigarettes. She lights the joint and they smoke it down while listening to the radio. As usual, Vincent is soon very high.

"You okay?"

"I'm fine," says Vincent. "I think I drive even better when I'm high."

"You're going a lot slower."

"Don't wanna give no cop a reason to pull us over."

Desiree nods. Vincent asks her to light a cigarette for him. She does and lights one of her own. Vincent opens his window for fresh air. When he closes the window again, Desiree says, "I had this terrible dream last night. You were in it."

"Well, I'm sorry if I did anything wrong."

"I forgive you," she smiles. "We were in Morningside Park again. And that dog, with the three legs, he was there too. Only this time, he got Clyde."

"What did I do?"

"You didn't do shit. Just stood there and watched."

"That's awful."

"I didn't do nothin' either. I was froze up and tryin' to scream with nothin' comin' out. And you were right there, just like before, only you didn't do nothin' but watch. Just watchin' and standin' and singing this song."

"Singing a song? What song?"

"I don't know... I couldn't understand it. Like it was in some other language or something."

"I don't know any songs in any other languages."

"It was just a dream," she says. "You were the one who saved Clyde. That's what's real."

"Damn straight," says Vincent. "Got the stitches to prove it."

"My hero," she says, sliding across the front seat, kissing his neck and then her hand on his leg...

Vincent does his best to keep the car steady and on course. He thinks that this is no doubt the best ride of his life.

CHAPTER TWENTY-ONE

It is late January and most of Montauk is closed for the season. One of the few hotels still open is the Montauk Manor, often referred to as the Castle. Built high on a hill during the Roaring Twenties, the Castle's ballrooms were routinely filled with the rich and famous. It was a grand resort that included polo fields and a golf course. Croquet was regularly played on the expansive front lawn. Today, such grandeur is long gone, found only in the faded photographs along the arched hallways leading to the empty ballroom.

"Dag," says Tyrone. "We goin' up there?"

"That's it," says Rosco.

Tyrone is sitting on a milkcrate between the two front seats of their rented van. Antoine is driving, Rosco riding shotgun. In the back, Tnuc and Cremator lie quiet inside their traveling crates. They have just turned onto the private road leading up to the Castle.

"Looks like that place from 'The Shining,'" says Antoine.

"It do," says Tyrone. "'All work and no play make Jack a dull boy.'"

"That nigga was off the hook," says Antoine.

"I like when the butler say he gotta 'correct' his wife and kid," says Tyrone.

As they drive up the winding road, the Manor looms higher and larger.

"I had another dream about Rum last night," says Tyrone. "I'm just remembering it now."

"What was it?" asks Roscoe.

"I can't remember it exactly. It was more of a feeling kinda dream... But I do recall that Rum had his leg back. He had four legs again. That much is clear."

"How you know it was Rum, then?" asks Rosco.

"It was Rum. I knowed it was him."

Antoine parks the van. They sit a moment in the nearly empty parking lot facing the front of the Castle. "Maybe Rum's ghost is up in there too," cracks Antoine. Maybe that's why you were dreaming about him last night."

"Alright, chill with that," says Rosco. "And don't neither of you be talkin' any junk once we get inside either. The place is gonna be crawlin' with crackers and we ain't in the 'hood no more. Got it?"

"Yeah, Rosco," says Tyrone.

Antoine nods.

"I'm gonna go in and see what up. You two wait here with the dogs."

"Damn! What the fuck?" shouts Tyrone.

Shooting out of the sky, a large seagull smashes into a light pole positioned just a few feet in front of the van.

"You see that?" says Tyrone.

"Fucking hole in one," says Antoine.

"Look, it's still alive," says Tyrone.

With one wing bloody and broken, the seagull flops about in a slow circle near the base of the light pole.

"Maybe I should go out and kill it," says Tyrone.

"What the hell for?" says Rosco.

"Put it out of its misery."

"Leave the fuckin' thing alone," says Rosco. "What I tell you? We not in the 'hood and we not gonna do nothin' but try and act as normal as we can without making anybody round here take any more notice of us then they have to. How it gonna look to some cracker to come out that door and see some nigga stompin on a seagull?"

"I got you, Rosco. I think he dead now anyway."

Suddenly, a second seagull swoops from the trees at the right of the Castle, bearing straight at the van.

"Fuck!" says Antoine. "He comin' right at us!"

At the last second, the seagull wheels up and over the hood of the van but not before leaving an egg-sized shit on the windshield.

"That was for us," says Tyrone.

"What you talkin' about?"

"I believe they was goin' after us," says Tyrone.

"You stupid," says Antoine. "What kinda birds gonna be attackin' three full grown niggas in a van?"

"White ones. White racist birds," says Tyrone.

"Stop talkin' junk," says Rosco. "No such thing as a racist bird. Now, you two stay put and I'll be right back."

Antoine and Tyrone watch Rosco cross the parking lot. When he's about half way along the walk, another seagull comes swooping. Rosco ducks and swats wildly at the bird. Like a dive bomber, the seagull wheels in a big arc before bearing down on Rosco, who is now on the run and flapping his arms to ward off the attack. As soon as Rosco makes it into the safety of the Castle, Tyrone and Antoine look at each other and burst out laughing.

"You see that nigga run?" says Tyrone.

"That Rosco can still jet when he have to!"

"Oh shit!"

"There's two of 'em now! What the fuck?"

One seagull seems to be chasing the other in a loose figure eight. The birds fly faster and faster becoming white streaks not ten feet from the ground.

"What the fuck they doin?"

"Shit if I know," says Antoine.

"They completely bugged out."

A third seagull swoops from the sky, screaming something in seagull language. As soon as this bird enters the picture, the first two commence to scream and chase him towards the tree line. But the third bird does not seek the safely of the trees. It wheels up towards the sun and straight down to earth, crashing in a great puff of white feathers on the brick walkway.

"You see that?"

"I saw it," says Antoine.

"He just killed his self."

"Word."

"What kinda birds go killin' themselves like that?"

"I never heard of no birds killin' themselves," says Antoine. "I don't think I ever heard of any animals that go killin' themselves. Maybe the fuckers are possessed."

"This place fucked up," says Tyrone. "I had a feeling about this place."

A golf cart comes up the roadway, driven by two Mexican groundskeepers. The groundskeepers park their cart in the center of the lawn. One points to the dead bird on the walkway. The other nods and gestures towards the dead bird by the light pole.

"What's up with them niggas?"

"They must work here," says Antoine.

The driving Mexican points at the tree line. Not a second later, another pair of screaming seagulls comes swooping into view. The second Mexican reaches down, pulling up a silver shotgun. He aimes and fires. Both seagulls fall from the sky in assorted pieces. The shooting Mexican smiles and his partner slaps him on the back.

Tyrone and Antoine have ducked down in their seats. They breathe heavy and wait. With no more shots fired, Tyrone peers over the dashboard.

"What they doin' now?"

"He musta put the shottie away," says Tyrone. "Now's our chance, let's get the fuck outta here."

"Can't leave Rosco."

"Yeah, you right."

Antoine sits up. The two Mexicans are out of their golf cart now, walking across the lawn. One carries a snow shovel and the other carries a large, plastic trash bag. They walk to the nearest carcass, scooping it up and into the bag.

Antoine rolls down his window. "Hey, yo!"

The Mexicans stop and stare.

"Excuse me," says Antoine. "We guests here. You mind tellin' us what's goin' on?"

"The birds," says the Mexican with the snow shovel. "Seagulls."

"Yeah, the seagulls. What up with them?"

"They drunk. They get drunk and go crazy."

"Drunk?"

"That's right," says the Mexican. "They get themselves drunk on the berries. It happens sometime when the weather turn warm and the berry fermenting. It don't take much to get them drunk."

"Like Mexicans," mutters Tyrone.

"Berries?" says Antoine.

"Yes," says the Mexican. "It usually happen much early in the year. Not in winter. But it be so warm for a week now. And the berry, they really, really like them."

"They love them," adds the trash bag Mexican.

"That's fucked up," says Antoine.

"Iss focked up," says the snow shovel Mexican. "But don't worry. We clean up good all the bird now. Should be no more drunk birds to bother you."

"Well, that's good," says Antoine. "Thanks."

"You're welcome, sir."

Antoine rolls up his window. After picking up all the dead birds, the Mexicans return to their cart and scour the tree line. But no more gulls have come forward. The Mexicans sit smoking cigarettes. A short time later, Rosco comes out the front entrance flanked by two large white men in black suits.

"This don't look good," says Tyrone.

"Just be cool," says Antoine.

When Rosco gets close to the van, he motions for them to come out. He introduces them to Norman and Henry. In addition to being exceptionally large beneath their tailored black suits, the two men have equally imposing thick necks and bald heads. The main difference between Norman and Henry is that Norman has a goatee and Henry has only a regular mustache. Norman and Henry have come to take Cremator and Tnuc to the kennels. With ease, the two men carry aloft the dog-filled crates from the back of the van. Passing the golf cart, they exchange Spanish words with the Mexicans who laugh loudly at a comment made by Norman.

"C'mon," says Rosco. "Grab the bags."

On their way towards the entrance, Rosco tells Antoine and Tyrone about the drunk sea gulls. It was Norman and Henry who sent out the Mexicans to deal with the birds after hearing what Rosco told them upon his arrival. Antoine and Tyrone politely nod at Rosco's narrative, and Tyrone mentions the sharp shooting Mexican with the silver shotgun.

"I told you, we wasn't in the 'hood no more," says Rosco.

"I had me a feelin' about this place," says Tyrone.

"Just remember what I told you," says Rosco. "We all gotta be chilled no matter how fucked up things seem around here."

Tyrone and Antoine follow Rosco into the castle. Inside, Rosco's shoes generate echoes in the otherwise silent entrance hall. The ceiling is high and arched. There are deep shadows in all directions except where harsh shafts of light cut from between the not so carefully closed curtains. Behind the reception desk, another Mexican in a green suit smiles and nods at Rosco. On the far side of the hall, a fireplace the size of Tyrone's apartment illuminates the faces of two old white men smoking pipes in great winged-back chairs. The old men have thick white heads of hair and blow white smoke. They do not turn, do not acknowledge the three negroes passing them by.

At the far end of the hall, a rather narrow hallway leads to their rooms. Rosco hands Antoine a room key. "You two are gonna share a room right next to mines," he says.

Antoine takes the key.

"And remember," says Rosco. "Don't' be playin' the TV or the radio on loud or be makin' any kind of fuss that gonna bring us the wrong kinda attention." Rosco stops at his room. "I'm gonna take me a shower and a nap. Just make sure you do whatever you gotta do to be ready at four."

"Okay, Rosco," they say.

"And I wouldn't go wanderin' around outside. Probably better stay put and we'll all move together."

"I ain't goin' nowhere," says Tyrone. "Not with them crazy ass seagulls out there."

"Yeah, alright then. Just lay low and I'll knock on your door at four."

Rosco lets himself into his room. Tyrone follows Antoine into theirs. Antoine flicks on the light and he crosses to the curtains, pulling them open wide to a breathtaking view of the sea beyond the great lawn leading from their terrace.

"I never been to no place like this before," says Antoine.

"Me neither," says Tyrone. "But I don't like it. I gotta bad feeling about this place."

"What's that?"

"Like it's fucking haunted or something."

"Nigga, you bugged."

Rosco screams. They can hear him through the thick walls and then even louder as he runs into the hallway. Antoine and Tyrone rush out to find Rosco in his underwear, his eyes bulging.

"What happened?" says Antoine.

"There was a fucking bat!" shouts Rosco. "A fucking bat in my room!"

Norman and Henry come running from the far end of the hall. They look at Rosco standing in his boxer shorts.

"What's the trouble?" says Norman.

"Somebody was shouting," says Henry.

"That was me," says Rosco, smiling. "There's a goddamn bat in my room!"

"A bat?" says Norman.

"A big, motherfucking black bat," says Rosco. "I went to open the curtain and the motherfucker flew right at me and all around the fucking room. I'm not going back in there."

"Terribly sorry," says Norman.

"First birds and now bats," mutters Tyrone.

Rosco stares at Tyrone, smiling.

Tyrone lowers his head. "My bad, dawgs," he says, just above a whisper.

Henry raises a walkie-talkie previously clipped to his hip. He speaks Spanish to the walkie-talkie.

Norman says, "It didn't bite you, did it?"

"No, but it could have," says Rosco. "I felt the wind from his wings, he was that fucking close."

"But you sure he didn't nip you?"

"I'm sure. I'd know if the fucker bit me."

"We'll get you another room right away," says Henry.

"I'm gonna stay with them," says Rosco.

"Are you sure?"

"Most definitely."

"Very well," says Henry. "And I will make it my business that you get duly compensated for such an unfortunate start."

CHAPTER TWENTY-TWO

Beneath the bill of a plastic marlin hangs a "VACANCY" sign. The Seaside Inn is a two-story structure of simple rooms with excellent views of the Atlantic Ocean. The rates plummet during the off-season.

Vincent pulls into the lot, parking beside a late model pickup outfitted with fishing poles attached to the front grill. The only other vehicle is a jet-ski mounted on an unhitched trailer. As Vincent opens the car door, Desiree says, "I'll wait here."

"Okay."

Desiree lights a cigarette. They exchange smiles through the window glass. Vincent crosses the parking lot and enters through the door labeled, "MANAGEMENT OFFICE." The front desk is empty. Vincent presses the button that reads, "Ring once and ONLY ONCE for Service." Vincent looks about the office. On the walls are framed photos of people smiling beside the hanging carcasses of upside-down sharks, in many of the pictures children holding their parent's hands, some licking ice cream cones, and pointing in disgust or glee at the lynched and bloody monsters of the sea. Vincent takes a close look at the photo of a young man playfully placing his head near the giant teeth of what appears to be a great white shark. Stopped in time with him, his girlfriend tugs at his sleeve. As Vincent continues to wait, he notices that in many of the shots, the same fisherman appears as a young man in the black and white photos and then older in color. Vincent wonders if this fisherman is still alive, still out killing sharks. He thinks about him, about Desiree's theory of the lines, all the slaughtered sharks, their lines intersecting with this one fisherman's line, so to speak...

As more minutes pass, Vincent begins to get impatient. He wonders if the bell is working. Maybe he didn't push it hard enough. He wonders if he should press again. Maybe he should leave and try another place. But Vincent has few options in this regard. A resort, Guerneys, is open but way out of his price range. The Montauk Manor is also open but that's where Rosco is staying, leaving only the Crow's Nest or the Memory Motel.

As Vincent turns towards the door, he hears the clearing of a throat. He turns to see a tall man sprouting a long, hillbilly beard, immediately reminding Vincent of the guys in ZZ-Top. "Can I help you?" In his hand is a coffee mug that states, "I HATE NEW YORK." As Vincent approaches the desk, he detects that both the mug and its owner are not filled with coffee. At first sniff, Vincent correctly guesses gin.

"I'd like a room, please."

"Oh, yeah? What for?"

"Uh—"

"Only kidding! King or Queer?"

"King, I guess."

"You guess? Don't you know what you are?"

"Excuse me?"

"I'm just fucking with you... You from the city? You sound like you're from Brooklyn or maybe the Bronx?"

"Hoboken."

"Oh, yeah. Same shit basically."

"But I live in the city now."

"Isn't that grand. Me, I grew up in Staten Island. But that was way before it went to hell. How I hate the fucking city. Can't stand the fucking place. How anybody can live there, totally fucking mystifies me. You like living there?"

"It's alright. I work there. Gotta pay the rent."

"I hear ya. Yeah, it must be tough on a young guy like you. Even if you wanna leave, what you gonna do? Jobs are hard to come by. Goddamn liberals, they sure as shootin' made sure of that. Which leaves poor fucks like yourself trapped workin' your ass off doin' somethin' you hate in a place you hate. I know it. I've been there, kid. And the only reason I'm here is my wife had a dollar and a dream. That's right. Hit the fucking Lotto and we bought this place. You know Montauk is the closest place in America to Ireland? Yep. You Irish? No, I didn't think so. Italian? Yeah, of course you are. With that shnoz what the hell else could you be? Other than a Jew—ha, ha—just kidding. I knew you was no Jew."

"So, about the room?"

"Yeah, sure. We got plenty of 'em. All with a view and a hell of a lot cheaper than Guerneys."

"Great."

"Must be great to get out of the city, huh?"

"Yeah, I guess."

"Fresh air. Peace. Quiet. Hey, you got a car alarm?"

"What? Uh-no."

"Good. Because if you did, I'd ask you to cut it off. Last guy out here from the city—his damn alarm went off in a high wind and kept me and the wife up near half the night."

"You'll have no such problem with me."

"Not that you'd need one out here anyway."

"I guess not."

"Only niggers you'll see out here are Mexicans. And, unlike your typical spic, they know their place."

"What?"

"You can sleep at ease out here, boy. Only coons you gonna see 'round here are the kind you make a hat out of."

"What the hell are you trying to say?"

"I'm just telling you like it is. It's different out here. You're free to leave your doors unlocked. You can walk at night without having to worry about being jacked up by a spade or a spic. Hey... Hey, where you goin'? What's wrong? Well, fuck you too then too. You Jew! You fucking kike bastard, you."

Vincent gets back in the car. He starts it up and pulls out of the parking lot. In the rearview mirror, he sees

ZZ-Top holding the door open with his coffee cup and flipping the finger with his free hand.

"What's wrong?"

"Nothing," says Vincent. "The place was a shit hole."

"Really? It looked okay from the outside."

"But rotten inside."

"Good cover—bad book."

"Exactly."

The Memory Motel is on Main Street with no views other than a gas station and a parking lot. A short strip of rooms is connected to the bar, the same bar the Rolling Stones once visited and wrote a song about while they were hanging out with Andy Warhol, who had a house by the beach.

"You think it's open?" asks Desiree.

"I hope so," says Vincent.

As Desiree accompanies Vincent inside, Vincent secretly hopes there is not another ZZ-Top kind of guy here too. The bar includes a jukebox and a scattering of mismatched tables and chairs. The jukebox is off. The TV behind the bar shows a hockey game. Two men sit at a table beneath the head of a moose. They are well past the half-century mark, dressed in expensive casual and obviously from out of town. They sip beer from glasses beside near empty bottles. Sitting on a stool is a young man wearing a flannel shirt and a dungaree vest covered in lewd patches. He's engrossed in the hockey game, slapping his palm on the bar at the action in the box. The bartender works a crossword puzzle on the counter near the register, his back to the customers.

As Vincent enters, harsh daylight momentarily floods the whiskey-colored air. The two at the table look up and then quickly away. Vincent and Desiree cross to the center of the bar, in front of the beer taps. Desiree glances at the guy slamming his palm into the bar.

Vincent says, "Excuse me?" And then, "Excuse me?" once more. The bartender turns around. Vincent does his damndest to look into the man's one good eye. Vincent remembers being told that if somebody has a "lazy" eye, the proper etiquette is to focus on the normal one. However, the eye in question is not lazy. It does not wander as lazy eyes are wont to do. Instead, it is completely unmoving, stuck in a fixed direction a good forty-five degrees from the bridge of the nose. Despite its fixedness, the eye is not glass. Living but aimed away like a chameleon's eye.

"Room or a drink?"

"Both," says Desiree. "Bourbon on the rocks for me."

"Me too," says Vincent.

"Comin' up."

"Yes! Oh, fucking yes!" shouts the hockey fan. "Hey, Bert? Another round!" He notices Vincent and Desiree. He nods his head at them. Vincent nods back. "You like hockey?"

"Sure," says Vincent. "But I haven't followed it in a long time."

"Islanders just won four to three."

"Great."

"And I just won a hundred bucks."

"Congratulations."

"Thanks. Hey, Bert, give these guys a round on me."

"Thanks," says Vincent.

"Sure," he says, turning back at Bert. "You get that? A round on me. That's for everyone. Them two too!"

The two men under the moose head thank the hockey fan. As Bert sets everybody up with booze, Desiree puts money in the jukebox. Much to Vincent's surprise, the first song is "Thunder Road" by Bruce Springsteen. Hearing the opening of the song, Bert turns up the jukebox from behind the bar.

"I love fucking Bruce," says Bert.

"I never heard him before," says Desiree.

"Why you put him on?" asks Vincent.

"I liked the name of the song."

"What you think?" asks Bert.

"He alright," says Desiree.

"Hey, Bert!" shouts the hockey fan. "Turn down the music! We on the TV!"

Bert cocks his head and grabs the remote, turning down the music and turning up the TV. On the screen, the local newscaster stands on the great lawn of the Montauk Manor. Beside him are Henry and Norman.

"So the gulls were drunk?"

"That is correct," says Norman. "The warm weather apparently fermented the fallen berries. The birds were completely intoxicated. Most of 'em just fell on the ground but some decided to take to the air."

"Not a good idea," says the newscaster.

"Not at all. A good number crashed into the castle and one died right on that light pole over there."

"Ouch!" says the newscaster.

"It wasn't pretty," says Norman. "But as soon as we figured out what was going on, we got rid of those berries."

"I didn't know sea gulls ate berries," says the newscaster.

"A gull will eat just about anything," says Norman. "Much like my partner, Henry, here."

The camera pans to Henry and back to the chuckling newscaster. "So there you have it folks. The drunken sea gulls of Montauk Manor."

The front door of the bar opens. Entering with the glare of the outside light are Henry and Norman. The entire bar stares at them.

"What the hell you all lookin' at?" says Henry.

"You were just on the TV," says the hockey fan.

"Really?" says Henry.

"Yeah, just this minute."

Henry goes to the TV but the news station has already cut to a commercial.

"Damn!"

"It'll be on at ten," says Norman. "We can catch it then."

"You think so?" says Henry.

"Undoubtedly," says Norman.

"What can I get you fellas?" says Bert.

"Nothing for us," says Henry. "I'm here to see him. Your name Vincent? Vincent DeRosa?"

"Yeah," says Vincent. "Why?"

Henry looks at Norman. Norman reaches into his pocket. He takes out an envelope, handing it to Henry who hands it to Vincent. Henry says, "You'll find everything you need to know inside."

"Thanks," says Vincent.

Henry and Norman leave. Bert turns the TV down and the jukebox up. Vincent opens the envelope. Inside is a pin. On the pin, the head of a pit bull clenching a rooster by the neck. There is also a paper with typed information. Vincent hands the pin to Desiree. She studies it a moment before handing it back to him. Looking up, Vincent realizes that everybody is watching him, including the two under the moose head who each give the "thumbs-up" sign with their fingers.

CHAPTER TWENTY-THREE

The phone rings inside Vincent's sleep. A naked heel to his head jars him to confused consciousness. The dream phone is still ringing. Vincent tries to focus despite his epic hangover, each ring of the ringer a hard whap on the nail being driven into his skull. With great effort, he rises to a sitting position, gently pushing aside the long dark legs draped across his chest. Desiree snores softly, oblivious to the phone. Vincent reaches for the receiver.

"Hello," he says, his tongue thick and sticky.

"This is Norman. We met yesterday in the Memory. Henry and I will be by in one hour. Be sure to be ready."

"Huh?'

"Be sure to be ready. We will not wait for you. Did you not read the instructions?"

"What? Oh, yeah. Right. Okay. I'll be ready."

"CLICK."

Hanging up, Vincent surveys the room. It is a wreck. The mattress is partially off the box spring. Desiree's feet are where her head is supposed to be. The bedside lamp is overturned. Clothes and a towel and the blankets are scattered and heaped about the floor beside empty and near empty bottles of beer. There is a hard, half eaten piece of pizza in an open pizza box on the rug near the bathroom door. Light filters in through the cheap cotton curtains.

Vincent turns his gaze to Desiree's long legs... To her ass... He takes in the view as disjointed images of last night tumble back at him, causing him to absentmindedly touch his cock and balls. He puts his free hand on the back of her calf. It is taut and strong beneath unbelievably soft skin. Vincent continues to touch himself and her, one thing leading to another with Desiree soon roused and up and on her hands and knees.

When they are done, Desiree stretches out across the bed, her head deep in the pillow, rushing back into the sleep she left just moments before. Stepping away from the bed in the direction of the bathroom, Vincent cries out in pain. Desiree turns her head to see. Vincent sits back down on the bed, his bloody foot in his hands.

"You okay?"

"Yeah," he says. "The light bulb was broke."

Desiree sees the overturned lamp and then the shards of the light bulb on the rug near the night table.

"How'd that happen?"

"I have no idea," says Vincent, grabbing a nearby towel and wiping his foot. "It's nothing. Just a small cut."

"Better wash it out good," says Desiree. "You want me to help you?"

"It's alright. I'm okay," says Vincent, rising once more and walking on the heel of his injured foot to the bathroom.

When Vincent comes back, Desiree is sitting up in bed, smoking a cigarette and watching music videos on TV. The sound of music is painful to Vincent.

"Can you put that a little lower?"

"Sure," she says.

"Aren't you hung over?"

"No. Not really. Maybe a little sleepy still."

"I feel like I got an anchor lodged in my head."

Desiree smiles. Vincent moves slowly about the mess of the room plucking out articles of clothing and putting them on.

"How's your boo-boo?"

"It's okay. Just a tiny cut."

"You want me to kiss it and make it better?"

"Always."

CHAPTER TWENTY-FOUR

The honk of a horn moves them to the next thing. Desiree kisses Vincent good-bye. She is wearing one of Vincent's T-shirts. Vincent loves seeing her in his shirt because it reinforces the notion of them being a couple.

"You sure you're okay with this?"

"Yeah. I'm fine," she says, touching the dog-fighting button pinned to his shirt.

"Okay, then," he says.

Desiree kisses him again. Vincent opens the door. The harsh daylight invades their cloistered world and, for a moment, Vincent finds himself inexplicably filled with sadness. How much better would it be to forget the whole thing, to turn back into the dark of the room and the warmth of this beautiful woman standing at the threshold...

The red minivan is waiting in the lot. Norman is behind the wheel, Henry in the passenger seat. Henry gets out to slide open the back door. Vincent climbs in beside another man who appears to have very little neck. Seeing him, Vincent immediately recollects a grade school janitor, a man they called Head and Shoulders. Back then, the thing to do was to wheel away Head and Shoulders' trash bin while his back was turned, prompting him to give chase and shout foreign words. What made it so much fun was the fact that Head and Shoulders had something wrong with his spine, causing him to run sideways like a crab. Years later, Vincent found out that Head and Shoulders was a concentration camp survivor.

Henry introduces them. "Vincent, this is Tito. Tito, Vincent."

Tito is wearing a pin with the image of a pit bull biting his own tail. Vincent shakes hands with Tito. It is a small hand but a strong hand. Once released, Vincent looks out his window to keep himself from staring.

They drive in the direction of the lighthouse. Gazing out at the passing trees, Vincent retains a certain fogginess of mind that softens all edges of the rushing world. He could easily fall asleep now. But he forces himself to keep his eyes open while allowing his mind to drift dreamlike over last night's adventures with Desiree...

Were they pirates? Or were they phantoms? What did they want? Where were they from? Where did they go to? Spooling into a rewind, Vincent recalls the bar, the heavy drinking and the late night mission to the beach. At first, their plan was to go see the Montauk Lighthouse. Desiree had never seen a real lighthouse before, much less one that was commissioned by the father of our country, George Washington. But it was Bert who quickly pointed out that it was too far to walk and they were in no condition to drive. Instead, he drew a map on a cocktail napkin leading to a not-so-secret lover's bench overlooking the ocean. In near darkness, they traveled hand-in-hand along a series of densely wooded paths, sometimes stopping to consult the map with a lighter before moving on in the direction of the thundering sea. As the crashing waves grew louder and louder, the forest gave way to scrub brush and high grasses until they found themselves out in the open on a high, wind-swept bluff facing the North Atlantic. They no longer needed the lighter to see the map. The moon and all the stars were out, casting a pale light on them and the surf below. Looking down at the beach, Vincent was reminded of "The Planet of the Apes," that last scene where Charlton Heston realizes he's back on earth because he sees the blown up Statue of Liberty. The lover's bench was easy to spot once they found themselves up on the bluff. As soon as they sat down, Desiree sparked a joint that they smoked while watching the waves crash and tumble. It was Desiree who first saw them coming.

"Hey," she said. "You see that?"

"What?"

"Over there."

"It's a boat," says Vincent.

"And there's another one out there too. See it? A much bigger one. Probably the boat they're coming from."

They watched in silence as the small dinghy slowly made its way towards the shoreline.

"You think they're pirates?"

"You so stupid," she said.

There were five figures in the dingy. They were a good hundred yards down the beach. Four of the five got out, carrying backpacks above their heads. The fifth motored back in the direction of the anchored boat offshore. Desiree and Vincent watched the four walk away down the beach. Not long after that, the offshore boat pulled its anchor, the sound of its motor fading fast and gone. After a moment, Vincent said, "What do you think that was all about?"

"They hustlers," she said.

"Drug dealers?"

"No doubt. It's the middle of the night and they sure as hell not here sightseeing."

"Makes sense. They probably didn't want to risk people seeing them come into town. I got the feeling everybody knows everybody around here.

"Hm-m."

"You think they're strapped?"

"Definitely."

"Imagine if we decided to go walking down on the beach rather than coming up here?"

"I'm glad we here," she said.

"I guess our lines weren't destined to connect."

Desiree smiled at this. "You don't let anything go, do you?"

"I've been thinking a lot about your line theory," he said.

"And?"

"And I think it makes a lot of sense. But..."

"What?"

"But what I don't get is how you can say you believe in God at the same time."

"What do you mean?"

"Well, if everything that is going to happen is happening because of the things that came before, then what has God to do with it?"

Desiree thought a moment, "Maybe he just started it. Started something he couldn't stop."

"Made a rock so heavy he couldn't lift it."

"What?"

"It's an expression. If God can do anything, can he make a rock so heavy that he can't lift it? You can't get a right answer. If he's God, he can do anything. And if he can do anything, he should be able to make a rock he can't lift. But if he makes that rock, then he's no longer God because he can't lift it."

"You talkin' junk."

"Oh, yeah?"

"Who says God gotta be able to do everything? Maybe all he ever did was get the ball rollin' and then quit."

"Quit?"

"Yeah. Why not?"

"That's good. So God's not dead. He's just retired."

"What's so funny? Stop playin' me."

"I'm not 'playin'' you."

"Then what you grinnin' at, fool?"

"I just think it's kinda funny. Somebody or something that powerful not doing anything with his power."

"That's why he God. Unlike people, he don't let the power get the best of him. He's able to turn away from it."

"Oh, you mean like power corrupts and absolute power corrupts absolutely."

"What?"

"Just another expression," said Vincent.

The car skids to a stop, dashing Vincent and Tito into the backrests of the front seats and snapping Vincent out of his reverie. Without looking back, the deer they just avoided continues on his run to the other side of the highway.

Norman cranes his head around, "You two okay?"

Tito nods.   Vincent exclaims, "What the hell happened?"

"Fucking deer," says Henry. "Montauk is lousy with 'em."

"Like cows in Calcutta," says Norman.

"Huh? What you talking about?" says Henry.

"The deers... They're like the cows in India. People starving to death while their sacred cows are free to walk up and down the streets."

"Oh, yeah. I heard of that," says Henry. "They crazy over there. I think some of 'em worship rats too."

"I never heard about that," says Norman.

"It's true," says Tito.

Slowing the car, Norman turns into a private road. Up ahead, a high fence and a locked gate, with a sign: "PRIVATE PROPERTY." Henry gets out and unlocks the gate, swinging it open to let them pass.   Once the minivan is through, Henry relocks the gate and gets back in the van.

"Can you believe this weather?" says Norman.

"Unbelievable," says Henry.

"I can believe it," says Tito.

"Oh, yeah?" says Norman.

"Yes, sir," says Tito.

"Of course he can believe it," says Henry. "Motherfucker's from Panama. No such thing as winter in Panama. Am I right or am I right?"

"You are right," says Tito.

The road is unpaved but smooth and level, the tires moving slowly, crunching the loose gravel beneath them. On either side, an orchard of leafless trees, their skeleton limbs pointing fingers in all directions.

"Where are we?" asks Vincent.

"We've just entered Camp Hero," says Henry.   "It used to be called 'Fort Hero' after General Andrew Hero back in 1929.   But then, during World War II, they renamed it Camp Hero.

"Is that so?" asks Tito.

"Yes," says Henry. "This entire area, over three hundred acres, was set up to fight off a German invasion with 16-inch guns inside reinforced concrete bunkers facing the sea. During the Second World War, the entire base here was done up to look like a New England fishing village. The bunkers had windows and doors painted on them with ornamental roofs and fake chimneys."

"Why would they bother to do that?" asks Vincent

"Nazi spies," says Henry.

"Fascinating," declares Tito.

"That ain't nothin'," says Henry. "It was during the Cold War when things really started getting weird."

"Bunch of balony," mutters Norman.

"Check that out," says Henry pointing to a gigantic radar dish. "Norm, stop the car."

As Norman puts the van into "Park," they all gaze out the windows at the radar dish.

"The reflector is forty yards long and weighs over forty tons," says Henry.

"What's it for?" asks Vincent.

"It ain't for nuthin' now," says Norman. "Just a big hunk a junk."

"They say it was once so powerful that it disrupted local TV and radio broadcasts," says Henry.

"Undoubtably to search the sky for Soviet bombers," adds Tito.

"That was the claim," says Henry. "But some people think it was much more than that."

"Fairytales," says Norman.

"Why must you always be so negative?" says Henry.

"I'm not negative," says Norman. "I just don't believe in it. That's all."

"The Romans didn't believe in Jesus either," says Henry. "And look where it got them."

"What are you talking about?" says Vincent.

Henry looks at Norman. Norman says, "Go on. Tell them. But don't get mad at me when they laugh at you."

"I will not laugh," says Tito.

"Thank you, Tito," says Henry. "Norm, we better get rollin' again. I don't think it's wise to tarry here too long."

As Norman drives the van forward, Henry continues, "The Montauk Project is believed to be an extension of the Philadelphia Experiment. Have either of you ever heard of the Philadelphia Experiment?"

"Not me," says Vincent.

"Nor I," says Tito.

Norman sniggers. Ignoring him, Henry says, "During World War II, in an attempt to make our ships undetectable to radar, an experiment was carried out in the Philadelphia navy yard on the USS Eldridge. But instead of making it invisible to radar, they ended up making it completely invisible by removing the entire ship from time and space."

"A porthole to the next dimension," says Tito.

"Exactly," says Henry. "But the crew? The sailors that returned to our dimension? They say they all went crazy. Completely lost their minds."

"The stress of time travel," says Tito.

"The Montauk Project is believed to be an extension of the Philadelphia Experiment. Working with super concentrated magnetic fields, the scientists sought to develop a new weapon that could drive an enemy insane."

"I can see it," says Tito.

"So what happened?" asks Vincent. "Where is everybody?"

"They shut it down," says Henry.

"How come?" asks Vincent.

"Nobody knows for sure. But there were rumors that they were using homeless people as guinee pigs."

"Did they not pay them?" asks Tito.

"I don't know, Tito. All I know is that the whole operation shut down or maybe went underground. Apparently, there's twelve levels of laboratories beneath the surface."

"We're here," says Norman, pulling into a parking lot already filled with cars and vans and trucks and trailers and a variety of mobile homes of various sizes and expense.

"It you're interested," says Henry. "I'll introduce you to Floyd Hunter. He once met a guy who escaped from the Montauk Project."

"I would be very interested to meet this Floyd," says Tito.

"Consider it done," says Henry.

"C'mon, let's go," says Norman. "It's showtime."

A fat man wearing an orange plastic poncho sits in a lawn chair, a shotgun across his knees. The fat man waves to Norman and Henry. They wave back at him. As Vincent and Tito climb out, Norman retrieves a pair of AK-47's from the back of the van, handing one to Henry.

They head across the parking lot onto a footpath, single file, with Norman in front followed by Tito, Vincent and Henry. Vincent wonders if this is anywhere near the lover's bench from last night. The trees look the same and the sound of the ocean is not far away... But there is no way to be sure, coming in from the highway like they did. Vincent remembers the cocktail napkin map. He hopes Desiree hasn't thrown it out. It might be nice to check out that bench in the daytime, maybe tomorrow, before they head back to the city.

Up ahead, Vincent can hear the noise of people and the noise of dogs. At the end of the path is second fat man holding a shotgun, also wearing an orange poncho. As they approach, he stands up to check each of their pins, making an "X" mark on a clipboard as they pass into the Circuit proper.

CHAPTER TWENTY-FIVE

There's a carnival-like atmosphere. People are glad-handing, slapping shoulders, smoking cigars and drinking glasses of whiskey and beer. No women but a handful of little boys, some of them young enough to play in a makeshift sandbox adjacent to the bar. On the other side of the bar is a booth offering hot dogs, hamburgers and philly steak sandwiches. In the center of the yard is the pit area, surrounded by two tiers of bleachers and protected from the possibility of rain by a red, white and blue striped tent top. Dashing through the crowd, one boy chases another into the pit where they wrestle and play fight. But this does not last long. This is not permitted. The boys are yanked out and rebuked with unkind words and hard pinches. Across the yard from the bar is a two-story bunker made of concrete. Near its top, two six by six foot openings face the sea. Across its bottom is a crudely painted frown, giving it an appearance of something vaguely Easter Islandish, an angry square head sprouting up from the earth. Vincent takes note of Norman, who has stationed himself in the left eye, AK-47 in hand, keeping careful watch on all the proceedings below. In the right eye hangs a shiny metal pail dangling from a pulley wheel as if it were at the top of a well. Henry has taken a spot by the side of the bar, his weapon slung over his shoulder while he sips club soda. In addition to Norman, Henry and the fat men in the orange ponchos, there are three blatantly armed Mexicans on guard at points of the perimeter.

For Vincent, the smell of booze in the air is a double-edged sword, a painful reminder of but also a promise of relief from the throbbing hangover waxing stronger by the minute. Once at the bar, Vincent is pleasantly surprised to see Bert, the chameleon eyed bartender from the Memory

Motel. Bellying up to the rail, Vincent nods at Henry and smiles at Bert.

"Well, hello," says Bert. "What'll be?"

"Hi," says Vincent. "How 'bout a shot of bourbon and a beer chaser?"

Bert draws a pint from the tap followed by a three-fingered shot of whiskey.

"Thanks," says Vincent. "And thanks for those directions last night. Your map was perfect."

"I wasn't sure if you two were gonna make it. You were pretty lit up."

"That we were," says Vincent, downing his shot, the hair of the dog searing and soothing his ripping hangover almost immediately. "That hit the spot." Vincent drinks from his beer. It is ice cold and delicious. He feels like a new man. "What do I owe you?"

"Nothing," says Bert. "It's an open bar. Grubs free too."

"You don't say," says Vincent, laying a five down for a tip.

"Thank you, sir," says Bert.

Vincent swivels on the barstool. He points a thumb at the Easter Island head. "So, what's that thing?"

"Army put it up during World War II. Used to have sixteen inch guns trained to the sea."

"Big guns, huh?"

"Yep. Kraut subs and V-Boats were all up and down the North Atlantic."

"So I've heard," he says, glancing over at Henry who gives him a one-fingered salute. "And what's all that stuff over there?"

"You must be new to all this."

"That I am," says Vincent.

"That there's the weigh and wash," says Bert. "That's where they weigh and wash the dogs before they roll."

"I get the weighing part," says Vincent. "But I don't get the wash. Why they gotta do that? Clean dogs fight better than dirty ones?"

"It's for foreign substances."

"I don't get you."

"I bet this is your very first time to a dog fight."

"That's right."

"Unfortunately, without the wash, you'll find all sorts of villains looking to get an advantage by rubbing in all kinds of toxic substances into their dogs. Flea powder, bug spray, liniments, you name it."

"Into their own dogs?"

"Yep. So when your dog bites 'em, he gets a mouth full of it."

"Oh!"

"Round here, we follow the Cajun Rules to the letter," says Bert, reaching for a pile of photocopied pamphlets. "Here."

After skimming the first page, Vincent puts the pamphlet back on the bar. He finishes his pint. Bert refills both glasses with whiskey and beer. Vincent feels a hand on his shoulder. He swivels, "Tyrone!"

"You made it," says Tyrone.

"Of course I did," says Vincent. "I told you I'd be here."

"I'm gonna be the first match of the day!"

"That's great. But where's your dog?"

"She comin'. She with Antoine and Rosco."

"Antoine? Doesn't he have practice?"

"He off for the whole week. He not allowed to practice 'cause of Regents tests. Nobody allowed to practice or scrimmage or they forfeit the season. Look, here they come now."

"Who's that other guy?"

"His name Munch. Jesse Munch. He real famous all along the Circuit."

"Your dog get washed yet?"

Tyrone tilts his head, smiles, "What you know about that?"

"I know a little something," says Vincent.

"I'll bet you do. Look, there they go now."

Coming around from behind the bunker is Rosco and a taller, white man with long, yellow hair—Jesse Munch, the Breeder. Following them is Antoine who has Tnuc on a short chain leash. Tito is also on the scene, checking out and adjusting the scale that hangs from the steel arm attached to a wood post set in concrete.

"Hey, I know that guy," says Vincent. "I rode up here with him."

"He's the referee," says Tyrone. "They say he's real good."

"The best," says Bert. "Tito is the best money can buy."

Tnuc's opponent, Sassy, is led to the scale by none other than the owner of the Seaside Motel.

"What up?" says Tyrone.

"Watch out for that motherfucker," says Vincent.

"Don't you worry. Tnuc's gonna eat her alive."

"I'm not talking about the dog. I'm talking about that ZZ-Top looking son of a bitch. I ran in to him yesterday. He's a real asshole."

"His name is McDonald," says Tyrone. "Jerry or Johnny or Jimmy McDonald. I can't remember his first name 'cause I be thinking Ronald McDonald. You know, like the clown?"

"He's a clown alright."

"He's the second. See that other guy over there? The older guy with the grey hair?"

"Yeah," says Vincent. "I seen him before too. Last night at the bar."

"Well, he the owner. His name is Seamus Doherty. And a very polite individual."

"The Nazis could be polite when they wanted, too."

Sassy is a black dog with ears chewed down to the size of corncobs. Her head and neck are covered with speckled scars looking like a tattoo of the Milky Way Galaxy.

"That's one game dog," says Bert.

"Is that right?" says Tyrone.

"You bet," says Bert. "Lost once when she was little more than a pup and never lost in twelve fights since. She a bottom dog, likes to break the legs."

"My Tnuc's a head dog," says Tyrone, proudly. "And I do believe she be keeping her legs today."

"Talk is cheap," says Bert.

"True dat," says Tyrone.

Sassy wags her tail as McDonald puts her in the sling of the hanging scale. Tito directs McDonald to stand away. Tito reads the weight and calls out, "Forty-two and one half!" Tito points a finger at McDonald who steps in to retrieve Sassy from the scale.

Next up is Tnuc who is put into the scale by Antoine. Tnuc weighs an even forty. Jesse Munch puts on a pair of Woody Allen glasses and examines the scale. He runs his hand through his hair and shrugs at Rosco who nods at Tito.

"What's up?" says Vincent.

"We lighter but we gonna take it no matter what. Tnuc, she ready. She gonna crush that bitch's head into oatmeal."

Antoine hands his leash to McDonald and McDonald does the same with his dog to Antoine. They lead the dogs to the washtubs. Tito stands between the tubs. He flips a coin. Antoine wins the toss. Tito goes over to McDonald. He has McDonald bare his arms to the elbows. Tito nods for McDonald to proceed. McDonald washes Tnuc in the first tub filled with soapy water with Jesse Munch watching every move he makes. After he's done, McDonald leads Tnuc to the second tub to rinse off the soap. After he's through there, Seamus Doherty steps up with a towel and a blanket. Tito examines the towel and blanket and hands them to Antoine who takes Tnuc out of the tub to dry her.

"How come they switched dogs like that?"

"Don't know," says Tyrone.

"You should," says Bert. "To keep the cheat off you, you have to know how the cheat is put on you!"

"Huh?" says Tyrone.

"If he washes his own dog, then it's that much easier for him to put on some kind of a rub. Don't make sense for him to put a rub on your dog if its his dog gonna end up biting it."

"Oh, yeah. I get you. And that's why he gotta use his towels 'cause maybe we could put somethin' on our own towels to rub into our dog."

"Exactly," says Bert. "You learn quick, kid."

"Yes, he does," says Vincent. "An excellent student."

Tyrone smiles.

"I see you got Jesse Munch in your corner," says Bert. "Nobody gonna put nuthin' over him no how. You can learn an awful lot from a man like Munch. He's one of the best."

"He is the best," says Tyrone.

"You may be right. I once saw him catch a guy who hid a rub in the hollow at the bottom of beer can. During the scratch, the handler asked for a drink and his friend handed him the can. The handler got all the rub he needed with that libation. But Munch, he spotted it and called him on it."

"Dag," says Tyrone.

"What happened to the handler?" asks Vincent.

"He never walked right again. Not him, his friend or the dog. And, believe you me, they all got off easy."

After Sassy is washed by Antoine, Rosco hands a towel and a blanket to McDonald. When McDonald is finished drying off his dog, Jesse Munch motions to Tito who nods and points a finger.

"What the hell he doin' now?" asks Vincent.

"Tasting," says Bert.

Jesse Munch is on his hands and knees besides Sassy. He licks and tastes Sassy's neck and shoulders, her hind quarters, legs, paws and ear stumps.

"Munch don't leave nothin' to chance," says Bert.

Finished with his tasting, Munch stands up, spits, and fixes his long yellow hair with a comb procured from his back pocket.

"There's an old saying," says Bert. "'The rub goes on after the wash.' Remember that, son, and always keep a good eye on your opponent's dog at all times. You're not always gonna have a man like Munch lookin' out for you. Hell, I once saw one sonofabitch holding a dog's tail while he was standing between his handler's legs getting counted out! Yep. Anything can happen and will happen if you're not on the look out."

CHAPTER TWENTY-SIX

"ALL BETS IN THE BUCKET!" declares Henry who's standing with his back to the concrete bunker. Holding "The Book" and a pen, his rifle over his shoulder, Henry looks up at Norman, who lowers the pail with a rope and pulley. Norman stops the pail chest high in front of Henry as a line forms to fill it with cash. The odds are even with the early money favoring Sassy because of her record and despite Tnuc's having been bred by Jesse Munch. Vincent watches the betting line from the bar. He's no longer feeling any pain. He is drunk and getting drunker but with enough wits about him to cut the whiskey and stick to beer.

"That's one loaded bucket," says Vincent.

"It sure is," says Bert. "And this is only the first roll."

"How much you think is in there now?"

"Hard to say. Anywhere from twenty to maybe fifty, maybe more."

When the last man on the line places his bet, Henry declares, "Last call! Last chance before the first scratch!" He waits a moment. He motions for Norman to pull up the pail. When the pail gets to the top, Norman removes the contents, sorting out the different denominations and placing them into a strong box on the floor by his feet. Once finished, he calls down to Henry, "Bills in the box!" Henry nods, pocketing the bet book and taking up his rifle. Norman moves back to the right eye, AK-47 in hand, his forefinger pointing just above the trigger.

The yard is buzzing with excitement. Even the dogs are hyped, howling and yapping in tandem with their master's anticipations, hopes and fears. All dogs not crated are on short leashes with some muzzled in heavy black leather, looking like dog world S&M freaks.

In the pit, Tnuc stands between Antoine's legs, wagging her tail. Sassy is between the legs of McDonald, the frayed ends of his beard caressing the galaxy of scars around her head. Each dog's nose is in a direct line above the scratch mark. The bleachers are completely full and people push close to the boards to find every available standing space. Vincent is next to Tyrone who's next to Jesse Munch, in Tnuc's corner. Tyrone holds the breaking stick in his hands, nervously grinding the paddle into the earth between his feet. Across the pit, behind Sassy's corner, Rosco stands next to Seamus Doherty. When Vincent and Rosco momentarily catch eyes, Rosco smiles.

At the center of the pit is Tito, wearing dark pants and a white shirt, his turtlehead riding close to the stiffly starched collar. Tito raises both hands for quiet. All present immediately comply.

"In this corner, hailing from Munch's Ramapo Mountain Kennels and weighing an even forty pounds, we have, Tnuc, on her first ever roll in this here Circuit!"

A round of applause is followed by Tito's up-stretched hands and silence.

"And in the opposite corner, with a record of eight and one, weighing forty-one and one half pounds, we have Sassy, hailing from the Doherty Kennels of Montauk!"

There is more applause, much louder from the hometown crowd.

Tito raises his hands for quiet. He looks to Antoine, "Ready?" Antoine nods. Tito looks to McDonald, "Ready?"

"Hell yes!"

"Gentlemen," says Tito. "Let 'em roll!"

In lightning spurts of fury and focus, the two dogs fly from between their handler's legs, their massive heads colliding at the center of the pit. The crowd laughs and cheers, stomping their feet. Both McDonald and Antoine are instantly hauled out and over the boards by a host of hands as Tito scrambles and flits to keep out of the path of the combatants. Right from the start, everybody knows that this is going to be a fight to remember. Even the other dogs sense this, barking and howling as if the world was about to end and despite the fact that they can see none of it.

Tnuc and Sassy are up on their hind legs now, jaws searching and snapping to lock onto the meat of the other.

"I thought their bitch was supposed to be a bottom dog," says Tyrone.

"It is," says Munch. "She's just feeling her way round first, lookin' for a weakness, maybe hopin' for an early turn."

"Tnuc ain't no cur," says Tyrone.

"I know it. We know it. But that black bitch there, she don't know it."

"She gonna learn real quick," says Tyrone.

"Maybe," says Munch. "But I can tell you right now, that bitch is all game. I don't see no turning in her neither."

"Oh, shit!" shouts Tyrone.

Sassy has a lock on Tnuc's nose. Blood spurts and sprays the sideboards. Men at the rail instinctively jump back as Tnuck twirls and bangs Sassy against the boards in a futile attempt to shake the lock on her snout.

"Looks worse than it is," says Munch.

"That's a lot of blood," says Tyrone.

"You ever get punched in the nose?"

"Yeah."

"Was there a lot of blood?"

"Yeah."

"Did you die?"

Calls for a scratch come from the crowd as the fight seems to stagnate. Tyrone looks to Munch. Munch says, "No need for a scratch. We alright. What I want you to do is go over 'round the other side so Tnuc can see you. And then I want ya to start screamin' her name. You got that?"

"Uh-huh."

"And if the roll takes her in other directions, I want you to keep yourself positioned in her line of sight. Just keep doin' it until that lock is broke."

Tyrone does exactly as he's told. Like magic, Tnuc charges in the direction of her screaming master, smashing Sassy into the boards and loosening the lock on her nose. Without a yelp, Tnuc twists herself free, in turn biting hard and deep into Sassy's shoulder. But Sassy doesn't yelp, doesn't turn, either. Sassy just takes the pain and drops and rolls and clamps on Tnuc's front leg.

"That don't look good," says Munch.

Sassy bites hard... The sound of a fibia cracking...

Despite the fracture, Tnuc does not turn. With redoubled fury, Tnuc snaps up along the shoulder to lock hard on an ear stump, sending her canines deep through gristle and meat.

Tito looks back and forth at Doherty and Tyrone. Munch tells Tyrone that now might be a good time for a scratch. Tyrone motions for the scratch and Doherty readily concurs. Tito allows the handlers and their seconds into the pit, the men quickly working their breaking sticks in-between teeth, slowly turning the paddles to unlock the jaws and pulling their dogs to neutral corners.

During the scratch the bucket drops and the betting is furious, with the heavy money dropping hard in favor of Sassy. Many who are not betting or running to the bar are crowding the two corners to get a look at the two dogs being feverishly attended to by their owners.

Tyrone has the medical bag wide open for Jesse Munch. Like a battlefield medic, Munch works deliberately and surely without emotion or loss of focus.

"Is it bad?" asks Tyrone.

"It's bad," says Munch. "Bone's fractured."

"What we gonna do?"

"Let's hope they quit first. Her shoulder looked pretty tore up."

"And what if they don't quit?"

"Then I suggest you quit."

"Quit? This is only her first real fight!"

"And it may be her last. But if you quit now, you can still breed her. This is one game dog, no doubt about that."

Tito breaks through the crowd. He says, "Two minutes."

Munch nods. He stands and looks at the other corner. They have already finished working on Sassy and are placing her back in the pit. With Sassy between his legs, McDonald forces a bold looking grin.

"What you wanna do?" says Munch. "It's your decision. She's your dog."

Before Tyrone can answer, Rosco says, "Rum fought and won and was a lot worse off than this bitch."

"True dat," says Tyrone.

"Hand me the thermometer," says Munch.

Tyrone takes the thermometer out of the medical bag. He hands it to Munch who promptly sticks it up Tnuc's asshole.

"If it goes much over 101.5," says Munch. "She'll go into shock and it won't matter how game the bitch is and you'll lose everything."

Tito returns, "Thirty seconds."

Munch pulls the thermometer, holding it to the sky to better read the numbers.

"What it say?" says Tyrone.

"You okay temperature wise," says Munch. "But I still suggest you quit now and breed her. No tellin' what kinda brood we can get outta a dog like this."

"Let her roll," says Rosco.

Munch makes a washing motion with his hands. "Alright then," he says. "It's on you."

Rosco and Tyrone hand Tnuc over to Antoine in the pit. Tito has to hold his hands up for long seconds before the frenzy of the crowd is abated enough to allow the handlers to hear the call.

"Gentleman, let 'em roll!"

Just like her granddad, Redrum, Tnuc barely moves across the scratch line before stopping and putting the broken leg forward. Going straight for this offering, Sassy hits that leg hard, gnashing and tearing at the bone like a greedy hyena. Without a whimper or bark, Tnuc endures this onslaught as if she's seemingly detached from the mayhem being loosed by the thrashing head. Then, as calmly as if she were bending to sip water, Tnuc lowers her head before suddenly striking with the precision of a rattlesnake. With her lower jaw on Sassy's right ear stub and her upper jaw at the center of Sassy's head, Tnuc sinks her canines deep and thoroughly into Sassy's skull with a horrible crunching sound that sends ribbons of blood running from ears, eyes, nose and mouth. With an extra shake to be sure, Tnuc tosses the carcass off to the boards, Sassy's legs and tail madly twitching and then still. With her front paw an inch or so off the earth, Tnuc stands on three legs, her tail wagging at the sight of Tyrone entering the pit.

CHAPTER TWENTY-SEVEN

Two local boys remove Sassy from the pit. They grimace while handling the dog, the fur saturated with drool and blood. Like grizzled veterans, Tyrone and Antoine exchange knowing glances: "we're not in the 'hood anymore." Unlike Harlem, the Circuit strives for proper decorum. Dead dogs are not hung from trees or tossed off rooftops. On the Circuit, all carcasses are either returned to their masters or buried in a communal hole.

Not far from the bar, Tnuc is on a folding table in the triage section of the yard. Her wounds have been cleaned and dressed by the deft hands of Jesse Munch, who has just finished injecting her with Azium and antibiotics to prevent shock and infection. In addition to his medical ministrations, Munch has been holding an impromptu dogfighting clinic, the gaggle of the hometown fans in awe and open admiration of his extensive knowledge and wisdom.

"Always have two," states Munch, removing the thermometer. "One for backup and one in the ass at all times, making sure to check it every few minutes. A dog's body temperature should be below 101.56 to keep 'em from goin' into shock."

As the fans murmur and nod, an older man addresses Munch: "At first I thought your bitch was gonna be a hard scratcher. But she turned out just the opposite. And she won. I don't recall seeing a slow scratcher beat such a hard scratcher like Sassy. Don't usually hard scratchers beat slow scratchers?"

"That's a very good question," says Munch.

The old man grins.

"In most cases, yes, a hard scratching dog has the advantage. First off, the hard scratcher is gonna wear down his opponent by hittin' him twice: the first impact outta the scratch and then a second wack when he hits the boards.

But, if your slow scratcher is not a cur, if she's all game like this bitch here, they often have a way of assessing their opponent and planning a strategy before any contact is even made.   You all saw that today.   Sometimes, you have to sacrifice a leg to save the body, to win the match."

"You mean she gonna lose her leg?" asks Tyrone.

"Did I say that?" says Munch, standing up straight, running his hands through his yellow hair. "Did I say that?"

The hometown fans frown at Tyrone. Tyrone shrugs.

Munch puts a hand on Tyrone's shoulder, "Don't worry, son, your bitch is gonna keep that leg. Of course, whether or not she's able to fight again—only time will tell. Gotta see how the bone sets after the cast comes off."

Bellying up to the bar, Vincent motions to Bert who sets him up with an ice cold pint of beer.   When Vincent reaches into his pack of Marlboros, he notices the funny cigarette. Now how did that get there? Desiree. She must have secretly placed it for him as a surprise. Vincent believes he is falling in love with her.   Downing his beer, Vincent decides that now is a most excellent time to enjoy such a thoughtful gift of smoke.

Feeling like a secret agent man, Vincent discretely slips away from the festivities, past the fat man in the orange poncho, across the lot, and along a narrow path leading to nowhere he knows. Not a few minutes later, without sight or sound of anything breathing, Vincent lights up the joint. He inhales deeply, blowing smoke up into the naked and gnarly limbs boughering about his head. He smiles, thinking about how earnest Head & Shoulders was to believe in Henry's story about the Montauk Project.   People will believe just about anything if that's what they desire to do.   Faith is never really blind because it always requires the focus of its desire.   Doesn't matter if it's God or the Devil or Space Invaders or the love of a loved one...

As usual, the weed is potent and Vincent's mouth has turned to glue. Another ice cold beer is most definitely in order.   Vincent heads back towards the Circuit on a stoned level of awareness, taking careful notice of the brush and the tangled branches, the sandy path and the blades of grasses and weeds struggling for light and space. Like the guy in Kung Fu, he feels "one with nature," and laughs at the memory of himself believing that was the coolest show of all time.

Passing by the fat man, Vincent is suddenly hurdled into a merciless present. His mind races. Either he is the focus of an elaborate and most unlikely prank or he's face to face with a very unpleasant and thoroughly threatening reality.

The fat man is dead. A gaping hole has completely obliterated his nose and right cheek. Thick, syrupy blood oozes along his face and neck and down the orange plastic poncho. The primordial fight or flight reflex kicks in. But there doesn't appear to be anybody around to fight or run away from.

A voice cries out from the wilderness: "BE STILL OR BE DEAD!" It is an amplified voice, a bullhorn voice. A voice Vincent will be sure to obey. Without turning his head, Vincent casts his gaze into the yard. He sees Antoine and then Rosco. Rosco has Cremator on a short leash. The dog is sitting and appears to be calm and in control. Over by the triage table, where Tnuc has been hooked up to an IV bag, Tyrone stands beside his dog. Standing next to Tyrone, Jesse Munch has a red dot in the center of his forehead. Jesse Munch is not the only human with a red dot. It seems that a series of red dots have alighted on various foreheads in the crowd. The red dots linger a moment and then haphazardly move about before landing on somebody else's forehead.

Vincent sees the body of Norman. He is bent over at the waist, his arms dangling down from the right eye of the bunker. There is a hole in the back of his head, his blood staining the cement in a dark cascade running into the frown at the base of the bunker. Norman's rifle lies on the ground where it fell from his hands after he was shot in the face. Norman's quick execution has made a powerful point on all those in attendance. Not far from Norman's rifle is the prostrate body of Henry. Face down, he still clutches his rifle above his head, a soupy pool of blood seeping into the earth on either side of his rib cage.

"BE STILL OR BE DEAD!"

"We hear you," shouts Jesse Munch. "Just tell us what you want and we'll do it."

"SHUT THE FUCK UP!"

The red dots continue to dart from one forehead to the next. Like most everybody else, Vincent has quickly figured out that these are the laser sights of anonymous marksmen. He sees a red dot flit and linger and flit from Rosco's head.

"NOW PAY CAREFULL ATTENTION! FOLLOW DIRECTIONS AND YOU WILL LIVE. MAKE A MISTAKE AND YOU DIE."

Vincent is determined to follow directions.

"IF YOU ARE ARMED, SLOWLY TAKE OUT YOUR WEAPON AND CAREFULLY LAY IT ON THE GROUND. PLACE ALL GUNS, KNIVES, RAZORS ON THE GROUND AT YOUR FEET. PUT ALL YOUR WEAPONS ON THE GROUND. DO THIS! DO IT NOW!"

A good number of the dogmen lay down pistols, knives, razors and black jacks.

"ALL DOGS NOT IN A CRATE MUST BE PUT ON A LEASH. DO IT NOW!"

Except for Tnuc, all of the dogs are in crates or on a leash already. Tnuc is still on the triage table with an IV tube running into his hind leg.

"ALL THOSE WITH DOGS ON LEASHES WILL PROCEED TO THE WALL AND STAND THERE WITH YOUR DOG."

"My dog's hurt," shouts Tyrone.

A red dot immediately appears on Tyrone's head.

"Just be cool," says Jesse Munch.

"YOU TWO BY THE TABLE, STEP AWAY FROM THE DOG."

Tyrone and Jesse Munch step back from the table. The red dot flits to Tnuc's ear followed by the percussion of concentrated air, the "PHHT" of a silenced shot: a bullet to Tnuc's brain. Tnuc drops her head. Her bowels empty. Tyrone cries out.

"NIGGER, BE STILL OR BE DEAD!"

Tyrone's eyes bulge with sorrow and hate and despite himself, the tears flow down his face like blood from an open wound.

"EVERYBODY WILL NOW STRIP! STRIP OFF ALL YOUR CLOTHES! EVERYTHING OFF. SOCKS AND SHOES TOO. DO IT NOW OR DIE."

Like everybody else, Vincent is numb with shock and fear. But unlike most everybody else, he is completely stoned, giving the current proceedings all the dread and wallop of a lucid nightmare.

"PUT ALL CLOTHING IN A PILE AT YOUR FEET. PUT WALLETS, MONEY CLIPS, WATCHES, CHAINS, RINGS, JEWELRY AND EVERYTHING ELSE OF VALUE IN A SECOND PILE AT YOUR FEET. DO IT FAST. DO IT OR DIE."

Seeing everybody naked, Vincent is reminded of the images of the concentration camps. He entertains the notion that he will soon be dead, that he is going to die today. He wonders if it might be better to revolt, to somehow try and fight this unseen enemy...

"EVERYBODY WITHOUT A DOG, SLOWLY WALK AWAY FROM YOUR BELONGINGS AND INTO THE PIT. GO TO THE PIT, NOW!"

Vincent joins the others inside the pit. Doing his best to make as little bodily contact as possible, he is both repulsed and secretly fascinated by the unlovely human nakedness. He also can't help himself from glancing at the horde of dicks all about him. Never in his life has he seen so many dicks. Never did he know how different they can appear from one another. As different as different faces can be...

Vincent takes notice of a young boy standing with his father, the father holding his boy by the shoulders. The varied forms of fear displayed by father and son are terrible to behold.

"BE STILL OR BE DEAD!"

Vincent notices that the red dots have alighted on four of the leashed dogs by the bunker wall. An instant later, the four dogs fall immediately followed by the other three dogs lined up beside them. Vincent calculates that there are only four shooters. All seven naked owners still hold the leashes of their dead dogs. One guy is wet with his own piss. Rosco is smiling and his grin is one of the scariest things Vincent has ever seen.

"ALL OF YOU BY THE WALL, STEP AWAY FROM YOUR DOGS AND GO TO THE PIT!"

Six of the seven move immediately. A red dot is trained on Rosco's brain.

"SOMETHING FUNNY, NIGGER?"

Still grinning, Rosco shakes his head and proceeds to the pit.

"BE STILL OR BE DEAD!"

"They gonna kill us all," somebody whispers.

"There's only four of 'em," whispers Vincent. "We can all rush them once they show themselves. They can't get all of us."

"Everybody just be cool," hisses Rosco. "All they want is the money. Otherwise we'd be dead already."

This last point seems to make sense since everybody has a good idea at the size of the treasure up in the bunker, not counting the rest of the loot laying out in the yard. Like an evil minded Tinkerbell, the red dots relentlessly race from one head to the next, reminding them all that death is very near. Out of fear and nervousness, somebody farts. But from it, no mirth is born. Everybody present is solely concentrated on survival.

Emerging from the brush they finally appear. Vincent is correct. There are only four of them. They are all extremely tall and, except for their boots and black gloves, they are all white—cloaked in the robes of the Klu Klux Klan. Their pointy hoods make them look even taller. Four white robed giants of the apocalypse. In their arms they carry long rifles with laser sights.

"Oh, shit," hisses Antoine. "It's the fucking Klan. We's fucked now for sure."

Each of the Klansmen takes a position facing the people in the pit. The shortest member who has to be well over six feet himself, speaks to them, only now without his bullhorn. "Be still or be dead," he says. It is a melodious voice. A voice that could easily be a lead tenor in the church choir. He nods to his henchmen before turning to the piles of clothing and valuables. As he does this, Tyrone is suddenly up and over the boards, a being full of fury and focus.

Tyrone doesn't make more than three yards before he is cut down by the, "PHHT, PHHT, PHHT," of the KKK's silenced long guns. The speaker, who has since turned back around, approaches Tyrone. He pokes a steel tipped boot under Tyrone's lifeless chin.

"You poor dumb nigger," he says. "You people just don't know how to listen, do you?" He looks up from Tyrone, his disembodied eyeballs more frightening than any red dot. "Now, the rest of you take notice. Be still, or be dead."

Carefully, but rapidly, the speaker goes through all the clothing, shaking each garment to see if anybody forgot to remove a wallet or cash. Nobody forgot. He then drops the wallets, cash, watches, rings and chains into a black plastic trash bag. He carries the bag back over to one of his henchmen before heading to the bunker.

He shoots open the locked door of the bunker. He heads up the stairs for the cash box. When he emerges from the bunker, he holds the box aloft for his confederates to see. This is his last move of the day. A shot rings out. It is a loud shot without the benefit of a silencer. The aim is true. The speaker falls and is dead.

Immediately following the first shot, another shot cuts down the tallest of the Klansmen, a flower burst of crimson staining the bright white of his hood.

The KKK is clearly the subject of an ambush, its two living members hitting the dirt, desperately seeking cover.

Vincent thinks to run, to run while the Klan is still pinned down. He sees Antoine a few feet away, eyes bulging and full of fear. He grabs Antoine by the arm. "C'mon," he says. "Let's get the fuck outta here!" This idea proves contagious. In the next few seconds, all the naked bodies go into motion, hopping the boards and fleeing in all directions.

As Vincent and Antoine race across the yard, Antoine cries out, stumbles, and falls. He holds his kneecap and screams. Vincent looks for blood, thinking he's been shot. But Antoine is not shot. He has caught and twisted his leg in a rabbit hole. The ball of his knee has been violently shorn sideways, the cartilage ripped, the pain extreme. More shots follow.

Not many seconds later, all the Klansmen are dead. Two men dressed in camouflage outfits appear, each cradling M-16 rifles.

"It's all over," says the one.

The naked people look at the two men, wondering what the hell is going on.

"My name is John," says the one. "And this is my partner, Johnny. It's all over now. You can go and put on your clothes and we'll try and sort this all out."

"Who the hell are you?" says McDonald.

"And you're very welcome, sir," says Johnny. "My partner and me are in the employ of an individual in your company."

"Body guards, huh?"

"So to speak."

Rosco comes over to Vincent and Antoine. "What happen? You hit?"

"I twisted my knee," says Antoine, tears flowing freely down his cheeks.

"Well, at least you not dead like Tyrone," says Rosco.

Tyrone! In all the chaos and fear, Vincent has completely forgot. Tyrone! Vincent goes to his body. The head is pulpy and torn and completely unrecognizable. Vincent looks away in despair while everybody goes about getting dressed in a stupefied daze. Never before has the putting on of shirt and shoes taken on such a significance.

John and Johnny drag the KKK into a heap near the front of the bunker, along with the strong box of cash and the garbage bag full of loot.

After getting dressed, the survivors assemble before John and Johnny. A stout and red-faced man steps forward, introducing himself as Patrick Gleason, Montauk Chief of Police.

"You got one fucking mess on your hands, chief," says John.

"A colossal fucking mess," adds Johnny.

"We all gotta just keep our heads here," says Gleason. "We gotta keep our heads, sort it all out and come up with some kind of a plan."

"Excellent idea," says John.

"A capitol idea," adds Johnny.

"You got any thoughts on the matter?" asks Gleason.

"First off. I think we should unmask these scoundrels in case anybody here might know who they are."

"Good idea," says Gleason.

John pulls off the first hood. Nobody can believe it. Gleason pulls off the three remaining hoods.

"They're all goddamn niggers!" shouts McDonald.

Like everybody else, Vincent crowds in for a better look. They are young darkskinned men, maybe in their mid to late twenties. One wears a doo-rag and another sports a single, tattooed tear below his eyeball. Vincent immediately recalls last night's mission to the beach... Desiree was wrong. Those guys weren't drug dealers. They were these guys. "Jesus Christ." The revelation that seeing is not necessarily knowing, that what he thought he saw last night is actually what he is seeing now, floods his consciousness.

Heads twist and crane as speculations and calculations disperse through the throng like a gargantuan sneeze. Suddenly, it is Vincent along with Rosco and Antoine, who is the collective focus of hard stares and not so secret accusations.

McDonald starts in first, pointing a finger directly at Vincent, "It's that fucking Jew right there. The kike tried to rent a room from me yesterday. He was acting all strange about it too."

"I'm not a fucking Jew, you racist shithead."

"Maybe you are and maybe you're not. But whatever you are, you're a motherfuckin' nigger lover who's part of this nigger gang here. He had a nigger girl with him in the car. Thought I didn't see that, did ya, ya Jew bastard."

Smiling, Rosco approaches McDonald, "Are you implying that myself or my friends here are part of this robbery?"

"Get away from me, nigger," says McDonald, turning to John and Johnny. "I say we string 'em up right here and now."

"Wait a fucking minute," says Gleason. "We don't have any evidence, any proof that they—"

"I got all the motherfucking proof I need. Just look at that fucking black bastard. He fucking can't keep the grin off his big nigger lips. He's been goddamn smiling ever since this whole thing started."

Rosco makes a step to McDonald but is stopped by John who places a hand on Rosco's shoulder. Approaching McDonald, Johnny says, "I'd prefer you to be quiet, sir."

"Fuck you," says McDonald. "Who the fuck you think you are anyhow?"

Johnny grabs a hand full of McDonald's foot long beard. Twisting the hairs up about his fist, he punches the nose with his free hand. As the nose pisses blood, John gives him a swift kick in the ass that sends him sprawling forward, face first into the dirt. Johnny steps over, putting the heel of his boot into McDonald's neck. "Like I said, sir, I'd prefer you to be quiet. Am I understood?"

McDonald nods his head while trying not to gag on his own blood. Johnny removes his heel. He jerks McDonald up by the hair of his head to a sitting position. He takes out a white handkerchief, handing it to him.

McDonald applies the hankie to his nose and remains sitting without further ado.

Johnny speaks: "The way I see it, you all were set up by one of your own. Most probably it's somebody right here, right now."

The crowd casts furtive and awkward glances, wondering and formulating likely and unlikely suspects.

"But it's not these boys here," says John, gesturing to Vincent and company.

"How can you be so sure?" says Gleason.

"Because we work for him," says John, gesturing to Rosco who continues to smile. "If it wasn't for him hiring us, you would all be dead right now... It's a strange world we live in, isn't it?"

"It sure is," says Johnny.

"So, whoever it is, it's most likely somebody from around here. A local," says John.

"You got any ideas?" asks Gleason.

"I gotta hunch," says Johnny.

"Go on," says Gleason.

"The way I see it, is that they were planning to kill you all."

"No doubt about that," adds John.

"And as soon as they got together all the money and loot, that's when they were gonna let you have it," says Johnny.

"That's when we figured we had to step in," says John.

"Why didn't they just kill us from the start," says Gleason. "Why wait?"

"Easier to get you to cooperate. Also easier to kill you quick while you were all in one spot. Otherwise, they start shootin' early and they got you all runnin' in all different directions and no tellin' how many of you would get away."

"With all of you corralled in the pit and dead together, they'd have plenty of time for a clean getaway," says John.

"I saw that Jew fella leave and come back right when all the shootin' first started," says Tito.

"Fuck you, turtlehead," says Vincent.

"He went off to smoke marijuana," says Johnny. "There was no more to it then that."

"My apologies," says Tito.

"If I can continue," says Johnny. "Thank you. Alright. So, the first thing on their agenda was to take out all your gunmen before anybody had any idea of what was about to go down. The fat men and the Mexicans went first. Then, they took out your inside muscle, the guy up in that window there and this guy over here on the ground. The thing of it is... The thing I find so peculiar is the fact that they all were cut down with a head shot. All of them except this one here who was apparently shot in the chest."

"That be, Henry," says Gleason. "He was a good man."

"The best," says a man with a mullethead hairdo. "God rest his soul."

"Is that so?" asks Johnny. "But that doesn't change the fact that he wasn't shot in the head, does it?"

"Head, chest—what difference does it make?"

John points his rifle, firing a round an inch away from the ear of the fallen Henry.

"What the hell you doin', mister?"

"That was a warning shot," says John. "The next one's going into the back of your brain. Now move your hands away from your weapon and turn around. Of course, if you're dead and you really can't hear me, I guess you won't mind me putting this slug into your skull just to be sure. You got two seconds..."

Henry moves his hands from his rifle. He turns around and sits up with his head down. He does not speak any words.

With the exception of John and Johnny, the small community stares at him in awe, completely flabbergasted at his treachery.

"This is your man," says John. "He's the one who set you all up. All he had to do was lay low, let these bastards do the dirty work, and then collect his share after you were all dead."

Johnny pulls out a large switchblade. He bends down, grabbing Henry by the hair. The blade shines as it passes quickly near his neck. But Johnny does not cut any meat. He slices through the front of Henry's jacket and shirt to reveal two plastic pouches, deflated of their bloody contents. Johnny rips the pouches away from Henry's body, tossing them on the ground. Vincent has seen pouches like that before in the theater when a character needed to be shot or stabbed.

"So what do we do now?" asks Gleason.

"That's the million dollar question," says Johnny.

"We should string up the son of a bitch and burn him alive," shouts the mullethead.

"Damn straight!"

"Cut his balls off first!"

"Make him eat his balls!"

"Scalp the bastard!"

"Cut out his guts like they did in 'Braveheart.'"

"Let's let the dogs go at him first, then cut off his balls, and then cut out his guts, and then string him up!"

"Gentlemen. Excuse me, gentlemen! Can I have a point of order here?" says John.

"Go ahead," says Gleason. "Everybody just shut the fuck up and let the man speak."

"Thank you. Of course, for the most part, my job is done here. My man is safe. We did what we had to do."

"You sure the fuck did," says Tito.

"Thank you, sir. Now, all of you, unlike me and Johnny here, have some other considerations, other possibilities to entertain. Namely, what do you do with the eleven dead bodies?"

"Eleven?"

"Yes. The two fat guys, the three Mexicans, the guy up in the window, the young black kid over there and these four in the Halloween costumes. That makes eleven, doesn't it?"

"Eleven, exactly," says Johnny. "But if you all decide to string this one up, well then, that makes an even dozen."

"The way I see it," says John. "You got two basic choices. The first choice is to come clean. We call in the state police. We answer all their questions. Let them sort it all out. For the most part, I'd say most if not all of you won't do any jail time."

"Jail time? What do you mean? We didn't do nuthin' wrong."

"Is that not a fighting pit over there? A pit used to fight dogs? Don't you all do some betting on the outcome of such fights?"

"That choice is out of the question," says Gleason. "I'm the fucking chief of police! Ritzo here is a scoutmaster. Christensen over there is the CEO of the Montauk Bank. Lewis is the head of the Suffolk County Municipal Association. And Floyd, Floyd Hunter, is the Superintendent of Schools! Not to mention all the out of town men, all respected members of their communities as well. Something like this could ruin us."

"You've got a point," says John. "As a former officer of the law, I clearly see your predicament."

"What's the other choice then?"

"You let us take care of it."

"Come again."

"You let me and Johnny clean up the mess. You all, right here, right now, take your dogs and go. After which, you keep everything that happened here today to yourselves. As long as you all agree to keep quiet about this, nobody else can do a thing to you."

"And, even if one of you is one day so stupid as to run your mouth," adds Johnny. "It won't mean much because there won't ever be no bodies to back it up."

"What about him?" asks Jesse Munch, pointing at Henry.

"We can take care of him too. We can make sure he is not a variable once you all agree to our terms and are no longer here to bear witness."

"And your terms?" asks Gleason.

"The cash box and the cash in the trash bag. All your personal items, you can keep."

"What? Do you realize how much that is?"

"I've got a pretty good idea," says John.

"A most handsome sum," says Johnny.

"That's outrageous," says Gleason. "So instead of being robbed by these dead niggers, we end up being robbed by you!"

"I beg your pardon," says Johnny.

"There's gotta be close to a million in that box alone," says Munch.

"Alright, listen up," says John. "A few minutes ago you were all rounded up like cattle for the slaughter and I'll bet every single last one of you bastards would have given up everything that you ever owned to be able to leave this place with not even the clothes on your backs. Think about that... Okay. So now, you're free, thanks to Rosco here. Our job is done. It has been done professionally and within all ramifications of the law. I have no problem turning this fuck here over to the state police and explaining every last one of our actions to them, the FBI, and the national and international media who will descend on this spot like a plague of locusts. I'm sober and clean and completely prepared to do that. To do the so called 'right' thing. That's choice number one. And that's exactly what we're gonna do unless we get properly compensated for choice number two. It's all up to you."

"Door Number One or Door Number Two," says Johnny.

"We'll give you a few minutes to discuss it amongst yourselves."

"It's a fucking shakedown," declares the mullethead.

"Yeah, it is," says Munch. "And I don't like being shook down any more than the next man. But I don't see any other way. I think we all can agree that we don't want no cops or newspaper people all up in this mess. A good number of us have families and assets to protect."

The mullethead speaks, "Why don't we just bury the bodies ourselves? Who says we need these two outsiders? We can do it all ourselves."

"And what about Henry?"

"We can take care of him too!"

"You willing to kill a man like that? Kill him in cold blood?" asks Munch.

"Hell, yes," says the mullethead. "He was gonna do the same to every last one of us!"

"Damn straight!"

"Scalp his ass and burn him!"

"String him up and let the dogs loose on him!"

"Shoot him in the nuts!"

"Hold on! Will you all just shut up a minute now please!" says Munch. "You're all letting your feelings take over your minds. We gotta tackle this conundrum with logic and common fuckin' sense. Just like you, I got a good number of notions that I'd like to employ on this dirtbag. But that's goin' with only my emotions. What am I? A woman? Sure, we can kill this fuck and bury or burn the rest of the bodies. We can do that. But then that makes us all witnesses, all accomplices. And as the days and months go by, all it takes is one drunken one of us to spill the beans to the wrong individual and we're all fucked. Also, you got your blackmail angles too. Those with the least to lose here might one day come lookin' for a pay off from those of us with the most to lose. Me? I say to hell with the money in that box, in that bag. Let them have it."

"He's fucking right," says Gleason. "These guys are professionals."

"But that's an awful lot of money!"

"And it's worth every cent if it pays for us all to go back to our homes and live our lives like nothing the fuck ever happened here."

There is grumbling and clearing of throats. Bert, the bartender, with an armful of whiskey bottles, passes them out among the crowd. Vincent takes a long swig and passes it on to the mullethead.

"So have you made up your minds?" asks Johnny.

"We got no choice, really," says Gleason.

"Any man not agreed to letting these two take care of it?" shouts Munch. "Alright then, it's agreed."

The mullethead steps up, "I have one more thing to add."

"Yes?" says John.

The mullethead kicks Henry in the face. But Henry does not cry out. Doesn't respond other than to allow the fast blooming bruise to blossom upside his cheekbone.

"I'd prefer no further violence," says John.

"May we proceed?" says Johnny.

"Go on," says Munch. "Let's get this over and done with."

"Alright, then," says John, taking out a notebook and a pen. "The two fat men? I need details regarding their jobs, if any, and family relations. Same goes for the Mexicans, the guy in the window and the black kid over there."

"Omar and Duke, they live alone with each other. They got no kin to speak of other than Omar's ex-wife who divorced him a good ten or more years ago."

"That's right," says Gleason. "They worked for me. Nobody's gonna miss them or the Mexicans. Norman? He worked for Henry. I never heard nothing about either of their families. And, for all we know, he could have been in on this too and got double-crossed by Henry in the end."

Henry does not react to this.

"I guess we'll never know," continues Gleason. "Now, with the young colored boy? That I can't speak of."

"He don't have no family," says Rosco. "His Moms died not long ago. That was it for him in terms of family."

"Well, that makes things all the easier," says John, closing his notebook. "I guess that's about it then. You all can gather up your belongings and your dogs and go on home. After you leave here, what ever happened here is like it never happened here. You will never see or hear from us again. Am I understood?"

"We understand," says Munch. "C'mon, let's all get the fuck outta here."

Johnny turns to Rosco, "Unfortunately, that goes for you too. After today, we won't be able to see you again either."

"Understood," says Rosco.

"But I'll be sure to leave you, leave on your service, the names of other men you might seek to employ down the line."

"Thanks," says Rosco.

In near silence, the yard is in motion with men and boys picking up and clearing out. Outside of the dead bodies and gore, it has the look of a recently finished family reunion.

Vincent finds Antoine by the fallen Tyrone. Vincent gently leads him away, allowing him to use his shoulder for support. As they exit the yard, Antoine turns towards Rosco who is still standing with John and Johnny. "You comin'?"

"I'll catch up in a minute," says Rosco.

Vincent and the limping Antoine progress slowly along the path as the last of the dogmen quickly pass them by without comment. Not long thereafter, the distinctive sound of a single shot echoes through the trees. Vincent and Antoine keep moving forward until they hear Rosco jogging up the path behind them. Without discussion, he moves to the other side of Antoine and together the three make their way out of the woods.

PART THREE

CHAPTER ONE

With the last period of the day over, the school empties out like a factory at closing time. A quiet ensues... Vincent remains sitting at his desk and the image of Tyrone's pulverized head comes to haunt him. Like a horrible pop song stuck in his brain, it plays over and over again, coming in and out of his consciousness without warning. Overwhelmed by the recurring horror, Vincent wonders how long it will last...

Vincent first hoped that Desiree would somehow make him feel better about it. Right after it happened, as soon as he got back to the motel, he told her everything that went down. He knew he could trust her. But after he told her, she went mute. She asked no questions and made no comments, neither of them talking for the entire ride back to the city. Feeling awful and wondering what she was thinking about, Vincent didn't think it wise to push her into talking. Better to let her say whatever she had to say in her own time.

After dropping Desiree off, Vincent had to return his father's car. He had originally planned to take Desiree to meet his family. He figured they might as well find out sooner rather than later. But considering the circumstances, he switched strategies, following the long ride of silence.

Strangely enough, Vincent was surprised to find himself looking forward to this visit. For Vincent, Hoboken had always been a place straight out of that Bruce song, "a town for losers," a place he forever sought to get away from. But then, just as he was crossing into New Jersey, Vincent felt a distinct sensation of relief. He couldn't figure out why this was so. He was still himself. Things that happened did not unhappen. Tyrone was still dead.

Walking in the front door, Vincent was likewise surprised to find that all the little things that had always annoyed him in the past were now a balm to his storm-racked psyche, a safe harbor of sorts, the contours of its shoreline clearly recognizable and inviting.

Although the entire family noticed a change in Vincent, they had no idea how or why it came to pass.

"You seem quiet," said his mom.

"He's just being a gavone," said his sister. "That's his third plate of macaroni."

"He's quiet because he's finally doing the right thing," said his father. "The boy has become a man. He's finally earning a real living. He's finally understanding what it's like to work and to have to pay the bills. To suffer the right way. He knows what I'm talking about."

With a small smile, Vincent looked up at his father.

"You see," said his father. "I know what I know."

"He's smiling to keep you quiet," said his sister. "That's what actors do, they act."

"I'm not an actor anymore," said Vincent.

"You see," said his father. "The boy has grown into the man. That acting stuff—that never was real. Sissy stuff, if you ask me. I know it. He knows it. It's as clear as the gravy on his chin."

"I don't think Robert DeNiro or Al Pacino are sissies," said his sister. "I'd like to see you say that to one of them... Right Vincent? What you think happen he said that to Scarface?"

"Scarface isn't real," said Vincent. "He's just a character played by an actor."

"That doesn't matter. Scarface is real. What difference does it make who played him?"

Vincent smiled at this. "Maybe you're right."

The door opens. Vincent looks up from his reverie. It's Steinberg, the basketball coach. "You busy?"

"No," says Vincent. "What's up?"

Steinberg closes the door behind him. He sits on a front row desktop, facing Vincent. He is a tall and imposing figure. He looks directly into Vincent's eyes. Vincent marvels at what a long face Steinberg has, the skin thick and rubbery, the ears and nose thick and long too. It is an imposing face, even more imposing than the person as a whole, a face impersonating a mask of some sort. Steinberg says, "Have you seen Antoine?"

"Not for a while," says Vincent. "He came in once or twice after Regents week and that was it."

"After he got hurt."

"Yeah."

"You see Tyrone at all?"

"He dropped out a long time ago. Right after that game we talked about in the bar."

"But have you seen him? Heard from him? I hear you two kept in contact."

"No. I haven't heard from him. I haven't talked to either of them in a while."

"You know what?"

"What's that?"

"I think you know a hell of a lot more than you're letting on."

"Oh, yeah?"

"That's right. There have been rumors. A whole bunch of rumors about you and your classes and about you and those two boys."

"Rumors."

"Where there's smoke there's fire," says Steinberg

"Sometimes, there's the most smoke when you're putting the fire out."

"I hear you're seeing Rosco's old girlfriend."

"Where'd you hear that?"

"I hear a lot of things. Kids tell me all sorts of things. I've also heard that Tyrone's dead. That he's dead and you know something about it."

"These kids can say the craziest things sometimes."

Steinberg stares at Vincent. Vincent looks right back at him. Now, he knows what kind of mask the face reminds him of. But it's not really a mask at all. Steinberg's face reminds him of an Easter Island head.

Vincent says, "That was a tough loss the other day."

"First time we got bumped in the first round," says Steinberg. "It's a season I'd like to forget. But I don't think I ever will."

"Yeah, that must have been tough on the rest of the team too, losing Antoine like that."

"I'm not half as worried about them as I am about Antoine."

"Yeah..."

"You know," says Steinberg, suddenly raising his voice. "I told you the last time. Most of these kids are living on the edge. The razor's edge. I said you were messing with their brains and I was right."

"You were right? Who the hell are you?"

"I'm somebody who's got your number. Yeah, sure, you come in here with great intentions, big ideas to help the poor ghetto kids. Like you're some kind of a one-man Peace Corps. But it don't work like that. There's no easy fixes. No magic bullet that's gonna solve all their problems."

"I never said there was."

"And now you've got one of the most gifted players I ever coached, a kid with a shoebox full of college offers, dropping out and strung out on the streets. Not to mention Tyrone who is most likely dead or worse."

"Don't try to pin that on me. Who are you to talk? You're a hypocrite."

"Hypocrite? I am and I've always been straight up with these kids. Sometimes I can help them and sometimes I can't. But, unlike you, I have never fucked them up."

"Oh, yeah? What about Rosco? Weren't you the one who got him started selling drugs? Yeah, I know some things too. You felt guilty, you felt real bad about what happened, so you tried to ease your conscience by giving the kid a bag of money so he could make a wonderful living selling drugs. I know all about that special gift you gave Rosco."

"I gave Rosco that money to get him the hell out of the city, away from all this shit. I had him all set up with his own place and a private tutor. The plan was for him to get his GED and then go to college—with or without basketball. And he, not me, fucked it up."

Vincent looks up and down the Easter Island head. It speaks the truth. Vincent says, "I didn't know that. I'm sorry."

"It was his choice. Whatever he is or is not, that's on him. I did what I could, what I thought would help him at the time. And maybe that was a mistake. I'm not claiming I have all the answers either. But, in the end, he made his choices and he had to live by his choices. We all do. And that's what I try to teach my players. Whether it's on the basketball court or out on the streets. It's all about choices and living with what you choose. It's the choice you make in the here and now that counts. And if you do end up fucking up, making the wrong choice along the way, still—all you've got is the here and now of the moment. The choice of the given moment. That's all they or anybody needs to know."

"Makes sense... I'm gonna give it some thought."

"You do that. In the mean time, I'm gonna ask you again: You hear or know anything about Antoine or Tyrone?"

"I hear that Antoine is working for Ivory White. The drug part, I don't know for sure. I know he smokes weed but—"

"I'm not talking about weed," says Steinberg.

"I can't say for sure. But I do know he's connected to that Ivory White."

"That's not good."

"No. I didn't think so either."

"Ivory used to play for me."

"I know."

"He is one of the most selfish individuals I have ever met."

"Then I can't really imagine him playing for you. From what I've seen, your team is big on passing, on team work."

"On the court, Ivory White did everything he was expected to do. Because he knew that by doing this I would play him. He was a strong athlete and he followed all my instructions to the letter. But everything he did on the court and in his life has been to satisfy himself with absolutely no regard to the feelings of anybody else. I think he's a classic sociopath. No real feelings of guilt or empathy."

"He seems to be close to Rosco."

"Only so far as Rosco fulfills a need."

"Interesting."

"Look, kid—I'm not an enemy. I hope you can see that. You're a smart guy, but you still got a lot to learn when it comes with dealing with these kids. You gotta understand that whatever you tell them, whatever you try and teach them, has the potential to act on them in ways you might not readily consider. Only with time and experience will you be able to really see what the hell I'm talking about. Until then, maybe try and go a little easy. That's all I'm saying."

"I hear you," says Vincent. "Thanks."

Steinberg stands. He offers his hand to Vincent. He says, "Alright then, I'll see you around. And if you do happen to hear anything on Antoine and Tyrone, let me know. Like I said, I'm not an enemy."

"I know it."

Steinberg leaves the room and Vincent stares at the door for a moment, wondering if he should have told him more. Not about Tyrone, but about Antoine. Maybe he could help in some way. But how? What could he do that Vincent couldn't do himself? "Just another white man," as Marisol would say. As maybe Desiree would secretly agree.

CHAPTER TWO

Vincent and Desiree's relationship had been strained ever since they got back from Montauk. But this strain was not directly connected to Tyrone's death or Antoine's injury. The strain came from the furious heat of Marisol's hate towards Vincent, whom she blamed for everything that had gone bad. Finding herself between two people she loved, Desiree was worn out by the constant conflict. It was the worst when the two were in each other's presence. But it wasn't much better when she was alone with either one of them.

With Marisol, Desiree always pointed out that Antoine and Tyrone would have gone to Montauk whether or not Vincent had gone himself. What's more, Desiree had been there too. If Vincent was guilty for not stopping them, then so was she, maybe even more so because she was Antoine's cousin.

Marisol would not hear any of this, "But he shoulda knowed. That cracker was they teacher!" Marisol needed a focus for her pain. Vincent proved the perfect target. Especially since Antoine's injury was not the only thing. In addition to quitting the team and dropping out, Antoine had started working for Ivory White as a hoe driver. And Marisol hated Ivory White as much as she hated Vincent.

Antoine, however, saw things from a different perspective. Driving hoes was easy work with good pay. All he had to do was drive the hoes to white tricks, mostly outside the city limits. It was easy. A hell of a lot easier than hanging dead dogs on the Losing Tree. After driving the hoes to their destination, he would chill in the car before driving them to their next "appointment" of the evening. There was never a problem with any of the johns. They paid upfront without a problem. Except when the two hoes went inside together, Antoine had the company of the free hoe to pass the time while waiting. At the end of the night, in addition to his pay, Antoine was also entitled to a free blow job. Antoine's friends were constantly bugging him to ask Ivory White if he needed any other hoe drivers. What other job offered such easy work and a blowjob at the end of your shift? Despite the perks and pay, Antoine was at first none too excited about his new employment. That is, until he started sniffing with the hoes. It didn't take long for Antoine to develop a habit. The coke was extremely potent. Ivory supplied it himself from his connect in Washington Heights. For Ivory, having his workers high was good business sense. It kept them alert with no chance of sleeping on the job in addition to keeping them unequivocally dependent on him. Ivory White was the company store: as long as they worked for him, they could always count on their daily supply.

Before Montauk, Antoine had never done a line in his life. Outside of weed, drugs were never a temptation. But after a short time driving hoes, he figured why the hell not? Basketball was no longer an option. The doctors told him as much. All of them. So why not check out what made the hoes so happy? What harm could a few sniffs do him? Unlike his first attempts with weed, the coke went to work on the very first try, immediately lifting his spirits and making the world electric with the present moment. Antoine couldn't get enough of the stuff.

Marisol had known Ivory White for years, as long as Desiree had known Rosco. Marisol was devirginized by Ivory White. Over the years, when they ran into each other from time to time, their exchange was never hostile. Ivory was always respectful as was Marisol in turn, their brief words akin to the words of people who knew each other from childhood but who were never really close. But when it became clear that not only was Antoine sniffing but being supplied by Ivory—Marisol flipped, confronting him in the middle of the street, in the middle of the day.

"Nigga, what the fuck is wrong with you?"

Ivory White had just gotten out of his car. He looked down at Marisol. "Excuse me?"

"You know what the fuck I'm talking about! You got Antoine all fucked up and—"

The mouth of Ivory's hand struck like a serpent, biting hard and steady into her windpipe and, like typical prey, Marisol froze up in unmitigated surprise and fear. Ivory looked up and down the street. He spoke softly, "Listen bitch, what Antoine chooses to do or not do is none of my fucking business. You got a problem with his choosing, you take it up with the nigga yourself." He let go her throat. As she gasped, he continued, "Because the next time you get up in my grill, especially out here in the street? I will hurt you. I will hurt you very badly."

Marisol looked up at him. She hated him. Ivory felt this hate and like a snake on a sunny rock, allowed himself to bask in its heat.

"You remember my dick, don't you?" he said. "Bitches never forget that first dick... Maybe I might have some work for you too. It could be a family kinda thing. You and Antoine would be together all the time. We can talk about that one day when you ready."

Controlling herself with great effort, stifling all instincts of fury and hate, Marisol pleaded with him, "Ivory, please. He's my brother. He don't deserve being like this. I'm just asking you, I'm asking you to just, this one time, to let this one kid go. Don't do this, don't let him end up like this. I'm just asking. That's all I can do. I'm sorry if I came at you the wrong way. I shouldn't have ever done that. But it's hard, Ivory. It's hard seeing your only brother going down like that. Please?"

Ivory White listened with his arms crossed. When she was through, he reflected upon what she said. But he didn't respond with words. Instead, he struck her with all his force across the side of her face. It was an open hand but it immediately swept her off her feet, momentarily knocking all sense from her head. Finding herself face down on the sidewalk, Marisol struggled to stand but another terrible pain stung her in the ass. Ivory had kicked her in the tailbone and again she went flying, this time into a pile of boxes and garbage set out by the curb. That's where he left her. That was his answer.

Unlike the black and blue on her face and ass, Marisol suffered the bruise of her brother's addiction far longer than any physical pain of her own. It was the age old pain of watching a loved one suffer without being able to help. A suffering of the heart that tainted all her hours with an unrelenting pressure that only seemed to be momentarily released when she was able to vent on Vincent, the root cause of all Antoine's afflictions. Ivory White was only a serpent who bites because that's what serpents do, they don't know anything else. But it was Vincent who had led Antoine into a garden full of snakes. It was Vincent who had allowed him to be bitten again and again. It was Vincent who had never warned the boy of the danger. It was Vincent, the white man, like all white men, whose smile disguised his evil doings.

In addition to Marisol's unrelenting hate, what further strained Desiree and Vincent's relationship was the change in Rosco. Since his return from Montauk, Rosco's attitude took an unexpected turn to the better, especially in regards to his son, Clyde. Almost on a daily basis, he met with the boy. But unlike before where it was a matter of Rosco giving him gifts or Rosco telling him not to walk on his toes, it was Rosco using their time together to just listen. He would encourage the boy to speak about what he thought about things, what he thought about what he saw, or what he heard, or what he could remember. Their relationship became defined by Rosco listening more than anything else. And Rosco took the same tack with Desiree, which unnerved her before secretly delighting her. But not in any sexual way. Not in a way where she considered fucking him again. Not that, not that yet. But, for the first time there came about a certain ease in their dealings whereby Clyde was the catalyst and focus of their interactions. Clyde never seemed so happy as when he was with Rosco. At first, it bordered on scary. But when it soon became evident that Rosco's love for Clyde was genuine, Desiree eased up and put away all fronts of frustration and anger.

For Vincent, this warming of relations between Rosco and Desiree couldn't help but fuel any dormant insecurities that he held along the way. Although not normally the jealous kind, Vincent found himself turning green on a regular basis. Which in turn irked Desiree to no end.

CHAPTER THREE

Outside the school, the air is white with snow. Falling fast and heavy, it covers the sidewalk and the tops of cars in an ivory shroud unsullied by the inevitable dirt and grime yet to come.

Vincent pulls the hood of his parka over his head. It has been getting progressively colder ever since he returned from Montauk. But this snowstorm has taken everybody by surprise. Vincent has never seen the city this way before. It is an unexpected delight. In addition to the visual element, Vincent also appreciates how the falling snow seems to quiet everything down. It is a thick and soft kind of silence. A dreamy silence in a dreamy world.

Vincent makes tracks first east on 114th Street and then north along Lennox. He is heading home. As he thinks about the beauty of the whitened cityscape, he is suddenly assaulted by the image of Tyrone's disfigured head. But Vincent doesn't resist. Instead, he dwells on the image. He allows his mind's eye to carefully examine the pulpy gore as if he were a medical examiner coolly appraising the next subject of the day.

Vincent wonders what it is that makes him think of such a terrible thing. Why does it, like the snowstorm, invade his consciousness without warning to cover up the rest of the world with its own reality? By what process or by what trigger do the so-called "normal" moments of our lives get suddenly eclipsed by a derailed focus of attention through either something tangible like the snowstorm or a memory of something horrible like Tyrone's head? How can the beauty of a snowstorm and the horror of Tyrone's head be related? Are they related? It does not seem so. Their only common element is the fact that they are both uncommon.

Something hits Vincent in the face. He is hit again, this time in the chest and thigh. Looking up, he sees them across the street, behind a parked car. His face is stinging but it is only snow. Vincent scoops up a handful of snow from the hood of a car and returns fire. It is excellent snowball snow—wet and easily packed tight. Vincent can throw hard and accurately. He is a master of the snowball fight. His first sally catches Marcus in the forehead. His second throw explodes in Rowland's ear. As they howl in surprise and pain, Vincent dashes across the street, a snowball in each hand. The two boys throw wildly. Two misses. Vincent walks their way, slowly, like Clint in "A Man With No Name." He allows them to reload and fire but they miss yet again. As they frantically stoop to form new snowballs, Vincent stops and fires, hitting them each upside the head. Vincent knows that these shots have got to hurt, he's not more than ten yards away. Vincent goes into a catcher's crouch, quickly forming a small pile of ammo. But Rowland and Marcus have surrendered. They hold their hands above their heads.

"You win! We give up," shouts Marcus.

Vincent smiles. "I'll give you ten seconds. Ten, nine, eight..."

Marcus and Rowland look at each other. They see Vincent standing in place, a snowball in each of his two hands, the hands bright red now from the cold.

"Six, five, four..."

"Oh shit," cries Marcus, finally realizing what's to come. "RUN!"

The two boys make a break for it. But Marcus slips and falls.

"Three, two..."

Rowland helps his friend up to his feet. Marcus looks back over his shoulder just in time to hear, "ONE!" and get blasted in the nose. A second shot hits Rowland in the back of the neck.

As they race around the corner, Vincent laughs an old laugh, a childhood laugh he forgot ever existed inside of him. His hands sting from the cold. He sticks them deep into the warm of his coat pockets. He walks smiling like a simpleton. He continues making progress homeward, the snow piling fast, his tracks fading fast and soon gone behind him.

Up ahead, on the corner of 119th Street, Vincent sees Rosco and Clyde. It is a peculiar sight because both Rosco and Clyde are walking on their tiptoes. Vincent wonders if this is some kind of demented scheme to shame the boy out of his habit. But what's even more peculiar is that Rosco is only wearing a sleeveless T-shirt. No hat, no gloves, just a wife-beater, jeans and sneakers. Vincent watches the two figures tiptoe across the street. At least Clyde is properly bundled up with a coat and a scully...

With one hand, Rosco holds his son's hand. In his other hand, he holds a gym bag with the Nike logo emblazoned across its side. Rosco looks up and down the sidewalk. He puts the gym bag down between his feet. He points at the street signs. Removing a small marbled colored notepad from his coat pocket, Clyde writes down the two cross streets. Rosco points at a "Botanica" on the far corner. But Clyde is not sure what he should notate. Rosco takes the pad from his son and makes the sign of the cross beside the address of the Botanica. He hands Clyde back the notepad. Rosco shudders. Squatting into a crouch, he scoops up snow. But not to make snowballs. Instead, he rubs the snow on his bare shoulders and arms, around his neck and ears and face. Clyde still holds the notepad and pencil while watching his father repeat the snow washing procedure.

Vincent decides he must do something because something is clearly not right with this picture. As he comes up on them, Clyde sees Vincent first because Rosco is still busy rubbing himself with snow.

"Hi, Clyde," says Vincent. "You okay?"

"I'm okay," says Clyde.

"Rosco?" says Vincent. "You alright there?"

Rosco looks up. Rosco grins and stands, picking up the gym bag and putting his free hand on Clyde's shoulder. He speaks to Clyde, "Go stand by that doorway for a minute." Clyde does as he's told, tiptoeing his way up the block to stand under the ripped awning of a burnt out Chinese restaurant.

"I don't have much time," hisses Rosco. "They're here."

"What? Who you talking about?"

"The Klan. They're here. They've made it here to the city. I don't have much time."

"Time for what?"

"Man, I'm burning up," says Rosco. "It's like I'm on fucking fire and God or the Devil has sent down all this snow to help me or mock me. How can I know?"

"You want me to take Clyde?"

"Take Clyde? Where you gonna take him? Pretty soon the motherfuckers are gonna be everywhere. Niggas gonna be strung up from every street light in Harlem."

Vincent takes note of a thin strand of spittle forming at the corner of Rosco's mouth. He must be on some kind of drug...

"I'm fucking sick... Hot all the time. Even now, which I know don't make no sense."

"I think you might have to go to the hospital," says Vincent.

Rosco looks over his shoulder. He points at Clyde. "In a minute!" he shouts. "Just wait right there and I'll be there in a minute!" Rosco stoops for more snow, rubbing it on his arms and neck.

"Hey, Rosco," says Vincent. "You gotta get yourself checked out."

"No time. Motherfuckers are gonna be here any time now. And I feel like I'm gonna burn up. What the fuck you think I'm gonna do? Give it all to them? Let them take it? Take me? Take my son?"

Like the witch's guards in "The Wizard of Oz," Vincent can see that Rosco is somehow being controlled by another force, a demented reasoning that mixes and merges with the "true" Rosco to produce an alternate Rosco who thinks he is being stalked by the Klan, or about to burst into fire, or both. But while this force has the ability to control his thought and actions, it still has not completely taken him over. In the space of seconds, Vincent can see Rosco going in and out, hopelessly fighting this force that seems to get stronger each time it comes into power.

"Look," says Vincent. "Why don't we take Clyde back home to his mom. We can get a taxi and drop him off and then take you straight to the hospital."

"You go near my son and I'll shoot you," smiles Rosco. "Yo, Clyde! C'mon, we going!"

On the balls of his feet, Clyde runs to his father's side. Rosco picks up the gym bag. He takes Clyde by the hand. He looks at Vincent and Vincent can see that the man is in some kind of agony, a lie of the mind that not only physically hurts him but is mentally terrifying him no matter how hard he tries to win back his old self.

"Where you going?" asks Vincent.

"East," says Rosco. "The rivers run in the east and in the west. They won't think to look east before west."

"Rosco," pleads Vincent. "Let me take Clyde back to his mom."

Rosco clenches his eyes. After an instant of intense inner struggle, he opens his eyes. "I'm really burning up," he says. "But we gotta run now. They gonna be here for sure come dark."

"Let me come with you!" shouts Vincent.

Rosco stops. He turns, "You follow me, you're dead. And no motherfucking Klan will be able to save you."

CHAPTER FOUR

Rosco was hit by a truck but not killed by the truck. The truck driver, George Maclean, had been making a delivery to the city for the first time. He got the job from his AA sponsor. Although Maclean was completely sober, he was unable to avoid hitting the man because the FDR drive was treacherous with snow. What's more, he wasn't even supposed to be on the FDR, because the FDR was only for passenger cars. The cop at the scene told him this as he handed him the ticket. But Maclean didn't care about the ticket, he was only concerned about the poor bastard he sent flying over the guardrail. Maclean told the cops that when he heard the blare of horns and saw the cars swerving, he figured there must be an ice patch so he tapped the brakes, slowing but not stopping, to give himself plenty of room to maneuver. What he didn't mention was that he at first thought it was some kind of hallucination, that maybe his dry drunk had begun to play tricks with his head, because how often do you see a naked black man kneeling in the center of the highway? Realizing it was no mirage, Maclean hit the horn and the brakes hard, sending the truck into a tailspin, the back end swatting the kneeling black man like a hard nut off a paddle. As the truck continued to spin, another and another car crashed and crunched in succession, causing a massive pileup where miraculously nobody got seriously hurt. Nobody but the naked black man.

The two cops first thought the truck driver was a DWI until his confused dialogue was punctuated by the sight of the naked man in the snow. The cops, Colon and York, soon realized that the man was Rosco. He was face up and still breathing, his arms and legs twisted akimbo, his dark red blood practically glowing against all the fast falling white.

But what stood out even more, what stood out so that you couldn't help but notice, was Rosco's erection, pointing straight up like an accusing finger at the low dome of heaven. Since the truck driver was present, the two cops refrained from crudely commenting on this fact. Instead, Colon threw a blanket over the body until EMS arrived to take him away.

At Harlem Hospital, the doctors were perplexed by a number of Rosco's readings and signs. But a young specialist, Doctor Tabor Lightbourne, had a hunch that the patient was also suffering from some kind of infection or virus. Her hunch was correct. Even if the truck never hit him, Rosco would have soon been dead due to the late stages of the rabies infection brought on by a rabid bat. According to Doctor Lightbourne, a bat bite victim will often be unaware of the bite, especially in a case like Rosco's where he was known to panic. "Their teeth can be very tiny," said Lightbourne to her wide-eyed nurse. "Quite often, one never even feels the nip. That's why it's so important to get checked whenever you find yourself in close proximity to a potentially rabid animal, most especially a bat in close quarters."

CHAPTER FIVE

Vincent ran all the way up the stairs. At the top, he pounded on the door. Someone opened it and he stumbled in, all out of breath. Beneath his coat, he was wet from sweat. Desiree and Marisol stood staring at him. They had just finished smoking a fat joint and the aroma filled the apartment. In a tumble of sentences, Vincent described Rosco and Clyde, how he saw them moving on their tippytoes with Rosco talking crazy.

Desiree listened as if made of stone, her gaze blank and pitiless. When Vincent finally finished, Desiree flew into a sudden rage. "Why the fuck didn't you call me?"

"I tried," said Vincent. "But it was busy. I tried every couple of blocks on my way back here. It was busy."

Desiree stared at Marisol. "You always on the phone!"

Marisol sucked her teeth, ignoring Desiree, and turning to Vincent, "Why didn't you call the police then? Isn't that what crackers do?"

"And tell them what? That there was some black guy in a t-shirt babbling about the Klu Klux Klan? I'm sure they woulda rushed right over."

"You see?" said Marisol. "That's his motherfucking attitude. Cracker never wants to take responsibility for nothin'!"

Vincent ignored Marisol, turning to Desiree. "I tried to talk to him. I tried but—"

"Why didn't you follow him then?"

"He was gonna shoot me."

"Fuck! I shoulda knew something wasn't right with that nigga!"

"The nigga and the cracker both," muttered Marisol.

Since the door to the apartment was still open, nobody noticed Clyde tiptoeing across the threshold until he suddenly appeared in their midst like Jesus to his surprised disciples after the resurrection.

"Daddy say he was gonna burn up. He wanted to take me with him across the river. But when we got there, he say it was too hot. He kept saying about being hot and about the clams coming to get us. So he took me back across the highway and told me to run. To run home because he was about to burn up."

Although Clyde never saw his father getting hit by the truck, he knew there was something terribly amiss. Clyde handed his moms the notebook. "He say for me to give this to you. He say you gotta take us far away to the jungle where the clams can't snatch me up."

It didn't take long to gather that Rosco had somehow lost his mind and had hidden a large amount of money beneath a pile of trash in an abandoned lot near East 138th Street.

"We better hurry up and get it before somebody else finds it first," said Marisol, paging through the notebook.

"She's probably right," said Vincent.

"Of course I'm right," said Marisol, flipping to the last written page in the notebook. "I don't know why he went to all the trouble of writing down his directions when all you gotta do is look on this last page to see where it's at."

"He was very confused," said Vincent.

"Nigga bugged outta his mind. Nigga's been bugged from the jump. Just that now the mask be off and it's obvious to even a child what's what."

CHAPTER SIX

Since there are no other next of kin around to decide otherwise, Desire had the body cremated. Not wanting the ashes herself, Desiree decided to give them to Rosco's old basketball coach because during the session with the undertaker, it struck her that the urn looked like a trophy. Rosco's last trophy.

There was no church funeral, only a brief memorial service at the Welden Funeral Home on East 116th Street. It is an awkward affair. It's here that Vincent first meets Desiree's mom, Delores, whose politeness hovers close to the border of icy hostility. Ivory White's presence in turn puts everybody on some level of unease, especially Marisol.

The basketball coach is the only one who speaks about Rosco's life and passing, "I can't say I really knew Rosco. But in the brief time that I did spend with him, I came to understand and appreciate his unique and prodigious passion. More than anything else, it was this passion that defined all that he did. Nobody, especially me, can ever judge where such passion ultimately led him, ultimately made him into what he was as a man and a father and a friend. But what we can do, what we can take with us from the short life of this passionate man, is the fire and the vigor that always burned bright no matter what the obstacle that lay ahead."

When Steinberg is through, Desiree makes a point of shaking his hand and thanking him for his words. He nods to her and quickly slips out before Vincent has a chance to shake his hand too. A long, ballooning moment of awkward silence is suddenly punctured by Delores. "That's it, then," she says. "Might as well go."

Outside on the sidewalk, while waiting for a taxi, Ivory White approaches Desiree. "I need to speak with you," he says.

"About what?"

"It's private business.   Business between me and Rosco and now you."

"Nigga, this is not the time nor the place.   What's wrong with you?"

"Is everything alright?" says Vincent, coming to Desiree's side followed by Marisol and Delores.

"Everything's fine," says Desiree.

Ivory White stares at Desiree for an extra second before turning up the block.

"What the nigga want?" asks Marisol.

"He didn't say.   But I got a good idea what it might be about."

Vincent, Desiree, Delores and Marisol share a cab to Desiree's apartment. When they get there, Aunt Gloria takes Clyde to the park, leaving the mourners free to indulge in wine and weed. Although mother and daughter have been smoking weed for decades, this is the first time they do so in each other's presence.

"It's alright," says Delores. "I know you get high and I know you been knowin' that about me for the longest. Sometimes you gotta just let things go. Especially if there's no real reason for holdin' on anymore."

This declaration brings an involuntary smile to Marisol's face. Marisol is always game for a smoke. Even if it's with Delores, for whom she still feels a strong resentment.

Much to everyone's surprise, it is Delores who not only brings forth the weed, but who proceeds to construct a finely rolled blunt. Vincent watches her remove a box cutter, a Dutchmaster cigar, and a bag of weed from her purse. She slits the cigar, emptying its contents on the Formica top table. From the rounded end, she pulls back the leaf and rips away a small rectangle of extra paper. She dumps a good amount of weed into the hollowed out cigar wrapper. She rolls it up and licks it closed. She hands it to her daughter.

"When you learn how to roll a dutch?" asks Desiree.

"Don't matter where I learned it. Go on, spark it up."

Desiree lights the blunt, taking two deep hits and passing it back to her Moms. The blunt makes its way around the table in silence.

Although it's a bit bizarre to be smoking grass with Desiree's mom, Vincent doesn't mind in the least. But, at the same time, he can distinctly feel the many currents of resentment flowing beneath the surface. Hopefully, the smoke will soon calm this flow...

"Clyde is growing so fast," says Delores. "It all goes by so quick sometimes."

"What about the other times?" asks Desiree.

"Yeah, well... Sometimes it goes pretty damn slow."

"What you talkin' about?" asks Marisol.

"Life," says Delores. "How it can go both fast and slow. And, in the end, it all ends, and the fastness and slowness just plain quits."

"That's deep," says Marisol.

"I was hardheaded and wrong about a lot of things," says Delores. "I made some terrible mistakes."

"Don't go there, Ma."

"And I'm sorry. I hope you know that. Both you and Marisol."

"We know it, Ma. Just forget it."

"And you were right. You were absolutely right to keep that child. I should never ever have said what I said... I guess I thought you—"

"Ma! Okay, alright then."

"Alright, then," says Delores, breaking into a sad smile.

Marisol turns on the radio. She works the dial until she gets a song by Mary J. They all groove on Mary J. When the song ends, Delores says, "She reminds me of Billie Holiday."

"I know her," says Marisol. "She from back in the day."

"From way back in the day. Back before me even."

"That is way back," says Marisol. "Oops, sorry. I didn't mean it like that."

"That's alright," says Delores. "I guess I'm old now. You hate to think it but it is what it is and nobody can't do a damn thing about it."

"I wonder what I gonna look like when I'm old," says Marisol. "I wonder if I gonna be all wrinkled up..."

"You stupid," says Desiree.

The radio commercial ends. The song, "Ain't No Stopping Us Now," begins to play. Desiree turns up the volume and begins to dance. She is soon followed by Marisol, Delores and even Vincent who proceeds to perform his interpretation of the George Jefferson. In total amusement and amazement, the three women watch the white boy pump and strut and pop out his ass, his hands tucked close to his body and his arms flapping like chicken wings, making a wide herky-jerky circle about the room...

"What the hell is that?" shouts Marisol.

"It's the George Jefferson!" shouts Vincent.

Although hilarious, his moves are not without skills.

"You go boy!" shouts Desiree.

There comes a knock on the door. But nobody hears it due to the loud music and the focus on Vincent's George Jefferson. More knocks follow, hard and steady. Desiree turns down the volume. They all stare at the door.

"Who?" says Desiree.

"It's Ivory," says Ivory White.

Desiree goes to the door. The others remain standing in place. Desiree opens the door.

"Can I talk to you a minute?" asks Ivory.

"Dag! Nigga, what you want with me?" asks Desiree.

"We need to talk."

"Alright, then. Fine. Talk, then."

Ivory White looks over her shoulder. "It's private."

Desiree does not want to be alone with him, if even for a minute. "Whatever you wanna say you can just go on and say it. We all family here."

"I have reason to believe that you got a hold of Rosco's bag."

"What bag you talking about?"

"Yo, I got no time to be talkin' junk. That bag was supposed to go to me. Rosco owed it to me and I plan on getting what's mines."

"I don't know nuthin' about no bag," says Desiree. "I wish I could help you on that but—"

"I ain't playin' around here, Dee Dee. I know you can appreciate that. I'm gonna get me my bag or else there's gonna be a whole mess of pain and sorrow."

"You threatening me?"

"I'm asking for my due. Nicely first and then not so nice later."

"And what you gonna do? You gonna fuck me up?"

"Nigga ain't gonna do nuthin'," says Delores, pulling a .38 snub nosed revolver from her purse. "I suggest you take your black ass back to the streets. Or else that same black ass gonna find a cap blown in it!"

"Okay, alright then," says Ivory, holding up his hands. "You got me, grandma. I ain't gonna mess wif you. I ain't gonna mess wif none of you all. I guess I just be going on my way then."

"Nigga, that's for damn sure," says Delores.

"Yeah, you right.... But, ah... Marisol? You want me to say, 'hi' to Antoine for ya? It's too bad he couldn't make it to the service. But I gonna be seein' him shortly."

"What the fuck that supposed to mean?" says Delores.

"Ask Marisol, she know," says Ivory, turning away.

Desiree slams the door, locks the locks. She goes over to Marisol, who stands with her face drained of color.

CHAPTER SEVEN

"We just gonna have to take the motherfucka out," says Delores.

"Ma, I never seen you like this."

"Oh, yes you have."

"Yeah, maybe. But not so cold. Not in such a... Such a calculating kinda way."

"The older you get the mo you get to understandin' that some things are best done by lettin' your anger help you focus rather than throwin' off your aim."

"You serious?" asks Marisol.

"As serious as cancer," says Delores. "I promised myself a long time ago that I would never let no nigga hurt any one of my family. So if anybody here don't want to know no more, they best be leavin' now or else they in it just by knowin' about it."

Delores looks hard at Vincent and he returns her gaze, acutely aware that Marisol and Desiree are also hawking him, waiting for a response. He tries to remain calm, to appear composed, despite that dropping feeling in his gut.

He says, "I'm not goin' nowhere. Not unless you want me to. But I'm also not gonna get mixed up in somethin' that's gonna put me in jail either."

"What the fuck is that supposed to mean?" barks Marisol.

"The plan has to be perfect or else I'm not in it."

"You hear this cracker?"

"He right," says Delores. "It's got to be foolproof. Can't be no reason for any mistakes."

"I can't believe we talkin' about snuffin' the nigga," says Desiree. "Maybe I should just give him the money. I don't need it."

"It ain't just about the money," says Delores. "He got Antoine under his thumb. And he ain't ever gonna let him go whether you give him the money or not. I know that nigga. I seen his kind. Know his kind. Only way to get a slave master to give up his slaves is to put him in the ground."

"True that," says Desiree. "But even then, Antoine still gonna be a slave to his habit. Especially since he went from sniffin' to smokin'."

"I can help him," says Marisol.

"You can try," says Desiree. "But that don't mean he gonna listen."

"You wanna help him, you gotta get him outta the city and into some kind of rehab," says Vincent. "That's the only way and even that way ain't for sure."

"What you talkin' about?" asks Marisol.

"You gotta get him away from the drugs and into a rehab hospital where they can treat him mentally and physically."

"Yeah, that might work for white folks and rich people, but we ain't neither," says Marisol.

"How much somethin' like that go for?" asks Desiree.

"Rehab? It costs a lot. Depending on which one you pick. The best ones can be ten, twenty thousand, maybe more—"

"You must be trippin'," says Marisol. "How they gonna charge that kinda money?"

"They do and people pay it."

"I got that. We got that right here in the bag," says Desiree.

There is a knock on the door.

"Who?" asks Desiree.

"Me Mommy! Me and Auntie and Antoine!"

"Just a minute," says Desiree, unlocking the locks and letting them inside.

Clyde stands between Aunt Gloria and Antoine, holding each of their hands. Antoine's hair is nappy and his clothes disheveled. Dark rings beneath his eyes reveal many days of sleepless nights.

"Auntie?" says Desiree. "Could you bring Clyde inside a moment?"

"Of course," says Aunt Gloria. "C'mon, angel."

Antoine smiles at Clyde, "See you, rookie star."

"Peace, out," says Clyde, tiptoeing away to his room with Aunt Gloria.

"He one crazy little nigga," says Antoine. "Peace, out. You hear him?"

"Look at you," says Marisol. "You a fuckin' disgrace."

"What? Why you gotta go and be like that?" says Antoine.

"Question is the other way around," says Marisol. "Why you have to go and be like that. You one sorry ass motherfucka... Things get a little tight and you crumble like a bitch."

"You funny," says Antoine. "She funny, ain't she?"

"Nothin' funny about it, child," says Delores.

"I hear you had Rosco carmalated," says Antoine to Desiree. "What made you wanna go and do that for?"

"Nigga, sit the fuck down and shut up," says Desiree. "We all here need to have a little talk with you."

"I'd like to do that, but I gotta bounce," says Antoine. "I just come by 'cause Ivory say you got some cash for me to pick up. He told me to pick it up and get it back to him real quick 'cause he in a hurry."

CHAPTER EIGHT

Although Vincent has never been late for work, this morning he is cutting it close. Passing through the small crowd of students smoking cigarettes, Vincent walks inside the school doors. Sampson, the security guard, waves for Vincent to come over.

Vincent approaches the security desk, "What's up?"

"Somethin' not good," says Sampson. "The principal told me to call her as soon as I seent you come in."

"Oh, yeah?"

"That's right. You in some kinda trouble?"

"Not that I know of."

"Usually when a teacher in some kinda trouble, she make me call her like that. Last time it happen, the resource room teacher was accused of stealing a microwave oven. Time before that, the gym teacher was caught jerkin' off in the girl's locker room."

"Thanks for the tip, Sampson."

"No problem, man. Good luck."

Stepping out of the elevator on the fourth floor, Vincent proceeds directly into the main office to move his time card. Stuck to the top of his time card, a yellow sticky note informs him to see Miss McCool immediately. After reading the note, Vincent is acutely aware that the secretaries in the outer office are staring at him.

The door to Miss McCool's office is ajar. Vincent knocks.

"Come!" says Miss McCool.

Vincent walks into Miss McCool's office. Although it is not a small office, it seems a bit cramped because of the number of people standing inside. Vincent recognizes Coach Steinberg, and Mr. Beasley, Dean of Discipline.

"Mr. DeRosa," says Miss McCool. "I believe you are already acquainted with Mr. Steinberg and Mr. Beasley."

Vincent nods, catching himself from staring at Mr. Beasley's cruddy red scalp peeking through an east-west swoop of greasy black hair.

"Will everyone please sit down," says Miss McCool. "Mr. DeRosa, I'm sorry to say that I've called you here to my office under some very serious allegations."

"I see," says Vincent.

"Do you know what I refer to?"

"No."

"Mr. DeRosa," says Mr. Beasley. "Did you not show the movie 'Scarface' to your classes?"

"You know I did. And?"

Mr. Beasley looks at Miss McCool before briefly throwing up his hands and crossing his arms.

"I'll bet you got beat up a lot as a kid," says Vincent to Mr. Beasley. "I feel sorry for you."

"Mr. DeRosa," says Miss McCool. "This is a very serious situation we have here. Please refrain from making light of these proceedings."

"Sorry."

"If I may interject?" says Coach Steinberg.

"Yes, go on," says Miss McCool.

"A number of my players attend DeRosa's class and on more than one occasion I have questioned them about what they were learning there."

"Why did you feel the need to question them?" asks Mr. Beasley, the Dean.

"Because I became uneasy, at first, regarding many of the things I was hearing."

"Of course," says Mr. Beasley. "Any decent educator would be alarmed, to say the least."

"But," continues Steinberg. "I then confronted Mr. DeRosa myself. And I have to say, while I did not agree with everything he had to say, I did come away thinking that he was trying to do the best that he could. In my mind, DeRosa is in no way negligent or incompetent in regards to his classes. In fact, if you'll check the records, he has the highest attendance and passing rate in the school."

"Of course he does," says Mr. Beasley. "But that's because he shows movies like 'Scarface.' Because he gives no tests, quizzes, or homework. Because he curses in class like a hooligan and allows students to do the same. Of course they show up to his class."

"I think I've heard enough," says Miss McCool. "So, with the exception of Mr. DeRosa, will you all kindly step outside while I take care of this. And thank you both for coming on such short notice."

As soon as they file out and close the door, Miss McCool removes a lighter and a cigarette from her top drawer. She lights up and puffs a number of times, her yellow teeth glowing in a wide grin behind the clouds of smoke. When Vincent takes out one of his own cigarettes, she reaches across her desk to light if for him.

"Thanks," he says. "Anybody ever tell you what beautiful hair you have?"

"Yes. Many times."

As Vincent savors the first few puffs on his Marlboro, he is clearly aware that his teaching days have come to an end. "I guess all I need now is the blindfold."

"Very good," says Miss McCool, smiling. "In a way, I'm gonna miss you, DeRosa."

"The feeling is mutual."

"But I really have no choice. You went too far."

"Maybe," says Vincent.

"What were you thinking?"

"I was trying, believe it or not, to teach them something new."

"Is that so?"

"Socrates once said that education is not putting knowledge into empty minds but instead allowing people to realize what they already know."

"And you think you're like Socrates?"

"I don't plan on eating any hemlock."

"But you will be banished."

"Fired, you mean."

"Exactly," says Miss McCool, smiling wide once more.

"I will not go quietly into that good night."

"Rage and burn, huh?"

"You know Dylan Thomas?"

"Let's cut the crap now, shall we?" says Miss McCool. "As of today, as of this very minute, you are no longer a teacher here at Wadleigh. As soon as you finish your cigarette, I will ring up security to have you escorted from the building."

"Understood," says Vincent. "But also understand that as soon as I leave the premises, I will immediately call the New York Times, the Daily News and the New York Post to inform them that a teacher has been the focus of an educational witch hunt. A teacher with the highest attendance and passing rate in the school. The papers will love that sorta angle, don't you think? Makes for great copy. By tomorrow or the day after, you'll have the TV crews waiting outside the building to interview all my students who will no doubt have a thing or two to say themselves. If it's a circus you want, a circus you will get."

Miss McCool stubs out her cigarette in the heap of ash overflowing from the swan shaped ashtray. She reaches into her drawer and lights another cigarette. "What do you want?" she asks. "Because there's no way I can let you continue to teach here."

"You can," says Vincent. "You have that power."

"True," she says. "But it would only weaken my power in the long run."

"Alright," says Vincent. "How about we make a deal then?"

"I'm listening."

Vincent puts out his cigarette in the dirty swan ashtray. "I walk. I walk outta here, right now and never come back. Only you keep me on the payroll for the rest of the year and through the summer. You can tell the staff and my students that I had some sort of problem with my teaching license. Nobody but me and you and I guess the payroll secretary has to know otherwise. This way, you're covered because I'm no longer teaching here and I'm covered because I'm getting paid until next September."

"Getting paid without working for it."

"I guess so. Yeah."

Miss McCool rises from her chair. She extends her chubby, nicotine-stained fingers. "Deal."

CHAPTER NINE

Marisol approaches the shining white Mercedes with the dark tinted glass. In the pocket of her coat, she fingers the box cutter. Antoine once told her that if you ever decide to carry a weapon, you best be ready to go all the way because more often then not, a nigga ends up getting cut by his own blade if he's not one hundred percent ready and willing to use it. Those are the rules.

She stands a few feet back from the driver's side window. The window glass slides down as the face of Ivory White confronts and, for an instant, nearly confounds her resolve. Marisol glances up and down the sidewalk. Nobody. She says, "Can I talk with you a minute?"

"What does it concern?"

"It concerns me and Antoine and that bag of money you be lookin' for."

"What in your pocket?"

Marisol removes her hand from her pocket. "Huh? My hand."

"You not lookin' to snuff me, are you?"

"What? No, I just want—"

"Chill, girl. I'm just playin' wif ya. Why don't you step around and come inside my office."

Marisol bends her head, looking inside the car. There is nobody but Ivory.

"Don't be scared. If I wanna hurt ya, I don't need to have you be sittin' in my car. In fact, that's the last place I'd choose to fuck somebody up."

The car is parked in front of a hydrant near the corner of 119th Street and Lennox. Marisol walks around to the passenger side. She hears the electric locks click. She pulls the handle to open the door. She sits down on the white leather seat while pulling shut the heavy door that clunks closed with the authority of a bank vault. The car stinks of Ivory's cologne. Although she does not recognize the brand, she knows it is not cheap, yet the scent still repels her because it's coming off his person.

"I'm gonna get right to the point," she says.

"Okay."

"I wanna work out a deal with you. I'm thinking I might know a way to get you your money."

"You were always a very smart girl."

"I'm just tryin' to look out for Antoine. And you know how I feel about him. Everybody do. So I'm thinking that I can help you if you be willing to help me, to help Antoine."

"What's the deal?"

"Okay. Okay, the way I see this thing workin' is for you to get what you want and me to get what I want. But, with that, we both gotta be willin' to compromise some."

"I'm always willing to compromise. That is part of doing business. Gotta compromise in this world or else you be stuck. Go on."

"Alright then," says Marisol, turning towards Ivory, looking him in the eye. "See, what they got in mind? Desiree and that cracker boyfriend of hers? They got themselves the notion that they can put Antoine into a hospital for drug addicts. A white folks hospital that costs mad money, like over fifty grand. Me? I be thinking that that's a complete waste of the money but they don't wanna be hearing that. The cracker, he say it's the only way to help Antoine. And Dee Dee? She be hangin' onto every damn word he be sayin'."

"Rehab, huh?"

"Yeah, that the word he used. Rehab."

"Okay. So what's your idea?"

"My idea is that with that kinda money, I could be using it much better. With fifty grand? I could take me and Antoine the hell outta here. I know some peoples in Jamaica. I'm thinking me and Antoine could start a new life there. Fifty grand down there like a million around here. I could open me up a little shop, a hair braiding shop. The white tourists pay mad money to get they hair braided. I figure I could open up a nice little shop for braidin' and nails and whatnot and hire the local girls for next to nuthin' to do it. Meanwhile, I'd be gettin' Antoine off the rock and back to smokin' weed because the weed downt there is da bomb. And dirt cheap too. I'd have that nigga so high he wouldn't be thinkin' of nuthin' but all the local pussy he be hittin' day and night."

"You really thought this out, huh?"

"Yes, I did."

"And what you're saying to me, is that you want me to give you fifty thousand dollars of my money to do it. Am I correct?"

"Yeah. That's right. But I seen that bag. There's gotta be five times that amount in there, maybe more."

"Closer to ten times."

"You would know better than me."

"So, if I give you fifty, I can keep the rest for myself."

"Yes. That's what I was thinkin'."

"Or else I could just snuff you and Antoine and Desiree and Desiree's kid and Desiree's Moms and Desiree's cracker boyfriend—slowly, painfully—to get it all without cutting anybody in. I could do that."

"Yeah. I guess you could. But that could get pretty ugly and very messy. Lot could go wrong or cause you some serious problems with a plan like that."

"So, for fifty large, you're gonna save me some serious potential problems."

"Yes."

"You know exactly where she keep the money?"

"No. She not stupid. Not even the cracker know. But I know a way how to get her to give it up."

"Go on."

"Alright then. Follow me with this... I arrange to take Clyde out to the park or the zoo, somethin' like that. But instead, I take him to a motel. At the motel, I call Dee Dee and tell her we been kidnapped. That they gonna snuff Clyde first if she don't bring the money straight over."

"I ain't goin' in for no kidnapping."

"You ain't gonna have to do nuthin' but pick up your money from me. I'm doin' all the leg work here. Listen, I been knowin' Dee Dee since we was little kids. I know how she thinks, what she gonna do. That money don't mean shit to her if you put it on a scale with her baby. And she trusts me. I'm probably the only person she trusts hundred percent in this world and that's including her Moms and the cracker. She gonna be told to come alone with the bag. As soon as she show up outside the door, she puts the bag down and the child comes out to her. Then, she gonna drive straight away."

"What about you?"

"Me, I be out as soon as you get your money."

"If something goes wrong, it's still a kidnapping rap."

"Nothing gonna go wrong. But, even if it do, you not gonna be in it."

"What you mean?"

"I gonna be alone with Clyde in the motel room. As soon as Dee Dee make the switch, I count out my fifty and leave the rest for you. All you gotta do is pick it up after she gone with the kid."

"What's to stop you from taking all of it?"

"For one, you can be close by, watchin' from a safe distance. And two: you will still have Antoine with you."

CHAPTER TEN

The Blue Spruce Motel is located about twenty minutes away from the George Washington Bridge. Flanking each side of the management office are two rows of standard sized rooms. Marisol is in Room 6-G with Clyde. Clyde watches cartoons on the TV while Marisol has her finger poked through the curtains, peeking out for Desiree.

About two hundred yards away, Ivory White sits inside his Mercedes Benz. He picks up the binoculars, focusing on the door of Room 6-G. He puts the binoculars back down on the dashboard. Ivory has been doing this, on and off, every five minutes for the past half hour. Antoine sits beside Ivory. Normally, Antoine would be wondering what the hell is going on. But Antoine has not been normal since he started smoking crack. Nowadays, his entire existence has completely paled in the pursuit of the next burning rock. Yet in certain moments of cruel illumination, Antoine has become keenly aware that he has lost all desire for all his desires. Like a butterfly pinned to the collector's corkboard, he writhes in anguish with the realization that he can never fly again because to escape would entail tearing apart his wings.

Desiree pulls into the lot driving Vincent's father's car. She parks, retrieving the Nike bag from the back seat. She goes to Room 6-G.

Ivory sees Desiree park the car. He grabs his binoculars. He sees Desiree remove the bag from the car, taking it to the threshold of 6-G. The door opens. The little boy comes out walking on his tiptoes. Desiree grabs him and they hurry back into the car. Marisol appears. She picks up the bag, taking it inside 6-G. Desiree drives away with her son. Ivory puts down the binoculars. He starts the car. He drives it down into the motel parking lot. He parks the car but leaves it running. He says, "I'll be right back. Sit tight."

"What's going on?" asks Antoine.

Ivory slaps Antoine with the back of his hand. "Are you a bitch?"

"What?"

"Answer me! Are you a bitch?"

"No!"

"Then do not question me like a bitch. Or I will treat you like one." Ivory gets out of the car and knocks on the door.

"Who?" asks Marisol.

"It's Ivory. Open up."

Marisol opens the door. She says, "You were supposed to wait for me to beep you."

"Shut the fuck up. Where's the bag?"

"It's over there," says Marisol, motioning with her head, her hands hidden in the front pouch of her hoodie.

The bag sits on the floor on the other side of the bed. Ivory goes to the bag. He bends to unzip the zipper. Delores steps out of the bathroom. She aims her .38 at Ivory's head. Ivory looks at the pistol. He looks at Marisol. "You gonna be one very sorry bitch."

Delores says, "Shut up."

Taking note that Delores is wearing rubber gloves, Ivory says, "What, you gonna shoot me now?"

"Go on. Give me a reason," says Delores. "Make one move and I will blow your motherfuckin' face off."

Ivory continues, "You bust that, there's gonna be a bang. People gonna hear it."

Marisol crosses behind Ivory. She touches the stun gun to Ivory's hip. Ivory is jolted with 300,000 volts of electricity. Marisol keeps her finger on the button until Ivory falls down. Marisol steps away. Vincent steps out of the closet. Ivory is on the floor, his arms and legs twitching. Delores keeps her .38 trained on Ivory.

Marisol says, "What you waitin' for? Do it now!"

Vincent swings the baseball bat across the side of Ivory's skull. Marisol quickly turns away. With the side of his face caved in, Ivory stops moving altogether. Vincent gets the duffle bag out of the closet. He places the bat and Marisol's stun gun into the bag.

Outside, Desiree returns, pulling up alongside the Mercedes. But Clyde is no longer with her. She has dropped him off with Aunt Gloria at a movie theater in Jersey City. Desiree knocks on the window of the Mercedes. Antoine looks at her in surprise. Desiree pulls open his door. She says, "Come on, Antoine. We gotta go."

"Go where? Where we goin'? Ivory told me to wait for him."

"I got no time to explain," says Desiree. "But somethin's gone wrong and the cops are on they way! Hurry!"

"But—"

"Did you hear what I said? They gonna be here in a minute!"

Desiree pulls Antoine out of the Mercedes and hustles him into her car. She drives to the PATH station. She hands Antoine the keys to her apartment along with a fifty dollar bill. She says, "Wait for me at my place. I need you to let in Aunt Gloria and Clyde when they get home. If you do this for me there will be another hundred for you when I get back. But that's only if you don't fuck up."

"What the fuck is going on?"

"Nigga, I got no time to explain it all to you now. But I need you to help me with this. I'm giving you fifty now and another hundred later and all you gotta do is shut the fuck up and do what I say. You in or out?"

Although Desiree knows he will spend that fifty as soon as he hits Harlem, she is also sure he will go straight to her flat in order to get the hundred promised. A true junkie, Antoine will do just about anything for the rock. Even if it means deserting his post in Ivory's Mercedes...

Meanwhile, Marisol and Vincent have put Ivory White into the duffle bag. Vincent zips shut the bag. Delores puts her pistol in her purse. Marisol peeps out the curtain for Desiree. When Desiree returns, they transport the Ivory White filled duffle bag into the trunk of the Mercedes.

Vincent gets behind the wheel of the Mercedes. Marisol and Delores get into the other car with Desiree. Better to have a lone white man at the wheel when you have a body in the trunk. No need to risk a DWB.

CHAPTER ELEVEN

Vincent fears the darkness beyond the reach of his headlights. Like a black hole, he feels himself being sucked inside to an obliteration beyond his imagining.

What the fuck am I doing? How did I get here? How did I ever allow myself to be a part of this? To plan and plot the murder of another human being. Even if it is justified. Even if it was either him or us. No way Ivory was gonna let Desiree keep that money. And even if she did give it up, there was still Antoine to consider. It's amazing how much weight he lost, how fast he went down. Now, at least, there's hope for the kid. Unlike Tyrone. Poor fucking Tyrone. I failed him. Marisol, bitch that she is, is exactly right about that. I was his teacher. I should have known better. At least there's still a chance for me to help Antoine. But to kill to do it? To become a murderer? Was that the right choice? Did I have a choice? Or was I just following a line that was set before I was born... What a strange fucking philosophy... Although it does have a certain impeccable sense to it... Who are we to think that only we, by the nature of our awareness, can control the world we exist in? The universe has existed and will exist long before and after I've come and gone and it's only my self important ego that makes me believe, makes me deceive myself into thinking that I have any options in the matter of things... The car's compass is pointing south-west. It shows the direction but it sure as hell doesn't steer the car. It's nine-twenty-nine. But that clock can't slow or speed up time. The speedometer says how fast but it's not responsible for the miles per hour. Maybe we are all like the clock and the compass, witnesses to what we do, but not in any way the author of our actions. Maybe, like the moon and the sun, we are nothing more than bodies in motion, made up of billions of atoms that have been following a course, reacting to the reactions that came before... If the moon could think (maybe it does think, why the hell not?) might it not believe it is revolving around the earth, pulling our tides, out of its own free will? If this Mercedes could think, might it choose to believe it chose all the many roads and places it has traveled to and from?

In the wake of three distinctive "pops," comes the shattering of glass and plastic and a sharp, searing pain up the side of Vincent's ass. As more shots follow, Vincent reacts, steering the car onto the shoulder and getting the hell out.

As Vincent stares into the glare of Desiree's headlights, Marisol says, "What the fuck that cracker doin' now?"

Desiree puts the car into park behind the Mercedes. "Somethin' wrong," she says as Vincent makes his way towards them in a kind of hippity-hop, his right, rubber-gloved hand clutching his ass. As the women get out of their car, another trio of shots crack through the night air. Not slowing his momentum, Vincent grabs Desiree and shouts for them to take cover.

"What the fuck goin' on?" whines Marisol.

"He's not dead!" says Vincent. "And he's got a gun!"

"Oh, shit! You bleedin'!" says Desiree.

Crouched behind the rear of Vincent's father's car, they look at Vincent's jeans, dark with blood. "We gotta get you to a hospital," says Desiree. "It hurt?"

"Hell yes, it hurts!"

"Let me see," says Delores.

Another series of shots ring out. They all duck and flinch.

"How many bullets that nigga got?" hisses Marisol.

"Probably fourteen," says Delores. "But I haven't been counting. Here, help me with his pants."

"Fuck! Oh, Jesus Christ... Go easy, will ya!"

"Typical cracker crybaby," mutters Marisol.

"Just shut up, will you," says Desiree.

"It ain't deep," says Delores. "Just a graze. You lucky."

"I feel lucky," says Vincent, wincing. "This has got to be the luckiest day of my life."

"Cracker crazy," mutters Marisol.

"We should still get him to the hospital," says Desiree.

"Can't do that," says Delores. "I can take care of it later."

"Later?" says Vincent.

"What you talkin' about?" says Desiree.

"We can't take him to the hospital 'cause that the easiest way for the cops to tie him to what we been doin' tonight. And, in case you forgot, we got us an armed and wounded nigga in that trunk to deal with," says Delores, removing a pair of rubber gloves from her purse. "Most important thing we gotta do, right now, is take care of business and get the hell outta here!"

"Ma! Where you goin'?"

"Stay here with him. Just do what I say now. We gotta get outta here and quick."

"She's right," says Vincent. "I'll be alright."

With her .38 in hand, Delores walks along the grass towards the Mercedes. She approaches the rear bumper from the right side. She fires five bullets into the trunk: one into the side panel and four in a line along the top of the trunk. Following her second shot, however, a shot in return blasts out of the trunk and into the heavens. But Delores doesn't flinch in her mission, reloading and returning fire with five more rounds of her .38. In the long seconds of silence that follow, Vincent, Desiree and Marisol make their way to Delores, the little gang of four staring in wonder at the bullet riddled trunk.

"What now?" asks Desiree.

"Now, we get outta here," says Marisol.

Vincent looks up and down the deserted stretch of road. Lucky it all started after they turned off the highway...

"Let me think this out a second," says Delores. "We don't wanna make any big mistakes we can't fix."

"Why the hell didn't you take his gun from him after you killed him?" asks Desiree.

"We thought he was dead," says Vincent. "I thought I killed him with the bat."

"But you didn't," says Marisol.

"You shoulda made sure," says Desiree.

"I never killed nobody before," says Vincent.

"It's my fault. I shoulda known better," says Delores, going around to the front door of the Mercedes.

"What you doin'?"

Delores takes the keys from the ignition. "What I shoulda done before. Make sure the nigga is dead."

As Delores puts the key into the keyhole, everybody holds their breath with the sudden realization that the body inside may still be alive.

When the trunk pops open, the trunk light illuminates the body bag. Near the middle, two small holes and a spreading stain of dark blood.

"Stand back," says Delores.

At the sound of her voice, the bag jerks and Marisol screams, hopping backwards. The rest of them instinctively scoot back away from the trunk. They stand in silence, holding each other, staring at the open trunk.

"Shit," says Desiree. "He ain't dead!"

"We gotta hurry and get this thing done," says Delores.

"What if he still has some bullets left?" asks Vincent.

"I don't think he do," says Delores. "But we gotta be careful just in case."

"Just go over there and finish the nigga off," says Marisol.

"I don't have any more bullets," says Delores.

A guttural grunt cuts through the night and into their hearts.

"Oh shit!" says Desiree. "This is so fucked up."

"We gonna have to strangle him or club the motherfucka to death," says Marisol.

"And quick," says Vincent. "Before somebody comes!"

"Let's find a rock or something and get this over with," says Marisol.

"I don't see any rocks," says Delores.

"Maybe we can club him with the car jack," says Desiree.

"Car's too new," says Vincent. "The jack is probably too small."

"Mister fucking know it all," mutters Marisol.

"The bat's still in the bag," says Delores. "We'll have to use that."

They decide to remove the body bag from the trunk. This way it will be more effective and accurate to destroy the head. Delores hands Marisol and Desiree each a pair of fresh rubber gloves. Since Marisol has the shakes, Delores has to help her put them on.

"Let's hurry," says Vincent.

As they drag Ivory over the lip of the trunk, he begins to squirm and moan inside the bag. But the gang of four does not turn from the job at hand. They know they are in very deep now and if they don't quickly finish up, their lives will be ruined in a jail cell or worse. The pain in Vincent's ass is but an afterthought now. Grabbing the zipper, he pulls and is struck numb by the mutilated meat of Ivory's head. While the other three look away in horror, Vincent focuses his gaze on the two dying eyes staring out from the fright mask that was once a face, "I'm sorry about this," says Vincent, the words coming out without consideration or forethought.

Ivory White's mouth forms a rictus, followed by a piercing shriek that sends Marisol spinning backwards, that makes Desiree clutch her Mom in an endless instant of shock and fear.

It is a terrible sound that confirms a horrible demise.

CHAPTER TWELVE

Desiree walks Clyde and Aunt Gloria to the door. Telling Clyde to be a good boy, she kisses him and she kisses Aunt Gloria. She thanks Aunt Gloria one more time.

"Oh, it's my pleasure," says Aunt Gloria. "It really is."

"I know... But I hate to be calling you last minute all the time."

"Oh, shew... You can call me anytime. Day or night. You know that."

"Well, thanks again. For everything."

After locking the door, Desiree returns to the Formica top table. It is eleven o'clock in the morning. A small pile of newspapers lies on the table. Beside the newspapers are a pair of scissors and a bottle of Elmer's glue. On the floor, leaning against the leg of the table, is a large piece of cardboard. Desiree flips through yesterday's copy of the Daily News. The phone rings. Her mother, Delores, speaks out of the answering machine. Desiree picks up the phone and tells her that Clyde just left with Aunt Gloria. Delores says she is on her way. Desiree cuts out the article from the Daily News. She proceeds to flip through the other papers, cutting out articles and carefully placing them in a pile on the Formica top table. She takes a moment to go to the kitchen and pour a glass of cold red wine. She turns up the volume on the radio. She is a big fan of R. Kelly. Not so much for the words he sings but for the way he sings them. He could be speaking in another language and she'd still like him. Probably like him even better that way... Listening to the music, Desiree thinks about Vincent. She thinks about fucking Vincent. She thinks how excited he gets and how his excitement fuels her own excitement more than anything else. Then, she realizes that this has been the longest time they have gone without fucking since they started fucking. Almost a week now. But a lot of shit has been going down lately. A lot of real heavy shit that would throw off even the most freaky of freaks...

Desiree looks at the photo of Ivory's car—the shot up windshield, the bullet holes in the popped up trunk, and the driver's side door still thrown open. It's hard to imagine she was even there. She picks up the photo, studying it closely until all she can focus on is the grainy black and white dots that make up the image. There is a knock on the door.

"Who?"

"It's me, Vincent. And your Mom."

Desiree goes to the door. She opens the door. She kisses her Mom on the cheek and Vincent on the lips. Under Vincent's arm are more newspapers. He places them on the Formica top table. "These are the ones from Jersey," he says.

"Anything in 'em?" asks Desiree.

"Plenty," says Delores.

"You seen them?" says Desiree.

"In the car," says Delores. "Your man here gave me a lift from 120th. At first, I thought he might be a cop but then, by the way he was honking on that horn, I knew he couldn't be no cop."

"Just some crazy white man beeping his horn," smiles Vincent.

"You said it, not me," says Delores.

"You all want some wine?" asks Desiree.

Vincent nods. Delores says, "Hm-m."

Desiree fills another two juice glasses from the jug stored in the fridge. She places them down on the table in-between the scattered pile of newspapers. As Vincent flips through the Newark Star Ledger, Delores shows Desire an article from the Record: "MEADOWLANDS MURDER AND MAYHEM." It is a two-page spread with a large photo of the shot up Mercedes along with a smaller insert taken from a decade old mug shot. Desiree examines the photos in horror and curiosity. She reads the headline, her lips moving to the words in her mind. Then, reading aloud, "'Harlem resident,

Ivory White, victim of grisly mob style execution... Police still trying to piece together the exact order of events..."

"They can do all the piecing they want," says Delores. "Just as long as they never find the gun, we be fine."

"Don't worry," says Vincent. "We solid with that. At least we got that part right."

Desiree begins cutting out an article. Vincent pulls out another story from the Newark Star Ledger. "Check this out," he says.

Delores and Desiree look at the photo of Ivory's carcass beneath an ambulance blanket, the dark pavement made darker where the blood ran hot and turned cold. Vincent points at the tips of a pair of shoes in the bottom left corner of the shot.

"I wonder who's feet they are?" he asks.

"Probably the cop or the ambulance man," says Desiree.

"Or the photographer," says Delores.

"I guess we'll never know," says Vincent.

The three begin to pick and cut and paste all the articles to the big piece of cardboard in very much the same fashion as a grade school social studies project. When they are finished, Desiree calls Marisol on the phone.

"We ready," says Desiree. "You all set?"

"Yeah," says Marisol.

"Alright then," says Desiree. "Come on over."

"Dee Dee?"

"Yeah?"

"You sure on this?"

"No. I'm not sure. How can I be sure? But we still gotta try. Or else it's all for nuthin'... You there?"

"Yeah, I'm here," says Marisol.

"Alright then, we waitin'. Let's do this." Desiree hangs up the phone.

"She comin?" asks Delores.

"Yeah," says Desiree, going to the fridge and getting the wine bottle to refill their glasses. "She seems a little shaky though."

"We all a little shaky," says Delores. "Be crazy not to be."

CHAPTER THIRTEEN

Desiree opens the door. She gives Marisol and Antoine a kiss and a hug. Vincent and Delores are standing near the Formica top table. In the center of the room, a chair has been placed facing the far wall. On the far wall, the cardboard display of Ivory White's demise is tacked up but covered over with a bedsheet. Beside it, a second cardboard display is likewise tacked up and covered by a sheet.

Desiree closes the door. Walking into the room, Antoine says, "What's up? What is this, a surprise party or somethin'? Whose birthday is it?"

"It's a surprise party, alright," says Marisol. "But it ain't got nuthin' to do wif nobody's birthday."

"Huh?"

"Nigga, just sit the fuck down," says Marisol.

Antoine looks to Vincent. Vincent says, "It's gonna be alright. Just have a seat so we can start."

"Start what?" says Antoine, allowing himself to be steered to the chair by Marisol. "What the hell is going on?"

"You is what's goin' on," says Delores. "You and me and all of us here. All of us here who love you and who are not gonna let you get hurt and hurt yourself no more."

"Oh, okay," says Antoine, smiling. "I get it. I know where this is goin'."

"Nigga, just shut up," says Marisol.

Ignoring Marisol, Vincent asks, "Oh, yeah? Where is it going, Antoine?"

"Somethin' to do with me and my issues."

"Issues? You beyond fuckin' issues. You a fuckin' crackhead!" says Marisol. "Look at your bum ass self! You a got-damn disgrace. Somebody get me a fuckin' mirror. Have you looked at yourself lately? Answer me, nigga!"

"I'm outta here," says Antoine, getting up from the chair.

Vincent reaches into his pocket. He removes a twenty-packet bundle of dime bag crack. "This is for you," he says. "But only after you sit down and let us finish here."

Antoine looks at the packets of crack. He cocks his head in the same way a dog does when finding something strange in his food bowl. "What's up with you all?"

"Just sit down," says Vincent, putting the crack back in his pocket. "Please trust me on this. Just sit and listen to and then it's all yours. No bullshit."

"That real? This ain't some kinda stupid joke?"

"No jokes. No bullshit," says Vincent. "I got two hundred dollars worth here for you as soon as we done. So as soon as we can get started, the sooner you can get your reward."

"Reward... You one funny ass white man," says Antoine. "I give you that."

"So, you ready?" says Vincent "We need your full attention and an open mind."

"Sounds like I'm back in class."

"Nigga, you gonna be schooled or you gonna be dead," says Marisol.

"Why you gotta be like that?"

"She loves you," says Delores. "We all do."

"And I love you all too. Even the cracker," says Antoine, smiling at Vincent.

"Thanks, Antoine," says Vincent. "Ready?"

"Yeah. Go on. Say what you gotta say."

Desiree removes the sheet from the Ivory White display. Antoine sits up in his chair, his eyes darting from the photos to the boldfaced headlines of murder and mayhem. Antoine gets up from the chair. He goes close to the display, reading one article and then the next. "What the fuck," he mutters. "When this happen? How come I didn't hear about this?"

"Because, nigga, you a crackhead," says Marisol. "When the last time you looked at the TV or a newspaper? All you be thinkin' about is your next rock."

Antoine sits back down in the chair, clearly shaken, at first shocked by the murder but then even more troubled by the fact that his supply line has been cut off forever.

"I know what you thinkin'," says Delores. "How the hell I gonna be able to score without Ivory. Then, sure enough, your mind first gonna lead you to us, to everybody you love and then to just about everybody you ever knew... You gonna be hittin' us all up for cash. Loans at first and then straight out beggin'. And when you used up all of that, you gonna commence to thievin'. You gonna do just about anything to get that next score. And that, that'll be the end of you. I know it. And, deep down, you gotta know it too."

"But we ain't gonna let that happen," says Desiree. "We love you too much to let you go out like that."

Antoine looks back to the display. "But how? Who?"

"That's not for you to think about," says Delores. "He was taken out so you could live."

"What you sayin'?" asks Antoine.

"We sayin' that the motherfucka had to be snuffed to save your sorry ass," says Marisol. "But before we go any further with this, you gotta get it through your head that you were never with the nigga in Jersey that day."

"That's right," says Delores. "If the cops ever do come around, asking questions, all you gotta remember is that you was never in Jersey. As long as you remember that, you be okay. We all be okay."

The realization suddenly hits Antoine. "You all had him snuffed... Or..."

The gang of four stares at Antoine. Marisol says, "All you gotta know is that the nigga is dead. He dead but you still be breathin'."

"You all snuffed Ivory?"

"He wasn't nothin' but a slave master," says Desiree. "A modern-day slave master who had to be taken out to save your ass and who knows how many others."

Antoine runs his hands around his head and then his palms over and down his eyes and face. Desiree removes the second sheet to reveal the other cardboard display. At the center of the collage are family snapshots. Surrounding the snapshots are the dozens of news photos and articles detailing Antoine's basketball days. Each clipping momentarily bringing him back, one after the other, to the memory of each specific glory. Along with Antoine, the gang of four likewise scans the clippings, the shared emotion in the room become palpable in the falling tears that give way to the suppressed weeping of first Marisol and then Antoine.

CHAPTER FOURTEEN

In a moment of clarity, Antoine understands how far he has fallen. He also sees that it's not much further to where Ivory White ended up.

"I think we should get going now," says Vincent.

Delores nods.

"Where we goin'?" asks Antoine to Marisol.

"You and him are gonna go and get you fixed up," says Marisol. "And when you better, I'm gonna be there to take you home."

"What?"

"I'll explain everything in the car," says Vincent.

"Hey, what kind of a setup is this? I ain't goin' nowhere I don't know where I'm goin' to."

"You goin' someplace that gonna cure your habit," says Marisol.

"What? You gonna get me locked up? You must be buggin. You think I gonna let you or anybody else get me—"

"You goin' to a hospital," says Delores. "A special kinda hospital that gonna help you get that monkey off your back."

"Like where Bobby Brown went to? A rehab?"

"That's right," says Desiree.

"I don't know about all of this," says Antoine.

"Nigga, you don't got to know nuthin' but the fact that you fucked up and you either got to get better or die," says Marisol.

"Hey, let's all calm down a minute," says Vincent. "Antoine, we're all here to help you. You know that. You also understand how fucked up your life has become. Am I right?"

"What you mean, 'fucked up?' I still maintaining. Yeah, I got me a little problem... Check that, maybe it's a big fucking problem. But it ain't nothin' I can't handle."

"Oh, yeah?" says Vincent.

"That's right."

Vincent removes the crack from his pocket. "I still owe you this. You still want it?"

Antoine stares at the bundles of crack. His soul salivating at the sight of his supreme desire. Antoine nods.

"Alright, then," says Vincent. "It's all yours. You can smoke it all up on the way to Veritas Village. That's the name of the rehab center. It's a good place, a solid place. I've been there myself."

Antoine looks at Vincent, seeing a side of him he knew was there all along but failed to notice until just this instant.

"No, it wasn't crack," says Vincent. "But I did get better. And you're gonna get better too. C'mon let's get goin'."

As soon as they cross the bridge out of the city, Vincent hands Antoine his first bag of crack. It is a charged moment for the two of them. Each of them realizing it is a turning point of some kind but a turning point around a blind corner. Antoine closes his fist about the tiny ziplock baggy. He covers this fist with the palm of his free hand. Looking out the window he says, "I never had no teacher like you before."

Vincent smiles, "I never had a student like you before either."

Antoine licks his lips. He looks out the window. He removes a short glass tube from his jacket pocket. Near one end, a clump of metal wool is stuffed inside to prevent the rock from shooting down the tube. Antoine puts the crack into the tube snug against the metal wool.

"Hey, can I ask you something?" says Vincent.

"What?"

"What's it feel like?"

Antoine doesn't have to think about this. "It's like you've been holding your breath your whole life and you suddenly come up for air. Your lungs and your whole body can't fucking believe how you've been missing out on this mad, intense, pleasurable feeling your whole life. But then, as soon as it hits you, it's gone again. Up in smoke. So the only thing to do is to get yourself back there and the only way to do it is to keep on smoking 'till you run out."

"Sounds like a heavy load."

"You know," says Antoine. "I'm gonna try. I mean, when we get to this place we're going? I'm gonna try real hard. Because I know what I did and what I'm doing to myself is gonna kill me. But, the thing is, I also know that there's nothing in this world that's ever gonna make me feel as good as crack does. And that's a fact."

Antoine fires up the rock with a butane lighter. There is a crackling sound and a chemical stench followed by the smoke running up the tube, down into Antoine's lungs and bloodstream... Antoine closes his eyes, the bliss overwhelming and complete.

It is not a long ride to Veritas Village. All along the way, Vincent keeps feeding Antoine the crack. When they exit the highway, Vincent hands Antoine a small bag of weed and some rolling papers. He says, "Desiree says you gotta finish the rest as a coolly. Be better that way."

"We here?"

"Almost," says Vincent. "You alright to roll it?"

"Yeah, I'm alright."

"You wanna beer or something?"

"Maybe a Pepsi."

Vincent drives the car into a strip mall. "You wait here," he says. "I'll be back in a minute."

"Alright, but give me the rest so I can set it up."

"When I get back," says Vincent.

Vincent buys a Pepsi and a quart bottle of Miller for himself. When he returns to the car, Antoine has a crazed look on his face and is shaking a leg.

"You okay?"

"Yeah. I'm fucking fine!"

"You're gonna be alright," says Vincent. "Just as long as you give it a try, you gonna make it."

"How the fuck you know that?"

"I guess I don't," says Vincent. "But that's what I hope. You have a strong mind and you're tough. And if you try hard enough, with those two things, you can make it through. That I do know."

"What were you addicted to? Cocaine?"

"Na," says Vincent. "Not that I didn't do my share of coke along with a bunch of other junk along the way. When I went in, it was for nearly overdosing on Valium."

"Valium? What's that?"

"It's a kinda pill."

"Oh."

"But, you know, my addiction wasn't the problem. My addiction was the solution. It's kinda hard to explain."

"I know exactly what you mean."

After getting back on the road, Vincent hands Antoine the last of the crack. Antoine crushes up the pieces, rolling it up with the weed into a fat joint.

"How come they call it a coolly?" asks Vincent.

Antoine shrugs, "The weed is supposed to cool you down. Make it easier so you don't crash so hard."

"Don't light that up just yet," says Vincent.

"Why not?"

"They got cops around here that are a half salute away from Nazi storm troopers. We gonna be there in a minute. You can smoke in the parking lot."

"What? You gonna let me light up at the rehab place?"

"Of course. Nobody will bother us there."

"What if somebody there see me?"

"It don't bother them none. They expect it."

In less than five minutes, they are driving up to the front gates of Veritas Village. After Vincent gives his name to the guard at the gatehouse, they proceed down a treelined drive to the parking lot. Set up on an old estate, Veritas Village sits at the top of a hill overlooking the Hudson River. When they park the car, Vincent nods his head towards the other parked cars in the lot. In most of them, there are two people, one of whom who is either drinking or smoking or sniffing some sort of drug.

"This is so bugged out," says Antoine.

"Yeah, I thought the same thing," says Vincent, drinking from his beer bottle. "And what I'm supposed to say now is: 'Go on and enjoy yourself. Because this is gonna be the last time you ever smoke crack for the rest of your life.'"

Antoine shakes his head. He lights up. Vincent can smell the sweet scent of weed being overpowered by the crack chemical smell. Vincent is curious about the crack. Although he has sniffed cocaine in the past, he wonders how much more potent crack can possibly be. Vincent tells himself that if Antoine offers him a puff, he will give it a try. But Antoine never considers such an option. For Antoine, Vincent no longer exists. Nothing exists but the moment's smoke filled bliss, a rapture that entirely eclipses the spinning world.

CHAPTER FIFTEEN

Desiree is reluctant to light the joint. She is reluctant because this is the first time she is going to meet Vincent's parents. She is also reluctant because she loves the "new car smell" and doesn't want to destroy it so soon. Paid for in cash, they bought the Jeep right off the lot. Neither Desiree nor Vincent has ever owned a brand new car before.

"What you thinkin' about?"

Desiree turns to Vincent. "I was thinkin' about lightin' a joint."

"Spark it up then."

"Maybe I'll wait 'till afterwards."

"Okay," says Vincent. "You nervous about this?"

"A little."

As they approach the George Washington Bridge, Vincent points towards the tenement towers built above the highway. "I remember when I was a kid, driving under these same buildings. I used to think it was so incredible that all these people were living above the highway while the millions of other people, people like me and my family, were passing below them each day in their cars and trucks... My father, he always used to say the same damn thing every time we passed this way: 'There's thousands of poor people living in the slums right above us, right now.' My father never used the word, 'ghetto.' Just, 'the slums.' As a kid, it was a haunting word for me. He used to tell me how dangerous the slums were. Places where poor and dangerous people live. 'And even though most poor people are good people, there's enough of the bad ones around to make the good ones afraid day and night.'"

"He wasn't too far off the mark."

"Yeah, but he's never really on the mark either. Just wait 'till you meet him, you'll see."

"Maybe I will light this joint."

As Desiree puts fire to the weed, Vincent's mind wanders from his own father to Desiree's father. "You ever think about your dad? Your real dad?"

Desiree cracks the window, blows smoke. She passes the joint to Vincent. "Not that much. I never knew him. Only stuff I know about him is what my Moms told me."

"What kinda stuff?"

Desiree smiles, "You are one nosy ass, ain't you?"

"I'm sorry..."

"I'm just playin' with ya... Dag..."

"He died when you were a baby, right?"

"Yeah. In Viet Nam..."

"He got drafted?"

"No, not really."

"Don't tell me he joined up?"

"No, he didn't join up but he didn't get drafted either. According to my Moms, he had three choices."

"Sounds like a fairy tale."

"It kinda is like a fairy tale... He used to work for the mob. The Italian mob."

"The mafia."

"Yeah. That's what my Moms said."

"What he do?"

"I don't know. My Moms didn't know either. He kept his business and family completely separate. But whatever he did, he got caught by the feds who gave him the choice of snitching, going to jail, or going to Viet Nam."

"I guess he didn't have too much of a choice then," says Vincent.

"I guess not."

"Must be sad not ever getting to know him."

"It's hard to miss what you never had... But I am thankful to him."

"For what?"

"Ever since I took over the apartment? Never paid rent. And every other month? I get an envelope of cash with no return address."

"Oh, yeah?"

"Yeah. Not so much, not like I can go crazy with it or nothin'. But enough to pay for my food and smoke, enough to live by, enough to chill by…"

"For real?"

"Yes. Whatever he did by not snitching definitely paid off. For me and Clyde at least."

"You think it's the mob taking care of you like that?"

"I know it is. My Moms, she don't like to talk much about it… But she told me that part."

"Do you think she gets an allowance too?"

"An allowance? You funny. Na, there's just one allowance. She used to get it first. Back when she used to live where I live now."

"That is sorta like a fairy tale. Whoever lives in your place, gets taken care of."

"I guess."

"When did your Mom move out?"

"Maybe a month or so before I had Clyde. Right from the beginning, she didn't want me to go through with it. We had all kinds of drama all through my pregnancy. But then, when she knew that there was nothing gonna stop me from having my baby, she handed me over the keys and told me about the rent and the cash envelope. Told it to me matter of factly, like she was giving me a shopping list or something. My Moms is funny like that. For months on end she near drives me outta my mind and then, suddenly, with no warning, she changes gears, tells me what she's gotta tell me and is gone."

"Where'd she go?"

"Who knows. I didn't see her again until Clyde was pretty near his first year."

"She wasn't there when you gave birth?"

"Hell, no. I popped that child out all on my own."

"What about Rosco?"

"That nigga was all up in his own shit. But let's not get on that subject right now."

Desiree flicks the roach into the wind. She turns on the radio, running through the stations for something she can listen to...

CHAPTER SIXTEEN

After parking the car, they share a quick glance before going up the front steps. The door isn't locked. Vincent passes inside. Desiree follows right behind, feeling a bit like a cat burglar or a cop.

Inside the living room, a local merchant shouts about installing storm windows. Vincent's sister, Gina, sits in front of the TV, talking loudly into the phone. Desiree notices the plastic saint turned upside-down on the end table. When Vincent lowers the TV, Gina looks up and, for a moment, loses focus of her phone conversation. Desiree smiles at Gina's surprise.

Gina speaks into the phone, "I gotta go." And hangs up.

"This is my sister, Gina," says Vincent.

"Hi, I'm Desiree."

"Hello," says Gina. "You're real pretty."

"Thank you."

"How the hell you get her?" asks Gina.

"Shut your mouth," says Vincent. "And try, just for once, not to be so much of a jerk. Okay?"

"Eat me, Vincent."

"Nice, right?" says Vincent to Desiree.

Desiree smiles, shrugs.

"Where's Ma?"

"She's in the kitchen, where else?" says Gina, picking up the phone again. "You know, you sorta look like that girl in that movie, 'Clueless?' You know, the black one?"

"What the hell is wrong with you!"

"I didn't see it," says Desiree.

"What?" says Gina to Vincent's glaring. "What? The girl in the movie was real pretty. So what's wrong with that?"

"C'mon," says Vincent to Desiree.

"It was nice meeting you, Gina."

"Yeah, me too," says Gina, dialing the phone.

Vincent's mother looks up from a steaming pot of linguine. "Oh, hello," she says, the steam further frizzing her already frazzled hair.

"Ma, this is Desiree. Desiree, this is my mom."

Vincent's mother wipes her hand on her Italy-map apron before taking Desiree's. Letting go, she picks up the wooden spoon again to stir the gravy.

"Smells real good," says Desiree.

Vincent's mother smiles.

Vincent says, "Where's Pop?"

"I think he's burning out back."

"Don't he know it's against the law?"

Vincent's mother gives Vincent a look.

Vincent rolls his eyes. He turns to Desiree. "You wanna go meet my father?"

"Sure," says Desiree.

A large branch from a tree rooted in the next yard overhangs in the center of Vincent's backyard. It is a small space filled with leafless rose bushes and a variety of religious statues. Standing on a stepladder, Vincent's father wields a wood rake, attacking the overhanging branch in an attempt to beat down the last brown leaves that failed to fall.

Vincent and Desiree watch him swat at the branch, the stepladder precariously tipping this way and that throughout the onslaught.

"He's completely nuts," says Vincent.

"What's he doin'?"

"You see that pile of leaves over there?"

"Yeah."

"He wants to make sure he got all the leaves before he burns 'em up."

"Oh."

"He's like that with everything. He's nuts."

Vincent's father is on the very top step of the ladder but still cannot strike down the two remaining holdouts at the tip of the branch. Vincent crosses around to the front of the ladder. Vincent shouts, "Hey, you need any help?"

But before Vincent's father can stop himself, his swinging continues on the down stroke, clocking Vincent across the side of his face and neck.

"Oh, my!" shouts Desiree.

"Fuck!" shouts Vincent.

"Shit!" says Vincent's father.

As Vincent's father examines the cracked teeth of his rake, Desiree takes in the three red lines running down Vincent's cheek, trying her best not to bust out laughing.

"I know you wanna laugh," says Vincent.

Desiree starts laughing.

Vincent's father says, "You okay?"

"I'm just great," says Vincent. "Nothing like being slapped in the face with a rake."

"Sarcasm," says Vincent's father.

"Oh, really?" says Vincent. "Is that what it is?"

"It's a crutch. Great men never use it. They don't need to."

"I guess I'm not a great man then."

"Not when you're being sarcastic," he says, turning to Desiree. "Hello."

Desiree shakes his hand. "Hi, I'm Desiree."

"I'm Victor. I'm Vincent's father."

"You gonna burn that pile of leaves?"

"As soon as I can get down those two," he says, pointing at the leaves with the handle of the rake.

"Hey, Vincent. Why don't you give your father a hand. I'll bet you can reach 'em."

Vincent stares at Desiree and looks at his father who hands him the rake. Vincent climbs up the ladder. "Somebody please hold it steady," says Vincent.

Both Victor and Desiree hold the ladder, making sure to be well out of the way of Vincent's swinging. Within three tries, the two leaves are mutilated and de-branched. Vincent comes down the ladder, handing the rake back to his father. His father in turn sweeps the remaining pieces of leaves into the leaf pile at the center of the yard. "Will you bring me the can?" he says.

Vincent goes to where the gas can sits on a small patio of red brick stones. He carries the can to his father. He takes Desiree by the arm back to the patio and together they watch as Vincent's father douses the leaves with gas.

"That's probably enough," says Vincent.

Ignoring his son, he empties the can before bringing it back to the patio. Reapproaching the wet pile of leaves, he pulls a book of matches from his pocket. He rips out a clump of matches. He stands back a foot. He strikes the matches, tosses the flame, and dashes to the patio as a ball of fire wooshes to the sky. While the leaves crackle and pop, the three of them watch the dancing of the flames. When Vincent lights a cigarette, Desiree pulls one of her own.

"What is it about fires?" muses Vincent.

"What's what?" asks Vincent's father.

"Most people like to watch them. Right? Campfires... Bonfires... Even house fires have a certain strange attraction... Maybe it goes back to caveman times... The fire kept us warm. Kept us safe from danger... What do you think?"

"Makes sense," says Desiree.

"It's gonna be the fire next time," says Vincent's father. "That's why."

"Huh?"

"The world is gonna end in fire. First it was the flood. But next time, it's gonna be by fire. Says so in the Bible.

"Even if that was true," says Vincent. "Why would we wanna look at the thing that's gonna end up destroying us?"

"Human nature. Why did Eve pick that apple?"

"I don't know, but I have a strong feeling you're gonna tell us."

"She picked it because she couldn't get her mind off of it. It obsessed her because she knew it would end up killing her."

"That don't make any sense," says Vincent. "Why, if she knew it was gonna kill her, go ahead and pick it and ruin everything."

"It's easy to be a Monday morning quarterback. But people have been forever doing things that they know are not only wrong but harmful, even deadly. Like that cigarette in your mouth."

"I like your statues," says Desiree.

"Thank you," says Vincent's father.

"Who's that?" she says pointing to the nearest one.

"That's St. Francis, the sissy. He also loves animals. My wife picked him out."

"It's Assisi," says Vincent.

"Right. He was."

"He's Saint Francis of Assisi," says Vincent to Desiree. "Assisi is a place in Italy where he was from."

"You've gotta lighten up some," says Vincent's father.

"Did you arrange them all like that yourself?"

"Yes, I did."

"You did a wonderful job," says Desiree. "I don't think I ever saw anything quite like it."

"Thank you."

"And him?"

"That's Saint Joseph. The husband of our Lady."

"Jesus's mother. That's her there, right?" says Desiree.

"Yes, that's right. But I got him much later. Just last year, as a matter of fact. When I was considering selling the house."

"You're gonna sell the house?" asks Vincent.

"Not right away," says his father. "Not until your sister is out."

"Does Saint Joseph have some sort of power with buying and selling houses?"

"Yes, he does," says Vincent's father. "Whenever you get ready to sell a house, you bury yourself a Saint Joseph in the backyard."

"Nutty, nutty, nuts..." mutters Vincent.

"You can make fun and belittle all you like," says his father. "But someday, someday you'll see the light."

"Who's that over there? I never saw someone nailed to the cross like that before. Is he related to the statue that I saw inside your house by the TV?"

"That's Saint Peter. Inside is Saint Anthony."

"But why are they both upside-down?" asks Desiree.

"Saint Anthony is upside-down because my wife put him upside-down because our daughter failed one of her classes."

"He's the patron saint of lost causes," says Vincent.

"But why put him upside-down?" asks Desiree.

"Because my wife is saying a novena to Saint Anthony for Gina to pass her class next time. And we keep him upside-down to make sure he follows through on his end."

"So when she passes the class, you put him back right-side up?"

"Exactly," says Vincent's father.

"Maybe we should go back inside," says Vincent.

"I've gotta wait for the fire to burn down," says his father.

"So what's going on with Saint Peter?" asks Desiree. "Not only is he upside-down, but he's also nailed to a cross."

"Saint Peter asked the Romans to do that. He didn't think he was worthy of being crucified in the same way as Jesus."

"I never heard of that before."

"You never heard of Saint Peter?" asks Vincent's father. "He's the one who holds the keys to heaven. After you die, to get in, you gotta get passed him first."

"No, I never knew that."

"He was also the first Pope."

Vincent says, "He was first a fisherman and then a disciple of Jesus. The idea of a Pope and all that kinda stuff only came years and years afterwards."

"What's your point?" says Vincent's father.

"No point, just giving her a fact."

"The most important thing about Saint Peter," says Vincent's father. "Is the fact that he denied Christ and wept bitter tears."

"Why is that?" asks Desiree.

"Stop egging him on," mutters Vincent.

"You gotta let all that sarcasm go, son. It's really no good for nobody," says Vincent's father, turning to Desiree. "Before he was crucified, Jesus told Peter that he would deny him three times before the cock crows. To which Peter said that he would never do such a thing but the very next day, after they dragged off our Lord, it was none other than Saint Peter denying he ever even knew Jesus to various no-goodnicks on the scene. He did it three times and when the cock crowed, that's a rooster, Peter heard the crowing and broke down and wept bitter tears."

"It's important to note that they were bitter," quips Vincent.

"That's right," says Vincent's father. "The bitter tears of guilt. Shame, remorse, regret... The backbone of all true religions."

"What about love and forgiveness?" says Vincent.

"Those are very important too," says Vincent's father. "But without guilt, forgiveness and love have no real flavor. It's the guilt that puts us above the animals. Guilt is the best thing a man can have going for him."

"But don't you usually feel guilty after you've done something wrong?" asks Desiree.

"I suppose so," says Vincent's father. "Most of the time."

"Then what good does it serve if the bad thing already happened?"

"When Vincent was a little boy—"

"Here we go," says Vincent.

"Let him finish," says Desiree.

"I guess he was about three or maybe four, he was fascinated by the stove top. It didn't matter how many times I told him to stay away from it. Didn't even matter how many times I spanked him. He was just obsessed with the stove top. Which you can understand if you put yourself in the mind of a little kid: seeing the blue flames shoot up like magic in a neat flaming circle... So one day I decide to let him go ahead and play with it. Only, before hand, I put the fire on a minute so the metal was good and hot. And I told him, 'Son, don't touch, it's hot. It's very hot!' And he just looked at me and looked at the stove and went ahead and touched it. The expression on his chubby little face was priceless! But he didn't cry. He just kept saying, over and over: 'HOT! HOT! HOT!'"

"You sure had a loving way with us kids," says Vincent.

"But you never touched that stove again, did you?"

"Nope."

"And guilt works the same sort of way. After we do something wrong, the guilt makes us unhappy about what we did. Otherwise, we'd be doing bad things all the time. Guilt is something that God puts in us that makes us different than the rest of creation. Guilt is the voice of God speaking to us, trying to keep us honest and correct."

"Like our conscience," says Desiree.

"Guilt is a big part of our conscience. Without guilt, you'd have no conscience because everything would be permitted."

"Do you think God ever feels guilty?" asks Desiree.

"That's an interesting question," says Vincent's father. "I know he feels sad when we do something wrong. And since he made us, maybe he does somehow feel a certain sense of regret over what we've done even though we did it ourselves... That's why I suppose he has to also be a very forgiving God too. He has to know our tendencies to screw up throughout our lives. Unless we become saints."

"Some of the most famous saints were incredible sinners first," says Vincent.

"You're absolutely right," says his father. "And?"

"Maybe God puts guilt in there as a form of revenge," says Vincent. "Maybe since we make God feel sad he in turn makes us feel guilty. And those saints like Paul with murder and blood on their hands? Maybe they feel so guilty about it that it gives them energy and incentive to become saints when they realize what they did."

"Even though once again you are trying to be sarcastic, you do have a point."

"I was just kidding," says Vincent.

"I know you were," says his father. "But even a fool can sometimes utter a truth or two."

"So you think God makes us guilty out of revenge?"

"I would never try to fathom the mind of the Almighty," says Vincent's father. "But I do know that he did say 'I am a vengeful God' in the Bible. That part does come to mind."

Gina appears at the back door. "Ma says dinner's ready! Hey, what the hell happened to your face?"

"Pop clocked me with a rake," says Vincent.

"You probably deserved it."

"Of course I did."

With the fire smoldering behind them, the three enter the house. The kitchen table is set out with a big platter of linguini and meat sauce, chicken cacciatore, and a jug of Gallo red wine. While Desiree goes to wash in the bathroom just off the kitchen, Vincent and his father wash their hands in the kitchen sink.

"Hey, hey, hey," says the father. "You only need one."

Vincent ignores him and continues to dry his hands with the two paper towels he's ripped from the roll.

"What happened to your face?"

"It's nothing, Ma."

"Daddy smacked him with the rake," says Gina.

"Victor!"

"It was an accident!"

"Can we just drop it?" says Vincent. "Move on to something else? Please?"

Desiree re-enters the kitchen. She sits down in a chair between Vincent and his father.

"Would someone like to say the grace?" asks Vincent's father. Following the pause, he says, "Vincent? Would you please say the grace?"

Vincent bites his lower lip. He says, "Lord, thank you for blessing us with the bitter tears of guilt that allow us to raise ourselves above the animals like this chicken here before us who was cut and killed so that we can live another day. Amen."

"Amen," says the father.

"That was the most retarded prayer I ever heard," says Gina.

"It was a sarcastic prayer," says the father. "But the Lord moves in mysterious ways."

"What's that supposed to mean?" asks Gina.

"It means that maybe God is saying something to Vincent with Vincent's own mouth."

"That don't make no sense neither," says Gina.

"Let's all eat," says Vincent's mom.

"Good idea," says Vincent.

Soon, the platters are passed and sacked of their contents, followed by the clatter of utensils, the sounds of chewing, and the swilling of wine from the short juice glasses. Talk is kept to a minimum, only enough to support the logistics of the meal, harkening back to bygone days when the rule, "No talking during dinner," had to be frequently repeated and periodically enforced with a slap to the skull.

Following the meal, strong coffee, sambuca and brandy are served along with a box of chocolate chip cookies and a choice of vanilla or chocolate ice cream.

"Feel free to Cosmo," says Vincent's father, undoing his belt and top pants button.

"It comes from our Uncle Cosmo," explains Vincent to Desiree. "He always used to unbutton his pants after a big meal."

"Then they would lay down on the floor," says Gina.

"Excuse me?" says Desiree.

"At Uncle Cosmo and Aunt Stella's house? If the meal was really big like on Christmas and Thanksgiving? Then everybody would go into the living room and lay down on the floor with their pants unbuttoned because they were so stuffed," says Vincent.

"And listen to Italian music," says Gina. "That was the only part I didn't care for."

"You should be proud of your heritage," says Vincent's father.

"Italian music sucks," says Gina.

"Watch that mouth," says Vincent's father.

"We used to have something like that too," says Desiree. "Only we called it 'niggaritus.' You know, after you ate too much food?"

Vincent chokes and his mother slaps him on the back.

Gina says, "I never heard of that before."

"It's an old expression from back in the day," says Desiree. "Sort of a joke on the idea that all black people wanna do is eat and lay back. So, after a really big meal or barbeque, you would pat your belly and say, 'I think I got myself a bout of niggaritus' and lay down somewhere to digest."

"Oh, like a disease," says Gina. "Like tonsillitis."

"That's right," says Desiree.

"Isn't that interesting," says Vincent's mom.

"What's that, Ma?" asks Gina.

"Vincent picked the chocolate and she picked the vanilla."

"Ma, what's wrong with you?" says Vincent.

"I was thinking the same thing," says Gina.

"I'm sorry," says Vincent to Desiree.

"Sorry for what?" says Desiree.

"Did I say something wrong?" says Vincent's mom.

"No, Ma. Just forget it."

"Don't tell me to forget it!"

"Alright, alright," says Vincent. "Just calm down, alright?"

"You see what you did?" says Gina. "You always do this."

"Alright, enough," says the father.

"I'm sorry. I'm very sorry," says Vincent's mom.

"No, it's fine," says Desiree. "Really."

"Look," says Gina. "You made her weep."

"Shut up," says Vincent.

"I am not weeping!"

"It's alright to cry," says Gina. "Go on, let it all out. That's what Oprah says."

"We don't care what the hell Oprah says," says Vincent.

"Watch that mouth at my table!"

"I love Oprah," says Gina. "What do you think of her, Dee? Can I call you Dee?"

"Sure," says Desiree. "I guess I like Oprah too. Although I don't really watch TV that much."

"I have to go to the bathroom!" declares Vincent's mother.

"Honey, it's alright," says Vincent's father.

"I have to go!" she shouts, moving out of the kitchen towards the bathroom.

"C'mon, Ma," says Vincent.

The slam of the bathroom door.

"It's all your fault," says Gina.

"Could somebody tell her to shut up, please?"

"She's right," says Vincent's father to Vincent. "It is your fault. Mostly."

"So I guess I should feel guilty now."

"Indeed you should," says the father.

"Indeed. Indeed. Indeed," sings Gina.

Long minutes of silence fill the kitchen as they sip their drinks while waiting and hoping for the mother's return.

Finally, Vincent gets up and goes to the bathroom. "Hey, Ma, you alright in there? Ma? C'mon, Ma. I'm sorry... Everything's okay. C'mon, Ma. Please? We got company here... Ma?"

Vincent returns to the kitchen. He sits. He shrugs. "She could be in there for hours," he says.

"She once slept in there," says Gina.

"Vincent," says the father. "Go back and tell her that Gina's gonna do her trick for her. Tell her that and she'll come. She's not that upset. She'll come for the trick."

"I don't feel like it," says Gina.

"I'm not gonna force you," says the father. "If you and your brother wanna ruin everything in front of our guest here—go ahead—there's nothing I can do to stop you."

"Gina, please. Do the trick," says Vincent.

"No."

"I'll give you ten bucks," says Vincent.

"Ten bucks? You gotta be kiddin' me."

"I'll give you a hundred," says Desiree. "I mean, if that's okay with your father."

"Fine with me," says Vincent's father. "If you've got money like that, then God bless ya."

"You serious?" asks Gina.

"Sure," says Desiree, reaching into her pocket and peeling off a hundred dollars from a roll of hundred dollar bills.

Vincent pours himself a full shot of brandy. He shoots it down. He says, "I can't believe you gonna take it."

"No, it's fine," says Desiree. "Really. And I'm sure it's well worth it."

"It is a great trick," says Vincent's father.

"Yeah, okay, whatever," says Vincent, pouring himself another brandy. "Why the hell not... Hey, Ma! C'mon out Ma! Gina's gonna do her trick for ya! Better hurry or you're gonna miss it."

The flush of the toilet is followed by the entrance of Vincent's mother into the kitchen. She nods and smiles at Desiree before taking her seat.

"Well, go on then," says Vincent.

Gina laces her fingers and cracks her knuckles. She kneels up on her chair. She makes a fist. She stretches open her jaws. She puts her fist to her lips. Like a snake, she very slowly and very steadily takes the entire fist into her mouth up to her wrist. She rises from her knees to stand on the chair with her fist completely inside her mouth.

As Desiree stares in amazement, the rest of the family starts clapping. Desiree starts clapping too. They all stand and clap and Vincent's father whistles loudly with his two middle fingers pressed on top of his folded tongue. Gina grins with the fist in her mouth but the grin doesn't look like a grin. The grin makes her face even more twisted than it already is. Following her bow, Gina slowly removes her fist from her face. Taking a napkin from her mother, she wipes her mouth and sits back down.

"That was incredible," says Desiree. "I never saw anything like it in my life."

"We're a family of many hidden talents," says Vincent.

"I am very proud of you," says Vincent's Mom to Gina.

"What about me?" asks Vincent.

"Of course, you too. I am very proud of you both. And so is your father. Aren't you, Victor?"

Vincent's father nods. He says, "So, son, how's work going?"

Vincent glances down at his empty glass of brandy and then back to his father. He says, "I'm sorta on a leave of absence."

"Leave of absence? What are you talking about?"

"I'm still getting paid. I'm getting paid for the rest of the school year and through the summer."

"I still don't understand."

"Dad... Mom... Desiree and me and Desiree's son, Clyde, are going to be traveling south."

"South? South where?"

"First to Florida to see Disney World and then Mexico."

"Mexico? For what?"

"To see the pyramids. Desiree just bought a new car so there's no worry about breaking down or anything."

"I thought the pyramids were in Africa," says Gina.

"They got 'em in Mexico too," says Vincent.

"I never knew that," says Gina. "Only thing I know about Mexico is Taco Bell."

"You don't know much," says Vincent.

"I didn't know either," says Desiree.

"How long you goin' for?" asks Gina.

"We're not really sure. We're gonna take it as it comes."

"Like an adventure," says Gina.

"That's right," says Vincent. "An adventure."

"You could be like the Blues Brothers. You ever see that movie? 'We're on a mission from God.' I love that movie."

"You're kidding," says Vincent's father. "He's kidding, right?"

"No," says Desiree. "We've planned it all out together."

"Why don't you just stay here," says Vincent's mother. "Hoboken has changed, Vincent. They say it's completely multicultural now."

"What is that supposed to mean?" says Vincent.

"Watch that tone!" says Vincent's father.

"I have to go to the bathroom."

"Here we go again," says Gina.

"Ma, wait. I'm sorry," says Vincent.

"Too late," says Gina. "Going, going, gone..."

There is a moment of silence following Vincent's mother's exit to the bathroom.

Vincent returns his father's stare. "What?"

"You must think I'm stupid," he says.

"I don't know what you're talking about," says Vincent.

"I'm talking about you," says his father. "Don't think I don't know what's going on here."

"Going on with what?"

"With you and her and that big roll of bills she flashed before... Paying a hundred dollars for the trick."

"You don't think it was worth it?" asks Gina.

"Be quiet," says her father. "As a matter of fact, why don't you excuse yourself."

"I'm not a little girl anymore. I'm not going nowheres."

"Look, Pop," says Vincent. "I don't know what you got in your mind, but whatever it is, it's wrong 'cause I'm not doing anything wrong."

"I don't know whether to call a priest or the police."

"What? What are you saying?"

"I'm saying your girl here needs a white man at the wheel to drive that brand new car of hers back from Mexico to Zululand. Okay? Less chance of being pulled over with junk in the trunk. Okay? Am I being clear now?"

"You're crazy," says Vincent. "C'mon, Desiree. We're outta here."

"Truth hurts, huh?"

"You are so far from the truth it's fucking ridiculous."

As Vincent stands, so too does his father.

"What, you gonna hit me now?"

Vincent's father rushes Vincent, grabbing him by the collar and jerking him around in a half circle. As Vincent tries to push him off, his father only tightens his grip. Almost a head shorter, the father pushes forward, sending Vincent up against the refrigerator, the magnets and clippings falling and scattering like leaves in a storm. Embarrassed and angered, Vincent comes down hard with his fists on his father's wrists, breaking the hold and sidestepping away from the fridge. But his father, a man well over sixty, is surprisingly agile, shooting off a left and a right to Vincent's head—the left missing on the bob but the right scoring a glancing blow off the side of Vincent's ear. Using what he learned from his opponent decades earlier, Vincent takes advantage of the opening gained by the overhand right, stepping in and sending a short left to his father's gut. But Vincent does not continue the attack. He steps back as his father grips the stove, sucking wind. Vincent looks to Desiree who is staring in disbelief. Vincent grabs her hand to lead her out of the house. But Desiree will not be led. She says, "Hold on, Vincent." She goes over to Vincent's father. She puts an arm on his shoulder. "Are you okay?"

Vincent's father looks up at her. He nods. Desiree helps him to a chair by the table. "Can you get him some water?"

"I'll get it," says Gina.

As Gina fills a glass at the sink, Vincent crosses to Desiree's side.

Vincent says, "I'm sorry, Dad."

Vincent's father shakes his head and begins to weep.

"Don't worry," says Vincent. "I'm not doing anything wrong. Not anymore. What you're thinking is just not true. Alright?"

"Just go on," says his father. "Just go."

"Here's the water, Daddy," says Gina.

Desiree takes Vincent's hand and together they leave the house.

After getting into the car, Vincent says, "I'm really sorry about all that."

"Don't worry about it. One thing just led to another. It wasn't your fault."

"I had no idea it would get so out of hand like that. I shoulda figured though."

"Hey! Wait," shouts Gina, running down the front steps.

Vincent opens his window. "What?"

"I wanna ask you somethin'."

"Is he alright?"

"Daddy? Yeah, he's alright. He'll be fine. He just drank too much I think."

"So what do you want?"

"First, I wanna say good-bye, you asshole."

"Good-bye," says Vincent. "Anything else?"

"How do you put up with him?"

Desiree smiles. "He's not so bad."

"I know you two love each other," says Gina. "I can see that. Daddy can't 'cause he's too worried all the time.

And sometimes, especially with you Vincent, you can't blame him for worrying."

"Yeah, ok, whatever," says Vincent.

"I love you," says Gina, wiping away a tear. "I love you both."

"We gotta get going," says Vincent. "I'll try and send you some post cards."

EPILOGUE

    As they pull away, Vincent watches his sister in the rear-view. After turning the corner they drive in silence but they do not drive very long.

    "What's that noise?" says Desiree.

    "What noise?"

    "That noise!"

    Vincent pulls the car onto the shoulder. The noise gets louder. The car cuts off. Vincent tries to restart the car. The car will not restart. Vincent tries again. No luck. Vincent looks over at Desiree. Desiree says, "What's wrong?"

    "I don't know."

    Vincent looks under the dash and pulls the lever to open the hood. He gets out of the car. He fiddles his fingers under the crack of the hood and the hood pops up. Vincent keeps the hood up with the thin metal bar. He stares at the engine. Desiree gets out of the car. She stands beside Vincent. She says, "So what do you think it is?"

    "I don't know..."

    "What are you looking for?"

    "I don't know. All I know is that this is what I've seen people do whenever their car cuts off on them."

    "And then what?"

    "I don't know... I guess we call a tow."

    "The car guy said I get free roadside assistance. How far are we from your parents' house?"

    "Not far. Why?"

    "Maybe we can go back and call and wait from there."

    "No way," says Vincent. "Look, there's a payphone just outside that store."

    After getting the roadside help number out of the glove box, Vincent crosses the street to the corner store. He buys a six-pack and asks for some quarters to use the payphone. He dials the 800 number, tells the service that he doesn't exactly know what's wrong. The car just stopped and now won't start again. After hanging up, Vincent crosses the street. He puts the thin metal bar down so that he can close the hood, gets into the car and tells Desiree, "They're coming. But it's gonna be like an hour."

"An hour?"

"That's what the lady said."

Desiree pulls out a joint from her pack of Newports. She lights the joint and Vincent opens two bottles of beer, handing one to Desiree as she passes the joint.

As the couple smoke and drink, they each think about different things, their minds bouncing from the past, present and future like molecules in a pot of boiling water. As usual, Vincent soon finds himself reflecting on his guilt over Tyrone and his guilt about having no guilt for killing Ivory...

"You gotta let it go," says Desiree.

"Huh? What?"

"I can see it in your face. You worry too much."

"Oh," says Vincent. "Yeah, you're right. I probably do. But doesn't it ever bother you?"

"What's that?"

"The stuff we did."

"I've done a lot of stuff in my life."

"No, with Ivory."

"It's not something I'm happy about. But I don't think there was any other way we coulda gone."

"Yeah... What about Antoine? You think he's gonna make it?"

"I hope so," says Desiree. "We did all we could for him."

"Hey, look at that!"

Coming down the road is a man riding a strange bicycle. He has a big, wide head with blue-black skin so dark it seems to glow from within. Sprouting from his head is a bush of wild dreadlocks and a long, natty beard. Not riding fast but not riding slow, the Rastaman rides with a steady, perfect control and a smile of utter serenity. Vincent and Desiree are mesmerized by the Rastaman and his bicycle. Like most bicycles, it has two wheels, handlebars and a seat. But unlike other bikes, the frame has been altered so that the Rastaman sits very high up in the air.

"Look how high he is!" says Vincent.

"He looks high alright."

"No, I mean he's really up there. His head's gotta be a good twelve feet from the ground."

"Must give him an excellent view of the world."

"Most excellent."

As the Rastaman pedals, he moves across the face of the earth. Desiree and Vincent watch in wonder, turning as he passes them by. It is a dreamy moment like a vision from a long gone reality, like one of those memories of early childhood that, in the act of remembering, is resurrected and relived for the duration of the remembering.

At the line of the eastern horizon, the Rastaman gracefully turns his bicycle in a perfect half moon, his speed steady and determined as he pedals back in their direction like a wish come true before you even thought of wishing it.

"I don't know why," says Vincent. "But he's just absolutely amazing."

"No need for why," says Desiree.

"I wonder how he gets on that thing," says Vincent. "He's gotta have a ladder or maybe a porch or fence that he climbs up to get on it and off of it too... Unless he just jumps down..."

"What are you talking about?"

"How do you think he gets on and off that thing? It's so high. It's not like a regular bike. He can't just hop on and hop off it."

"I don't see the question at all."

"What do you mean?

"The start and the finish don't matter when you're enjoying such a fine ride. It's only the ride. That's all there is for as long as you're riding. The beginning and the end? They've come and they're gonna come and there's nothing you can do about them. But the ride, the ride is all that there ever is because you're still moving for as long as you keep on moving."

The Rastaman passes into the frame of Vincent's open window, his thick legs methodically pumping the pedals, the rest of him high and momentarily out of sight. But as he continues towards the far edge of the world, his shaggy head is suddenly lit up by the setting sun, a blazing black bush of dead hair and old light.

THE END

Acknowledgements: Love and thanks to my wife, Deirtra, my children---Taber, Dakota and Max---along with my family and friends who have always offered understanding and support. Also, to all my students whose struggles and triumphs over catastrophe have given me hope and inspiration. It has been a blessing and an honor to learn from them.